ROBERT, MY SON

OTHER WORKS BY HENRY DENKER

NOVELS

I'll Be Right Home, Ma
My Son, The Lawyer
Salome: Princess of Galilee
The First Easter
The Director
The Kingmaker
A Place for the Mighty
The Physicians
The Experiment
The Starmaker
The Scofield Diagnosis
The Actress
Error of Judgment
Horowitz and Mrs. Washington
The Warfield Syndrome
Outrage
The Healers
Kate Kincaid

PLAYS

Time Limit!
A Far Country
A Case of Libel
What Did We Do Wrong
Venus at Large
Second Time Around
Horowitz and Mrs. Washington
The Headhunters
Outrage!

ROBERT, MY SON

Henry Denker

W.H. ALLEN · LONDON
1986

Printed and bound in Great Britain by
Mackays of Chatham Ltd, Kent
for the Publishers, W.H. Allen & Co. Plc
44 Hill Street, London W1X 8LB

British Library Cataloguing in Publication Data

Denker, Henry
Robert, my son.
I. Title
813'.54[F] PS3507.E5475

ISBN 0-491-03743-0

The author wishes to express his gratitude to Dr. Lloyd M. Caplan, Medical Director, Desert Hospital Psychiatric Assistance Services, Palm Springs, California, for his help and advice on the scientific portions of this novel. And, for her excellent and constructive editorial contribution, to Frederica Friedman.

CHAPTER 1

Soundside Marina was closed and deserted. It appeared ominous in the grim, cloud-shrouded dawn. The water, black and angry, beat against the pilings, a film of old oil forming rainbows on its surface. The wind swept across Long Island Sound. Heavy with moisture, it felt like light rain on Claire Ward's face as she stood on the dock, staring out at the dark sky. Beside her, her husband, Don, felt her shudder. He put his arm around her. Her kind of cold could not be warded off by a comforting arm or the tweed coat wrapped around her. It was fear. If her son, Robbie, was out there, he was lost. Not only hidden by the dark night but swallowed up by the angry waters.

Detective Frank Melendez stood alongside them, speaking into his walkie-talkie from time to time.

"Where the hell is that police boat?" Melendez demanded. "You said it was on the way half an hour ago!"

There was some cross talk back which neither Don nor Claire Ward could make out. But it obviously infuriated Melendez, who replied, "Look! You know what exposure can do in this kind of weather. And we don't know how long the kid's been out there!"

More cross talk.

"What do you mean, we don't even know if he's out there?" Melendez replied angrily. "We found the stolen car here. His father has a boat at this marina. That boat is now gone. Two plus two equals four! He is out there somewhere!"

* * *

It seemed that hours had gone by. It was less than thirty minutes. Through the mist of early morning appeared the silhouette of a vessel, which played a powerful searchlight across the darkness in their direction. A voice came over the water by bullhorn. "Detective Melendez?"

Melendez shouted back to acknowledge.

"Any instructions? Any direction?" the voice asked.

"Just sweep the area. It's a Hobie Cat. Eighteen-foot." Melendez turned to Don Ward. "What color was the sail?"

"Mainly blue, with red, orange, and yellow stripes."

Melendez relayed the information and asked, "Anything said about a copter?"

"Not till this mist lifts," the bullhorn responded.

"Okay. Get going!"

Claire could make out the shadowy form of the police boat as it turned to head out into the Sound. Its searchlight probing ahead of it, as if cutting a path, it started away, the throb of its powerful engines growing fainter as it disappeared into the mist once more.

A police car pulled up behind them. One of the officers emerged, carrying a paper bag with containers of hot coffee. He passed one to Claire, one to Don, but used the third one to lure Melendez away from the Wards. Once at a confidential distance, the officer spoke. "We got another report. That kid is really on a tear."

"You mean he's not out there?" Melendez asked.

"I mean he damn well may be out there. But before that, even before the stolen car thing, he may have been spotted walking the Windsor Street bridge railing."

"How do you know?"

"Duane was thumbing through the nine-elevens to make up the daily report. Earlier last night there was a call from someone who lives on Windsor. A kid about sixteen was spotted walking the rail. The caller said he stood there, balancing himself, while two trains went by underneath."

"No jumper," Melendez concluded.

"Evidently just wanted to see if he could balance himself against the rush of wind as the train went by. When our checkup got there, the kid was gone. We think it was the Ward kid."

"Could be." Melendez agreed. "Could be."

He did not attempt to drink his coffee but tossed the container *in the direction of the dark water. He seemed even more harried than before. He turned his walkie-talkie on again. "Melendez. Spot anything?"*

"Not a thing."

"Nothing at all?"

"Nothing."

"Well, keep at it," Melendez said, because he could think of nothing else to say that would not admit the feeling of defeat that was beginning to grip his stomach. His wife always said, "Frank does his best detecting with his stomach. What he feels there generally turns out to be his best hunch."

Now he was wishing it were not so.

They heard a car pull up behind them and stop abruptly. They both turned, saw a man getting out. Don recognized him.

"Dr. Rissom?" he called.

Rissom approached him. "I couldn't stand just waiting. I had to be here. Anything?"

"Not yet," Don said, unwilling to accept Melendez's fatalistic attitude.

"And Claire?" Rissom asked.

"Barely holding on."

"I thought so," Rissom said, reaching into his pocket for a small white envelope. "Try to get her to take this sedative."

Don went back to the car. Claire sat still and stiff, staring.

"Take this, darling," Don said softly.

"It's a sedative, isn't it?" she demanded belligerently.

"Dr. Rissom brought it for you."

"My son is out there. And no matter what they find, I don't want to be asleep when it happens. If there is joy, I want to feel it. If there is pain, I want to know it. Else I am not truly a mother, and never was. Never was."

She began to weep.

He edged in beside her, embraced her, spoke softly into her ear. "Claire, darling, listen to me. You may not have given birth to him, but you gave him all the love, care, and attention that any child could have. You gave him more of that than most mothers. Because my damned job took me away from him so much."

He stared out at the mist, at the dark waters of the Sound as he said, "In a way, if anything happens to him now, it's only right that it's because of something that I bought him. It points the finger to where the blame really belongs. Me! So don't go accusing yourself. And don't punish yourself now by refusing this pill. Take it."

He brought the pill to her lips. She turned her head away, protesting, "I want to know the truth the moment they know it."

He knew it would be futile to persist. He left her, sitting there, staring.

And thinking. Thinking of how it had all begun. Of her resolve and determination to be the perfect mother. To give some child the peaceful, happy home which she had been denied because of her parents' stormy divorce and their bitter custody battle.

Unable to conceive a child of her own, Claire Ward had been extremely conscientious about being mother to a son who had been handed to her sixteen years ago, when he was only two weeks old. To raise him, she had retired from a successful career as an ingenue on a popular daytime soap opera. She had read, studied, inquired, attended lectures on mothering because she was determined not to fail in this, the most important role of her life. But there had been times in those past sixteen years when she felt she was still the actress, playing the role of a mother instead of being one. She had never quite felt fully qualified, as if she had missed something magical that took place in a woman by living through nine months of pregnancy.

Her problem was aggravated by her husband's devotion to his career. They had met when she was on that soap opera and he was a rising young television executive in daytime programming.

Even then he used to boast, "One day I am going to be president of this whole damn network!" Ever since, he had been making his way steadily up the corporate structure, like a climber carefully ascending the sheer glass walls of a modern skyscraper. It was a treacherous journey that could be thwarted by any number of uncontrollable factors.

The farther he rose, the greater the pressure, but conversely, the more consuming his ambition. It meant late hours at the office. Not to mention sudden frequent trips to the West Coast to rescue television productions that were "in trouble." That two-word phrase was dreaded by Claire and, later, by their son, Robbie. Whenever some show out West was "in trouble," Don Ward was the man sent out to set it right.

At one time she had been tormented by suspicions that those trips to the Coast were actually a cover-up for an affair Don was having with some younger, perhaps prettier woman. He did not act like a man involved in an affair. At least she could not detect any of the so-called signs. But then how would she really know? She had come from an early broken home, and her experience with marriage was almost totally limited to those in soap operas, where infidelity was a necessary way of life.

After a time she had realized that her only rival was his work. She was convinced of that when he was as eager as she for them to have a child. He had dedicated his career to what he could do for their son when they had one. Except that they never did. Not one of their own.

They both had entered their marriage with the romantic dream of a home in the suburbs, a family of two perfectly beautiful children, one boy, one girl, both as rosy-cheeked and golden-haired as Claire. But despite all the probing, testing, specimens, X rays, and time spent on gynecologists' tables, she had not been able to conceive. They had sex under the least romantic of conditions, at hours prescribed not by passion but by doctors. Still, she had not become pregnant. After two years, the doctors concluded that for some undetermined reason, Claire and Don were unable to conceive a child.

To relieve Don of any further pressure, Claire pretended to accept the situation. She devoted herself more intensely to her career. But they realized how deep was her psychological need when Evvie Troy had her baby. Evvie had been associate producer on Claire's soap opera until she left to have her baby. But they remained close friends. Claire lived through Evvie's entire pregnancy, went shopping with her to outfit the baby's room, selected wallpaper, furniture, the bassinet, the layette.

Evvie called her just before Harris took her off to the hospital to deliver.

"Well, Claire, this is it!" Evvie said, trying to sound buoyant and unafraid. "See you later."

Evvie delivered only hours after reaching the hospital: a seven-pound-two-ounce boy. The first person she called was Claire Ward. That conversation ended with Evvie's insisting, "I can't believe it. You've got to come see my son!"

Don had his secretary send flowers. Claire went down to the local jeweler's shop to pick out a silver porringer and have it engraved "H. W. T." for little Harris Wadsworth Troy, Jr. She made the jeweler rush the engraving because she wanted to take it with her to the hospital.

Claire picked up the gift the next afternoon on her way. But as she came within sight of the hospital, she pulled her car over to the side and turned off the motor. She sat there until without being conscious of pain or grief, she found herself sobbing.

A passing patrol car stopped. One of the officers approached her. "Something wrong, lady? Can we help?"

Tears streaming down her face, she shook her head.

"If you're in trouble . . ." he continued.

She shook her head to discourage any further questions. She turned her face away until the officer got back into the car and they took off.

How could she tell him, or anyone, that she found herself unable to visit her close friend, unable to share with her the joy of having given birth to her first child?

Finally she turned her car around and drove back home, circuitously, through streets with which she was only vaguely familiar. She was almost as reluctant to go home as she had been to go to the hospital. The phone would undoubtedly be ringing. Evvie would be asking, "Where are you? I thought you'd be here at feeding time so you could see him, even hold him."

She forced herself to drive home. She could hear the phone, faintly, from the garage. She resisted, then finally answered it.

"Claire? What happened? We were expecting you, Harris Wadsworth, Junior, and I," Evvie joked. "He was very disappointed. Not that it cut into his appetite. They talk about feeding on demand. This little one doesn't demand. He just takes. Drained, I feel absolutely drained." But she laughed proudly.

Claire tried to laugh along with her. She hoped she was giving one of her better performances.

"I was just about to leave the house when the phone rang. You remember Curt Hammerstein? Handles the Procter and

Gamble account. He insisted I come in to audition for a series of new commercials. I couldn't talk him out of it. So I raced into the city. Did the audition. Raced back. I won't get it, of course. But I had to do it so as not to offend Curt. After all, they're the network's biggest client. But I'll be by, don't worry."

When Don came home, she told him. It was not easy. Especially about having to lie and using him in that lie. "I was jealous. So jealous I sat in that car, on a nice, bright, sunny day on a pleasant street in a lovely small town, and cried. When the police stopped, what was I supposed to say? 'My friend has had the baby that I can't have. I don't want to see her baby. I want to see my own baby!' I want—"

Unable to continue, she found herself crying again. Don took her in his arms.

"Claire . . . honey . . . please. It's only natural to be a little jealous. . . ."

"Jealous? I hate her, I hate her baby, I hate—"

"You know you don't hate her or that baby. Or anything, except the fact that we can't have one. Well, this settles it. I am not going to let this thing eat you up. We are going to adopt a baby. Maybe two or three even."

He used his silk pocket handkerchief to wipe away her tears. "Tomorrow you'll go to the hospital. You'll see Evvie; you'll hold that baby. Knowing that soon, very soon you'll have one of your own. We should have done this months ago."

She nodded, sniffling to overcome the crying. "Okay. Tomorrow I'll go. I got the nicest silver porringer for him. Monogrammed and everything."

"Terrific!" Don said. "Now let's go out and have a nice dinner at that French place in Darien."

She found herself unable to go to the hospital the next day. Or even on the third day. They spoke on the phone each day, but sensing something was wrong, Evvie no longer insisted Claire come visit at the hospital.

Once Evvie came home, it was less difficult for Claire because by then she and Don had taken the first step toward adopting a baby of their own.

* * *

With that had begun a whole new battery of tests of a different kind. Their private lives were probed: education; financial standing; emotional stability; family and ethnic background. A woman visited and although she gave no outward signs of disapproval, her quizzical looks seemed to find fault with the way Claire maintained their comfortable home.

Claire was questioned in detail about her fitness for motherhood. Was she emotionally prepared without undergoing the nine months of slow, gradual acclimatization? Had she made a study of the care, feeding, and health of newborns? The woman probed Claire's early childhood. The fact of her broken home was revealed. The woman made no comment, merely jotted a note on her interview sheet.

When the woman finally left, Claire called Don at the office. Over his secretary's protests she insisted on speaking to him at once.

"Failed. I failed again," she lamented. "I'm sorry."

Nothing he could say helped assuage her fears or diminish her sense of guilt.

That night they had a late dinner again. Ever since an enticing hint from Ed Brady, Don's boss, that soon there might be a significant shift in the executive echelon at the network, Don had been leaving for the office earlier each morning, coming home later each night. He wanted to be there before eight in the morning to get the first look at the overnight ratings. He stayed late so as not to miss any important meetings. Claire continued to console herself with the hope that when he had advanced high enough, he would be able to control his time to suit himself and her, too.

That night, late as it was, Don spent hours reassuring Claire after her disheartening interview with the woman from the adoption agency.

"Honey, where are they going to find a better mother than you?" Don tried to comfort her. "Capable. Dependable. Highly intelligent. Sensitive. You've gone through all those damn tests and experiments to try to have a child. Who's shown more desire, more sincerity? Did you tell her about that?"

"Yes, I told her."

"Did you tell her you just gave up a starring role on one of the top-rated shows in daytime? How many actresses in this business would have done that?" Don said, growing furious in defense of his wife.

"I think it only made things worse. You know how civilians are about people in show business? They think all we do is screw around. With other women's husbands," Claire said. "But the worst part was when she asked about family background. I had to tell her about my parents' divorce and that terrible custody fight. I don't think she liked that."

"It wasn't your fault your mother and father had a nasty divorce. What did she say?"

"She didn't say anything."

"Then how do you know she disapproved?"

"Just a feeling, that's all."

He embraced her to comfort her. "Angel, where in this whole world are they going to find two people who can give a child more love, a nicer home, a brighter future?" he asked. "They're lucky to have applicants like us."

"Still . . ." she started to say, but he smothered the words by kissing her. Which led to more impassioned kisses and eventually to making love.

After he fell asleep but she still lay awake, she tried to perform the same accounting he had done, adding up all her qualifications for motherhood. Still, she came up short. She fell asleep protesting: *Because I know what childhood unhappiness is, I am determined to make my child happy, to give him or her the most secure home, the best environment.*

She woke during the night, weeping.

After eighteen days of self-recrimination, after accepting that motherhood was not for her, that she should once again devote herself to her career, perhaps even expand it, forget television, and go all out for a big part in a Broadway play, a neatly typed letter arrived in the mail.

Dear Mr. and Mrs. Ward:

Since you have passed all our tests and satisfied our requirements as potential adoptive parents, we are pleased to inform you that you have been placed on our approved list.

In the usual course of events you may expect to hear from us about a child in about six months, or possibly sooner.

Claire called Don at the office to announce the news. To celebrate, Don managed two tickets to the hottest musical on Broadway, with dinner at "21" beforehand. All on his network expense account, of course. Throughout the performance Claire sat there, not thinking her usual *I could do that role far better.* Instead, she exulted, *Let her have it. I'm going to be a mother, finally!*

At the disco after the show Claire danced with more energy and abandon than usual until Don joked, "Darling, for a woman practically five months pregnant, you're taking too many risks. Cool it, babe."

That night when they made love, without any hope that it might lead to her pregnancy, they enjoyed each other more than at any time during the ordeal of the past two years.

CHAPTER 2

One day the adoption agency woman called to inform Claire that there was a possible baby.

A boy!

Claire had never thought in terms of the baby's sex. All she wanted was a baby, to love, to care for, to cherish, and to raise. But in answer to that question on the application form Don had indicated his preference for a son. At the time Claire feared it was a risk to be so specific; perhaps the agency would consider it a negative factor in their approach to adoption. But no. It had evidently taken it into its considerations. So here it was. The day, the time, and a baby boy.

They went to see him for the first time at the hospital in New York. He had been isolated from all the other infants in a small private room. He was a tiny red-faced little thing, hardly more than a handful, with the slightest wisp of dark hair on his pink scalp. He seemed well formed, with no forceps marks or other blemishes or discolorations of birth.

Uncomfortable, ill at ease, Don tried to joke. "With his face so wrinkled and almost bald he looks like a little old man."

Claire had controlled her first impulse, which was to pick him up. Sensing that, the nurse said, "Go ahead. It's all right."

Claire lifted him gently out of his white crib, blanket and all, and held him to her.

"Would you like to feed him?" the nurse asked.

"May I?"

The nurse disappeared for a few moments, during which the infant turned his face toward Claire's breast, declaring his hunger. The nurse returned with a small bottle of white formula. Claire eased the nipple into the infant's mouth. Instinctively it began to suck eagerly.

The nurse watched, encouraging. "He's a fine baby. Healthy. And unusually active. You can tell from the first day what they'll be like. And he's an exceptional one. You're very lucky people."

"What about the mother?" Don asked.

"Oh, you can't see her," the nurse protested.

"I asked, what *about* her?" Don corrected.

"The lady from the agency will explain all that." As if Don had just broken the rules, the nurse indicated that Claire had better hand the infant back. Reluctantly Claire obeyed.

Once the door had eased shut, Claire reprimanded him in a whisper. "You shouldn't have said anything. Now you've ruined it. And he was such a lovely baby."

"It was a natural question. I'm sure they get it all the time."

They were summoned to the office of the agency in the main building of the hospital. There the investigator who had caused Claire such earlier distress greeted them.

She was no longer inquisitorial but appeared warm and most friendly. She explained the infant's background as fully as she had been able to obtain it. The mother was a young woman of twenty-one. She had been educated in public schools through high school. She then took secretarial training. She had been employed in the same office for two and a half years when, as a result of a brief affair with her married boss, she had become pregnant. For religious reasons her family objected to an abortion. She had carried to term, without incident, and been delivered of this healthy baby boy. There was nothing in her medical record to indicate that any of her habits or any medication she had taken would in any way adversely affect the future health of the child. If the Wards would like, after they had several days to make preparations, they were free to take him. All remaining legal and paper work would be done afterward.

"I can be ready tomorrow," Claire blurted out.

The woman smiled. "I'm afraid not. There are more things to prepare than you expect. Bottles, formulas, diapers, a crib, medications for emergencies, a pediatrician. And oh, by the way, it's always a good idea to have your own doctor check out the baby first—just to be sure."

The examination by Dr. Rissom, a private pediatrician recommended by their own physician, substantiated what the agency had said. This was a perfectly healthy, robust little boy, not only meeting but exceeding all physical and neurological standards. Obviously a full-term infant, of good weight. All in all Rissom felt that Claire and Don were an extremely fortunate young couple.

Two days later Don Ward drove his wife and his new son home from the hospital. Her seat belt securely in place, Claire sat clutching the infant to her breast. Don drove slowly, staying in the right-hand lane of the highway at so slow and safe a speed that all other drivers passed him impatiently. He kept his eyes on the road ahead, except when glancing into his side mirror and his rearview mirror to make sure no careless driver would hit the car and endanger its precious cargo.

He did not relax until they had the infant safely in his crib in the upstairs room they had converted into a nursery. The infant had slept through it all, unaware of the sudden change he had made in the lives of these two people.

As Don stood over the crib, looking down at the sleeping infant, he smiled and said, "How are we ever going to tell him?"

"About being adopted?" Claire asked.

"No, about what his father does for a living."

They both laughed.

"The way the networks are going, maybe by the time he grows up there won't be any television," Claire said.

"So what? As long as there's you, as long as there's him, we'll get along," Don said, and embraced her.

While they were in each other's arms, Claire whispered in Don's ear, "We *are* going to tell him. About being adopted. I would never want him to find out in a way that would hurt him."

"Of course, we'll tell him," Don said.

The infant was making sucking motions and beginning to squirm in his sleep.

"He's hungry again. I'd better feed him," Claire said, slipping out of Don's embrace.

Gradually, slowly, with the encouragement of her mother, friends, and Dr. Rissom, Claire overcame her fear that she would, in some unintentional way, harm the infant. Once she relaxed, she began to enjoy him. As did Don.

They watched him grow as if observing a miracle. His every small achievement became an act of genius. Turning over by himself, crawling, rising from the floor, walking finally—all were cheered as if performed for the first time in human history.

Making sounds, learning to form specific words, talking, recognizing colors, letters of the alphabet, reading one-syllable words became undeniable corroboration of previously suspected brilliance. At the network Don Ward became a bore, extolling the mental and physical attributes of his son.

Nor was it all paternal pride and exaggeration. For if one were to judge by all the books on child rearing and development, little Robbie Ward had accomplished everything earlier than other normal healthy children.

That became even more marked when Robbie entered the period of infancy which the books designated as the terrible twos, that time in an infant's development when, by reason of being able to locomote on his own, he declares himself a free human being, no longer dependent on the will of another person. And when the answer to every question is a loud "No!," sometimes accompanied by gestures of anger and defiance.

When Robbie Ward reached that period of his young life he was even more independent than most other youngsters. He was self-assured where other two-year-olds were usually peevish. He was also self-reliant, never dependent on the companionship of other children. But when he found himself in their company, at a park playground or later in nursery school, he was the child to whom all the others gravitated and whom they imitated.

More than once his nursery school teacher had said to Claire, "That son of yours is a born leader. It isn't something they develop; it's a special talent they're born with. Inherited. Takes after his father, I guess."

"Yes, takes after his father," Claire said, secretly amused.

The week of Robbie's fifth birthday Claire brought up a subject that she had not mentioned to Don for some time.

Five was the age recommended by some books as the proper first time to tell a child that he had been adopted. At such a young age the concept would not make a significant impression. But it did serve to introduce the word as well as the thought. It would have to be reintroduced at the age of eight, at which time the child was more able to comprehend.

They decided that on Sunday, when both Don and Claire were sure to be home, they would tell him. It did not happen on Sunday because late Friday afternoon Don called and regretfully informed her, "Hon, I'm on my way to the airport."

"Oh, no!" Claire protested. "This is the Sunday we were going to tell Robbie—"

He interrupted, "I know. But Lester Barton is threatening to walk out on *Way of Life.*"

"Again? They renegotiated his contract only last April," Claire protested.

"Sure. But the new ratings came out this week. *Way of Life* is in the top ten. Nothing can make a star more greedy. So I have to fly to the Coast and put out the fire."

Claire knew it was futile to ask, but she did. "How long will you be gone?"

"Hon, I've got to save the show. We don't have too many in the top ten."

"Of course. Have a safe trip," Claire said.

Sunday. Claire celebrated Robbie's birthday with him, her mother, and four children from his nursery school class. There were matching colored streamers, tablecloth, and napkins. Funny hats. Gifts for each child. Messy hamburgers. Birthday cake and ice cream. Milk was more honored in the spilling than the drinking.

By the time they all had left, it was late on that spring Sunday afternoon. The last of the setting sun was filtering through the delicate branches of her favorite white birch on their well-tended back lawn. Claire gathered her handsome young son in her arms, sat in the cushioned dormitory alcove of their living room, looking out at the pleasing scene. As she tousled his soft black hair, she thought: *How lucky. In this game of chance called adoption we were fortunate enough to hit the jackpot. A handsome child, happy and smiling, a bright child, a loving child, yet so mature and forthright.* What that nursery school teacher had said three years ago was true: Her Robbie was a leader, with such enthusiasm, ingenuity, and determination that other children followed him without questioning.

She hugged him so tightly he squirmed to be free. She smiled; he would never get over wanting to be independent. Even at the age of five he was his own man, his own little man. She permitted him to slip out of her arms. He went back to the new challenging construction toy Don had sent up for his birthday from F.A.O. Schwarz. Robbie handled it with an intensity and dexterity Claire credited to his superior intelligence.

Feeling that way, she decided to perform the agreed-upon ritual despite Don's absence.

"Robbie, darling . . ."

The boy half turned from his toy but continued to work on it.

"Come here, darling. Mommy wants to talk to you."

As simply as she could, she proceeded to tell him how not all babies come out of their mothers' bellies, as he had been told in school. That some babies, some very precious and lucky few, were chosen by their mommies. That he was one of that precious and lucky few.

He pretended to listen, but his eyes and mind were on the half-finished construction toy he had left on the living room carpet. He slipped out of her arms again and went back to play. She felt that he had not heard her at all. But then the book had warned that no child of five truly understood or was impressed by the facts of adoption.

That had been eleven years ago. Since then Robbie had been made well aware of his adoption and had coped with it in his usual style, with maturity and confidence. He had seemed to gain strength from it, being better adjusted than most of his peers.

He was not only an outstanding student, but the youngest first-string quarterback in the entire county prep schools league.

The judgment made by that neonatal nurse at the hospital so many years ago was more than corroborated by his football coach, who was Robbie's most enthusiastic supporter. He had already alerted a number of college coaches to the potential of this outstanding young man.

CHAPTER 3

Staring out at the dark, threatening waters of Long Island Sound in the misty air of early dawn, Claire Ward was now forced to confront a painful truth. To ask herself: Do sixteen years of love, devotion, pride, and joy all end here in this forlorn deserted marina?

Was it only a brief six months ago that their dream had begun to come apart? Yet they were unaware of it. Should they have suspected then? Could anyone have known that that single unusual episode was actually only the first of a number of Robbie's increasingly dangerous and symptomatic manifestations?

Surely not his mother. And surely not on the first day all this began.

She could remember now only too well that she had been directing the rehearsal of another production of the Towne Players, the local amateur dramatic group she had formed practically single-handedly.

"Let's take it from Amanda's entrance," Claire Ward ordered. "And this time we'll run through the entire scene without a break. And without our books."

There was a groan of protest from the stage of the empty Civic Auditorium. To which Claire responded, "We've been at this long enough for you to know your lines. So without the books, if you please! Ad-lib if you go up. But no books!"

Her volunteer cast dropped their battered playscripts on the tables and chairs in the makeshift rehearsal set, determined to brazen it out.

Claire whispered to her assistant, "If they falter, throw them their lines. I want to keep this run-through moving so I get some feel of the tempo of the entire scene." She raised her voice, "Okay! Ready! From the opening of the door, go!"

She began pacing up and down the aisle, listening, watching, making mental notes as the scene progressed.

Just turned thirty-nine, Claire Ward was still naturally honey-haired. Tall, she possessed a figure kept youthful and firm through regular exercise and the active life she had maintained.

"Mrs. Ward . . ." The hushed voice of her young apprentice interrupted with an air of great urgency.

"Later!" Claire said in an impatient whisper so as not to distract her cast.

"Mrs. Ward, it's important."

"I don't want this scene interrupted."

"But the police—"

Claire turned to face the tense young apprentice. "Audrey, did you say 'police'?"

"They're on the phone. It's about Robbie."

"Robbie? *My* Robbie? There must be some mistake!"

"Robert Ward, they said. Three twenty-seven Cedar Lane."

"Robbie's never been in any kind of—" She turned to her assistant. "Keep them going till I get back."

She raced out of the auditorium.

On the thirty-third floor of the Intercontinental Television Network, high above the Avenue of the Americas in Manhattan, a tense meeting, which had commenced at three in the afternoon, was still in progress. Don Ward was standing before a wall-size chart which was divided into the prime-time periods for the television week. He was explaining the arrangement and the logic of the new network schedule for the ensuing season. Each program on the chart was printed on a large card that could easily be pulled out of one slot and slipped into another, so that the entire week's schedule remained fluid, until all the concerned executives had reached a consensus.

Nine executives, eight men and one woman, Emily Grant, sat

studying the huge chart. Some had cocktails in hand; some held sandwiches, which they were too preoccupied to eat, despite the fact that it was now almost nine o'clock and they'd had no dinner.

Don stood before them. Tall, distinguished, he still possessed virtually the same physique he had had in college, when he was a member of a midwestern basketball team that had gone to the semifinals of the NIT in his last year at the university. It was on that trip to New York and Madison Square Garden that he took time off to visit all three television networks to inquire about a job after graduation.

At the first network, because of his handsome face and rugged build, he was sent down to the casting department. But he made it quite clear that he was interested only in the executive training program. He was determined to be in management. Now, at age forty-one, black hair graying just the slightest bit, he was in the upper echelon of Intercontinental, and headed higher.

At the moment it was his assignment to sell to the other executives a new prime-time schedule which had been designed by Ed Brady, president of the network. Brady, in his turn, was seeking to move up to the presidency of the parent company. If Don Ward carried out this duty to Brady's satisfaction, he might be in line for the top post at the network once Brady moved up.

Don was bringing to bear all his charm, which was considerable, and all his persuasive powers, which always worked wonders on reluctant stars, belligerent producers, and unhappy advertisers.

"Tuesday night and Thursday night are drama nights. But Sunday we have to go comedy early to have a shot against *Sixty Minutes.* If we can eat into *Sixty Minutes,* we have a chance to crack the whole CBS lineup for the night. So it's comedy all the way. And we've gone to tremendous expense. Some of you haven't seen the pilot of *Ain't It the Truth,* but it is funny. F-u-n-n-y." Don spelled it out. "We've put together a top team of comedy writers, the best director, and two young comedians we think will be the biggest thing since Milton Berle and Sid Caesar in the old days of live TV. And the demographics are right. We'll be hitting the young age group."

At that point the door to the conference room eased open. Don saw his secretary, Jeannie, peer in; her look warned of trouble. Grave trouble. Don glared at her, demanding immunity from all interruptions. At the same time his mind performed some East-West mathematics. Nine in the evening New York time was six o'clock Los Angeles time. That could mean, probably did mean, something had gone wrong with the new pilot being shot out there. Most likely the producer wanted to know if he could incur the expense of shooting another day, or should he try to rush things and wrap tonight? Either way spelled added costs. Overtime was cheaper than extending shooting, which might not even be possible if one of the necessary actors had another commitment tomorrow. But such an emergency was insignificant compared to a scheduling meeting which could determine network operations and profit for the entire next year.

Don assumed Jeannie would read all that from his forbidding look. Still, she persisted, her look a warning that could not be ignored. Don was forced to say, "Study this lineup. If you have any suggestions, Ed is always open-minded, as you well know."

This, despite the fact that all of them had been put through many an uncomfortable hour for having dared question the judgment of the network president.

Don rushed to the door, slipped through to confront his secretary in the anteroom. "Damn it, Jeannie, you know better than to break into a scheduling meeting!"

"It's your wife."

"There's nothing so impor—" Don interrupted himself. "She hasn't been in an accident, has she?"

"It's Robbie."

"What happened to Robbie?" Don Ward demanded, suddenly hoarse with anxiety.

"Your wife said he's being held by the police."

"Police! What the hell is she talking about?" Don demanded.

"He's being held by the police, and they won't release him without you," Jeannie said. "I explained about the meeting, but Mrs. Ward said the police are adamant."

"Police . . . Robbie . . . They're out of their minds! Robbie's never been in trouble in his whole life. Did she say what kind of trouble?"

"Something about driving."

"He's not allowed to drive; he's too young!"

"I think that's the trouble."

"Look, Jeannie, get back on that phone, and tell them I'll be there as soon as I can. But I can't leave this meeting. Brady wouldn't like it, wouldn't like it at all."

"I know," she said sympathetically. "Okay, I'll call her back."

CHAPTER 4

It was almost eleven o'clock when a network limousine delivered Don Ward to the New Canaan police station.

He found Claire exhausted, her face tense and drawn as she sat on a hard wooden bench in the waiting area. He kissed her hastily, asking, "What happened?"

"Robbie. He took your car. Was driving with that Susan Spencer he's so crazy about."

"He can't drive alone. He's only got a learner's permit!" Don protested.

"That's not all," Claire said hesitantly.

"Was he in an accident? Is he all right?"

"*He's* all right. But your Mercedes isn't."

"Okay. Tell me. What happened?"

"He veered off the Merritt Parkway. Hit a tree."

"And my car was totaled," Don concluded.

"Not quite."

"Wait'll I get my hands on him!"

"Now, Don, wait."

"Don't start protecting him. If it was up to you, he'd get away with murder," Don said.

"You're the one who indulges him. Expensive gifts. Football games. Baseball games. Always in the network's box seats. The best restaurants. On the network's expense account. Talk about spoiling—"

Don changed the subject abruptly. "We'd better talk to whoever's in charge."

The police sergeant led the way down the jail corridor past several cells, all of which were occupied. At the fifth and last cell Don Ward saw his young son sitting despondently on the thin, ragged mattress of an iron frame cot. At the sight of his father Robbie jumped to his feet and grasped the bars of the cell, imploring, "Dad?"

"Not yet," the sergeant said. "This way!" He led Don to the door at the rear of the building. He shoved the door open. He indicated that Don take a look. In the light that shone through the open door Don recognized his red Mercedes. The left fender was crumpled, sharp edges of raw metal protruding manacingly. The door on the left side was sprung. The front wheels were bent out of shape, one tire blown out.

"Did my son do all that?"

"He sure did. If he and the girl hadn't been wearing seat belts, I don't have to tell you what would have happened. So this wasn't just a harmless prank. That's the reason I kept him in a cell till you got up here. To impress on him the seriousness of it. Now let's get him out."

Don Ward, his son, Robert, and his wife, Claire, stood before the desk of the admitting sergeant, who sat on an elevated platform like a judge holding court.

"Robert Ward, I want you to know that technically I could charge you with auto theft as well as driving without a license. Not to mention reckless endangerment. If it weren't for the intervention and the pleas of your father and mother, I would charge you. Now I want your promise that you will never again do such a thing. Because if you do, it will go hard for you, very hard. As it is, consider yourself on parole as long as you exhibit good behavior. Understand?"

Fifteen-and-a-half-year-old Robbie Ward, black-haired, sober-faced, handsome, standing taller than his mother and almost as tall as his father, nodded gravely. He was rugged and strong for his age, well built. While his jeans fitted snugly around his lean hips, his broad shoulders strained his letter jacket, which he had earned while still a freshman at Canaan Prep. He had already outgrown the jacket, and he was only starting his sophomore year.

Since he did not resemble his mother, most people assumed he took after his father's side of the family. That resemblance was the result of careful matching at the adoption agency.

"Mr. Ward," the desk sergeant said, "we'll release the boy into your custody. But first I would like a word with you in private." He gestured in the direction of a side room.

Once they were secluded, the sergeant said, "Look, I intentionally gave your kid a rough time. To put the fear of God into him. Of course, I couldn't charge him with auto theft. It was your car. I said that to scare him. For two reasons: First, so he'll never do such a foolish thing again; second, because that boy of yours is important to this community. He's the model other parents hold up to their kids. I mean, a boy just starting his sophomore year and already first-string quarterback on the Canaan team, kids look up to him. So I don't want him setting a bad example. Now don't you or your wife undo my work by going easy on him."

"I promise you we won't," Don said.

"Another thing," the sergeant said, "with a kid like him, the time's going to come when he's considering colleges. I can't keep people from gossiping but no kid in this town is going to have a police record if I can help it. Besides, he's going to be in line for football scholarships. We expect him to go to one of the big schools. Ohio State, Michigan, UCLA, Texas. He's got what it takes, that son of yours."

Don nodded, smiled modestly because he knew it was expected of him. But he was thinking: *My son is far too bright to go to any football factory. He is not going to feel like an indentured servant who thinks that his future depends on playing football.* Don himself had gone through college on a basketball scholarship and knew the pressures if a man wanted to be a good scholar as well. However, to humor the police sergeant, he said, "Thanks. I appreciate that. And I'm sure when Robbie's a little older, he will, too."

"I hope so," the sergeant said. "Oh, by the way, another word of advice: Don't put in a claim with your insurance company. Pay for the damage yourself. No matter what it costs."

"I know. They'd cancel my policy after a claim of this size," Don said.

"Even worse, they'll go digging into the circumstances. That could lead to all kinds of trouble. Robbie would lose his learner's permit. He might not get another one for a year or more. After all, he could have been hurt, and that girl, too. Her father was steamed as it was, threatening all kinds of action against Robbie. So I would advise keeping this quiet. Very quiet."

There was no discussion, no rebukes during the ride home from the police station. Claire drove her station wagon, Don sitting alongside. Robbie sat behind them, silent, guilty.

Just as Claire turned into their circular driveway, Don said, "Robbie, take a shower. Get to bed. But we're going to have a talk in the morning. Understand?"

"Yes, sir," Robbie said.

Don knew his son was sufficiently chastened, for he addressed his father as "sir" only under very special circumstances, of which this was surely one.

Claire steered the wagon into the left area of the three-car garage, which had been designed and built to seem like one wing of the two-story gray fieldstone and white wood Colonial-style home. With its spacious surrounding grounds the Ward home was considered an estate by some. The cost, when they bought it, far exceeded Don's salary and financial stature. It was made possible by an interest-free loan from the network. Another of the tempting and enslaving perks that insured executive loyalty.

They knew Robbie was asleep when the usual thumping bass beat that accompanied the rock music had finally and mercifully ceased from his room above.

Claire felt free to give vent to her fears. "I can't understand it. He's never done anything like this before."

"He's never been fifteen and a half before. Or had a girl friend to show off for. But he's learned his lesson. It won't happen again," Don assured her.

"Thank God it wasn't more serious."

"Drugs, you mean."

That was the single greatest fear which haunted all parents in this affluent Connecticut suburb.

Don embraced his wife to reassure her. "Don't worry, darling. We brought him up right. In fact, sometimes I think, being the terrific boy he is, he must take a lot of kidding for being so straight."

"Yes, we've been lucky, very lucky," Claire said.

"What does that mean?" Don demanded angrily.

"What I said. We're very lucky."

"Why not say what you really mean?" With exaggerated emphasis he laid out each word meticulously, "We are very lucky that Robbie is so well adjusted *despite* the fact that I'm away on business so much. Well, maybe I have been. But he seems able to manage. And damn well, to judge from his grades, his athletic achievements. He won the Freshman Citizenship Award, didn't he? I wouldn't exactly call him deprived. So don't lay any guilt trip on me. I happen to be in a highly competitive business. But it pays off. And it'll pay off a hell of a lot more very soon."

Since she had not blamed him, or even intended to, Claire simply stared at him and thought: *He feels so guilty he doesn't realize he's the one doing all the accusing.*

"So I've been away a lot more lately," he continued. "Okay, I promise, no matter what happens at the network, I'll spend more time with him from now on. Maybe I can even arrange to take him along on one of my trips to the Coast."

Claire did not respond, not even to point out that he had made such righteous paternal resolves before and failed to keep them. He was devoted to an industry and a career which demanded not only most of his time but somehow always when it was most important to be with his son.

"Once we get the network back into competitive position, I can ease up. We'll have more time together as a family."

"Yes, darling, of course." Claire pretended to agree. She knew that the battle among the networks was so fierce that it would never let up.

What troubled her more than she cared to admit, even to her husband, was the nature of Robbie's escapade earlier this evening. It was not only unlike him, but dangerous. In sports he had always been flamboyant, bold about taking risks. As a quarterback he was known as a scrambler, willing to run the ball and take punishment doing that. God knows, she had come away from several games with tight knots in her stomach. But in all other areas of his life Robbie was quite cautious. No, she decided, *mature* was the better word. It was the word used about him constantly, by his teachers, by his coaches, even going back to his early days in Scouts and at camp.

Why now this sudden impulsive, dangerous adventure? Was it only to impress a girl with whom Claire knew him to be in love? Or was it more?

She could not sleep for worrying. So, quietly as she could, she slipped out of bed, went down to the den, and tried to read herself to sleep. She was still awake at dawn when Don found her there.

"You, too?" he asked. "I tossed and turned all night. It's completely unlike him. I kept telling myself it's only a single incident. But then I asked: If it is only one incident, why am I so worried?"

When Robbie came down to breakfast, Don directed him into the den. Chastened, more restrained, and even more respectful than usual, Robbie complied.

"Now, son, what do you have to say for yourself?"

"I'm sorry. 'Specially about your car. If you want to, take the cost of repairs out of my allowance. Or even my savings. I'll understand."

"Robbie, you don't have enough savings to cover the damage. But that's not the point. You endangered your life. You endangered that girl. Why?"

Robbie looked away, blinked, but did not reply.

"Robbie?" His father persisted. "Why? To show off? There must be better ways. Safer ways."

"I wasn't showing off," Robbie said. "It wasn't for her. It was for—for me."

"For you? What does that mean?"

"Didn't you ever get the feeling that you could do anything in the world? Didn't you, Dad?"

"We all have ambitions, daydreams."

"I mean more than just dreaming. I mean *knowing* you can do it. *Anything. You own the world.* Nothing is impossible for you. In fact, the more impossible it seems, the more sure you are that you can do it."

Don reached out gently to turn his son's face to him. He looked into his blue eyes. He saw there a conviction that forced him to forgo any further questions about his son's motives in the unfortunate event.

"Next time you get a feeling like that, think before you do anything dangerous. Promise?"

"Yeah, Dad, I promise."

"Okay, son," Don said, releasing him.

Alone, Don pondered Robbie's strange explanation. Accustomed as he was to his son's boundless enthusiasm, Don had never heard him express himself in quite those words before.

Growing up, Don thought, *he's growing up.* Then comforted himself by thinking: *It's a phase. It'll pass. It'll pass.*

Robbie biked off to school. On the way he almost precipitated an accident with a southbound car by passing a red light. He had not meant to. He had simply been unaware of it. The driver shouted threats and curses at him. But Robbie ignored them. He was too engrossed in his own thoughts to pay attention.

He kept reliving that terrible moment when the car suddenly veered out of control, shot off the Merritt and into that tree. Fortunately he braked in time; else it could have been more serious. Fatal even. He was frightened. Not only of the possibility of injury or even death. But of the thing, the impulse, the . . . the . . . There was no word in his vocabulary to explain it. The feeling that took possession of him. Exciting, exhilarating, it was a fire that took over and made him feel that he stood atop this world and could do anything. Anything!

It was impossible to explain. No one understood, Not his friends. Not even his Dad. It had better remain his secret. He must try to control it whenever it happened.

CHAPTER 5

Andrew Slattery, B.A., M.A. in education, Ph.D., dean of Canaan Preparatory School, was a tall, spare man with a bald head tanned from exposure during his daily one-hour afternoon run. School meetings were scheduled around that religiously adhered-to ritual. While many considered it a personal indulgence, his own private self-serving theory was that his perseverance served as an example of personal discipline which had a beneficial effect on the entire student body.

His rigid routine resulted in a wiry leanness that, at first glance, made him appear a more ascetic and forbidding individual than the pleasant, concerned educator he was.

On this afternoon, precisely at three-thirty, as was his habit, he had retired to the small private dressing room that adjoined the school gym. He had dealt with all the complaints and suggestions of the faculty and felt free to take his plain gray sweat suit out of the metal locker when he was interrupted by a knock on the door. Unused to disturbances of any kind at this hour of the afternoon, he called out, impatiently, "Yes?"

The door opened briskly. Robbie Ward entered, speaking hurriedly, for he realized he was intruding.

"Mr. Slattery, this will take only a minute, but I have to say it. We must do it. I don't see how we can refuse. Not after what I saw on television last night."

"Ward." Slattery made it a point to address students by their last names. He felt it treated them like adults. "Can we discuss this later? Say an hour from now?"

"That's the whole damn trouble!" Robbie Ward responded.

Taking that as personal criticism, Slattery flushed in anger. "See here, Ward, I am not in the habit of being addressed in this fashion. If you have any grievance about this school, your teachers, or me, there is a proper time to voice it. Either an hour from now or first thing tomorrow. Good afternoon!"

Slattery brushed past Robbie on his way to the door.

"Damn it, Mr. Slattery, people are dying!"

The intensity in young Robbie's voice made the dean stop, turn back, and ask, "People dying? What are you talking about, young man?"

"Didn't you see it? Last night on television? Those film clips of people, kids, babies with their bellies hanging out from hunger? They were dying, or dead, right in front of the camera."

"Yes, yes, I saw it. It was dreadful," Slattery agreed.

"But still you're going out on your run like it's not happening."

"What would you expect I do about it?"

"Something. Anything!" Robbie said.

"Our government is sending food. Other governments are sending food," Slattery pointed out.

"Not good enough."

"What would you suggest?" Slattery asked, more in impatience than curiosity.

"Sir, Friday afternoon, before the game, I would like to get on the microphone and say a few words to the crowd. The students will all be there. A lot of parents. I would like for the whole team to back me up and for us to ask that Monday every student and his or her parents bring some good, nourishing food to school. Canned or in cartons, so it's not perishable. Food they take off their own pantry shelves, so it feels more like a sacrifice instead of just driving down to the supermarket and laying out a few dollars to buy it. I think that would be good not only for those starving people but also for a lot of overfed people around here. I would like permission to do that."

Touched, Slattery reached out to put his hand on Robbie's

shoulder. "Robert, if that's what you'd like to do, we'll do it."

"Thank you, Mr. Slattery."

Andrew Slattery started on his usual itinerary up the incline known as School Hill. Instead of listening to one of his familiar tapes of string quartets on his Walkman, he allowed the earphones to hang loosely around his neck. He was thinking that Robert Ward was quite a special young man with great potential for good.

There was a light rain falling Friday afternoon. Because of the weather, the crowd was smaller than usual. But as arranged, Robbie Ward, in his football uniform, helmet under his arm, stood at the microphone, flanked on both sides by his teammates. He spoke to the people in the stands, who huddled under umbrellas.

"Fellow students, parents, and spectators, our whole team is asking for your help. Not for ourselves but for babies, kids, young people our age, and people of all ages who right now are suffering in Ethiopia. Not just going hungry. They are way past that. They are starving. We can help feed them. So we are asking: When you leave this stadium, go home, find the most nourishing food in your kitchens and pantries, and bring it in to school on Monday morning. Mr. Slattery arranged with the government to have it shipped to Africa. Now, since this is a rainy day and less than our usual crowd, I want each of you when you get home to call at least one friend and tell them to do the same. We thank you. And now, guys, let's go!"

Shouting the Canaan battle cry, Robbie raced out onto the field, his team following.

On Monday morning there was a serious vehicular tie-up extending from the front entrance of Canaan Prep down the block and around the corner for two blocks beyond. The police had to be called out to direct traffic.

Cars pulled up at the school building. Drivers and passengers, old and young, students, their parents, people not connected with the school opened their car trunks to unload shopping bags of canned and packaged goods.

Before the day was over, mounds of food became mountains. National Guard trucks were commandeered to haul the food off to points from which they would be sent to Stewart Air Force Base, where they would be loaded onto air force planes for the mercy flight to Africa.

By midday several television stations had dispatched crews to Canaan to cover the event. With Robbie standing alongside him, Dean Slattery was interviewed. He presented Robbie as typical of what Canaan students were like and of what most young Americans were like, given the inspiration.

At the network everyone on the executive floor dropped in on Don to enthuse. "Hey, Don, that's your son, isn't it?"

Though he was bursting with pride, Don pretended to accept their enthusiasm and praise with diffidence.

That night, while the Wards were at dinner, the phone rang. It was for Don. A police sergeant was on the phone.

"Mr. Ward, Sergeant Lister. Remember, I read your son the riot act after he cracked up your car? Well, I just want to tell you I saw him on the TV tonight. Man, am I a judge of character? Was I right in handling that thing quietly?"

"You sure were, Lister."

"Give my best to the boy. And tell him this is more like it. It's what I meant by serving as an example."

Robbie had gone up to bed before Don allowed himself to say, "Best of all, he was so modest about it."

"I never thought about organizing anything like that, did you?" Claire asked.

"No. But that's the kind of boy he is. I have to say it. Honey, knock wood. We are the two luckiest parents in this whole world!"

CHAPTER 6

"Mrs. Ward, this isn't the usual monthly parent-faculty conference," Dean Slattery began. "But then what I want to discuss with you isn't very usual either."

Claire Ward stiffened slightly, for Slattery's stoneblue eyes and his severely lean face seemed to warn of trouble.

"Robert has always been a super young man here. Dean's list in his freshman year. And he'll make it again this semester. A fine athlete, a real leader. But in recent weeks Robert has done several things that have caused me to do a great deal of thinking."

"If you're referring to that incident with his father's car . . ." Claire began to defend her son.

Slattery anticipated her. "Yes, that started me thinking. But what really convinced me was his recent inspiration to collect food to feed starving Africans."

"I don't understand," Claire said.

"That act was most constructive. The other was not. Yet to me both have one significant thing in common. They are expressions of a young man with an overactive, restless mind. Evidently we do not offer him enough of a challenge. He needs something beyond our exacting curriculum. So I am about to suggest that we direct his abundant energies into more demanding and productive channels."

"But if you don't offer it here . . ." Claire protested.

"There is a program down in New York. At Columbia University. It admits unusually bright high school students into certain college courses."

"Let me understand," Claire said. "Robbie would attend classes at Columbia?"

"Yes, as if he actually were a college freshman," Slattery replied.

"Could he do that while carrying his full schedule here at Canaan?"

"All students in Columbia's Double Discovery Program do that," Slattery replied.

"And still keep up with his football? That's a big part of his life," Claire said.

"Don't we know," Slattery said, smiling. "We're expecting to win the private school league championship this year because Robbie's our quarterback. Don't worry about it, Mrs. Ward. I've already talked to the coach. The team doesn't practice on Mondays. So if Robbie takes a Monday and Wednesday course, he'll miss only one afternoon of practice. And the coach said Robbie's backup needs all the work he would get on Wednesdays."

"Well, if the coach feels that way . . ." Claire said.

Realizing she was still tentative about his suggestion, Slattery urged, "Mrs. Ward, believe me, I am not trying to push Robbie beyond his abilities. I have never before made such a recommendation about a second-year student. But that son of yours has more energy, mental and physical, than any student who's come through here in my time. Give it some thought. Talk to your husband."

Still somewhat apprehensive, Claire nodded hesitantly. She would only concede: "At times Robbie has a lot more energy than we can cope with."

Don Ward had a network limo drive him up to 116th Street and Broadway. It was an undistinguished part of New York City, an area of old tenements, small, modest apparel shops, and neighborhood food markets which had grown up around ancient Columbia University. The university itself was a strangely cohesive mix of stately beaux art renaissance structures interspersed with newer modern buildings that seemed to be intruders. The venerable institution was a microcosm of New York itself, where the old and new were thrown together.

The slip of paper Jeannie had handed him said only "Ferris Booth Hall, Double Discovery Program. Mrs. Prentiss." He knew he should have talked to the woman himself. But as with most things not immediately connected with network business, very efficient Jeannie had handled it.

Ferris Booth Hall proved to be one of the newer buildings. Which meant it lacked the feeling of warmth that wear, use, age, and original architecture imparted to the ancient ones. He took the elevator to the fourth floor. Found the office of the Double Discovery Program.

Mrs. Prentiss was a young, light-skinned black woman, nice-looking, pleasant, slender, and almost tall enough to be at eye level with Don. Jeannie had obviously prepared the way well for him.

"So you have the world's brightest son, Mr. Ward," Mrs. Prentiss said, smiling.

"Jeannie always says that. I don't know if she's trying to flatter him or hit me up for a raise." They both laughed. "But he *is* bright."

"We'll need his academic record, of course," Mrs. Prentiss said. "But first we'd like to know what his outlook is. We don't have unlimited facilities. And we have to be sure—"

Don felt compelled to interrupt. "He's not applying as a charity case. I can pay. No matter how much it costs."

For the first time Mrs. Prentiss ceased smiling.

"Mr. Ward, in our program no one pays. We accept young people on only one basis: ability. Plus their potential for the future. We aim to train the brightest and the most promising young people for whatever constructive contribution they can one day make to society at large. That's our only demand."

"Sorry about that," Don said. "But I thought—"

"No need to feel self-conscious, Mr. Ward. Most people make the same assumption: that everything has a price."

The moment of tension receded when she smiled once more. "Now, a few basic requirements. We'll need this application form filled out"—she handed Don a blue mimeographed form with many questions and blank spaces—"plus a transcript of his school record and some letters of recommendation. We'd also like to know his preference for a course. Advanced math. Sociology. Physics. Chemistry. Biology. English and composition. Philosophy—"

It was Don's turn to smile. Mrs. Prentiss interrupted herself "Did I say something amusing, Mr. Ward?"

"Knowing Robbie and his aptitudes, I can hear him now, 'Why can't I take *all* those courses?' And he'd be damned good at them, too."

"If he's only half as confident as his father, he'll do very well here," Mrs. Prentiss observed dryly.

Damn it, Don rebuked himself, *shut up and listen more. This isn't a network meeting. You don't have to score points.*

Aloud he said, "Mrs. Prentiss, please don't hold anything I say against Robbie. He's actually a very modest kid for all his accomplishments. I'll guarantee you'll like him."

"Well, we'll see about that," Mrs. Prentiss said, secretly amused at Don's inability to be less than ebullient on behalf of his son. "Meantime, submit the form and his transcript."

She rose from her chair, indicating Don had used up his allotted time. Don started for the door. He had his hand on the doorknob when she stopped him.

"Mr. Ward—" He turned back. "One thing I forgot. Where do you live?"

"New Canaan. But we'll arrange to get Robbie back and forth. Don't let that be a factor in your evaluation."

"But it is. You see, the program is limited to young people who live *in* New York City. Our federal grant specifies that."

The look of sudden disappointment on Don's face made her suggest, "If he could move into the city, stay with relatives perhaps. Anything that would give him a city address . . ." She left her suggestion hanging unfinished.

Between them passed looks that said, *Work it out. Your son seems like the kind of young person we're searching for.* While he responded, *Don't worry, I'll find a way.*

The meeting on the thirty-third floor was coming to a close. Ed Brady had made one of his usual locker room-type pep talks, promising his executive staff lavish amounts of additional development money with which to experiment on new programming for the upcoming season. They departed enthused, leaving behind them on the conference table an array of plastic cups half filled with cold coffee and wet cigarette butts.

Brady seemed relieved that it was over. He resented the fact that Don had lingered after all the others left.

"Yeah, Don?" Brady asked, hoping Don would not attempt to pin him down to specifics since he had never secured such an appropriation from the directors of the parent company. "Something troubling you?"

"Ed, I don't like to ask . . . but the apartment the network provides for you here in the city—"

Surprised, Brady stared across the highly polished conference table, "Oh, Christ, don't tell me, Don. I never figured you to be one of those—"

"One of what?" Don asked.

"Okay," Brady said, his disappointment quite obvious. He reached into his pocket, took out a single key hung on a gold key ring. He tossed it onto the table. It slid across the highly polished surface so swiftly that Don barely caught it before it could fall to the carpeted floor. "Just don't get into any trouble. Next thing you know she's pregnant. Which leads to all kinds of complications. Especially these days when they insist on having the baby. Who is she, Don?"

"Wait a minute! Do you think I'm asking for this key so I can take some girl up there for a matinee?"

"Then what?" Brady asked, his usually florid face redder than ever.

"It's about my son—"

"Robbie?" Brady asked, even more surprised. "Don't tell me that at his age—"

"For God's sake, Ed, just listen instead of making assumptions. Nasty assumptions!"

"Okay, kid, I'll listen." The use of the word *kid* was Brady's way of indicating their relationship was restored to that of mentor and protégé.

Don began to explain about Columbia, the Double Discovery Program for gifted students, the need to have, if only for record purposes, a New York City address.

Before Don could finish, Brady was laughing. "Is that all? You want to know what I thought. I thought it was Emily Grant. She's quite a piece. I've often thought about her . . . well, never mind. Of course, you can use the address for Robbie. It's about time that apartment was used for something besides—" He paused and laughed once more. "Come to think of it, in a way it's the same thing, except this way we're screwing the government!" He laughed more heartily as Don tossed the key back to him.

CHAPTER 7

Robbie Ward stood outside Ferris Booth Hall, grasping the envelope containing his school record and other papers. Claire nudged him with a gentle "Fourth floor, Robbie. Let's go."

"I'm going up there myself."

"There's really no need . . ." she started to say.

"But there is," Robbie insisted. "If I'm going to do this, I'm going to do it on my own."

"Okay." Claire agreed reluctantly. "I'll wait in the car." She watched until he disappeared into the dark corridor.

"So you're Robert Ward," Mrs. Prentiss said. As she read through the credentials he had presented, she cast sly, perceptive glances at the young man who sat across from her. He was handsome as well as bright. His father had not exaggerated. His grades, the letters of teachers' recommendations, especially Dean Slattery's letter about Robbie's food campaign, proved that he was the kind of student she was seeking.

He seemed mature beyond his years. Since he was physically big as well, he could pass for seventeen or eighteen quite easily. That resolved one of the questions which had concerned her. She did not like to integrate into a group of college freshmen a student so young that he would feel out of place and unable to participate in the give-and-take of normal class procedure. She had to be concerned about the emotional as well as the academic qualifications of her special kind of student.

Young Robert Ward was eminently qualified on all counts.

During the first week Claire drove Robbie down to Columbia on Monday and again on Wednesday. On the first day, while waiting out his two-hour session in English and composition, she browsed among the university buildings, dropped into the student lounges, listened to the students' chatter, was amused sometimes, startled others, but also impressed.

She spent Wednesday in the huge Columbia library. She was delighted to find an updated edition of a history textbook she had used during her own college days. As she thumbed through it, she was surprised to discover how much further advanced college students were today than in her day. The world, too, had changed a great deal. But the problems had not. In her version of the text the last war referred to had been in Korea. This new volume dwelt on Vietnam, unrest in Latin America, Soviet expansionism, the Middle East.

The world—soon it would be Robbie's world—was becoming ever more complex, more threatening. She closed the volume feeling depressed.

At the end of the second week of auditing the class in English comp, and after Robbie had submitted his first assignment, Claire was called into conference by Mrs. Prentiss to receive his professor's evaluation of Robert Ward's work.

"I have to read this exactly as it was dictated by Professor Gilman."

Claire sat up a bit stiffly. Don had warned her, as he had been warned, Double Discovery reserved the right to evaluate and expel any auditing student at any time if he or she did not keep pace, by missing classes, failing to hand in assignments, or falling below acceptable college-level work. Claire was prepared.

"I am reading now," Mrs. Prentiss said. "Quote 'This student, Robert Ward, exhibits a most unusual ability to express himself in writing. I have seen an occasional auditing student in the past who exceeded some of the freshmen in my course. But this is the first time one of them has exceeded the entire class. His ability to use and spell words correctly (a rare feat in these times, I might add) and to formulate mature thoughts and express them in a coherent and forceful manner is quite astonishing.

" 'His understanding and criticism of the eventual effect of the mass media on a democracy, its impact on American thought and international affairs are so well researched, so thoughtful and mature in its conclusions that I am taking the liberty of submitting it to a student writing competition.

" 'In my years of university teaching I have only once before come across a mind so brilliant at such an early age. And that man is now a special presidential envoy to Central America and being mentioned for the post of ambassador to the United Nations.' Unquote," Mrs. Prentiss said.

She smiled. "You will have to apologize for me to Mr. Ward. When he raved about Robbie, I put him down in my mind as a vain, overly proud father. Now I realize he has every good reason to feel the way he does. You've got a remarkable young son there."

Greatly relieved, Claire said, "Yes, we are lucky. Very lucky. Robbie's adopted, you know. And I often think, of all the babies in this world we might have been given, how fortunate we are that it was Robbie."

Claire smiled sheepishly before she said, "I don't dare say this to my friends, especially my friends in show business. They always keep asking me don't I miss it. Wouldn't I love to go back to acting? And I want to say yes, I miss it. But I would miss even more having a son like Robbie. It was worth every sacrifice I ever made. But they wouldn't understand."

CHAPTER 8

In Robbie's third week in the Double Discovery Program Claire's mother came down with an illness that required hospitalization. Divorced, living alone, and in her sixties, she depended on Claire for both help and companionship.

In order for Claire to be free for most of the afternoon, she and Don decided that she would drive Robbie into New York for his classes. But after class he would take the subway down to Don's office and wait until his father was free to leave for home. Robbie would take enough homework with him so it wouldn't matter if Don were late. If Don had to make a hasty, unscheduled trip to the Coast, Robbie could take a commuter train or get a ride home with one of the other network executives who lived in Connecticut.

The first two times the arrangement worked well, though on the Wednesday Don worked so late that Jeannie had to get Robbie two hamburgers and a shake to tide him over until Don was free to leave. But Robbie spent the afternoon and early evening in the network library, doing his assignment for English comp and his homework for Canaan Prep.

On the Monday of the fourth week Robbie became bored. He had no more assigned work to do, so he slipped out of the network office and was gone until almost eight o'clock. Don had been ready to leave long before.

"Son, I've been waiting! We could have left an hour ago if you'd been here. Where were you?"

"Oh, just hacking around," Robbie said.

"Well, next time look at your watch once in a while."

"Sure," Robbie said.

He concealed from his father the real reason for his tardiness. In the afternoon he had taken the subway down to Greenwich Village. On his way back, confused by the unfamiliar designations of subway trains, he had inadvertently taken one that carried him out to Queens. But it had been worth it. He had discovered Greenwich Village. It was fascinating and exciting, peopled by strange, intriguing, and colorful characters. He would go back, he knew that.

On the following Wednesday, when his mother dropped him off at 116th Street and Broadway, Robbie waved to her as usual.

She called a reminder to him. "Don't forget. Be on time in case Dad can get away early."

He nodded, smiled, started up the university steps briskly and across the campus in the direction of Hamilton Hall, the English building.

But as soon as Claire drove off, he turned back and headed for the subway. Mindful of her warning, he had decided to cut English comp so he could spend the entire afternoon in Greenwich Village and still meet Don in time.

The ride down on the noisy, dirty, swaying subway train seemed interminable. Unused to such forms of transportation, Robbie felt confined, almost claustrophobic. He was relieved to climb up out of the dank tunnel to the sounds of the traffic and human voices on Sheridan Square. He wandered the streets, studying all sorts of unfamiliar people: young people with stiff, eccentric spiky hairdos; old people—lifelong residents of the Village who hobbled along on tired, blue-veined legs and hugged to themselves grocery bags which were never large or very full.

Perhaps, Robbie thought, they bought enough food for only a few days at a time, fearful that they might not live longer. Or else they feared being mugged. Or was it that they could not afford to buy more at any one time? He had heard on the radio, seen on television depressing news stories about the struggle many retired people had to subsist on Social Security and measly pensions. It might be an excellent subject for a future paper in his English course, which at that moment he should have been auditing.

He would have to ask the nice blond girl who sat next to him in class what their next assignment was. She was older than he by three years and very maturely developed. Ridiculous as it might seem to anyone else, he had contemplated asking her for a date. For she always treated him as an equal. And she did have those nicely developed breasts, far more developed than Susan's.

Bewildered, he stared into the window of a shop that sold water pipes and other paraphernalia for using illegal drugs. From across the street a loudspeaker fixed in the transom of a record store blared forth hard-rock music. He passed on to gaze into other shop windows that sold the latest in rock-style clothing for those young who liked to mimic their idols. Compared to all this, Canaan was dull and unexciting.

When the din of the rock music came to an end, Robbie heard the softer sounds of a different kind of music. The melody of a guitar floated from the open door of a small old coffeehouse bar. He lingered in the doorway to listen. The place was dark, lit only by candles on the little tables. A few of the tables were occupied by young people dressed in jeans or leather, with denim jackets or vests. They nursed glasses of wine or coffee in tiny cups. The only light that emanated from the ceiling was the pale blue spotlight that fixed on the guitarist who sat on a plain wooden chair in the center of the simple stage.

Robbie listened appreciatively and went in. *Very good guitar,* he thought. *Nice voice, too.*

He found a tiny marble-topped table barely wide enough to accommodate two cups and saucers, an ashtray, and a sugar bowl. A young waitress approached. Even in the dark he could see coffee stains on her wrinkled uniform.

"Cappuccino? Espresso?"

Entranced by the music, he said, "Yeah."

"Yeah?" she questioned. "Which?"

Since it was the last one mentioned, he said, "Espresso." He had never had any before, but she was not insisting that he drink it, only that he order it.

He became more deeply entranced by the music, for the man played excellent classical guitar and sang softly in pleasing Spanish. The waitress set down his tiny cup of steaming and fragrant black liquid, more pungent than the coffee his mother served at home. There was a sliver of lemon peel on the saucer.

"That'll be a dollar fifty," she said.

"Okay."

"Rule of the house. Pay on being served," she insisted.

He dug into his pocket, felt for and found two single dollar bills. He laid them down on top of the check. She took the money and left with no intention of returning with any change. He tasted the coffee. It was hot and bitter. *If this is espresso, who needs it?* he thought. Having paid for it, he felt free to ignore it. He left the table to edge closer to the low platform that pretended to be a stage.

The thin dark guitarist brought his number to a close with a sudden long crescendo. Robbie began to clap in appreciation. As if he had reminded them that applause was obligatory, some of the others joined in with weak, scattered handclaps. The guitarist smiled at them sardonically. When he directed his smile toward Robbie, he seemed more sincere.

"You play?"

Robbie nodded.

"Would you like to?"

Again Robbie nodded.

The man handed the instrument over to him. Robbie took it gingerly, noticing that the man's hands trembled as he released the guitar to him.

"You don't have to be nervous," Robbie said. "I'll be careful with it."

The guitarist smiled indulgently. Robbie took the man's place on the platform and began to play.

The man listened for a few bars, seemed impressed. "Your own composition?"

Robbie nodded.

"Excellent. Very original."

He slipped quietly out of the blue spotlight and in the direction of the men's room. Robbie noticed that another man followed, only to emerge moments later. Finally the guitarist returned.

He waited respectfully until Robbie finished his song. While the audience applauded politely, the man reached for his instrument. Robbie handed it back carefully but noticed that this time the man's hands no longer trembled. Robbie resumed his place sitting on the edge of the platform, content to listen. The man played more serenely now.

Robbie listened even more intently, studying the man's nimble fingering, until he became aware of time. He looked at his watch. Already past six. He had better head for the uptown subway. And this time make sure he took the right train. But he realized first he had better make a stop in the men's room.

The toilet was dark; it stank. The tiles on the floor were damp and smeared by shoes tracking over careless urine. He was relieving himself when he heard the door open behind him. He half turned, to see the same man who had followed the guitarist into the men's room.

"Nickel bag?" the man asked.

Robbie had heard enough, read enough, to know what the man meant.

"No, thanks, I'm not a user," he said, zipping up his fly.

"Then what do you want?" the man challenged. "You a plant, or something?"

"I just came in to hear some guitar," Robbie said, trying to push past the man to get to the door. In so small a room it was impossible to avoid physical confrontation.

The man seized Robbie's arms, held him close, while he studied his face.

"You a cop? A narc? Dressed up like a student?"

The man's suspicious, angry eyes searched Robbie's eyes, seeking confirmation of his accusation.

Forcefully Robbie broke free. As he turned to the door, the man swung out, catching Robbie across the face. Robbie felt pain and a gush of blood from his nose. He lashed out in retaliation. He struck the man on the side of the face, hurling him back against the wall. The man slid slowly to the damp floor. Robbie turned to the door to escape. The man reached out to grab him by the ankle. In the same move Robbie flung the door open and fell forward.

"Grab that son of a bitch!" the man cried out. "He tried to rob me."

Robbie leaped to his feet, only to be confronted by half a dozen men, who rose up from their tables to attack him.

There was no time to think, only to act. Robbie jumped forward at the closest man with more power and force than he had ever used to throw a block on the football field. He stunned the man, bowling him over, causing him to fall in the path of the others. Then Robbie catapulted over him, scattering the others.

Between him and the front door was now only one man. But he held a knife in his right hand.

Robbie knew he had no choice. If he tried to outmaneuver the knife wielder, it would give the others time to recover. Instinct told him: *Attack! Go at the man and take your chances!* He leaped toward him. When the man lunged at him, Robbie pivoted as he was used to doing when he avoided would-be tacklers. He barely eluded the man's hand, which swung out, slashing at Robbie with the long, sharp knife.

Robbie sensed the knife cut through something but felt no pain. He hit the man with a body block, sending him crashing against one of the tiny marble-topped tables, which collapsed and shattered under the impact. Robbie hurtled past the man, out the door and into the cool autumn evening. He started running desperately, trying to remember if he was going in the right direction for the uptown subway.

He was. He jumped down the stairs two at a time, not daring to look back until he had reached the bottom. He was not being pursued. But he noticed that homegoers emerging from the train climbed the stairs slowly, looking back at him strangely. He ignored them. They could not have guessed that he had just escaped a dangerous encounter, perhaps even a fatal one.

Instead of feeling frightened by that realization or even relieved, Robbie was exhilarated. It was another triumph.

When he pushed onto the crowded uptown train, passengers seemed to draw back to avoid him.

Only when he was able to see his reflection in the dirty car window did he realize why. From his nose down his face was covered with dried blood. When he examined his arm, he discovered that the knife, which had missed his flesh, had slashed a long, clean cut in the luxurious Italian leather jacket his father had brought him from one of the expensive shops on Rodeo Drive in Beverly Hills.

Robbie tried to dismiss it by thinking, *What the hell, it's only another bribe he brings me every so often to make up for being away so much.*

Once back at the network Robbie stopped at the men's room on the thirty-second floor to wash up and remove all signs of blood from his face. He examined himself closely in the mirror. His nose was not broken. His face was red, bruised, but looked little different from the effects of an afternoon of strenuous body-contact football practice.

He was ready to go up to the thirty-third floor and his father's office.

On the ride home his father asked no questions. Fortunately the knife slash was in the right arm of Robbie's jacket and shielded by the door. So his father never even noticed. Robbie was sure when it became necessary to explain he would have an acceptable story.

One thing he had not planned on.

CHAPTER 9

"Mrs. Ward, this is Mrs. Prentiss. At Columbia Double Discovery Program." Her firm voice identified itself over the phone.

"Oh, yes, of course, Mrs. Prentiss. How nice to talk to you again," Claire said.

"I'm afraid not. Usually I don't make personal contact. Just a letter will do. But since Robert is such an unusual young man, I couldn't let this go by without more direct contact."

Claire felt her throat tighten. She could hardly respond. "Is there some trouble?"

"Mrs. Ward, has Robert been ill lately?"

"Some minor football bruises. But otherwise he's been fine. Why?"

"Your son has missed his last three auditing sessions," Mrs. Prentiss informed her.

"That's impossible!" Claire protested. "I drove him down myself each time. He had to be there!"

"He wasn't," Mrs. Prentiss said firmly. "So, according to our rules, he must be dropped from the program."

"But I thought he was doing so well."

"He was. Until this happened."

"I'll get to the bottom of this. I'll find out what happened. I'm sure there's a good reason."

"It won't change anything," Mrs. Prentiss warned. "If he

wishes to reapply next year, we might consider him again. But for this year he is out. Sorry."

"I see," Claire said, in a soft, defeated whisper.

She hung up the phone. Her first impulse was to call Don. But she refrained. Don's business problems were heavy enough. This could wait until he came home.

She sank down onto the dinette chair. Suddenly all her other plans and chores for the day became unimportant. Even visiting her mother, shopping for her, preparing her meal seemed irrelevant. Her first thought about Robbie was: *He doesn't like to lose; he's not used to losing.* Being dropped, expelled, could destroy his morale. What a critical time of his life to suffer such a rejection.

But why? What had he done those afternoons after she had left him at Columbia, after he had waved good-bye to her, smiling, always smiling? Where had he gone?

She was startled suddenly by a disturbing thought. Something that she had noticed but that Robbie had passed off with an excuse that seemed logical at the time. That long slit in the sleeve of his leather jacket. The one she'd had mended at the tailor shop that did Don's clothes. It was a long, sharp slit. Even the old tailor had remarked on it. She went to the hall closet where it hung. She examined the sleeve. The tailor was right. It was too clean a tear to be caused by being caught on a locker room hook, as Robbie had explained.

She came back into the kitchen, absentmindedly went about making notes of things to buy for her mother's next two days' meals. Until she stopped writing and sat there thinking.

Her concern was not due to distress over the effect on Robbie. It was not even her concern about protecting Don from this news until his day was over. It was herself. Now she knew why.

This was the second unusual event in the last few weeks. The second time that Robbie was not acting like the Robbie she was used to. This time it was not something that Don could shrug off by saying, "He's a fifteen-and-a-half-year-old kid wanting to show off for a girl."

It was a pattern of conduct different from any Robbie had ever exhibited. Before she could become obsessed by the thought, she reminded herself she had duties to perform: shopping for her mother; her daily visit; her afternoon meeting at the hospital about the benefit she had promised to organize for them. Then she had to drop in at Village Furniture to talk Mr. Yodelson into lending the Towne Players the couch and two easy chairs she needed for their new production. Yodelson always grumbled, but he always came around in the end. He simply loved the theater.

As the afternoon wore on, though she fulfilled all her obligations, and did so in a manner to conceal her concern from everyone, that shocking phone call from Mrs. Prentiss proved a distressing, ever-present counterpoint to her entire day.

"I can't believe it!" was Don's first angry response. "I'll call Mrs. Prentiss in the morning. She'll reverse her decision."

"She won't," Claire warned.

"Claire, honey, I know how to deal with people, all kinds of people. It's my job! I can do it!"

"Not this time, Don. I could tell by her voice. This is final."

Don slowly rotated his cocktail glass, letting the pimento-crowned olive spin around. His silence was acceptance of her appraisal. He asked quietly, "Did you talk to him? Did you ask him why?"

"I thought we should do it together."

He looked across at her, noticed something in her eyes that made him ask simply, "Claire?"

She knew what the question was. She felt forced to answer. "Yes," she said. "Yes, I'm scared."

"He must have some explanation."

"I'm still scared," she said. "Somehow this is different. And I don't know why."

"A kid suddenly playing hooky. I don't like it either. But it's nothing to be scared of. We'll talk to him."

She called up to Robbie. He came down, entered the den, asking, "Dinner ready?"

"Son, sit down," Don said. The tone of his voice made Robbie realize this was not the usual call to dinner.

"Yes, sir."

"Son, if there's something you're into, some kind of trouble—"

"I am not on drugs," Robbie said firmly.

Don glanced at Claire, then looked up into Robbie's eyes and studied them for a long time before he said, "Okay. I accept that. You are not on drugs. But where have you been these last few days?" When Robbie hesitated, Don continued: "Your mother got a call today. You've been dropped from Columbia."

"Oh?" Robbie said in a small, hushed voice.

"You want to tell us about it?" Don asked. "About what happened those days between when your mother dropped you at school and you showed up late at my office?"

Robbie felt a burning embarrassment, was unable to respond.

"What about those things you told me on the drives home? Those things you said happened in class? Funny things. Serious things. What other students said, what you said," Don challenged. "They were all lies, things you made up?"

Robbie blurted out, "The things I made up were a hell of a lot more interesting than what happened in that class!"

"Was that it?" Claire asked. "You were bored?"

"Yes! Bored. Bored in class. Bored waiting around until Dad was free to drive me home. Just plain bored!"

"Where did you go? What did you do?" Claire asked.

"The Village. Walked the old streets. Narrow, crooked streets, crisscrossing each other. All kinds of restaurants. Bars. Coffeehouses. Lots of interesting people down there. Some good guitar, too. Rock groups. Lots of drugs. But I swear I didn't get into any. I swear!"

"I believe you, son," Don said. "But you realize this is a failure. A big failure. Since it's outside your regular schoolwork, it doesn't have to appear on your college entrance applications. But it would have looked great to have a recommendation from Columbia."

"Yeah" was all that Robbie could say.

Claire tried to ease her son's painful embarrassment by saying quietly, "Dinner's ready."

"I don't think I want any dinner. Can I go up to my room?" Robbie asked, chastened.

"If you'd rather," Claire said.

Robbie started for the door when Claire asked, "Robbie that rip in your suede jacket—*was* it from a hook in the locker room?"

He turned to look at her, considered perpetuating his lie, but then admitted, "A knife slash. I had a fight down there."

"A fight? Against a man with a knife?" Claire asked, terrified.

"Yeah," he said, and continued out the den and up to his room.

As if suddenly reminded, Don said, "Hell! Ed Brady!"

"What's he got to do with this?" Claire asked.

"Because we used his apartment address to make Robbie eligible, he's declared himself in on this. He keeps asking how Robbie is doing. He got a tremendous boot out of that professor's report. Even said maybe we'd use Robbie in the newsroom this summer. What am I going to tell him now when he no longer sees Robbie around the office on Mondays and Wednesdays?"

In a moment he improvised. "I know! I'll tell him Robbie's coach said he had to attend football practice every afternoon or be dropped from the team."

He could tell by the look on Claire's face that she disapproved.

"What do you want me to do?" Don demanded angrily. "Tell him that Robbie got expelled, kicked out? After all the trouble we went to? One little lie isn't going to matter!" he insisted. But it was obvious he too was uncomfortable with it.

After a long, disapproving silence Claire said, "It's not like Robbie to cut school. To go down to a place like Greenwich Village on his own. To get into knife fights. He could have been killed."

"Claire, honey, you'll have to get used to the idea that he can't live his whole life in the protected atmosphere of an upper-class suburb and a select private school. He's at an adventurous age. He wants to get out and explore this world, lousy as it is. But he's got to discover that for himself."

"Yes, you're right, darling."

Claire pretended to agree. But within her something kept protesting: *It isn't just growing up. I'm his mother. I know him better than anyone. He is not the same boy. Something's happening, and I'm frightened.*

CHAPTER 10

"I wish Dad had been here today," Robbie said as he sank into the front seat of his mother's station wagon. "I mean, that fourth quarter, wasn't that something?"

"The best you've ever been, darling. Completing six out of seven passes in a single quarter. And it puts you into the championship game. Dad would have been proud. Very proud. We'll tell him all about it when he gets home for dinner," Claire said.

"*If* he gets home," Robbie said.

Ever since he was dropped from the program at Columbia, Robbie had become more dependent on his football accomplishments for self-pride and satisfaction. It would have meant a great deal to him to have had his father there, Claire knew.

She pulled the wagon away from the curb in front of Canaan Prep stadium and started down the street, which was arched over with tall maples almost shed of their late-autumn leaves of red and gold.

Disturbed by Robbie's silence, his unaccustomed lack of exuberance, she said, "He did call. He said they were having—"

Robbie anticipated her. "I know. The new fall lineup is a disaster, and they have to do something. Which means they will buy some lousy old movies and have the *Tuesday Night Movie of the Week,* and the *Wednesday Night Movie of the Week.* And the *Thursday Night Movie of the Week.* Well, if they put on some decent programs instead of all that junk—"

"Robbie, you shouldn't talk that way about your father's profession. It's the way he earns his living."

"And the way we can afford a big house, two cars and the way he's going to pay for my college education. If I hear that once more . . ." But he gave up protesting.

They both were silent until Robbie exploded suddenly. "Why does it take all those meetings? I've met some of those executives You ask me, one idiot in a darkroom could come up with better programs. All that crap!"

"Robbie!" She reprimanded him as she stopped at the red light. She waited diligently before making her right turn. She was not so meticulous when driving alone but tried to set a good example whenever Robbie was in the car.

She could hear the phone ringing as she slipped the key into the lock of the door leading from the garage into the kitchen. Leaving the key in the lock and pushing by Robbie, she rushed to the phone. She hated those times when she picked up the phone just one ring too late, to hear nothing but a dial tone. She would usually spend the next hour trying to figure out who might have called and about what.

She seized the phone and, breathless, said, "Hello?"

She was rewarded by Don's comforting voice. "Angel? How'd it go?"

"Go?" For the moment she was confused. Had he asked her to do some errand and had she forgotten?

"The game, the game," Don insisted impatiently. "How was he?"

"Terrific, as usual. Coach said we could begin thinking about football scholarships even though he's only a sophomore."

"You know how I feel about that," Don said. "MIT wants to give him a scholarship, fine! But football, uh-uh. Is he there? Let me talk to him."

"Robbie! Dad. He wants to talk to you." She was relieved as well as pleased. All during the game and on the drive home she had worried whether Don would remember, no less have time, to place a call.

Robbie came to the phone. His resentment obvious, he said only, "Hi."

"Hi, laddie. Mom told me you were great. I sure wish I could have been there. But you know this business."

"Yeah, Dad, I know this business."

"I guess this win puts you into the championship game two weeks from now," Don said cheerfully, hoping to offset the coldness in his son's voice.

"Yep," Robbie said, the monosyllabic answer indicating to Don that he had failed his son once more.

"Look, son, tell you what. Sunday afternoon you and I will go to the Giants-Packers game over in New Jersey. We'll sit in the network box. How about that?"

"Okay." Robbie agreed with no enthusiasm.

"Robbie, I explained why I couldn't be there today. Some very important decisions had to be made about fill-in programming. It was a crucial meeting."

"I understand," Robbie said, making it clear that between understanding and accepting there was a wide gap.

"Let me talk to your mother."

"Sure."

"I love you, Robbie, you know that, don't you?"

"Yeah." He turned to Claire. "He wants to talk to you." He did not wait to hand her the phone but started out of the kitchen.

"Don?"

"He's pretty upset, isn't he?"

"Yes, he is."

"I'll make it up to him."

"If we live long enough."

"What does that mean? Don demanded, his guilt emerging as anger.

"It means, darling, that you already have a lot of making up to do."

"I can't help it. It's the nature of the business." He realized he was shouting and lowered his voice. "Look, I promised to take him to the Giants game on Sunday. I'll make a big occasion of it. I'll have a network limo pick us up and take us out. We'll sit in the network box. I'll even take him down to the locker room afterward so he can meet some of the players. Maybe I'll have his picture taken with the Giants quarterback."

"Good," she said, and hung up.

She wondered: Was her husband so much in love with his

work or with the perks that came with the job? He enjoyed saying, "I'll have a network limo pick us up," or, "We're having dinner at 'Twenty-one.' " Or Le Cirque. Or whatever the in place was at the moment.

Claire ofttimes thought: *We're not rich. Don just likes to live as if we were. And the network makes it possible.*

Well, she resolved, two weeks from now Robbie's championship game, network problems or no, his father was going to be there! Even if she had to call Ed Brady and insist!

The rain started Saturday night. It was still raining Sunday morning. Despite the weather, Don and Robbie went to the Giants game. In a network limo.

The Meadowlands field over in New Jersey was drenched, the water inches deep on the playing field. When a man was tackled, he slid fifteen feet before coming to a stop. When a pass was missed, the ball did not bounce but lay there in a pool on the sodden Astroturf.

It was a bad game, badly played. Don became increasingly aware that Robbie showed little enthusiasm. He had even passed up the hot dogs, which he usually loved.

Midway through the third quarter Robbie said, "Let's get out of here."

"Don't you want to meet any of the players?" Don asked.

"No. Let's go."

Don had the network limo drive them back to Connecticut.

On the way Don tried once more to apologize for missing Friday afternoon's game. He failed. They rode through the rain in silence. The spacious rear compartment of the limo seemed small, too small for its two passengers.

During the long silence Robbie thought: *Maybe it was a mistake, all a big mistake. Maybe my father is too busy ever to have had a son, adopted or otherwise. Or maybe*—the thought did occur to him—*if I had been my father's real son, things would be different.*

At that moment Don intruded. "I'm going to be at your playoff game. Did Mom tell you?"

"No," Robbie said. "I guess she didn't want to promise too much."

The rebuke in the phrase *too much* compelled Don to reply, "Son, I don't miss your games because I want to. When you grow up and have kids of your own, have the responsibility of supporting them, you'll know exactly how I feel."

"Why do I have to grow up to know how you feel?" Robbie asked. "I know now."

Those words made Don swing about in his seat to stare at his son. "Meaning?"

"What you said it means," Robbie replied. "I'm not really your son; I'm a responsibility."

Hurt and angry, Don replied, "Responsibility and love are all part of the same thing. If I didn't love you, would I work so hard to send you to an expensive private school? If I didn't love Mom, would I feel responsible for her? You understand that, don't you, son?"

"Yeah. Sure." Robbie agreed for fear he would say something that would make his father feel even more guilty. For Robbie had learned that whenever he made his father feel guilty, somehow he ended up feeling less secure himself.

Days, weeks, sometimes months would go by, and he would never consider the fact that he was adopted. Only when he felt deprived would he wonder: *How would they treat me if I were really their son?*

How many times when he was just hacking around with the other guys had he discovered they had exactly the same complaints about their natural parents. He had heard them gripe, "Can't do nothing. Can't go anywhere. Without their asking, 'Where have you been? What did you do?' Half the time they must think I'm on drugs or something. They don't trust me at all."

And those kids weren't adopted, had no private fears of their own, as he did. Still, when something happened, as on Friday afternoon, when he had excelled and his father was not there to see it, that same question kept coming up.

Of course, it was good to have Mom at the games. She was always there. She never would really learn what football was all about. But Dad knew. He was an expert. Years ago he was on the sports side of the network and covered NCAA games as an associate producer. He knew when a play worked to perfection, and why. And when it failed, and why. He could talk football with you, even help you with your game.

But not if he wasn't even there to see you play.

During the long, silent drive home through the heavy rain, Don Ward kept thinking: *I know how he feels. I should know. When I was starring in basketball back in high school in Clinton, Iowa, my biggest booster was my dad. So I know what it means to a boy to have that kind of moral support. But things were different then. My dad ran his own lumberyard. He was his own boss in a business which was never plagued by emergencies. In four years he never missed one of my home games. And hardly any of our away games. But things were different back there.*

There must be something I can do to make up . . . something.

CHAPTER 11

Late Monday afternoon Don called. Claire could tell from his voice how excited he was.

"Is he there?"

"Up in his room. Doing his homework. To the loudest rock music I've ever heard. Why?"

"Put him on the phone!" Don insisted.

"Don, what is it? What happened?"

"You'll find out!" he said, teasing with a laugh.

Once he heard Robbie's voice, Don said, "Laddie, what would you say if I told you that there is a possibility of getting two seats to the rock concert of the Morbid at the Civic Center next Friday night?"

"Dad, are you kidding? They're scalping tickets at forty and fifty dollars apiece."

"Damn right they are. But my son, and any girl of his choice, are going to be right there."

Beginning to grow skeptical, Robbie asked, "Dad, is this another one of your promises?"

"Promises? I am sitting right at my desk holding in my hot little hand two tickets that say 'Row F. Seats one-ten, one-eleven.' How about that?"

"Terrific!" Robbie replied, half turning to his mother. "Did he tell you? Tickets to see the Morbid Friday night!"

"Son, son, you haven't heard it all," Don said. "Through my same contact here at the network I have arranged for me to introduce you to Killer Kane after the show."

"Dad, now you've got to be kidding. Everybody knows that Killer gets so exhausted during a concert that he doesn't see anybody!" Robbie said. "It's been in all the columns."

"Robbie, it wasn't easy. I had to use a lot of muscle to arrange it. But Friday night, when I take you into his dressing room, you'll see."

"Wow! I better call Susan."

"Right!" Don said, exuberant now. "One thing before you do, son. Forgive me for not being at last Friday's game?"

"Sure, Dad, I understand."

"Okay, laddie, as long as you understand."

Late Friday afternoon Don had to fly down to Washington. The network was facing serious objections from several government departments over a film about nuclear war. The film was already in the can and had cost four million dollars. So when Ed Brady said, "Don, I can't trust anyone else to get us a clearance. But you can do it. You always do," Don had no choice but to go.

Claire rolled up to the center. She could sense the tension in the air. The doors had not yet been opened. Young people, several thousand of them, crowded around the entrance. Many sprawled on the ground or the concrete steps. The air was heavy with the oversweet odor of marijuana.

With considerable concern and disapproval she noticed a number of wild hairdos among the young. Many of them, both boys and girls, imitating their rock idols, had their hair dyed in patches of bright red and garish purple. Some, in addition, had their hair lacquered into spiky points that stuck straight up like the prongs of an ironwork fence.

Claire tried to minimize all of that by consoling herself with this thought: *It's a different generation. I'll never understand them. But I won't stop worrying about them either.*

Mindful of the tragic event not too many years back when almost a dozen youngsters were trampled to death at a rock concert, she resented that the doors had not yet been opened.

So, after she had dropped Robbie and Susan with all the appropriate warnings and admonitions, she pretended to drive off. Instead, she parked down the street, where she could watch the progress of events in her rearview mirror.

Soon the doors must have opened, for she noticed that like grain being sucked into a funnel, the young people began flowing into the auditorium. Her fears at rest, she started her wagon and took off for the dress rehearsal of her newest production. She would be late. But let them wait. Robbie was where he wanted to be, and safe.

The air hung thick with smoke that wafted about in the blinking, blinding psychedelic lights that radiated from the stage. The Morbid was into its third set for the evening. More than an hour of heavy rhythmic music and wild suggestive lyrics had brought two thousand young people to a pitch of excitement. Stamping their feet in unison, they sang along with Killer, the Morbid leader, until his voice was almost blotted out. Robbie and Susan rose to their feet to join in. Soon others around them rose. Before long the entire audience was on their feet, clapping, singing, stamping until the members of the Morbid were watching their audience more closely than their audience was watching them.

"I can do that!" Robbie said suddenly to Susan.

"Do what?"

"Play better rock guitar than Killer Kane!"

"Robbie, are you crazy?" Susan protested.

"I'll show you if I am!"

Intoxicated by the fervor surrounding them, and with his own natural impulsiveness taking control, Robbie shouted out loud, "I can play the best rock guitar in the world!"

With that he sprang from Susan's side, forced his way to the aisle, fought his way down the stairs toward the stage. He had to push through couples who were dancing on the steps and in front of the stage.

In a single leap he bounded up onto the stage. He confronted Killer Kane, who was dressed in black shiny leather, bristling with bright steel decorations, buttons, stars, tiny spikes. Killer's hair stood on end, lacquered into weird, ugly shapes. His face was painted with wild surrealistic dabs of dead white makeup mingled with red that pretended to be blood. His eyes were painted with concentric alternating circles of white and black so that his pupils seemed to be the bull's-eyes of two targets.

By staring at those pupils, Robbie knew that Killer was high on something, completely in the grip of that something even more than the rhythms which he himself had created.

But Robbie was possessed by compulsions of his own. He reached out for Killer's guitar, shouting over the deafening music, "I'll show you how to play rock!"

To protect his costly instrument, Killer swerved and turned to avoid Robbie's grasping hands. But Robbie pursued him. Suddenly they both were grappling over the guitar until Killer called out to his drummer, "Dinty! Help!"

The drummer bolted down from his platform to attack Robbie. When the audience realized one of their own was outnumbered and in danger, young men began to leap up onto the stage to join in the combat. In seconds the frenzy that had been loud, violent music had become a hand-to-hand battle between audience and musicians.

Driven by the impulse to take possession of that guitar and demonstrate his own virtuosity, Robbie struck at Killer Kane again and again. He landed his sharpest blow alongside Killer's head, knocking him to the floor. As Robbie reached for the guitar, Killer drew out from under his black leather vest a chrome-plated .38. He pointed it toward the ceiling and fired. Two shots. The sound reverberated deafeningly through the auditorium, multiplied in resonance and impact by the loudspeaker system.

Those sounds brought a sudden silence and a terrible sense of reality to the frenzied place. All fighting ceased. The fear of imminent and deadly danger had restored a sense of sanity.

Robbie drew back slowly, tense with an awareness of how close to being injured or killed he had come. A fraction of change in the angle of the gun, and he might have become its victim. As if coming out of a trance, Robbie asked himself: *What am I doing here? What happened?*

The sirens of approaching police patrol cars made the audience straggle back to their seats. Some of those onstage were still leaping into the pit as the police burst into the hall.

The police lieutenant in charge ordered them all to remain where they were. He mounted the stage and began an inquiry. First he demanded, "Where is that weapon?"

No one replied. He insisted, "There's a weapon in here. And I demand to see it!"

Killer finally surrendered his gun.

"You got a permit for this?"

"Yeah. It's in my dressing room."

"Get it!"

"I'll get it." Killer's agent, Tony Ferrante, volunteered, heading offstage.

The lieutenant took possession of the weapon and turned to probe the events that led to the riot. It did not take long to reconstruct what had happened. Even Robbie's contemporaries were forced to admit that he had been the cause of the trouble when he leaped up onto the stage to grapple with Killer.

"So you see," Ferrante tried to explain, "all my client did was try to stop the riot. And he did not shoot *at* anybody. He was very, very careful, considering the circumstances."

The lieutenant finally relented. "Okay. You guys pack up, leave town, and we'll forget this whole thing."

"Wait a minute," Ferrante intervened. "What about this kid?"

"Look"—the lieutenant tried to mediate—"nobody got hurt. Let's forget it."

"The hell you say!" Ferrante protested. "What if it's in the papers or on the television news that there was a riot at a Morbid concert? You know what that means? We'll be barred from booking lots of cities. And there are arenas and stadiums where they won't let us in. Unless we put up big deposits against possible structural damage. So we ain't going to just forget it! We want the blame where it should be. We want this kid prosecuted. And we might also sue for damages!"

"If you insist on pressing charges . . ." the lieutenant said.

"Charges is exactly what I insist on pressing!" Ferrante said. "Hold that kid!"

For the second time in only weeks Don Ward was summoned to make a late-night visit to a police station to redeem his son. This time the police lieutenant was less cooperative, warning on the phone that an irate citizen pressing charges was not something the police could gloss over with a mere warning.

"Mr. Ward, we know how to take care of rambunctious teenagers up here. But this is different. There was an assault. There was almost a riot. Shots were fired. And this agent is screaming bloody murder."

Don's first demand was to see his son. They brought Robbie out from the cell in which he had been held to satisfy the vengeful demands of the Morbids' agent. Don examined him carefully, face, eyes, neck. He wanted to make sure that Robbie did not need medical attention.

"What happened?"

"I just wanted to get up on that stage and play guitar with the group," Robbie said.

"And start a riot?"

"I swear I don't know how that happened. Suddenly I was on my way up to that stage, knowing only one thing: I could play that thing better than Kane, better than anybody."

Better than anybody. The words registered on Don. It was a frequent phrase of Robbie's. Used in connection with football or Robbie's academic achievements, it always amused Don, almost made him feel proud. Somehow not this time. However, he was convinced of one thing. His son did not act out of malice or evil intent. Still, there were the consequences of a near riot to deal with.

"You wait here, son. I have to talk to that man."

Tony Ferrante was small, slight, dark-haired, attired in a black silk designer-tailored suit, as if in deliberate contrast with the garish costumes of the Morbid. When he faced Don Ward in the private interrogation room, he assumed his toughest negotiating attitude. His sharp features were set in what seemed an implacable pose. But the slight film of perspiration that shone on his olive skin gave Don a hint of how to attack the problem.

"Mr. Ferrante, I'm Robbie Ward's father. I understand you waited just to talk to me."

"I certainly did. Do you realize what your son has done?" Ferrante demanded in his most outraged tone of voice. "He is responsible for starting a riot that not only broke up my clients' concert but blackened their reputation and jeopardized their ability to earn a living. It will be difficult now, very difficult, to book them into any big arena or concert hall. The loss of income could run into millions!" He emphasized, "Millions!"

"I see," Don said gravely.

"Okay, as long as you understand that. What do you intend to do about it?"

"I don't know. I wasn't prepared for anything like this," Don said.

"Well, *get* prepared, Mr. Ward. Because I have already spoken to our lawyer, and we are going to file a suit against you Monday morning. For assault. Damage to expensive instruments. Physical injury to Killer Kane. Damage to professional reputation. Loss of future earnings."

"That's pretty serious," Don said.

"You bet your ass it's serious," Ferrante said.

"Look, mind if I talk to your lawyer?" Don asked.

"Be my guest. If only to get straight on one thing. *We* are not kidding. And our *lawyer* is not kidding," Ferrante said.

"Can we get him on the phone now?"

"Sure. He's home. I just talked to him."

The lieutenant provided his own office and telephone. When Don indicated it would be best if only he and Ferrante were privy to the conversation, the lieutenant obligingly left.

Ferrante made the call. "Mr. Casey, I have here with me the boy's father. He is willing to talk a deal. He seems like a nice man, so go easy with him. But remember the damage to our clients."

With that preamble he handed the phone to Don. Before Don could say more than an interrupted "hello," he heard the pontificating voice of attorney James Casey.

"Mr. Ward, I find this to be a terribly distasteful business. I mean, here is a young man fifteen, sixteen years old getting into a riot, being arrested, doing all that damage. And now faced with a long trial that is sure to attract lots of publicity, distasteful publicity. A matter like this wouldn't come on for trial for a year or more. Just the time when that young man would be applying to colleges for admission. He *is* planning to go to college, isn't he?"

"Yes, yes, he is," Don said, retaining his calm, for he recognized the obvious attempt to blackmail him into a settlement. He dealt with Casey's type of show business laywers daily, knew their threats, real and invented, their tactics, their innuendos. He permitted Casey to continue.

"But I'm a father myself. I know how you must feel. So I have prevailed on Ferrante and Killer to be reasonable. I think I can keep them from proceeding with a lawsuit if you decide to be reasonable, too."

"Just what do you consider reasonable, Mr. Casey?" Don asked.

"I think for, say, fifty thousand dollars, they might be willing to forgo suing you," Casey said, sounding quite practical now.

"Fifty thousand." Don pretended to consider.

"It doesn't all have to be cash. We can work out some arrangement. The important thing is to protect your son from any more detrimental publicity. These days colleges do not like troublemakers," Casey emphasized. After a brief pause, during which Casey assumed that Don was considering his offer, he prodded. "Mr. Ward?"

"Mr. Casey, now that we know each other you don't have to be so formal. You can call me Don."

"Very good, Don. Don . . . Don Ward?" Casey asked gingerly.

"That's right, Mr. Casey. Don Ward. Vice-president of Intercontinental Entertainment. Wonder World in Florida. Pacific Wonderworld in California. And many many other entertainment enterprises. Now, I happen to know your clients are booked solid for the next fifteen months. Because the network is negotiating for a possible special with the Morbid for Halloween 1986. So don't tell me about the bookings you stand to lose. And don't try to hustle me for a bribe. Because if you want to play hardball, I can show you a trick or two. Understand, Counselor?"

There was a pause on the other end of the line. When Casey spoke, he no longer sounded pontifical or even practical. He was just plain scared. He said only, "Put Ferrante on."

With a puzzled look Ferrante took the phone which Don held out to him. Ferrante said only, "Yes, Mr. Casey," and was met by a loud, angry attack that Don could hear standing feet away from the phone.

Ferrante tried to interrupt and explain, but Casey kept right on. Finally Ferrante had an opportunity to reply.

"How the hell was I supposed to know? There's a million Wards in the phone book. . . . Yes, yes. I understand. . . . Yeah. . . . Okay . . . okay . . . right . . . right. I'm sorry, I said I was sorry . . . Yeah, I'll do that. Right away."

Ferrante was sweating profusely by the time he hung up.

"Mr. Casey says in view of the entire situation we should forget this whole thing. Just shake hands like it never happened."

Ferrante held out his hand. Don considered rejecting it but finally shook the thin, cold, damp hand. As they did, Ferrante asked, "The deal for Halloween '86, that's still viable, isn't it?"

"Yeah," Don said. He was not going to punish his network because of Ferrante's greed. "Just one thing. Our network deals do not provide cocaine. You have to supply your own."

"Sure, Don, sure, I understand. You got to be clean all the way. I respect that."

On the drive home Don felt comforted having his son safe and unharmed by his side. But he could not help thinking that having the muscle to blackmail the blackmailers was one of the network's perks. He reached over to pat him on the thigh.

"Robbie?"

"Yeah, Dad?"

"Son, what really made you do it?"

"I felt the beat, the urge. And it just happened. I wasn't looking for trouble. I never expected to start a riot. It just . . . like I said, it just happened."

"Shots were fired. Someone could have been killed."

"Yeah, I know."

"Well, at least no one was seriously hurt," Don said. "Still, I want Dr. Rissom to look you over just to make sure."

Rissom had done a complete check on Robbie Ward. Aside from some bruises on his arms and his chest, he found nothing wrong. But he indicated that Robbie wait outside while he talked to Claire.

"Robbie got off pretty lightly. To judge from the injuries I treated on two other boys, it was a terribly dangerous situation," Rissom said.

"We know," Claire said. "Frankly Don and I were terrified when we learned the whole story. Robbie, of all boys, to do such a wild, irresponsible thing. It's so unlike him."

"Claire, what about his cracking up Don's car?" Rissom forced her to consider.

"Yes, there was that." She agreed. "It does seem that suddenly he's changed. What's happening to him?"

"I don't know for sure, but I could offer an educated guess."

Rissom swung about in his swivel chair, reached for Claire's hand, and held it in a fatherly fashion.

"Now don't become upset, my dear. But what we have here is a terrific young man. Excellent scholar. Superb athlete. In the best of health. Then, lately, he gets involved in two episodes, which are not only unwise but dangerous. Now why does a boy do something like that? He wants attention. I think he's crying out for it."

"Dr. Rissom, I've given up my career to raise him. If it's attention he wants—"

Rissom interrupted. "Claire! You're his mother, true. And very devoted. But forgive me, you are *only* his mother. He has a father, too. Who is rarely there for him. Who is too busy or too far away to go see him play football. Or join in other father and son activities. It's not enough for a father to *say* he's proud of his son. The son has to see approval and pride in his father's eyes when he's just accomplished some special feat.

"I think Robbie has decided, perhaps unconsciously: *If doing everything perfectly won't get my dad's attention, maybe doing things wrong, or dangerous, or illegal will do it.* Frankly that's my reading of the situation."

Claire nodded, thoughtful and terrified. "That man had a gun. Robbie could have been killed."

"Yes, kids will run all kinds of risks to get attention," Rissom said gravely. "Try to convince Don that no matter what it takes, he should be at Robbie's next game. After all, it's for the championship of the league."

"He wants to, believe me. But you know the business he's in."

"Claire, make sure he's at that game," Rissom insisted.

* * *

As soon as Claire left his office, Rissom followed his usual procedure of making his notes on the patient's chart while the case was still fresh in mind.

He entered his findings on Robbie Ward's chart. Noted the location of each contusion and described its characteristics. Indicated that no treatment or medication was necessary. Then, as he was about to close the folder, he stopped and added one more note: "The patient's newly observed tendency to precipitate dangerous situations, without the intent to do so, will bear monitoring. It is very puzzling and disturbing."

CHAPTER 12

It was a brisk, sunny morning in November, this last Saturday of the month. The prep school league restricted its schedule to six games, beginning late in September and ending with the second Friday in November. The Saturday morning two weeks later was scheduled for the play-off between the teams that ranked one and two at the end of the regular season. Robbie's team ranked second only because he had had to miss one game early in the season when he had a severe attack of tonsilitis. Except for that loss they would have had a perfect record and been tied for first.

But they would have their chance today. Robbie rose earlier than usual, earlier even than on other game days. He was too excited to sleep, too anxious to prove himself. He lay in bed pondering the game, analyzing his opponents, planning his strategy, hoping the coach would let him call his own plays instead of sending them in from the bench.

The most powerful offensive weapon his opponents, Hallside Academy, had was a big fullback, heavy enough, strong enough to be playing college ball. He had already been granted a scholarship at Ohio State for next year. On sheer power he was good for five or six yards on a play. And if, by skillful blocking, his team opened a hole for him, he could go all the way. He was strong enough to break tackles and fast enough to avoid most of them.

The trick, Robbie knew, was to hold that fullback in check often enough to get possession of the ball. Then Robbie could operate, throwing passes to his two wide receivers, who were as good as any in the league.

Fortunately his opponents' pass defense wasn't as solid as it could have been. He would nibble them to death with short passes, for which he possessed a special talent. It required an agile, heady quarterback with quick reflexes to use the short pass effectively. Even some college quarterbacks never mastered the art.

It was something Don had started to teach Robbie when he was barely eight years old and he'd already exhibited excellent athletic coordination and aptitude. Don had taught him. Look up and throw. Pivot and throw. Throw from any angle, but quickly. Before the defense could organize. Yes, Robbie determined, he'd nibble them to death today. He was determined not only to win but to show his dad. To show his dad. To show his dad. It became an endless refrain, which finally caused him to slip out of bed and find out: Was Dad really going to be there today?

Barefoot, his new pajama bottoms trailing his feet, Robbie had started toward his parents' bedroom when he became aware that his father's voice was coming from the floor below. Robbie started down the stairs. The swinging door between the dining room and the kitchen was closed. But he could hear his father's loud, angry voice.

"Sorry! Get someone else to fly out. Look, Ed, this is one time I can't. I owe it to my son. Get hold of Harry. Or Pres. There must be someone else who can hold her hand and sweet-talk her. Look, promise her a feature or a new pilot. No, Ed, I can't. Loyalty to the network? Ed, I'm talking about loyalty to my son. Thanks, Ed, thanks. I'll make it up to you some other time. Listen, I'll be back here right after the game. About four o'clock. Call me. If you're still having trouble with her, I'll fly out tomorrow."

Robbie realized that his father had been talking to Ed Brady, president of the network. If he would refuse Brady, there could never again be any doubt in Robbie's mind about how much his father loved him.

I'm talking about loyalty to my son. Robbie repeated it to himself several times. He liked the sound of it. Responsibility was one thing, but loyalty meant more, much more.

Robbie determined that today he would exceed any performance he had ever given on the football field. He would also make it up to his father for all the trouble he had caused in recent weeks.

His mother sat in the stands with all the other team parents. But because of Don's expertise, accumulated during years of sports coverage, the coach invited him to sit on the team bench.

It was a cold, sunny day, one of those fall days when the clarity of the air made the sun far brighter than usual. Which meant it was a bad day for passers and pass receivers. A receiver running out and cutting back to receive the ball found himself looking right into the sun's glare.

On his team's first possession of the ball Robbie threw three passes. Two of them were lost in the glare of the sun and dropped. The third went for only eight yards, and the team had to kick the ball away.

Robbie was forced to sit on the bench and watch with great frustration as Hillside, led by that fullback, racked up yardage on the ground, three, four, five yards at a clip. They not only worked their way downfield steadily but ate up the clock. Every minute they were in possession of the ball meant another minute that Robbie's team was prevented from scoring. A long, slow drive down the field could eat up seven or eight minutes. Two such drives could consume a whole quarter.

Get the ball, get the ball, Robbie kept urging. *Stop that big son of a bitch, and get me the ball!*

The Hillside players scored on their first possession. They were leading by 7 to 0 when they kicked off to Canaan. Since the sun was still behind Robbie and in the eyes of his receivers, the coach reverted to their ground game. With Robbie handling the ball skillfully, giving it off to his running backs they managed two first downs. They were gaining confidence in their ability to move the ball on the ground.

But on the next play the tailback started around the right end. The defensive tackle, anticipating the play, caught up with him, failed to tackle him, but, in swinging out, ripped the ball loose from his grasp. The ball bounded crazily on the frosty turf. Robbie dived for it, but a Hillside lineman blocked him out while another fell on the ball.

Again Robbie was forced to watch from the bench as Hillside ground out yardage with play after bruising play aimed at the Canaan line, which was beginning to feel the relentless pressure of the heavier team.

It went that way through the first quarter and into the second. Midway through the second quarter the score was Hillside: 14, Canaan: 0. In the second quarter the sun, which had punished his receivers in the first, frustrated Robbie, who had to stare into the bright sun to find his receivers. With time running out in the half, short passes would not do, so he went for long ones. His vision limited by the glare, he failed to connect for any appreciable gains. When the teams left the field, the scoreboard read: Hillside: 14. Canaan: 0.

In the locker room the coach made his methodical analysis of the weaknesses that had surfaced in the first half. He did not dwell on the superior weight and manpower of Hillside but kept insisting, "We must stick with our game plan. And we must not beat ourselves. That fumble broke up our rhythm, our momentum. We can't afford any more mistakes. We must play errorless fundamental football. Run to set up Robbie's passes. Pass when they least expect it. Got that, Robbie?"

"Yes, sir," Robbie said, but his mind was on other strategies.

"Okay, let's go," the coach said. "Gather 'round." He gestured them to assume a circle and hold hands, a ritual they always did before leaving the locker room for the playing field.

All 37 young men formed a circle, reaching out to hold hands. Only Robbie refused to comply.

"Robbie," the coach ordered.

"Wait just a minute!" Robbie said. "Holding hands isn't going to do it. Shouting isn't going to do it. Victory yells aren't going to do it. You guys want to win this game, get me that ball! Stop that big, stupid son of a bitch they call a fullback. You ends, cut in, hit him before he gets to the line of scrimmage. You tackles, instead of letting him punish you, you punish him. Hit him hard. Get him behind the line of scrimmage. Wear him down. Slow him down. But get that ball for me, and I'll win this ball game for you. Because when I get that ball, I am going to short pass them to death. No nice high beautiful spirals that get lost in the sun. Short, low passes a man can see. Out to the tight ends. Just over the line to the wide ends. Never in the same place twice. I will drive them crazy. Just get me that ball!"

He looked toward the defensive team. "Okay, guys?"

"Okay!" a number of them shouted back.

"Now," Robbie said, reaching out his hands to join the others.

In a large circle, holding hands, the entire team chanted the school cheer in unison. They ran out of the locker room, yelling as they went. The coach stood at the door watching. Robbie was the last of them. The coach swung out to slap him warmly on the back.

"Wait'll I tell your father. Boy, is he going to be proud of you!"

Fired up by Robbie's outburst, the defensive team played beyond its capabilities at the opening of the half. Hillside took the ball on the kickoff. But after grinding out three first downs, the Canaan line began to catch the fullback before he could break into the clear. Hillside was forced to punt.

Now when Robbie ran out onto the field, he did so with confidence and determination. *Watch me, Dad. Watch those short passes you taught me. I am going to nibble them to death, nibble them to death. Five yards, six, seven. But I'm going to drive them crazy. Just watch me, Dad!*

Slowly, with precision and complete control, Robbie ripped off gain after gain. When he was on the Hillside thirty-four, and he had drawn the secondary in to try to break up his short passes, he threw a long, high one to his wide receiver, who gathered it in unimpeded and went in to score.

Robbie held the ball for the extra point. His kicker made it good. The score was now 14 to 7. Canaan was on the way back. Robbie Ward felt confident, supreme. No one could stop him now. When his teammates came back into the huddle, the bigger men, the seniors, playing their last game and tasting victory, pounded him on the back.

He was again what local sportswriters had dubbed him: "the kid in control." They were predicting that the coach would be able to build a dynasty around him. He glanced over toward the bench. He saw his father smiling, exchanging words with the coach, who was jubilant. This was the greatest game of Robbie's young career. More important, he was doing it in front of his father, the one person in this world whose love and respect were vital to him.

I want to show him. He made a special effort to be here. I'll make him glad that he did.

It was midway in the fourth quarter. Canaan had tied the score on the opening play of the quarter, had forced Hillside to punt again. Robbie was once more in possession of the ball. This drive could put the game away.

Without varying his strategy, he peppered them with short passes and used runs only to pin down the defensive line. He worked the ball down to the fourteen-yard line. His long pass was batted away in the end zone. His short pass for a first down was dropped when the receiver was hit. The coach sent in word to go for the field goal. Robbie balked but finally acceded to the coach's strategy. A three-point edge this late in the game, and with the Hillside offense so well contained, was a safe bargain.

Robbie held the ball; the kicker's leg flashed by him crisply. When Robbie looked up, the ball was sailing between the goalpost. Hillside: 14. Canaan: 17. The game was as good as won.

On its last possession Hillside had been forced to kick again. The final minute had begun to tick away when Canaan took over. There were only seconds remaining. From his huddle Robbie glanced at the sidelines. He saw his father beaming, the coach alongside sharing his pride. Robbie thought: *I'll give them one more big play to smile about. Why not? On this day I own this team. They'll do anything I ask.*

He glanced at the clock on the scoreboard at the end of the field.

Fourteen seconds to go. Enough time to send them all home talking about Robbie Ward's daring as well as his skill. It would look great in the local newspapers. It might even be mentioned on television when the sports reporters read the local scores, as they did on Saturday evenings. Especially this Saturday since this was for the league championship.

Today, no matter what I do, it's going to work. Today I can do anything! He had never experienced such a sense of omnipotence in his young life.

He gathered his team on the Hillside forty-two-yard line. It was second down, seven yards to go, with only fourteen seconds remaining on the clock.

"What do you say, guys, we go out in a blaze of glory?" Robbie challenged. "What's the last play in the world they would expect right now?"

"Not fall on the ball?" his tailback said. "Everybody does that."

"Exactly. So I say, let's go out with a play that'll make them talk about us for years to come." When no one ventured a guess, Robbie grinned from behind the ribs of his plastic face mask. "A long pass. One last touchdown pass."

"They'd sure as hell never expect that," his tight end said, beginning to share Robbie's enthusiasm.

"Then that's what we do!" Robbie said, smiling.

He lined up his team in their usual formation. Both Don and the coach rose from the bench to see what they expected would be the last play of the game. Nothing exciting, they knew. A routine hand-off or Robbie just dropping on the ball right behind the line of scrimmage. They both were totally surprised to see Robbie take the ball from center and fade back. Don assumed his son was fading back to run across the field and eat up the remaining seconds.

But no. Robbie was fading back to throw. He did throw. Routinely one of Hillside's defensive ends had faded back with Robbie's wide receiver. He was there to leap up and intercept the high spiral Robbie had thrown. He raced down the field, catching Robbie's team completely off guard.

Robbie was the only one who had a last desperate shot at him. He lunged for him but fell short. The last Robbie saw, looking up from the ground, was the blue-clad legs of the Hillside runner as he crossed the wide whitewashed stripe that was the goal line.

The kick, which was automatic, was completed after time had run out. There was no chance for Robbie to recoup from that disastrous blunder.

The scoreboard was a blur before Robbie's tear-filled eyes. *Hillside: 21. Canaan: 17.*

Robbie started toward the locker, ignoring the words of consolation being showered on him. Don tried to put his arm around him. Robbie shrugged him off violently. When the coach tried to console him, Robbie avoided looking at him, staring down at the turf and desperately trying not to cry.

CHAPTER 13

Robbie could feel his cleats scrape grittily on the hard concrete of the tunnel, so different from the soft turf of the playing field. He heard the harsh sound of his teammates' cleats. He dared not look up. Helmet dangling from his sweaty hand, he trudged into the overheated dressing room, which stank of liniment and youthful sweat. Head down, he was unable to look around. After previous games there had been joking, exultant shouts, hard but good-natured slaps on his back. Not this time.

He had just opened the door to his locker when Roger Ames, fullback, and a senior for whom this had been his last game, reached him.

"Look, kid, I know—"

"I am not a kid!" Robbie turned on him.

"Okay, okay. I just wanted to say—" Roger continued.

Before he could, Robbie leaped at him, flailing with right and left hands, one of which landed high on Roger's head, the other on his jaw. The fullback, taken by surprise, was thrown back against the metal locker but recovered and struck back on his own. Despite his superior size and weight, he could not overcome Robbie or diminish the fury of his attack.

Younger, smaller, Robbie kept punching fiercely, in a frenzy so unnatural to him that it took the coach, aided by three teammates, to subdue him finally.

They had to hold him down for several minutes before he could regain control. Only then did the coach signal the other boys to release him.

"Robbie?" he asked, greatly concerned.

Robbie turned his head away to avoid him.

"What's come over you, boy?" the coach asked sympathetically. "Just remember, it was only a game. And Roger wasn't blaming you. He was trying to console you. So I would like you to apologize to him. Both of you, shake hands, and forget this."

Roger Ames stood over Robbie, holding out his hand to lift the younger boy to his feet, as he had done on the field many times when Robbie was tackled after a pass. Robbie ignored the outstretched hand. He got up on his own, brushed by Roger, headed for the shower. Roger rubbed the side of his jaw where Robbie's most painful blow had landed. "I never knew he was so strong."

"I've never seen him like this before," the coach said. "Something's happening to that boy."

The Wards' station wagon was parked at the curb outside the stadium exit. Claire sat inside; Don was leaning against the front fender, waiting for Robbie to appear. The coach came down the concrete walk first.

"How's he taking it?" Don asked.

"Not well, not well at all."

"He's too much a winner to take a defeat like that lightly."

"He had a little—a little misunderstanding in there," the coach said.

"What happened?"

"It would be better if he told you himself." He started down the street toward the faculty parking lot.

Minutes later Robbie appeared, dark hair still glistening damply, his handsome face ruddy. Above his right eye he bore the red welt left by Roger Ames's fist. Don assumed it was a game-incurred bruise.

Robbie slipped into the front passenger seat as usual. He avoided looking back at his mother. Gave no sign of greeting to his father.

To break the tension, his mother said, "Robbie, dear, your seat belt."

"Who cares?" he mumbled.

"*I* care!" she said, angered by his response.

Making eye contact with her in the rearview mirror, Don warned her not to pursue it. They were under way before he asked, "Anything said after the game?"

Robbie did not reply, only dug his fists deeper into the pockets of his letter jacket and slumped lower in his seat.

"Your father asked you a question," Claire said.

Don's look rebuked her, but it was too late. Robbie turned on her. "Okay! So he asked me a question! What do you want to know? Was anything said in the locker room? No! N-O! No! Nothing was said. Nothing!" He was shouting in an angry, intolerant way he had not done for several years, when they used to dismiss such conduct as early teenage rebellion.

Again Don signaled her in the mirror: *Let him be.* She fell silent, distressed but silent.

It was minutes before Robbie exploded again. "I could have killed that son of a bitch! If they'd let me alone, I would have!"

Startled by his son's fury, nevertheless Don asked only, "Who?"

"Roger."

"Roger?"

"Ames, Ames!" Robbie shouted intolerantly. "I could have killed him. After what he said."

Spurred by her son's unusual ferocity, Claire asked, "What did he say?"

"What did he say?" Robbie echoed, turning to confront her. "He called me kid. I am not a kid. I am fifteen and a half, going on sixteen!"

"And that made you so angry?"

"It was what he said after that. He said, 'All I want to say—' "

"Yes, but what did he actually say?" Claire asked.

"I didn't give him a chance. Because he was going to say that if I'd given the ball to him, he could have won the game. That I lost it. Well, I don't let any big, stupid fullback talk that way to me. Lucky for him they grabbed me. I was going to kill him . . . and I could have, I could have."

Neither Don nor Claire spoke a word in response or recrimination. They only exchanged looks in the mirror that agreed, with alarming concern. This was yet another episode of Robbie's atypical, aberrant behavior in the past weeks.

They had turned off the highway before Claire felt compelled to break the depressing silence.

"You were terrific. You can't let one bad play spoil everything."

"Stupid! I was stupid! I have always been stupid!" he exploded. "I don't know why, with all the other kids you could have picked, you chose me!"

Both Don and Claire instinctively stopped breathing for a long, painful moment. Their eyes met in the mirror. There had been disagreements and arguments among them in the past. Times when Robbie wanted to do something that "all the other guys do" and Don or Claire had refused permission. Which was usually followed by pouting and "If you really loved me, you wouldn't treat me this way." Or even "If I were your real son, you wouldn't treat me this way." By now they were used to hearing it, and Robbie was used to saying it. All three of them realized those words were spoken in moments of juvenile anger.

But this was the first time Robbie Ward had ever taken the blame upon himself.

Claire could not restrain herself. "Don't ever say that. Don't even think it. We picked you. We're glad we picked you. We are very proud of you. And you are not stupid. You are one of the top students in your class, and your grades prove it. They admitted you to special classes at Columbia, didn't they?"

"And I got kicked out, didn't I?" he countered.

"Not for being stupid," Claire pointed out.

"I lost that game by being stupid. All I had to do was fall on the ball. But I didn't. Stupid! Stupid!"

There was no further discussion in the car. Don suggested an early dinner at Robbie's favorite restaurant, where the roast beef was thick and tender and the hot fudge cake was oozing with chocolate sauce. But the boy declined brusquely, almost rudely.

When they arrived home, he refused any dinner, went up to his room, not only closed his door but locked it. Claire made another attempt to call him down to the table; he refused to answer. She went up, leaned against his door, asking, "Robbie, do you hear me?"

"I hear you."

"Time for dinner," Claire said.

"I am not coming out of this room!" he declared with finality.

She came away from the door, distressed yet in a strange way considerably relieved as well. She could not understand why. But that seemed less important than the fact of feeling less concerned.

Don had closeted himself in the upstairs den to read a dozen scripts, all of which were the standard Hollywood half hour comedy drivel. They fell into one of four overdone formulas. Situations based on supposedly cute and hilarious misunderstandings that hinted at innocent sexual infidelity. Ones in which nine-year-old children were smarter than any adult. The third group dealt with the conflict between the generations. The fourth group were fantasies in which ghosts appeared in quite solid form to torment living humans. All this was supposed to delight the audience.

Surely, Don thought, *there must be some other, fresher comedy format that would make more sense.* But he plowed through nine of the scripts before he gave up. Not one showed any promise. *And they ask what's wrong with network television,* he thought. When Claire summoned him to dinner, he regarded it as a rescue call. On his way down he stopped at Robbie's locked door. His son refused to answer.

"Robbie," Don called once more, then decided: *He'll come down on his own. With his ravenous appetite, he can't resist.*

All through the simple dinner Claire had prepared, neither of them said anything. They both were listening for familiar sounds from above: one of Robbie's rock albums, which he always played too loud and on which they had to ask him to turn down the volume. But they heard nothing. Not the sound of his own guitar or the thump of the beat. Don suddenly pushed back his plate.

"I'd better go up and talk to him."

Once Don had left the table, Claire could abandon all pretense. She found herself on the edge of tears. There had been disappointments and arguments in this house before between them and Robbie. But for some reason this time seemed different, far more serious and distressing. She could not explain it. It was only a vague feeling.

Don found Robbie's door still locked. He listened but heard no sound. He knocked. There was no response.

"Robbie? Son? I want to talk to you."

Still no response. He knocked again.

"Go away!" came the answer finally.

"Son? Please?"

"I don't want to talk!"

"*I* want to talk," Don persisted.

"What do you want to tell me, how stupid I was?"

"I just want to talk. Open up. Son?"

Some moments later Don heard the door being unlocked. He turned the knob, opened the door. He looked in. The shades had been drawn. The room was totally dark. Robbie was sitting at the foot of his bed, still wearing his letter jacket.

He was staring at the opposite wall, where his team's schedule was posted in big type on a poster the school had printed for display in local stores to drum up ticket sales. Robbie had inscribed the score of each victory. Before yesterday he had inked in the championship game in the big, bold strokes of a black marking pen. Don saw that instead of today's score his son had printed the word *S T U P I D* across it in large, angry black letters.

"Son . . ." Don began, expecting the boy would turn toward him. But Robbie turned farther away in an obvious attempt to ignore him. "Son, we have to get this thing in perspective. But we can't unless we talk about it."

"What good is talking about it? We lost. *I* lost. It was my own stupid fault. I can never go back to that school again."

"Come now, let's not get hysterical. You made a mistake. One play out of fifty. That's all it was, one bad play."

"It cost us the game; it cost us the championship!" Robbie exploded.

"Want to hear what your coach said to me?"

"No!" Robbie shouted.

"Well, I'll tell you anyhow. He said, 'That son of yours learned a very valuable lesson today. It'll make him a better player, a smarter quarterback for next year.' "

"There's not going to *be* any next year!"

"Now look," Don said, close to losing his temper, "I don't want to hear that kind of talk in this house. Monday you will go to school. You will finish this school year. Next year, when you're a junior, you will be the quarterback again, and you *will* win the championship!"

Outside the door Claire listened and shook her head as if pleading: *Now, of all times, Don, darling, don't lose your temper with him.*

But Don was demanding, "Did you hear me?" His son refused to respond. Don ordered, "Look at me when I'm talking to you!" When Robbie refused to turn to him, Don said, "Okay, when you're ready to talk, I'll be in the downstairs den."

He almost collided with Claire as he charged out of the room. There were no words between them. Only her look of reproach, his look of anger. He lunged by her, heading for the stairs.

For a moment she hesitated, then decided to go in. She said not a word to Robbie, only embraced him. He tried to pull away, but she held his head against her breast.

"I know how you feel, darling. But in time you'll be able to see this for what it was. Just another football game."

"It wasn't just another game. It was *the* game. For the championship," he protested.

"There'll be other years, other big games. And you'll win them."

"No, I won't!"

The same fear she had suffered earlier gripped her once more. Why, today, was he so insistent on making everything sound so dismally final? She held him tighter.

Soon he said softly, "I wish he hadn't been there."

"Who?" she asked.

"Him."

"Your dad?"

"Yes, my *dad,*" he said, enunciating the word with a degree of vehemence.

"You wanted him there. He had to turn down Brady to be there. And you know what a sacrifice that is," she pointed out.

"If he hadn't been there, it wouldn't have happened," Robbie said.

She turned him about, raised his face to look into his eyes. "Robbie?"

"I wanted to show him. I wanted him to be able to tell them at the office Monday. About his son and the great game, how he won the championship, that one last play, a forty-seven-yard touchdown pass. I wanted to make him proud. Make him feel that he did pick the right little baby that day."

"Robbie, darling, one game, one play isn't going to change the way your father feels about you. He's very proud of you," she assured him. "Besides, don't you ever think of how *I* feel about you? I love you, and I'm proud of you, too."

"It's not the same," the boy said. "I always have you. But he's away so much and always has things on his mind. The only way I can get his attention is to bring home a paper with an A on it. Or show him some clipping about me from the local paper. So today, because he was there and I had this tremendous feeling that I couldn't do anything wrong, that I couldn't fail, I thought, today I would show him. But I didn't . . . I didn't. . . ."

"Robbie, come down and have some dinner. You'll feel better."

He interrupted by shaking his head.

"I'll make you anything you want. Or would you like to go for pizza? I'll drive you over."

"Uh-uh. The other guys might be there."

"You'll have to see them Monday."

"I told you I'm never going back to that school!" he said firmly.

"All right." She placated him, certain that by Monday he would go off to school on his bike as usual.

She fully expected that about nine o'clock he would be hungry enough to ask for some supper, possibly even pizza.

She had underestimated the depth of her son's despair, the stubbornness of his resolve never to go back to that school again.

CHAPTER 14

On Sunday Robbie remained secluded in his room. When Claire called him for breakfast, he responded by calling back to say he had already had breakfast early. The kitchen revealed no signs of it. Don tried to eat but finally gave up.

"What's he doing up there?"

Claire could only shrug, greatly worried. "He's never been like this before. On any other Sunday he'd have been up and out, practicing or biking over to round up some of his friends for one of his projects."

"I'm going up and talk to him."

"You might only make it worse," she warned.

"What does that mean? *Talking* might make it worse? Or *I* might make it worse?"

"Darling, promise you won't get angry. . . ."

"Angry about what?" he asked, already angry.

"Don, what he did yesterday was . . . was done to . . . well, he missed you so much at the other games that yesterday, when you *were* there, he wanted to put on a show for you. So if you go up and talk to him, that'll only make his failure seem worse."

"You're saying I can't talk to my own son?"

"I'm saying you have every right to talk to him, just don't, that's all."

"A hell of a situation. I can talk to hundreds of network affiliate executives, to trade associations, government agencies, and sponsor groups. And I am damn good at it. But I can't talk to my own son without making matters worse." He rose suddenly. "I'm going for a drive! Maybe even stop at the club and hit a few."

He left, slamming the door that led from the kitchen to the garage. Claire was very familiar with her husband's two antidotes for frustration and anger. Driving alone, which he did so aggressively that she often feared for his safety. And tennis at the club. It was one game which allowed a player to vent his anger and possibly even to improve his game.

Once Claire heard his new Mercedes back out of the garage and growl hostilely down the quiet street, she thought: *Maybe I can coax Robbie down to eat.* Then, because she unconsciously feared failing, she compromised by thinking: *His appetite is so ravenous he'll get hungry and come down on his own. Then he won't feel I'm pressuring him.*

She busied herself with the Sunday *Times.* That fat, bulky paper, which on Sundays seemed to be sold by the pound, presented one consolation. It was great if you needed to waste time. Section after section. News. Arts and Leisure. Business. Sports. Magazine. Book Review. Travel. Real Estate. Want ads.

Today the *Times* proved a boon as she settled down to outwait her son and her absent husband. This week the *Times* contained a bonus for her. Though it was barely the end of November the spring Fashions of the *Times* section, a thick, colorful magazine on women's fashions, was included.

Claire leafed through, looking for a suitable evening gown to wear at the network's annual affiliates dinner, in Las Vegas this year. She found nothing that pleased her. She realized that her concern for Robbie rendered her too anxious to be pleased. She tossed the section onto the ottoman, but being glossy and slippery as Teflon, it slid off to the floor like a colorful snake. She made no effort to retrieve it.

Instead, she went up the carpeted stairs, along the carpeted hall to listen at Robbie's door. She heard nothing.

"Robert? Robbie?" she asked softly. Then a bit more loudly: "Robbie!"

"Yes?" he responded abruptly.

"It's long past breakfast."

"I'm not hungry," he called through the door.

"What would you like for lunch?"

"I said I'm not hungry!"

"You will be an hour from now."

"If I am, I'll let you know."

Gingerly she tried his doorknob. It did not yield. He sometimes locked his door for privacy. They always respected that, so she did not persist. She turned away, more troubled than before. She tried to reassure herself: *Tomorrow he'll have to go to school. That will bring him out of it.*

The next morning Don woke early, showered, dressed, and reached the dinette table before seven o'clock. He wanted to be in time for the eight o'clock coffee meeting at the office to discuss the overnight ratings on Sunday's shows. On every Monday that Don was home, he fully expected Robbie to be not only at the table by now but finishing a rather substantial breakfast. Not so today. Don turned to Claire, who was sectioning his grapefruit for him.

She explained, "He's a little late today."

"Well, get him down, and if he hurries his breakfast, I'll drop him at school. He'll never make it by bike and still be there on time."

Claire answered softly, hoping to avoid a confrontation, "He says he's not coming down."

Don rose, demanding, "What do you mean, he's not coming down?"

"He—he says he won't go to school."

"I put up with his sulking all day yesterday. But today he is going to school. He's going to face the other guys. And his coach. The longer he puts it off, the worse it's going to be."

"I tried to tell him. . . ."

"You know your trouble, Claire? You baby that boy. He's fifteen and a half years old. When I was fifteen, I worked three afternoons a week. My father didn't shell out seven thousand dollars a year to send me to a private school. Seven thousand dollars *after* taxes yet! Well, you can indulge him, but not me. I'm going up there!"

"Don, no!" she protested. "If you go up there . . ." But she left her threat dangling because he turned to confront her.

"If I go up there, *what?*"

"I don't know," she admitted. "Just don't go up there."

"Why not?" he asked, softer now, because beyond concern, he detected fear in her eyes.

"Because this time he's—he's different."

"Different how?"

"I don't know."

He embraced her. She trembled. More than frightened, she was terrified.

"Claire? Darling?"

"I just have this feeling. This is no time to try to force him to do anything."

"I promise not to get angry. I'll just go up and talk to him quietly. In the end he usually does what I ask. He's a good kid. A terrific kid."

She finally nodded and released him.

Minutes later he was back down.

"What did he say?"

"I couldn't even get in to talk to him," Don admitted. He glanced at the kitchen clock. "I've got to get going. You drive him to school."

She tried his door again. It was still locked. "Robbie, dear, you have to eat something. Please?" She waited. He did not answer. She grew frightened. "Robbie? Answer me!" She was on the verge of tears, and it was evident in her voice.

It must have touched him for she heard his door being unlocked. He opened it partway, looking out at her. Through the narrow opening she could see his bed, with the cover and the sheets so twisted and disarranged that she knew he had spent a tormented, sleepless night.

"Robbie, please come down, have some breakfast."

He only shook his head.

"You can't stay locked up in your room forever."

"Why not?" he asked.

"Don't talk like that!" she said, fear making her appear angry. "Don't even think like that!"

"I do," he said, flat, listless, devoid of any emotion.

The tone of his voice, remote, detached, caused her to push the door open and embrace him so suddenly he could not resist.

"Darling, it's going to be all right. Dad says you played magnificently. He's proud of you, Robbie, very proud. He wanted to tell you, but you wouldn't let him."

Robbie did not respond. Not by word, not by relaxing the rigid attitude of his young body.

"Robbie? What is it, son?"

In a child's small voice he whispered, "I'm afraid."

"Afraid of what the guys on the team will say?"

He shook his head.

"Afraid of what your coach will say? He's already told Dad that this will make you a better quarterback next year."

Again he shook his head, staring beyond her.

"Robbie! Look at me!" she insisted.

He turned to her. His blue eyes were the eyes of a fearful young boy. She embraced him, pressing his handsome face against her, as if the warmth of her body could ease his fears.

"Robbie, what is it? Tell your mother."

"What makes me so afraid . . . I feel like I'm in a strange place. . . ."

Those words, so foreign in thought from this son whom she had known ever since the second week of his life cut into her like a scalpel.

"What do you mean, Robbie, 'a strange place' ?"

He shook his head. "I don't know."

He slipped out of her embrace and closed his door against her.

Throughout the day those words—*I'm afraid*—clung to her like a thorny vine from which she could not disentangle herself. Her son had never said that before. Far from it, he had always been a boy whose danger lay in the fact that he had no fear. He was aggressive, compulsive about the dangerous challenges, seeking rather than avoiding them. He had certainly never said he felt as if he were in a strange place. What was strange? This house? How could it be? He had lived in it from the time he was five, when Don had been promoted to the high salaried upper echelon position at the network. This had been Robbie's home for nearly eleven years.

A strange place?

CHAPTER 15

On the morning of the third day, before Don left for the office, there were no more long discussions about it. He said only, "At least see if you can get him back into his routine again. Then going to school will be part of it."

"I'll try," Claire said.

Don snatched his attache case and a heavy envelope of scripts he had brought home to read. He was at the door when he turned to ask, "Are you sure he said he felt like he was in a strange place?"

"Yes, quite sure."

Don shook his head but said no more.

After he left, Claire went up to Robbie's room, knocked, tried the door. It yielded. The room was still dark, still silent. *Mournful* was the only word that came to her mind. Robbie lay on the bed, atop the twisted, disarranged sheets. He did not acknowledge her presence.

"Robbie, dear, the best thing for you would be to face it. Get dressed. I'll drive you to school. If they joke or tease you, you'll just have to take it. And you can. You're a very strong young man. You brought that team to the championship game. Don't forget that. Please, son, take a shower, get dressed and let me drive you to school."

Following Don's suggestion, she went into his bathroom and

started his shower. She waited. After minutes, which seemed much longer, he finally stirred. His arm slid away from his eyes. He sat up on the side of the bed. He rose to his feet and started to the bathroom. When she heard the change in the sound of the shower, she knew he was under it. Greatly relieved, she went down to prepare his breakfast.

"It's a little late," Claire said. "I'd better drive you to school."

"No, I'd rather bike over, like always," Robbie insisted.

Good, she thought, Don was right. Just get him to resume his routine. "Of course, darling, bike over, like always."

She watched from the front window of the living room as he biked down the circular driveway, turned and was off to school. She was relieved, greatly relieved. The crisis, depressing as it had been, was over. She could resume her own busy routine.

I'll do it, Robbie kept telling himself. *There'll be some nasty wisecracks. Roger will surely make some. Especially after the way I slugged him. He won't forget that. But what the hell, I don't give a damn. Let 'em. I'm not doing this for myself. I'm doing it for Mom. And Dad. They've been too good to me for me to give them such a hard time. And as Dad said, do it and get it over with. Okay, I'll get it over with!*

But as he turned the corner onto the school street and caught sight of the few stragglers who were running to beat the last bell that rang out over the quiet neighborhood, Robbie braked his bike to a sudden stop. He dropped his feet to the pavement to balance himself and stared at the parking lot, where all the other bikes were left.

Then, instead of starting into the parking lot, he turned and pedaled past the school.

When Canaan Prep originally was laid out, a small athletic field had adjoined the main building. But a dozen years ago with the influx of so many families it had become necessary to preempt the athletic field for a larger school building. The new stadium was now a block away.

Robbie pedaled up to the stadium, which from the outside appeared to be a gaunt steel skeleton of beams and struts supporting long green wooden benches, surrounded by a high chain-link fence. Careful to avoid the sharp, rough extrusions at the top, Robbie scaled the fence and dropped gracefully to the ground below.

He walked out onto the football field. The soft turf did not feel the same as when he wore his football cleats. He began to run. He raced down the field as swiftly as he could, gradually feeling the burden of Saturday's defeat fall away.

Instead of shrinking and hiding, he felt strong, bold. Felt the full vigor and confidence of his youth. He turned to gaze up into the stands, and he could visualize the spectators there.

They cheered his every move. He took a position in the middle of the field and simulated bending behind the center. He took the ball, pivoted, threw a short pass, and another, and another. Bit by bit he overwhelmed Hillside, shredding the pass defense.

"Quick hands," a local sportswriter had written about him.

"Swift release for a high school player," another had said on the radio. "Some lucky college will get Robbie Ward soon."

In his mind he began to replay the last moments of Saturday's game, simulating all his movements. As he did, the stands seemed fuller, the cheers louder, even louder than they had been on Saturday.

There were now only fourteen seconds left to play. Canaan had the ball on Hillside's forty-two-yard line again. He assembled his team in a huddle. He knelt in the midst of them, on one knee, as was his habit.

"Okay, guys, let's not try anything spectacular. We just win the ball game and the championship. You just protect me, and I'll fall on the ball. We run out the clock. And by the time I get up we'll be the champs. And boy, will my dad be proud!"

He took up his position behind the absent center. He barked the signals loudly, looking from one end of his team to the other to mislead the opposition. Then he received the ball from the center, cradled it securely in his arms to prevent a fumble, and dropped to his knee, surrounded by his teammates.

The whistle sounded. The game was over. There was a thunderous outburst from the stands. They had won! They were champions of the prep school league!

Around him he could hear the crowd cheering. He could feel his teammates slapping him on the back, Roger Ames more than anyone. Now they were lifting him to their shoulders. They were carrying him off the field in triumph. He waved to his dad on the bench, to his mom in the stands. They waved back, Mom smiling broadly, Dad holding his hands above his head, clasping them in a gesture of victory.

The feeling of fantasized elation slowly ebbed away. He knelt there on the cold November ground, on a bare spot where too many cleats had shredded the turf, and there was only brown earth. No cheers. No triumphant parade across the field. No smiling Mom. No victory signs from Dad.

He asked himself: *Why didn't I do that on Saturday? It would have been so easy. So easy. Why do I have to keep trying to excel? And at everything? And always the hard way, the dangerous way?*

Why? To make his father proud? So he would feel it had all been worthwhile?

Had what all been worthwhile? Robbie asked. *For taking me in as an infant, bringing me up, giving me all the best things in this life? In a word, for adopting me? Was that what it was all about?*

Why this sudden obsession with being adopted?

Because for them to have adopted him, someone else had to get rid of him, give him away. Why? Was there some defect in him even as an infant that made whoever she was give him away? As if she'd known that, when confronted by crucial moments, such as on Saturday, he would fail?

Cold, alone on that stadium field, he had never felt so adopted in all his fifteen and a half years.

When he opened the door from the garage, his mother cried out, "Robbie!" She rushed from the living room to embrace him and kiss him. "I was so worried."

He did not respond.

"Dean Slattery called. You weren't in school today. Where were you? What did you do all day?"

"I went to school. I just couldn't go in," he said.

"You will. Tomorrow," she reassured him.

He brushed by her without a word and made his way slowly and silently up the stairs. She heard him close his door and lock it.

He was secluded in his dark room again.

CHAPTER 16

"Darling, you can't baby-sit him as if he were a two-year-old," Don said. "We've done everything we can. He's got to get over this by himself. So you do what you have to. Shopping. Rehearsals. Luncheons. Mainly get that new dress. This is a very important cocktail party. All the brass from the parent company will be there. I want you to knock 'em dead!"

"All right, Don, I'll find something striking," she said.

She was approaching the shopping mall where both Saks and Bergdorf had branches. Suddenly she took her foot off the gas pedal and allowed the wagon to slow down. It was a precipitous act, totally unpremeditated. The driver in the car behind her honked angrily in protest, then swept wide to her left, and passed her, his horn blaring. Claire ignored him. She turned off at the next exit, pulled to the side, and stopped.

She was trembling. She was aware of a pain, a vague pain, in the pit of her stomach. She tried to relate it to events of the morning. Unfortunately there was nothing different about this morning. Robbie had remained in his room, refusing to go to school again. When she knocked on his door, he responded in desultory monosyllables. But he made no move to come down for breakfast or get ready for school.

So this morning had not been unlike any other recent morning.

Except . . . She suddenly realized. That last time she stood at Robbie's door, knocked, and told him that she was going shopping he did not respond at all.

Why his lack of acknowledgment? Had he wanted her to go out? To give up bugging him? Or was it something more? Had he wanted to be left alone in the house? And if he had, why?

She knew now why her trembling. Why her pain. God knows, she had heard enough about it, seen enough about it on the local television.

Suicide. Teenage suicide. Boys, and girls, Robbie's age, fifteen, sixteen. It was the current scourage of the upper-class suburbs.

Not Robbie, she protested. *Not my son.* He had always been so full of life, of plans, of ambitions, drive, and ideas. It could never happen to Robbie.

Yet the dread feeling lay in the pit of her stomach like a hard, deadly tumor. She recalled the words of one surviving mother being interviewed on television who said, "We never suspected . . . he never said anything . . . never gave any indication. . . ."

Claire threw her car into gear, raced across the overpass to the other side of the highway, and sped toward home.

The speed at which she drove reflected the terrifying thoughts that cascaded one upon the other until she was near panic when she turned the corner to their street. The squeal of her own tires forced her to slow down. She barely managed to control her speed as she drove into the garage. She leaped out of the car, slamming the door behind her. She burst into the house, calling, "Robbie! Robbie!"

She bounded up the stairs two at a time, ran down the hall to his room, where she leaned breathlessly against the door. "Robbie! Robbie!" She pressed against the door to keep from trembling. She felt the sweat trickle down between her breasts.

"Robbie!"

"Yes? What?" he finally responded.

She heard him unlock the door. She threw it open. She found him in darkness again. She embraced him and began to weep. Startled, he drew back from her.

"Mom?"

"Nothing, darling. Everything is all right, all right."

But she continued crying.

* * *

Dr. Rissom leaned in Claire's direction, took her hand, and said, "I wish I could say your fears are exaggerated. But I've had two cases in the last few years myself. It happens. We can't close our eyes to it. However, you won't help things by becoming overwrought yourself. From what you describe, it sounds as if Robbie's in a depression. Understandable, of course. He feels he's disgraced himself in front of all his peers."

"He won't let anyone explain or console him. He's totally withdrawn. I can't reach him. Don can't reach him."

"This may call for outside help."

"Psychiatric help?" Claire asked.

"Yes. Psychiatric help," the doctor said. "I know someone I would recommend. A woman. Excellent. Expert. Very good with young people. Talk it over with Don. Let me know, and I'll arrange it."

Claire nodded. "I'll talk to him tonight."

Once she had left, Rissom took down a psychiatric text intended for the professional use of physicians. He glanced through the index. He refreshed his mind on the symptoms. Yes, he decided, this would indeed take outside help.

It was past eleven when Don returned home. It was apparent from his exhausted appearance, the disarray of his tie, his wilted collar that he had had a rough day. When she embraced him, she was struck by the heavy smell of tobacco. Since he did not smoke, she knew that he had spent the entire day and evening in the company of network executives who did. She would not hang this suit back in his closet without sending it to the cleaners.

She desperately wanted to discuss Robbie with him. But clearly tonight was not a good time.

Claire woke suddenly in the middle of the night. The other side of the bed was empty. Thinking Don might have gone to the medicine chest to get an antacid, as he often did when he had too much to drink, she called, "Darling? Don? You all right?" When he did not answer, she slipped out of bed.

She found him in the den, a shadowy presence in a dark room.

"Don?"

"Yeah. I wake you? Sorry."

"Something go wrong today?"

"We took a beating in the sweeps. There was hell to pay." He pressed his fist into the pit of his stomach. "I need some milk."

"You might need an X ray more."

"No," he said firmly.

"How can you be sure?"

"I had a complete GI series last week."

"You never told me."

"It's part of the executive health plan at the network." He was lying. She knew it. He must have had symptoms. But she chose not to argue about it.

"What did they say?" she asked.

"I'm fine. Doctor said I just have a sensitive stomach. Then he made a bum joke. He said the best series on our network was our GI series."

It was over the nonfat milk, which Claire always bought to preserve her family's health in the battle against cholesterol, that she felt free to mention the events of her own distressing day. Her fears. Those terrifying thoughts which had made her race home that afternoon. She mentioned her visit to Dr. Rissom.

Don reached across the dinette table to pat her hand. "Darling, you're Robbie's mother. You're terribly concerned about his welfare. Well, so am I. But being a mother, you are always spelling out the worst possible scenario. He made a bad decision during a football game. So he's brooding. He'll get over it. But you don't help by becoming hysterical."

"I am not being hysterical!" Claire protested, her voice rising.

"There. You see. You're getting hysterical now. Don't forget, you're the mother who used to sit by his crib at night in those first days because you once read an article on crib death. He didn't die of crib death. And he's not going to die of this!"

Despite that, Claire insisted, "Dr. Rissom thinks he needs professional help."

"Professional help? A psychiatrist? What's a psychiatrist going to tell him? That it's all my fault? That I've been away too much? Because I want to make sure my wife and son have the best of everything?" he demanded.

"Is that it, Don? Is that why you resist Robbie's getting help? Well, maybe it isn't your fault. Maybe it's mine," Claire said.

"Yours?" Don asked, no longer defensive or angry.

"When something like this happens to your son, you do a lot of thinking, a lot of soul-searching."

"Claire, what are you talking about."

"Remember when we adopted Robbie how many of our friends said that right after a childless couple adopts, the wife often becomes pregnant. That the wife's sterility was psychological. She was afraid to become pregnant. Well, I expected to become pregnant after we got Robbie. When I didn't, I began to wonder why. Was I afraid? Once I learned I was fully capable of taking care of an infant, what was there to be afraid of?

"Then what was it? I used to think about that. In the last few days I've thought about it much more. And I think I was unconsciously refusing to become pregnant because underneath I always wanted my career more than I ever wanted a child."

"If you felt that way, you wouldn't have undergone all those tests. Done all those crazy things the doctors made us do," Don protested.

"I think I did all that only to cover up my guilt."

"And if you did, what's that to do with Robbie?"

"We shouldn't have raised him as an only child. I should have become pregnant. Or we should have adopted a second child and even a third."

He took her gently by the arms, looked down into her moist eyes. "Honey, you're so worried about Robbie that you're over-dramatizing this whole thing."

She shook her head. "I'm frightened, Don. He's not the Robbie we're used to. Something is different. Very different."

"Tell you what I'll do. I'll talk to Brady first thing. I'll tell him for the time being I have to be relieved of any trips to the Coast. I want to spend more time with my family."

"Don!" she interrupted tensely. "Dr. Rissom said he's had two cases of teenage suicide in the last year!"

"All right. Okay. If you want to consult a psychiatrist, go ahead," Don said. "But we'll pay for it ourselves. I don't want to put it through the network health plan."

"Of course not," Claire said bitterly. "After all, that's how Ed Brady checks up on the families of his trusted executives.

And we wouldn't want him to know we have a problem, would we?"

"He doesn't like executives distracted by family problems. Kids on drugs. Wives on alcohol."

"Of course not," Claire said sarcastically. "That is reserved for stars."

CHAPTER 17

Dr. Sabrina Belmond listened intently, from time to time jotting down a note on her yellow pad. She was a woman in her early forties, with pulled-back jet hair, lightly streaked by gray, and a finely shaped face. Though she was tall, her body was nicely proportioned and quite feminine.

When Claire completed her recitation of the events that had led up to Robbie's strange conduct of recent days, Belmond asked, "And your son has never before exhibited such conduct?"

"Never. If anything, he's usually too active. He's the leader, the instigator. His coach says he's the most mature fifteen-year-old he's ever coached. To Robbie nothing has ever seemed impossible. Until now. This is the first time I've ever heard him say, 'I'm afraid.' "

"Did he say what he's afraid of?" the doctor asked.

"No. He didn't seem to know. And then he said, 'What makes me so afraid . . . I feel like I'm in a strange place.' His words terrified me. They still do."

"Uh-huh," Belmond said, making another note. "Tell me, Mrs. Ward, is your son really as terrific as you're trying to make me believe?"

"You can ask anyone. Ask Dr. Rissom. He knows Robbie well. Remember, two months ago, the food drive at Canaan Prep that tied up traffic for a whole day, that resulted in truckloads of food for the starving people of Africa? That was Robbie's idea. He started that whole drive by himself."

"Quite a remarkable young man, your son," Belmond observed.

"I don't say he's perfect. There are times, well, he tends to brag a little. And once when he was thirteen, some of the kids in his class dared him to . . . you know the bridge over the railroad tracks on Windsor Street?"

"Yes."

"They dared him to walk the rail of that bridge while the train was speeding by underneath."

"Did he?"

"Robbie never said a word to me about it. But one of the boys told his mother, and she called me."

"I see," Belmond said, making another note. Claire strained to see what the doctor had written down. At that moment Belmond looked up to catch her. "Anything else, Mrs. Ward?"

"Well, lately . . ."

"Yes, what about lately?" Belmond asked quickly.

Claire recounted Robbie's experience at Columbia, stressing how well he had done there until he began cutting classes and ending up with his adventure in Greenwich Village.

"Is that all?" Belmond asked. When Claire hesitated, the psychiatrist said, "Dr. Rissom mentioned having to examine your son after that near riot lately at the Civic Center."

"Oh, yes, that," Claire admitted. "Well, that was an impetuous thing. Robbie never intended any harm. He was just carried away by the music. The beat, as they say."

"Uh-huh," Belmond said, and made another note. "How is he with material things? Does he use them well? Take care of them? Or is he careless?"

"He's very possessive of his things. Sometimes he asks for more than Don and I would like to give him. But once he gets them, he takes extremely good care of them."

"You said, 'once he gets them.' I assume that means he generally gets what he asks for," Belmond observed.

Taking that to be a critical comment, Claire said, "He's not the kind of boy to whom you have to say, 'Robbie, if you want a new stereo, you'll have to improve your math grades.' He gets As in math. And in almost everything else. He also excels in sports. So there's no reason to deny him anything."

"And it also makes up for his father being away so much," Belmond commented.

"It's the nature of Don's business." Claire defended him staunchly.

"Mrs. Ward, please don't interpret my every comment as criticism. I'm only trying to get a complete picture of your son before I see him. Do you give him a reasonable allowance?"

"Going to Canaan Prep, he has to be able to keep up."

"Does he hoard his allowance or tend to spend it all?"

"What difference does that make?" Claire started to protest but then admitted, "Sometimes he overspends. Last year his first time when he was quarterback for a whole game and they won, he took the whole squad out for hamburgers and shakes."

"The whole squad?"

"Thirty-seven of them."

"That must have depleted his allowance for quite a time," Belmond remarked quietly.

"He—he had to call from the hamburger place for me to come down and bail him out."

"Mrs. Ward, has your son ever evidenced any previous periods when he seemed very unhappy, downcast, reclusive?"

"No, this is the first time," Claire responded quickly. "Of course, like all young people, he does worry a little at exam time. Or before a big game. And before he started going with Susan Spencer, he used to worry about getting dates. You know how young boys are."

"Yes, of course." Belmond agreed but then asked, "Susan Spencer, is she the girl who was with him when he cracked up his father's car?"

"How did you know?" Claire started to ask, but then realized, "Dr. Rissom told you about that."

"He thought I should have a complete history."

"Well, yes, Robbie did have that accident," Claire conceded.

"Now, as to your husband's reaction to all this . . ." Belmond said.

"I'm afraid Don isn't very keen about Robbie's having treatment, psychiatric treatment. He's sure Robbie will snap out of this on his own. It's just a matter of time."

"Time . . ." Belmond repeated in her uncommunicative way, which was beginning to unnerve Claire. "Mrs. Ward, I think you'd better tell your husband to call me," Belmond said with a directness that indicated it was more than a suggestion.

"And if he refuses?"

"He loves his son. I don't think he will refuse."

Claire Ward had left. Sabrina Belmond reviewed her notes. Then she placed a call to Dr. Rissom.

"Fred, I've just seen Mrs. Ward. What she told me substantiates what you thought. The things she's proudest of can be the most dangerous. Her son is overly bright, overactive, overimaginative and has a tendency to be prodigal with money. Lately he takes physical risks that tend to be quite dangerous. A very significant set of symptoms. But I'll have to know a great deal more to make a sound diagnosis. Which is most essential in a case like this."

"Keep me apprized," Rissom insisted.

"I will. Meantime, I would say nothing to his mother or father," Belmond warned.

"Of course," Rissom agreed. "Let me know if I can be of help."

"Dr. Belmond, I appreciate your seeing me outside your normal hours," Don Ward began, "but in my business—"

She smiled. "I know. I have several patients in your business. Now then . . ." she invited him to talk.

"Doctor, will what I say to you be considered absolutely confidential?"

"Of course."

"Even from my wife?"

Belmond paused for the slightest instant before nodding. For Don's request had opened avenues she had not yet considered in this case.

"I think Claire's exaggerating this whole thing. You know how mothers worry. Every childhood fever is the highest ever recorded in medical history. Every illness can be terminal. In the very early days she used to sit by his crib and watch for signs of crib death. Did she tell you she'd been an actress, still dabbles in local theater? I think it's given her an overactive imagination. She's always making more of a thing than it deserves. Robbie's a bright, active boy. He's a terrific quarterback. Okay, so he made one mistake and lost the championship of the prep school league. Of course, he feels terrible. And he doesn't want to face the other boys. I don't like it. But I understand it. Claire, on the other hand, has to magnify it into something it isn't. So if you could"—he groped for a word that would minimize the problem without demeaning Dr. Belmond's profession—"if you could see her through this until Robbie comes out of it, I would appreciate it." Then he added, "At your usual fee, of course."

He felt he had made an adequate presentation of his view of things until Dr. Belmond asked, "Now do you want to talk about your son?"

"I've already told you . . ." He started to protest.

"Mr. Ward, you're aware, aren't you, that your son is in a deep depression? I've seen teenagers in depressions not nearly so obvious who are a serious danger to themselves."

"I know what my wife told you, but I tell you that with Robbie any such fear is ridiculous!"

"He's got all the signs. Refusal to eat. Brooding. Isolation. No sense of self-worth. Fear. The world's suddenly become a strange and unmanageable place to him."

"I admit he's depressed. But dangerous?" Don doubted it.

"Mr. Ward, have you ever been confronted by a similar situation before?"

"He's never been like this before," Don admitted.

"I mean, have you ever experienced such a situation before with a parent perhaps? A family member? An uncle? An aunt? Someone close?"

Don searched his memory, then shook his head.

"What about your wife's side of the family?"

"Not that I know . . ." Don started to say. But he interrupted himself. The import of Belmond's question had suddenly become clear to him. "Just one minute, Doctor. Are you trying to say that Robbie's condition might be hereditary?"

"Our recent studies indicate that conditions such as alcoholism, suicide, depression can be genetic in origin."

"Impossible!" Don protested.

"There are considerable data to prove—"

Don interrupted. "Doctor! In Robbie's case that would be impossible. Didn't my wife tell you?"

"What?"

"Robbie is adopted. Nothing in my family history or in Claire's could have any effect on him."

"Adopted?" Belmond considered it soberly. "Interesting that your wife never mentioned that."

"Why should she? He's as much our son as if she'd given birth to him."

Not exactly, Belmond thought, *but it's too early to probe that subject now. I devoutly hope it eventually proves to be unnecessary as well.*

"Mr. Ward, it's important, very important, that I see Robbie as soon as possible."

"He won't even come out of his room to eat. How am I going to get him out of the house to come see you?"

"Has anyone asked him?"

"Of course not."

"He might be relieved to talk to someone whom he doesn't feel he's disappointed or betrayed by losing that game," Belmond suggested. "Ask him."

Don finally nodded.

"It would be best if he called me himself to set up the appointment."

"I wouldn't hold out much hope for that. Not in his present state of mind."

Don was at the door when a sudden impulse seized him. He turned to look at Belmond, who was on her feet now. She was tall, with a good figure, a feminine figure, a good face, not so much pretty as handsome, bespeaking warmth and honesty. No wonder people trusted her, he thought.

"Doctor, would you consider doing some television commercials? We have a sponsor looking for someone with authority and warmth, sort of a female Walter Cronkite, to sell a line of female sanitary products. . . ."

Belmond smiled and shook her head in a way that made Don feel foolish. He apologized. "Sorry. But in our business we have to pursue all the angles."

"Yes, I know," Belmond replied. "Ask Robbie to call me.

Don't expect he'll say yes at once. Give him time. At least a few days."

"We're not saying you have to, son. But if you'd like to, if you feel you want to talk to someone, here's her name and number."

Don placed a small piece of paper on the rumpled bed alongside his son. Robbie did not acknowledge him. He stared through the darkness of the curtained room at the poster on which, a few days ago, he had printed, in large black letters, STUPID.

As Don had agreed with Claire, he did not urge or argue. He left the room. Outside the door Claire waited, listening tensely. Her look to Don was an entreaty. His response was a shrug of worried futility.

The next two days proved a time of watchful waiting for Claire. She dared not leave the house except for the most urgent shopping. She spent her time in the kitchen preparing Robbie's favorite foods. But she could not tempt him down to eat. She waited for him to come out of his room. To go to the telephone in their bedroom. Or, more likely, to the private phone in the upstairs den, where Don did most of his business calling. Waiting and listening had now become Claire's two main activities.

At the end of the second day, just before Don was due to arrive home, she was in the kitchen preparing dinner. She thought she detected movement in the bedroom above her. She put aside her paring knife, carefully, so as not to make a sound. She went quietly to the foot of the stairs. She heard him come out of his room. He was going down the hall to the den. It could be for only one reason. He was going to place a confidential phone call. To Belmond, she devoutly hoped.

That evening the first thing she whispered to Don, even before kissing him, was "He made a call today."

"To whom? That Susan girl?"

"I think to Dr. Belmond. He may be coming out of it."

"Good," Don said. "That girl, did she ever call?"

"Four times. He won't talk to her."

"Maybe if I got his coach to call," Don suggested.

"He did. Robbie won't talk to him either."

CHAPTER 18

Dr. Sabrina Belmond sat at her desk, studying Robbie Ward. He was handsome; his mother had not exaggerated about that. Despite his weight loss of recent days, he was obviously physically developed beyond his fifteen and a half years. His face, as she expected, presented the signs of a depressed child. He was ill at ease, silent, withdrawn, isolated. She could have picked him out of any room of normally active boys his age. He stared down at his hands, which rested in his lap until he began to rub them along his thighs as if trying to remove some unwelcome substance from his fingers.

"Robbie . . . may I call you Robbie?"

He shrugged. It was of no consequence to him.

"Robbie, do you know why you're here?"

He nodded but still did not speak.

"Is there anything you'd like to tell me?"

"Not really," he said.

Frustrating as that reply was, it did not discourage Belmond. She had heard that same reply too many times from her own teenage son and daughter. There seemed to be a universal network for the interchange of adolescent language so that by some mysterious means all young people spoke in the same phrases. "Not really" was now their standard form of saying, "No, and don't pry into my life."

"Robbie, is there anything *you* want to ask *me?*"

"Not really."

"I know about that forward pass," she said, to elicit his reaction.

He looked away and dispensed with the subject in a single word: "Stupid."

"You don't strike me as a young man who does stupid things," Belmond said.

"It didn't work. That made it stupid." He was silent again and staring.

"Robbie?" she prodded.

"Look, I don't think this is going to work either." He started to rise.

"How do you know," she asked, "if you don't give it a chance?"

"Because it can't change anything. What's done is done," he said. "Besides, I know all about doctors like you. I had a friend went to one for a whole year. Nothing happened. Except he wound up on pot. Which he was on in the first place."

Then Robbie admitted softly. "He ended up hanging himself in his closet. So . . ." He never finished that sentence. Instead, he rose from his chair. Belmond waited to see if he would leave. He turned toward the door as if to go for it. Instead, he began to pace, angrily, speaking in a staccato rhythm that matched his pacing.

"So you want to look inside my head. What do you expect to find there? Some dark, hidden secret? I did a dumb thing because I *am* dumb. What's the big secret about that?"

Before Belmond could respond, he preempted her. "Yeah, I know. A young man like me doesn't do dumb things. Well, it didn't seem dumb at the time."

"How did it seem, Robbie?"

He turned on her fiercely. She stared back. Slowly the anger in his eyes seemed to drain away until all that remained was the exhaustion of sleepless days and nights.

"Yes, Robbie?" Belmond asked softly. "How did it seem?" She waited. When he did not reply, she suggested, "Like the most terrific, sensational play of the year? The greatest play you ever made? That any league quarterback ever made?"

He studied her. How did she know the feeling? She met his

inquiring look, thinking: *If he's what I suspect, this should encourage him to open up.*

"Yeah," he admitted, "that's how it felt."

"Exactly how, Robbie? Tell me. I'd like to know."

As much to defuse his pent-up nervous energy as to avoid making his confession eye to eye with her, he added spasmodic actions to match his erratic pacing. She watched him pick up random objects, then discard them. A pencil from her desk. An ashtray from an end table. A note pad from the chair at the head of her patients' couch. A shiny steel mobile of a balancing tennis player, which a patient had given her.

To Belmond, his moves and actions were important, symptomatic.

"How did it feel? How did it feel?" Robbie whispered to himself until in full voice he exploded, "You have no idea how it felt! Like being on top of the world! I owned everything I could see. I had these ten guys working for me. Doing whatever I asked them to do. And doing it right. Nobody, nobody else in the whole school, in the whole league, in the whole world could make them work together like I did.

"Because they respect me. Look up to me. Fifteen and a half, and these guys who are bigger than I am, older than I am, seniors, they were doing what *I* wanted them to do. I owned them. That's how it felt! So I said, 'I'll give the school something to remember! I'll be Joe Montana on the Forty-niners. Or Jim Plunkett! Or Joe Namath! I'll be better than all three of them rolled into one.

"What would *they* do in a spot like that? Fall on the ball! No! What kind of way is that to win a game? Falling on the ball! Go out in a blaze of glory! Give them something to remember! That's how it felt! Yeah, that's how it felt," he said, his face glistening with sweat from the inner excitement he experienced in reliving that moment.

"Ninety-nine times out of a hundred I complete that pass," Robbie said. "What right did that idiot defensive end have to be out there anyhow? Any end with a brain in his head would know I would never pass in a spot like that. That was the whole idea. It was so unexpected. Such a brilliant surprise play!"

He became conscious of holding her little desk calendar he

had picked up. It interrupted his train of thought. He handled it clumsily, finally putting it back to be rid of it. He stared at it.

Belmond could read his puzzled thought, *Why did I pick that up? Why couldn't I remember doing it?*

"They all think I won't go back to school because I'm ashamed. I'm not going back there because I'm too good for that school! There are lots of schools that'll be glad to have me. Lucky to have me! I can play quarterback for any prep school in the whole country. And later I'm going to college. One of the big ones. I'll play in the Rose Bowl one day! In the Super Bowl!"

Belmond noted: *He thinks of himself only in superlatives. He can do anything. Including the impossible.*

"My dad wants me to go to an Ivy League school. Says I can't get a good education at some football factory. Who needs a good education? I can make millions playing football! Millions! Do you know what Steve Young got for signing with the USFL? Forty million dollars! And he wasn't as good at fifteen as I am. I'm going where the money is. I'm going to have it all!"

The confident gleam in his blue eyes was that of a supreme young warrior in his moment of triumph.

Belmond sat back in her chair, observing: *Significant how he can go from depression when he came in to a high state of elation within a matter of minutes. Doubtless will relapse into depression either while here or when he reaches home. As long as he is communicative, I'd better make the most of it.*

"Tell me, Robbie, how do you stay in such terrific physical shape?"

"Work at it. I run a few miles every day. Even in the rain. Holding weights in my hands. One thing a quarterback needs, big, strong hands."

"Do you take anything?" Belmond asked him.

"You mean, drugs? Do you think I'm crazy?"

"Some athletes take steroids to increase their muscular development."

"They're not good for you. I read up on that once."

"Oh? Where?" Belmond asked.

"Public library. It said in those articles that steroids can cause all kinds of physical damage later in life. So I said, 'Not for me.' "

"Do you spend lots of time in the library, Robbie?" she asked, pursuing a fresh and unanticipated concern.

"Whenever there's something I want to know about."

She felt somewhat uneasy now. If Robbie were to become curious about his own condition and look that up in the library, it could seriously impede his treatment. She had had cases where the most dangerous crises had been precipitated by bright, intelligent patients who explored the psychiatric literature. Always they concluded that they were suffering from the worst manifestations and were doomed to the most hopeless prognosis.

For a young man in Robbie's condition it could prove dangerous, sending him into an even deeper depression.

Yet she had no means of prohibiting him without arousing even greater curiosity in his highly intelligent, if disturbed, mind.

"I think that will be all for today, Robbie."

The boy smiled.

"Something funny, Robbie?"

"That friend I told you about . . . the one who smoked pot . . ."

She noted that significantly, he did not identify his friend as the one who had committed suicide.

"When I asked him about what it was like to go to a shrink, he told me that one thing was always the same. When your time is up, they tell you. He was right. You people don't give anything for nothing, do you?"

"You were very curious, weren't you? About shrinks, what they do, what they say," Belmond pointed out.

"Look, lady, you're not fooling me. I only asked Hubie about his shrink because I was curious. Well, I'm curious about lots of things. Like the space shuttle. I asked our science prof a lot of questions about that. Questions he couldn't even answer. That doesn't mean I want to be an astronaut. The same with this. Just because I asked Hubie questions doesn't mean a thing. Nothing! One thing sure, I am not crazy!"

"Your mother tells me that since you haven't gone back to school, you spend your time up in your room. Which is always dark. You don't play your guitar anymore. Or your stereo."

He shrugged, admitting that.

"What *do* you do, Robbie?"

"I don't know. . . . I . . . just . . ." He looked away from her before admitting, "They think I'm up there in my room sleeping all the time. But I'm not. I hardly sleep at all. That's why I feel so tired all the time."

"Do you feel tired right now?"

"Yeah."

"What else?"

"Dumb."

"Just dumb?" She prodded.

"No. Terrible. Terrible about what I did in that game." He paused, turned away from her gaze. Then he confessed, "I don't know why anybody even bothers about me."

"Shouldn't your parents bother about you?"

"I'm not really their son. Did they tell you that?"

"Yes. Is that why you feel so terrible? So afraid? That after that dumb thing you did they'll turn you out?"

"Mom'd never do that!" Robbie protested.

"And Dad?"

Robbie did not answer.

"Has your dad ever said anything like that? Ever threatened you?" Belmond asked.

"No."

"Then why are you so afraid that he might?"

"Because if I had a son who'd done such a dumb thing, I'd turn him out."

"Would you? Really?" she asked.

Robbie looked down at the carpet, scuffed it with his shoe, then said, "No. I'd feel sorry for him. I'd figure he feels miserable enough, worthless enough, a blowout, a disaster. Maybe I'd feel he'd be better off—" Robbie stopped abruptly.

"Better off how? Robbie?"

"Better off . . . dead," he said softly.

"Is that what you think about when you're up there alone in your room?"

"No!" he protested instantly. Then, in a voice barely audible, he admitted, "Sometimes . . ."

If pain could be personified, its expression would be young Robbie Ward's face in that moment.

"Is this the first time you've ever told that to anyone, Robbie?"

He nodded.

"Thank you for being truthful with me, Robbie. It makes it possible for us to work together. Now, one thing more you can do. Try not to spend your time in that dark room. Get out. Get some exercise. Think about going back to school."

"I do. But the longer I stay away the worse it gets. Until now . . ." He indicated how hopeless it seemed.

"It will be easier tomorrow than the day after. Easier this week than next week. Try, Robbie, try," she urged.

"I'll—I'll try. . . ."

He started for the door, stopped, looked back at her.

"Yes, Robbie?"

"You will help me, won't you? I mean, not so much for me, but for them. My mom and dad. I know how this is tearing them up. And I wish I could be different. But somehow . . . Look, you've got to help me. Because I can't help myself. I can't!"

His blue eyes showed more desperately than his words how much he wanted help.

"I'll help you, Robbie, I will," Belmond promised.

CHAPTER 19

After a long day plagued by many emergencies Fred Rissom was finally able to lock his office door and sift through the phone messages that had accumulated. The one he chose to return first was Dr. Belmond's call.

As soon as she answered, he asked, "Well, what did you find? What's your assessment of the boy's condition?"

"He's obviously depressed. Yet he has moments of elation that are almost delusional. He fluctuates between the two in a very disturbing way. He is bright, extremely so. I sense an enormous intelligence and sensitivity. Frankly, though, I haven't been able to make a definitive diagnosis," Belmond said.

"Definitive . . . between?" Rissom asked.

"Between a bipolar affective disorder—"

"Manic-depressive?" Rissom asked, alarmed.

"Yes."

"Or?" Rissom pursued.

"Schizophrenia."

"Oh, God," Rissom reacted. "That's—that's untreatable, isn't it?"

"Treatable, yes. Curable, probably not," Belmond said. "However, I can't even begin to treat him until I make a diagnosis. Because unfortunately the treatment for the one condition can be very counterproductive if used on the other. A mistake in diagnosis can lead to disastrous consequences."

Rissom absorbed that distressing news before saying, "To think, I've been treating that boy since he was six years old and never detected anything."

"Both illnesses often don't present until the mid-teens and usually even later."

"There must be something we can do," Rissom insisted.

"I'll put him on an antidepressant meantime," Belmond said. "That's safe, no matter what the diagnosis. But I want to be sure that he has no other chemicals in his system. No drugs of any kind. Especially not steroids. He says no, but I want to be sure. So check him out."

"No problem," Rissom said. "I'll have him in tomorrow."

"But most important, I must talk to his parents. There are steps we have to take, possibly legal steps."

"Legal steps," Rissom repeated. "Surely you're not thinking of committing the boy."

"No, no, I'm not," Dr. Belmond said.

"My husband had to fly out to Chicago." Claire apologized to Dr. Belmond. "They're shooting a new series out there, and there's trouble."

"I wish he were here. This might be a bit too much to take on your own, Mrs. Ward."

"I'm not a hothouse flower," Claire protested. "Or your typical housewife either. I've been around. I've supported myself ever since I was sixteen, doing bit parts in television. So I may be tougher than you think."

After her first defensive protest her fears surfaced. "Besides, it can't be all that bad. Dr. Rissom said his physical checked out well. Perfect, he said. And you've seen Robbie only twice."

"I had my suspicions the first time. His second visit served to corroborate them."

"All right, tell me," Claire said, clasping her purse so tightly that Belmond could see her knuckles turn white.

"Mrs. Ward, relax. You won't help by developing symptoms of your own. Your son is going to need understanding, cooperation. And a great deal of love."

"We've given him all that," Claire protested.

"It will take even more now," Belmond said, her strong black eyes fixing on Claire. "Because his is not the kind of case that moves in a straight line. There may be progress and then reverses. There may not be any progress for a time. Until it seems there will be no progress at all."

"*Are* there cases like Robbie's where there is no progress at all?" Claire dared ask.

"We're a long way from drawing any such conclusions. In fact, it would be wise not to draw any just yet."

"But you sent for me, said you wanted to discuss his case. . . ."

"Yes. I have a feeling that all during the years you and your husband have looked with such pride on Robbie as an extremely bright, overachieving leader among his peers he has actually been waiting to explode. Like in that championship game."

"That was the only time," Claire protested.

"What about the time he cracked up his father's car? And the knife fight in Greenwich Village? That riot he precipitated at the rock concert? His vicious attack on his teammate who was trying to console him? It's all part of a pattern. The significant thing is these episodes all exposed him to danger. In their exuberance, manics tend to court danger, physical and otherwise. Yet this is only half of his problem. The other half is the depressions that alternate."

"This is the first time that's ever happened to Robbie."

"The first *severe* depression," Belmond corrected. "The others, being minor, passed unnoticed. But even if this was the first, every illness presents itself for the first time. Even cancer. The problem is, such a depression as he is now undergoing may be a forerunner. A hint of what may come."

Despite her effort to control her fear, Claire began to weep silently, tears tracing down her pretty face. She made no attempt to wipe them away.

"Mrs. Ward, in a situation like this I find that parents immediately assume the worst. Before we assume anything, let's complete our investigation, apply all our diagnostic skills to the known facts, and decide what to do. Because there are things that can be done."

"Just tell me what to do," Claire said.

"It is very important to discover if in Robbie's family history there is any close relative, mother, father, uncle, aunt, close cousin, who was alcoholic, depressive, manic-depressive, or suicidal."

"Suicidal?" Claire repeated, betraying her worst fears.

"Mrs. Ward, don't blame yourself for thinking of all the possibilities. Even the worst. It's the age we're living in. It is crucial to discover Robbie's family history."

"He's adopted, you know. The papers are sealed by court order," Claire pointed out.

"Of course. So you'll have to consult your lawyer. Even go to court. Discuss this with your husband as soon as possible."

As Claire rose to go, she said, "Well, at least—" She stopped precipitously.

"At least it's not something that *you* did wrong," Belmond anticipated.

Claire nodded.

"The first thing all parents assume is that their child's condition must be the result of something they've done wrong. Between old-fashioned myths about psychiatry and millions of how-to books about bringing up children, parents think that they are responsible for every difficulty. Not so. Children are born with many of their problems. It simply takes time for them to surface. Talk to your husband. Then call me."

"I will," Claire promised.

"Mrs. Ward, I know that finding Robbie's natural mother will be emotionally difficult for you. But if at all possible, I would like to interview her, ask her about her family history. It could prove crucial in your son's treatment. Find her. Convince her."

"I knew it," Don exploded in a controlled but angry whisper so that he could not be overheard by Robbie, who was up in his room. "First you consult Rissom, then he says consult this Dr. Belmond, and now she wants to open up the whole adoption procedure. There's going to be no end to it. I say now what I said before. Give the boy time, and he'll work his own way out of it."

"Don!" Claire said. "No! He will not work his way out of it. Rissom doesn't think so. Belmond doesn't think so. He needs help."

"I don't see how losing a football game can suddenly become a life-and-death crisis!"

"Belmond called it the precipitating factor," Claire said.

"Belmond . . . Belmond . . . a woman we didn't even know a week ago has suddenly become the most important person in our lives. Why? Suppose she's wrong. She doesn't know Robbie like we know him. And now she's saying open up the whole adoption situation? Not me. Sorry!" Don said, adamant.

"Don, please?" Claire persisted.

"Before we do anything as serious as finding Robbie's natural mother, opening up what might be a painful and destructive situation, let's get another opinion. And this time not through Dr. Rissom. I'll get the name of a good psychiatrist from one of the network's medical authorities. Okay?"

"Okay," Claire agreed because it seemed the only way to prevent Don from foreclosing all consideration of further professional help for Robbie.

"And this time," Don warned, "I'll do all the talking. I'll present the case. I'll bring Robbie in. And I'll get the doctor's findings and conclusions firsthand."

"All right, Don, fine. Do that. Just as long as we do something. I have this terrible feeling that time and our son's life are slipping through our fingers. I have this feeling . . ." she said, then turned away to hide her tears.

He took her in his arms. "Claire, baby, don't let them panic you. It can't be as bad as Belmond says. If it were, we would have known or at least suspected. He's been our son for fifteen years. Surely we know him better than some strange woman who talks to him for a few hours."

"That's what I keep telling myself," Claire said, but then admitted, "I would never have guessed that he'd react this way. So how well do I really know him? How well do you know him? Really?"

Because he could not answer honestly, Don said, "That's why I'm saying let's get a second opinion."

Dr. Alexis Cooper, consultant to Intercontinental on all medical news and dramatic programs, had recommended three names to Don Ward: two women and one man. Because Don secretly felt that female psychiatrists tended to respond too emotionally to such situations, he chose the man, Dr. Ralph Christian.

A man in his early sixties, Christian was white-haired, small, portly, and given to the habit of constantly readjusting his spectacles, which never seemed to settle at a proper angle on his patrician nose. He did so many times while evaluating Don's recounting of the events leading up to Robbie's present condition.

Christian listened, nodded from time to time, readjusting his glasses. When Don completed his presentation, Christian said only, "And you say your son is adopted?"

"Yes."

"Uh-huh," Christian commented noncommittally. "Well, of course, I would not venture an opinion without seeing the patient."

"Naturally," Don agreed.

"I'll need about two hours," Christian said, looking through his appointment book. "Say, Thursday, at four?"

"I'll make sure he's here, Doctor."

On Friday morning, when Don returned to his own office after a long session with the vice-president of miniseries and movies of the week, he found Jeannie's message on his desk: "Call Dr. Christian. Important."

Christian was with a patient, so it wasn't until after lunch that Don was able to reach him.

"Mr. Ward, I had a most informative session with your son. He is a very interesting young man. Very bright. Very challenging, too. Because he is the kind of patient that brings out the best in a psychiatrist. I mean, he's the kind worth saving at any cost. Real possibilities in that young man. Real possibilities."

"Thank you," Don said. "But your diagnosis. What do you think we should be doing for him now?"

"On the basis of the facts as I gather them from you and from Robert and my observation of him, I would say a diagnosis of either schizophrenia or a bipolar affective disorder is possible. That means manic depression, Mr. Ward."

"I see. And how does one treat these?" Don asked.

"Your son mentioned seeing Dr. Belmond. I know her only by reputation. Hers is excellent. I don't know what advice she's given you. But if it were up to me, before you do anything else, I would get the medical history of the natural mother. It might prove crucial in making the proper diagnosis."

"Open up the whole adoption situation," Don said, to make absolutely sure he understood.

"It is vital, in order to avoid the complications that might result from a faulty or mistaken diagnosis and treatment."

"I see," Don said reluctantly.

"By the way," Christian added, "from the manner in which your son spoke of Dr. Belmond, he seems to trust her and he likes her. I would suggest you continue his treatment with her."

"Yes, of course. And investigate his natural mother. Thank you, Doctor, thank you very much."

CHAPTER 20

As an affirmation that adopting Robbie was something they both had wanted with equal commitment, Don and Claire determined they would visit the adoption agency together.

The personnel had changed completely since the last time. The present head of the agency was Mrs. Lena Betancourt. She was a small woman, dark-haired and slightly plump, with a pleasant and appealing, if not a pretty, face. *Motherly* was the word Claire settled on for her, encouraged that such a woman would be understanding and helpful in their present crisis. Mrs. Betancourt listened with considerable interest, reacting with sympathetic nods and sounds as Don related the history of the events which precipitated their visit.

"Ah, too bad. Fortunately we don't have many such cases. We select our children as carefully as we can. And"—she could not permit the opportunity to pass without defending her institution—"we always do as careful a check as possible on our mothers. The fathers, too, whenever that is feasible. However . . ."

"What we need now is information about Robbie's natural mother," Don said.

"I'm sure you saw all that at the time of Robbie's adoption," Mrs. Betancourt said.

"Dr. Belmond would like her family history as well," Claire pointed out.

"Family history," Mrs. Betancourt repeated, becoming discernibly resistant. "You understand the restrictions under which we operate."

"Yes," Don said, "but in such a case, where family history is crucial to making a differential diagnosis, I think you should relax your rules."

"It's not a question of what you think or even what I think, Mr. Ward. There is the law."

"Law or no law, we've got to discover the woman's whereabouts!" Don said, no longer asking but demanding.

"Don, please." Claire tried to placate him.

"When my son's health is at stake, I don't choose to be polite or diplomatic. Two doctors have said we need that information, and I intend to get it!"

"Not without a court order," Mrs. Betancourt said, rising to her full five feet three. "Now, if you would like to review the original health record of Robbie's natural mother, I can show you that. But nothing more. That is state law. And also an unbreakable rule of this institution."

Don was about to refuse, but Claire intervened. "As long as we're here, we might as well."

The anonymous record of the woman who had given birth to the baby boy now known as Robert Anson Ward revealed that she was in good health throughout her pregnancy, had good medical care, delivered without incident a full-term six-pound-two-ounce infant, whose Apgar tests showed him to be neurologically excellent at the time of delivery. The woman had no history of any life-threatening health problems in her youth.

Nothing was known of the father, except that he was roughly thirty-seven years old and, on the basis of the mother's information, in good health, married, with three children, all of whom were apparently normal.

There was also a certificate, prepared by the agency's doctors, which testified to the good health of the woman during pregnancy and at the time of delivery.

"Comforting," Don said, "but not what Dr. Belmond needs."

"I'm sorry," Mrs. Betancourt said, "but this is as far as we can go. It's up to the courts now."

* * *

The legal procedure required long, detailed affidavits from Don and Claire Ward and an even longer one from Dr. Belmond explaining the psychiatric elements of Robbie's case. Plus a statement from the adoption agency that it would interpose no objection if, in the opinion of the court, revealing the mother's identity was justified in this case.

Two days after the affidavits had been submitted, the Wards' attorney, Ed Hillman, called.

"Claire? Don home?"

"He's on the Coast. Won't be back till Sunday."

"Too bad," Hillman said. "Under pressure from one of my partners, who knows Judge Carmody well, he agreed to hold a private hearing in chambers tomorrow after his regular court session."

"Why a hearing? You prepared all those affidavits."

"Some judges are sticklers about anything to do with kids. I guess I'll have to put it off. Too bad."

Before he could hang up, Claire said, "We can't put it off. I'll go. Anything Don would say, I can say."

"I'll check with the judge's secretary, but he asked for *all* the parties."

"That doesn't mean Robbie, does it?" Claire asked, even more anxious now.

"No, no, no," Hillman reassured. "I'll get back. By the way, how is Robbie?"

"I don't know," Claire confessed. "I think he's coming out of it. Or maybe I'm being optimistic because I don't know what else to be."

The same degree of change in Robbie's condition that Claire had noticed was also evident to Dr. Belmond. However, in her mind, and in her notes, she did not describe that as improvement, only as change. She was handling this case gingerly. She was waiting for that genetic information.

The hearing took place in the chambers of Judge Julian Carmody. Carmody, a lean man, sixtyish, with a puckered face, seemed to be tasting something bitter as he leaned back in his old leather chair. He picked up the papers his secretary had set before him. As he scanned them, he appeared surprised because Claire heard him say, "Oh, this matter. All right, let's get on with it," as if he had neither the time nor the taste for such a petition.

As succinctly as possible Ed Hillman set forth the facts in the case, for it was obvious that Carmody had only scanned the affidavits, not studied them.

Carmody was silent, looking from Claire to Belmond. "I asked that the father be here, too."

"He's in California on business," Claire said.

"If this were my son, no business in the world would keep me away," Carmody remarked acidly. "Not if the situation is as serious as you'd have this court believe."

"He is in a business which makes enormous demands on his time," Claire tried to explain.

"What kind of business?" Carmody demanded.

"He's a television network executive. Vice-president."

"You mean it actually takes grown men to put that crap on the air?"

Claire did not reply, though she had more than once reprimanded her son for using that same word about his father's business.

"Maybe that's your son's trouble. Maybe you don't have to find his natural mother after all." But then Carmody turned from being the disgruntled television viewer to the more moderate and understanding judge. "Look, Mrs. Ward, I happen to believe that one of the most delicate relationships in our society is the triangle which joins an adoptive child, adoptive parents, and natural parents. It is fraught with great danger. I have seen children track down natural parents who want nothing to do with them. I have seen natural parents who want to find adopted children who refuse to see them. And I have also seen adoptive parents badly hurt in the process.

"What if I sign this order and the agency, in compliance, gives you this woman's last known address, then you do find her, but she refuses to see Robbie or you?" Carmody asked.

Dr. Belmond interjected, "Your Honor, there is no need for the woman to see either the boy or his adoptive parents. I'm the one who needs the information. As I stated in my affidavit, if I am to treat the boy conscientiously, I must know certain things about his medical history. And that includes everything I can learn about his natural mother and father."

"Then there would not necessarily be any need to bring the parties together?" the judge asked.

"It might not require more than a single interview, and I would conduct that if you so order," Belmond stated.

"Well . . ." Judge Carmody considered it. "I don't want to put too many restrictions on this." He picked up his pen and was about to affix his signature to the document when he stopped, glanced at Dr. Belmond, and asked, "You affirm that you need this information before you can make a differential diagnosis?"

"Yes, Your Honor," Dr. Belmond said.

The judge scrawled his signature in the blank space provided, blotted it carefully, and handed it to Ed Hillman, who took it with a great sense of relief.

As they were leaving, Judge Carmody called to Claire, "Tell your husband to get some honest work somewhere instead of what he does now."

CHAPTER 21

"Emily Birch, 1277 Rosemont Avenue" were the name and address typed out on the letterhead of the adoption agency. It was handed to Don and Claire Ward by Mrs. Betancourt, who seemed reluctant to surrender it.

Rosemont Avenue was a street in the Washington Heights section on the Upper West Side of Manhattan, near the George Washington Bridge. Years ago it had been a comfortable middle-class neighborhood. Now it was an area of old run-down houses of weathered, dirty tan brick. The cars on the street were parked so tightly it seemed they had set down roots in the asphalt. The language heard was mainly Spanish.

They located 1277. They stood outside, staring at the old building, hesitant to enter.

"It's a place to start," Claire said.

They mounted the single step and entered the small foyer, where mailboxes lined the wall. Some boxes had had special locks superimposed over them to thwart rifling by thieves who preyed on Social Security and welfare checks.

Don had to light a match to read the names on the boxes. They were mostly Spanish refugees from South and Central American tyrannies. There was no name that even faintly resembled Birch.

An elderly woman, carrying a frayed cord shopping bag sagging with groceries, entered the dark hallway. Startled to discover them, she pulled back, protecting her possessions. Once they passed her suspicious inspection, she stopped to unlock her mailbox. It proved to be empty.

"Ma'am . . . madame . . ." Don addressed her, thinking a woman so old might well have lived here the past sixteen years.

The woman stared at him, tense and defensive again.

"You live here a long time?" Don asked.

"Too long," the wizened old woman said. In those two words she confirmed by her intonation that she was Jewish, a remnant of the time when this neighborhood had been populated mainly by the middle class.

"May I ask you a question?"

"What harm can it do?" the woman said, holding her bag of groceries closer to her as if fearing they might be stolen.

Claire realized it was not that she specifically suspected them but that she suspected everyone. An unfortunate state of mind, inculcated by big-city crime.

"Sixteen years ago there was a young woman who lived in this house. Her name was Emily Birch. Did you know her?"

"Birch?" the woman pondered. "Birch . . . that's not a Jewish name. You sure she lived here?"

"That's the name she gave. And this is the address," Don said.

"Birch . . . Birch . . ." the woman kept repeating. "Who knows a Birch? And sixteen years ago? I can't remember some things that happened only yesterday."

"Think! Please! It's very important," Claire begged.

"Important." The woman dismissed the word, adding, "These days nothing is important except unemployment and the Russians, and what happens on the soap operas. It's some world," the woman said.

"Emily Birch." Don persisted. "We have to find her because our son is sick. He needs her help."

"You got a sick boy?" the woman asked sadly. "I know how that is. I had a son, Irving, he was so sick . . . was before even penicillin . . . they couldn't do nothing for him." Her eyes, which had been watery from age, now began to blink, and she sniffled back her tears. "Nothing worse than for a mother to bury her own child . . . nothing."

"Then please help us if you can. *Emily Birch,*" Claire repeated.

"You like a glass of tea?" the woman asked suddenly. "Come. We'll talk, maybe I'll remember."

She used her key to gain admittance to the inner hallway. It was even darker there. Claire could barely make out the small white floor tiles that had once been so neatly arranged and kept meticulously clean with daily mopping but were now cracked or missing and had not felt a wet mop for weeks.

Don sought to ease the woman's climb by taking her shopping bag, but she only clutched it more protectively. Slowly following the woman as she labored up three flights of stairs, they finally arrived at her door. She had to unlock four locks before gaining admission. They followed her into the flat. Though it was dark, the smell was sweeter than the heavy, rancid odors that had assailed them on their climb.

"You'll sit, I'll heat up the teakettle," she said. She showed them into a small living room, filled with large overstuffed pieces covered with brocaded velour on which the pattern had begun to unravel. The arms of the sofa and the chairs showed worn spots. This furniture, Claire thought, must have been here through all this woman's married life. Forty years? Fifty? There were some photographs on the small table against the wall. They were yellow from age. The subjects were dressed in clothes of many years ago.

One photo stood apart from the others. A boy, even younger than Robbie, wearing a prayer shawl and a little black skullcap. Claire could not resist picking it up. She was suddenly surprised and guilty when she heard the woman say, "Irving, my son. Thirteen and a half. And such a boy. Brilliant in school. But the doctors couldn't do anything. Specialists. From three different hospitals. And they couldn't do anything." She sighed heavily, the sound as fresh and racked with pain today as it had been so many years ago. "So sit. I'll make some tea."

She disappeared into the kitchen. Don looked at Claire. He made a gesture indicating that he had no hope of discovering anything here. They had best extricate themselves as soon as courteously possible.

The woman reappeared with a small tray on which were three steaming cups and a plate of cookies. She handed them each a cup and saucer, offered them some slices of lemon, and finally a small china cup with a white substance in it.

"Take. Take. It's not sugar, but just as good. My doctor says I can't have sugar anymore."

Before they could ask, she started thinking aloud. "Birch . . . Birch . . . let's see. On the first floor was in the front the Rosens and the Winokurs, and in the back the Levins and the Schwartzes . . . no, the Schwartzes was before. Sixteen years ago was the Samuels. He was in millinery. Then, when millinery got bad, he went into sportswear. . . ."

Don began to exhibit an impatient look, which Claire recognized. With a sharp glance she forbade him to interrupt. If it took hours, Claire was determined to ferret out any bit of information that might lead them to Emily Birch.

The old woman had searched her memory, going from floor to floor, apartment to apartment, recalling each family name and dropping some bit of information about them. She had finally reached the fifth and top floor and identified each of the four families that lived on that floor. Then she finally admitted, "Birch . . . Birch . . . I don't remember any Birch. Not in this house. You sure you got the right address?"

"Twelve seventy-seven Rosemont," Claire repeated.

"Right address, wrong house," the old woman said, shaking her head. "As one mother to another, believe me, I'm sorry."

"Thank you anyway," Don said, anxious to escape this place, which depressed him so.

"Leave your phone number. If I remember, I'll call you," the woman said.

Don was reluctant, but Claire seized the opportunity. As she handed their number to the woman, she said, "Please? Anything at all that might help."

"I'll do my best. Tell me, what's wrong with *your* son?" the woman asked, anxious to compare his symptoms and diseases with those of her own long-dead child.

Under pressure from Don, who resented anyone's finding out about Robbie's condition, Claire evaded. "It's very complicated."

"Whatever," the old woman said. "These days doctors can do a lot. God bless you and your boy."

"Thank you. You've been very kind," Claire said.

"Kind." The woman disparaged her. "What good is kind if I couldn't help?"

Owlish, puzzled, Herb Bannerman, head of research for Intercontinental Television, stared through his thick glasses at Don Ward, incredulous as he questioned, "The Manhattan telephone book of sixteen years ago?"

"Yes, Herb," Don said. "The Manhattan telephone book of sixteen years ago and seventeen years ago and fifteen years ago."

"And if I finally succeed in getting them?"

"Herb, do me a favor. Don't ask questions. Just get hold of those books. And do this yourself. It's very important. Look up everyone in those books with the name of Birch. B-i-r-c-h."

"Name like that can also be spelled B-*u*-r-c-h," Herb pointed out.

"No, this is spelled B-*i*," Don insisted, but then relented. "Okay, with an *i* or a *u*."

"And you want a list of all of them with their phone numbers," Herb assumed.

"No, just the one who lived at Twelve seventy-seven Rosemont Avenue," Don said.

Herb was about to ask, but Don preempted him. "Herb, don't try to outguess me. Just do what I ask. Please! It is important!"

Because it was taken for granted around the network that Don Ward was on his way up to the presidency, Herb Bannerman said, "Of course, Don. Anything you say."

The next afternoon, when Don returned from a long, heated lunch meeting with the rest of the brass, he found Herb Bannerman waiting in his office.

"Well?"

"It wasn't easy to get New York Telephone to dig out phone books of sixteen years ago. But I said the network needed them in order to be accurate on a documentary we were doing."

"And?"

"Don, there are twenty-one Birches with an *i*. And nineteen with a *u*. But none that lived at Twelve seventy-seven Rosemont."

"That's impossible!" Don exploded. "She lived there. That was verified by the—" He stopped short of revealing the reason for his concern.

"I could photocopy the pages," Herb offered. "You can see for yourself there was no Birch by any spelling at that address."

"No, no, don't bother," Don said, trying to make Bannerman's failure seem less distressing than it was. "And thanks, Herb. I would appreciate it if you would keep this confidential. FYI. Okay?"

"Okay, Don."

Don had only one remaining hope.

Jim Brennan, chief of security at the network, a giant of a man, white-haired now, had for years been a detective on the New York City police force. When Don put the problem to him, Brennan said that a trail sixteen years old and cold was virtually worthless. Especially since no such person as the Birch woman was registered by the phone company as having lived at that last known address.

"You can't search the whole country to find a woman about whom you really know nothing."

"You mean there's no way . . ." Don asked.

"Mr. Ward, you know if there were, I'd do it for you."

"I know. Thanks, Chief. If anything does occur to you, please let me know."

"Sure, Mr. Ward, sure."

But in his own mind Don had eliminated all hope that any help would be forthcoming from Brennan.

Dr. Belmond would have to risk treating Robbie without knowledge of his natural mother's medical history.

CHAPTER 22

He had decided not to tell Claire of his futile attempts. What would it accomplish, beyond adding to her torment? He was already distressed by the change in her these last few weeks. She was thinner, tenser. Her fair skin stretched like a mask over her delicately shaped face. She seemed almost to be mimicking Robbie's symptoms.

But that evening, after dinner, once Robbie had gone up to his room, spurred by the honesty that had always existed between them, Don felt compelled to tell her.

"Bannerman couldn't find anything. And Brennan says—and he's a man with lots of experience in missing persons—he says it's impossible. We have virtually nothing to go on. He says she must have used a phony name and address."

"Yes, she must have," Claire agreed. Then said, "Don't be so discouraged, darling. It may not be necessary to find her after all."

"Why not?" Don asked. "Belmond said—"

Claire signaled him to lower his voice. "Don, haven't you noticed?" she asked in a whisper.

"Noticed what?"

"How well Robbie ate tonight. And another significant thing. He had his window shades up today. Two very important signs. Don, I think he's coming out of it. In fact, I called Dr. Belmond, but she's not taking any calls today. I can't wait for her to get back to me so I can tell her. She'll probably say, "Forget about that woman."

"That'd be a relief," Don said. "Say, maybe I should go up and talk to him, encourage him."

"I'd wait for Belmond. If things are getting better, we don't want to upset them," Claire cautioned.

Don agreed, sadly, "Sixteen years he's been my son, now I have to get a doctor's permission to talk to him."

"Darling, it's not a matter of getting permission. Just be thankful he's coming out of it. Let's not pressure him."

The next morning, just as Don was leaving by taxi to catch an early train, Robbie came down to breakfast at seven. On days when Don was due to fly to the Coast, he went into the city by train so as not to be burdened with his car. And he left earlier, commuter trains into New York notorious for always being late whenever they were not canceled.

"Hi, Dad," Robbie said shyly. But he did smile, the first time in weeks.

"Morning, son!" Don embraced his son and kissed him on the cheek, a procedure with which they had been accustomed from those early days, when Robbie was fed his breakfast in a high chair and Don was fifteen years younger and a striving junior executive.

Don's first impulse was to ask, "Going back to school today, son?" But he stifled that in deference to Claire's glance, warning him not to rush things. Instead, he said only, "Great to see you at the breakfast table, Robbie, boy. I won't be home tonight."

"I know," the boy replied. "Another trip to the Coast."

"Yeah. Say, tell you what. When school is out, maybe the Christmas holidays, what if we all go out to the Coast? Maybe sneak a few days in Palm Springs. Or else take in the Rose Bowl game. We've got the television rights this year. I could get passes to the press box. How would you like that?"

"Hey, terrific! Real neat!" Robbie said, exhibiting enthusiasm for the first time.

Between Don and Claire passed the most hopeful look they had had reason to exchange in many anxious days.

"Okay! I'll start working on it today," Don promised. He hefted his overnight bag and a brief case bulging with memorandums, scripts, and proposals for new television series. Claire preceded him to open the front door.

There they had a brief whispered conversation.

"He's like a new boy," Don said.

"Isn't it terrific!" Claire replied. "He's coming out of it. Finally."

"Without pressing, encourage him to go back to school, darling," Don said. "That's the real hurdle. To get him to face his classmates."

"I just hope they understand," Claire said.

"They will. Enough of them called to ask about him when he didn't show up," Don said. "I'm sure they'll be very understanding."

He started out to the driveway, where the taxi was waiting to take him down to the train.

Claire busied herself in the kitchen, a hundred times fighting off the nagging need to go up and suggest Robbie set out for school. But she refrained, even doing the breakfast dishes by hand to occupy her time. She listed her chores and appointments for the day: shopping for groceries, her meeting of the Towne Players. She had neglected those duties during the worst of Robbie's depression. And there was Mercy Hospital, which was still after her to create and stage its benefit show in its drive to buy a new and very expensive piece of sonar equipment.

It would be a relief, Claire thought, not to sit here like a jailer wondering what her tormented son was doing alone up there.

When Robbie came down, he was dressed for school, in his usual jeans, plaid shirt, and letter jacket. His hair was glistening wet, properly combed and brushed. Thank God, Claire thought, that boys had given up those wild, weird hairdos of recent years. If a boy wasn't into hard rock these days, he presented a fairly decent appearance.

"Robbie . . . are you going to school?" she ventured to ask.

"Yep," he replied a bit sheepishly. "Finally going back."

"If you like, I could drive you," she volunteered impulsively.

"No. I'll bike over. Like always."

"Good! That's the best way."

"I'm sorry, Mom. Sorry I gave you and Dad such a rough time."

"That's okay, darling." And she embraced him.

While he was still in her embrace, he said, "One of the reasons I want to go back, I've got a terrific idea I'm going to lay on those guys. About next season. With the guys we got who are juniors this year, we can win it all next year. So what I'm going to do is, since by league rules we're not allowed to do spring training, I'll get our guys to practice on our own. Without the coach. After all, they can't stop a bunch of guys going out and practicing, can they, especially if it's not on school grounds?"

"I don't think so. Especially if the coach is not involved." Claire encouraged him.

"Then, comes our opening game, we'll be ready! Real ready! And this time we'll go all the way. All the way!" he enthused. "We'll win it all."

"I'll bet you will, darling." She kissed him. "Have a good day in school!"

She watched from the living room window as he biked down the circular driveway, turned and was off to school. She went directly to the phone. She dialed. She was rewarded only by Belmond's voice on her answering machine.

"I am busy just now. If you leave your name and number, I will call you back at the first opportunity. Thank you."

"This is Claire Ward. I must talk to you as soon as possible. Five-five-five-six-seven-five-two."

She glanced at the kitchen clock. It was only ten to eight. Did Belmond have such early patient hours? Perhaps a patient who worked in the city and could keep appointments only in the very early morning.

Claire busied herself stripping the beds and changing the linen. Lily always did that. But Claire needed things to do to pass the time until Belmond called back. It couldn't take very long. After all, an hour lasted only fifty minutes. And Belmond was already into the hour when Claire had called.

It was past ten before the phone finally rang.

"Mrs. Ward, this is Dr. Belmond. You called. And from the

sound of your voice you seem anxious about something. Sorry I couldn't get back to you sooner, but I had an emergency. I've been out of the office."

"Nothing too serious, I hope," Claire said.

"I'm afraid you'll read about it in the newspapers" was all Belmond said by way of explanation. "Now, your call? Something go wrong?"

"No, no," Claire was eager to reply. "Something went right. *Everything* went right."

"Good," Belmond said, but with a certain inflection that demanded more information.

"Robbie came down to breakfast on his own. Then he showered, dressed, and started off to school. All without a single suggestion from Don or me," Claire reported proudly.

"Did he say or do anything more than that?" Belmond asked.

"Oh, yes! He's coming around to his old self again. I can see signs."

"Exactly what signs, Mrs. Ward?" Belmond asked, betraying no hint of her professional reaction.

Claire told her of Robbie's plan to institute an unofficial training program for his football squad. That was the old Robbie. The leader. The innovator.

Throughout, Belmond kept inserting those nonrevealing "uh-huhs" that in medical school doctors must be taught to take the place of informative conversation.

"I tell you, to see him this way again is a relief. A blessing," Claire said.

"I can understand why you feel that way, Mrs. Ward."

"Then we no longer have to try to track down his birth mother, do we?"

Instead of replying, Belmond suggested, "Mrs. Ward, because of my emergency, I've canceled all my appointments for the day. So I have some free time this afternoon. Can you drop by? Say, at a quarter to three?"

Feeling she was being reprimanded, Claire conceded. "Yes, of course. Quarter to three." She hung up the phone. The relief she had enjoyed when she watched Robbie bicycle off to school had been replaced by a heavy feeling that slowly turned into pain in her belly.

* * *

She arrived at Dr. Belmond's office a full forty minutes early. She waited impatiently. She thumbed through old magazines, too concerned even to read the captions under the cartoons. Finally she tossed her magazine aside and surrendered to the thoughts and fears that crowded her agitated mind.

She had been so sure that once Belmond had heard the good news about Robbie, she would be willing to forget about his natural mother. But instead, it had seemed to strengthen her insistence.

Last night and this morning Claire had felt so free again, so relieved. Now she felt worse than at any time since Robbie had first been seized by his depression. Had Belmond discovered something in the course of Robbie's visits that was far more dangerous than she had yet revealed to them? Mainly, why had Belmond reacted with such strange reserve and severity to Claire's good news about Robbie?

All her thoughts, hostile and fearful, were suddenly brought to a climax when the door to Belmond's inner office opened and she said, "Mrs. Ward, please. Come in."

In her anxiety to comply, Claire rose swiftly, dropping her purse, which burst open and spewed out lipstick, compact, keys, shopping list, credit cards, and all the other articles it contained. Claire had to get down on her knees to gather them up, at the same time apologizing. "I'm sorry. I'm terribly sorry."

Once Claire had collected everything and regained her composure, she smiled nervously at Belmond. "I suppose you're reading all kinds of things into what just happened."

"I know you're anxious about coming here. Anxious about waiting. Anxious to get in to see me and ask me lots of questions. So, in your anxiety, you dropped your purse. Which under trying circumstances, all women sometimes do. Including me. Now come in, and let's talk."

Once Claire was at ease, Belmond asked, "So Robbie followed his usual morning routine and went back to school without any suggestion on your part. Well, it proves the antidepressant medication is starting to work."

"Medication or not, the important thing is he's the old Robbie again."

"You're right, Mrs. Ward, that *is* the important thing."

"Then why do we still have to find that woman?"

"Mrs. Ward, describe what you call the old Robbie."

"He's eager again. He has innovative ideas. Like running football spring training without the coach. And he'll do it. Because the boys admire him. They trust him. They follow him. Even boys older than he is. That's the Robbie we've always known," Claire said.

"And the same Robbie who just went through a siege of depression that required a strong antidepressant to overcome," Belmond pointed out. "So I still need that woman's help if I'm to know how to treat your son."

"But if he's better, why does he need treatment?"

"Because in his case getting better may be part of the disease," Belmond pointed out. "His ups as well as his downs, when they go to extremes, may be Robbie's illness. Find that woman, Mrs. Ward. She is the blueprint to his condition, his diagnosis, and his chance of being cured."

CHAPTER 23

Belmond's words from an earlier session stayed with Claire all during the drive home: *You must both understand, there is a risk in treating Robbie without a definitive diagnosis. Treatment for one type of mental difficulty may be totally ineffective for the other. May be even counterproductive.*

Totally ineffective, even counterproductive—the words unnerved her. As much as, perhaps even more than, Belmond's disturbing reaction. Rather than be encouraged by Robbie's improvement, she considered it a sign that his condition was worsening.

Claire conjured up all the things she should have said if she had thought of them in time: *If the medication works, isn't that enough? If Robbie is acting as he did before all this started, what more proof do we need?*

By the time she rolled into the garage, she felt exhausted from the emotional drain of that disheartening session. She let herself into the house, noticed that Lily had been there, done her usual thorough housecleaning, and left. Claire went straight up to their bedroom, lay down on their bed, kicked off her shoes, and soon fell into a deep sleep.

When she woke it was already dark out. Must be almost five-thirty, possibly six, she thought. Robbie should be home by now. She listened for some sound of him. She recalled he had said that now that football was over, he was going out for basketball. Knowing how diligent he was, he had probably stayed late to get in some extra practice.

"Robbie," she called out.

There was no answer. She sat up, suddenly tense. She called again. Again no answer. She went out into the hallway. She listened. No heavy beat of rock music. He was surely not home yet. She started into her bedroom, but as if some presence had reached out to tug at her sleeve, she stopped. She turned back toward the door. All the feelings that had tormented her after the session with Belmond suddenly seemed to come alive again.

The same fears she had lived with during the days of Robbie's depression were gnawing at her again. The familiar pain in her belly gripped her once more.

She could not resist. She approached Robbie's door cautiously, on stockinged feet. She tried the door, expecting it to be locked once more. It opened easily. She looked in. The room seemed to be in the same tidy condition in which Lily would have left it. Slowly, with great hesitancy and fear, Claire dared approach Robbie's clothes closet. The door was closed. Lily always left it closed. Robbie hardly ever did. Though he might have, if . . . if . . . She reached out. The doorknob felt cold to her hand. She gripped it, turned it, slowly pulled it open.

His clothes were hanging neatly, as Lily always left them. The drawers of his built-in chest were firmly closed, not partly, with a sock or shirt caught in them.

Everything neat, everything in place, yet she began to tremble. The accumulated fears of many days, the thoughts that had tormented her, the stories she had heard on television, read in the local papers, of mothers who had found their sons or daughters hanged in their own closets, suddenly came crashing in on her.

She felt herself trembling so violently that she sank down onto Robbie's bed. She had to cross her arms and grasp them with her cold hands to hold them still.

She was sitting that way when she heard the back door open and slam shut. The familiar sound was reassuring. Robbie's sound. Robbie's sound when he was his usual active self. She heard him call out, "Mom?"

"Yes, darling, I'm here. Upstairs."

He came bounding up the stairs to meet her as she came out of his room.

"Gee, Mom, you all right?"

"Of course, I'm all right. Why?"

"You look so . . . like you'd seen a ghost."

"I'm fine," Claire said, forcing a smile. She kissed him on the cheek. "How did it go today?"

"Terrific! They elected me captain of the junior varsity basketball team," he boasted. "But I'll make the varsity soon, and when I do, I'll show them a thing or two. You know, basketball teams need quarterbacks, too. They call them playmakers. And I can do it. You'll see, Mom, I can do it!"

"Of course, you can, darling."

She kissed him again. Despite all of Belmond's warnings, she loved it when her son was so exuberant. Relieved, she went down to start their dinner.

She found the note stuck to the hood over the electric range. It was on a slip from those little pads Don brought home from the office. Slips with adhesive on one edge, so you could stick the note anyplace and it would remain there. Lily's way was to stick them on the range hood.

Claire pulled the slip off, read it quickly, and was about to discard it as unimportant. She did not know any Mrs. Birnbaum. The phone number was not familiar. So it was probably a solicitation of some kind. But in the middle of cooking she realized that the name Birnbaum did register with some familiarity. She dialed the number in Manhattan.

On hearing the woman's "Hello?" with that upward lilt on the second syllable, Claire identified the voice. It was the woman who lived on Rosemont Avenue.

"Hello, Mrs. Birnbaum. This is Mrs. Ward, returning your call."

"Oh, yes. Hello, darling, how are you?"

"Fine," Claire said, puzzled. *Surely she hasn't called to inquire about my health.*

"And your nice husband? A handsome man. My Morris was like that. Handsome and nicely dressed. But that's not why I'm calling."

"Mrs. Birnbaum, why *are* you calling?"

"You and your husband were asking about that girl Emily Birch?"

"Yes," Claire said eagerly.

"Wasn't any," Mrs. Birnbaum said.

"What do you mean, there wasn't any?"

"Birch there wasn't. Biegenwald there was."

"I don't understand."

"Four C, the fourth floor in the back, was a family named Biegenwald. German people but very nice. I mean quiet people. People who went to church every Sunday. They kept to themselves. They had a daughter. Her name was Emily. Then they moved away very suddenly. Personally, you ask me, I would say the girl got herself in trouble. You know what I mean?"

"Yes, yes, I know what you mean." Claire agreed, to hurry the old woman along.

"Wasn't like today. Today an actress gets pregnant without getting married, she makes a public announcement and gives interviews. Some world, eh, Mrs. Ward?"

"Yes, yes, some world. Now what about the Biegenwalds?"

"Like I said, they had a daughter Emily. And with a name like Biegenwald, why shouldn't she change it to Birch? 'Specially if she gets herself . . . you know what I mean?"

"Yes, Mrs. Birnbaum."

"If it helps you, I'm glad. But if it doesn't, don't hold against me what I said about that girl. Far as I know, she was a nice quiet girl, and I was sorry for her," Mrs. Birnbaum said.

"Yes." Claire agreed. "So was I. Thank you, Mrs. Birnbaum, for remembering and for calling."

"Not at all, glad to help. Take care of yourself and of your husband. I looked at him I saw my Morris, *olev hasholom.*"

"Biegenwald?" Herb Bannerman said, as he stared at the slip Don had handed him. "I'll check it out with the phone company."

"Quickly," Don urged.

Within the day Herb Bannerman called back. "Don, yes, there was a Biegenwald listed at that address in the Manhattan phone book sixteen years ago."

"Now we're getting somewhere!" Don said, encouraged. "Find

out when they moved and where to. The phone company ought to have that."

"*They* do. And *we* do."

"Terrific! Where, when?"

"They moved the same year. They had a change of number from Manhattan to Queens. Address Twenty-one-twenty-seven Vickers. In Long Island City. That number was good for two years. Then they moved again. But this time no forwarding number."

"At least we have a place to start," Don said. "Herb, thanks a million. I'll never forget this."

"Nothing at all, Don, glad to do it, any time," Herb said. He hung up feeling he had scored some points with the potential future president of the network.

"Biegenwald?" Brennan, chief of security, considered. "Well, that's a lead. Give me a few days, Mr. Ward."

"Take all the time you need, just hurry!" Don said, smiling. Then added: "It's important, Jim, very important. Please, do what you can."

In the ensuing four days Brennan called on those men in the New York City Police Department who had been his colleagues in the old days. He imposed on Missing Persons. He arranged for two of his own men to search all the files. One trail led right back to the adoption agency. Which was no help at all.

But on the fifth day an officer making a routine check of admissions to all city hospitals at that time came up with an entry that mentioned the name Birch, Emily.

An Emily Birch had been admitted to emergency at Bellevue Hospital. That event coincided with the date when the Biegenwald family moved away from Long Island City.

Brennan called Don Ward's secretary, asked for an appointment, and stressed that he would like it at a time when Mr. Ward would not be under pressure from telephone calls from the Coast.

At ten-thirty the next morning he was summoned to Don's office and was immediately shown in. Don was standing at the expanse of wall window that looked out over the west side of

Manhattan. On this bright, clear end-of-winter day, it presented a view far beyond the Hudson River and many miles into the Jersey countryside.

"Well, Jim, what did you find?"

Instead of answering directly, the chief asked, "Mr. Ward, this Emily Birch, she a relative of yours?"

Phrased that way, and considering her relationship to his son, Don found himself unable to answer at once. Then he said, "Why? Should that matter? Did you find her or didn't you? That's the real question."

"Well, in a way we found her."

"What do you mean, 'in a way'?" Don asked, provoked by Brennan's strange response.

"We've been able to track her as far as emergency admitting at Bellevue," the chief said. "I didn't want to go any further without letting you know."

"Why not?" Don asked. "It's important that I find her."

Instead of explaining in words, Brennan placed on Don's desk a thin file, containing very few pages. But evidently it was the complete history of Emily Birch as far as he could discover it.

"If I can be of any more help, let me know, Mr. Ward."

Don waited until Brennan left before he ventured to pick up the file. He opened it. On top was a photocopy of the record of admission of a patient named Emily Birch to Bellevue.

Emily Birch had been admitted to emergency after a psychotic episode which terminated when she attempted suicide by trying to jump from the Queensborough Bridge. Taken in charge by two New York City policemen, she was brought to Bellevue. There she was kept under heavy sedation for several days. When she was able to be interviewed by staff psychiatrists, they found her to be delusional, very depressed, so suicidal that she was forcibly restrained until she could be transferred to Rockland State Hospital.

The record ended there. Don sat stunned, unable to answer the insistent buzzing of his secretary. When she received no response after her fourth very long buzz, Jeannie knocked on the door, asking, "Mr. Ward, are you all right?"

He was barely able to answer, "Yes . . . I'm . . . all right."

"May I come in?"

He nodded and only then realized she could not see that. So he said weakly, "Yes, Jeannie. Come in . . . come in."

She opened the door and entered in her usual brisk way, only to stop abruptly and ask, "Mr. Ward, what is it?"

"I . . . it must have been that last cup of coffee . . . those damn morning coffee sessions. Too much caffeine."

"Shall I call first aid? Would you like a sedative of some kind?"

"No, Jeannie. I just need a little time alone. So no calls."

"Of course." She backed out of the room slowly, staring at him.

He sat there, perfectly still. Until the sweat started. He could feel it seep out of his forehead, could feel his cheeks grow damp. His shirt collar was suddenly too tight. He pulled it open so violently that he ripped off the button. He swung his swivel chair around to stare out of the window at the vast view but saw nothing.

He could not assemble his thoughts. They were a tangle. *Robbie. Dr. Belmond. Claire. Robbie, Robbie, Robbie.* His first impulse was to call Claire. He decided against that. Why terrify her as he had been terrified? There must be a considered and logical step to take at such a time. One thing he knew: He must pursue this information to its ultimate end. Only then would he be able to discuss it with anyone, especially with Dr. Belmond.

He sat there taking deep breaths, waiting for the oozing perspiration to abate. When his collar felt cold and damp against his neck, he knew that he had stopped sweating and was experiencing only the aftereffects. He mopped his face dry. He pulled up his tie, closed his buttonless collar, and made every effort to look as neat as he usually did. But his fingers felt thick and unmanageable. He knew that he could not trust himself to drive in this condition.

He lifted the phone. "Jeannie, get me Security."

In a moment he heard Brennan. "Yes, Mr. Ward, can I help you?"

"Would you do me a favor, a big favor?"

"Drive you up to Rockland State?" Brennan had anticipated him.

"Yes, please. I would appreciate it."

"Of course, sir, I understand."

CHAPTER 24

On any other bright end-of-winter day the drive up to Rockland State would have been a scenic pleasure. But on this day Don Ward saw none of it. Not the sun, not the hint of fresh greening of the countryside, not the blue sky or the racing clouds.

Brennan drove in silence. He made no effort to ask or comment. Don appreciated his consideration. When they arrived, Brennan asked only, "Make it on your own, Mr. Ward?"

"Yes. Sure. I'm . . . fine . . . okay."

Don insisted on seeing the superintendent of the hospital. Told he was not available, he finally settled for a Miss Sampson, the woman in charge of institutional records.

She was a black woman, petite, with silver-rimmed spectacles. She seemed no more than in her mid-twenties but was older, the deception based on her diminutive size.

"Yes. Can I help you in any way?" she asked.

"For certain reasons," Don began, "it is very important for me to find a woman who was a patient here fourteen years ago. I've got to know when she was released and, if possible, where she went. At least her last known address."

"Are you an attorney?" Mrs. Sampson asked.

"No."

"Do you have a court order requiring us to open our confidential records to you?"

"I know your records are confidential. But this is important, urgent! We need the information. We need to find that woman," Don insisted.

"We have many requests for information. And they are always important and urgent," she replied. "Usually we do not release it except to an attorney and then only with a court order."

"Look, lady"—Don began to lose his temper—"my son's life may be involved. I've got to have the information. *Now!*"

He had bolted out of his chair and was leaning across the desk in a menacing attitude. Mrs. Sampson did not draw back or appear intimidated. She said softly, "Look, Mr. . . ."

"Ward! Donald Ward! And I need that information," he insisted.

"Mr. Ward," she said in a calm tone intended to restore him to a less agitated state, "I don't wish to be difficult. But what you're asking is against our rules."

"Lady, I have no time or patience to go getting court orders!" Don protested. "My son—" He broke off, settled back in his chair and felt the sweat beginning to run again.

Quite sympathetically Mrs. Sampson asked, "Would you care to tell me how our fourteen-year-old records could affect your son's life?"

He stared at her compassionate brown eyes behind her silver-framed glasses.

"Yes," he said, "yes, I would care to tell you."

As briefly as he could, and for the first time, he was able to talk to someone other than Claire about Robbie and about the dangerous possibilities involved. When he finished, Mrs. Sampson said, "Would you mind if I called Dr. Belmond?"

"No."

"Do you have her number?"

Don reached into his pocket for the little black book in which he had the phone numbers of all those people important in his life. Stars. Directors. Writers. Studio executives. And Dr. Sabrina Belmond. He passed the book to her, a confession of his own disorganized state. She found the number, dialed, waited, and was rewarded by an answer.

"Dr. Belmond?" he heard the woman ask. "I am Dorothy Sampson, in charge of records at Rockland State. I have here in my office a man named Donald Ward, who is seeking information about a former patient. He says it is in reference to his son. Is a Robbie Ward a patient of yours?"

"Yes, he is."

"Would information of a past patient be of vital importance in your treatment?"

"Is the patient the boy's natural mother?" Belmond asked.

"So Mr. Ward says."

"Then, yes, the information is of vital importance, and I would appreciate it."

"If I release it, would you send me a letter on your professional stationery making an official request?"

"Yes, indeed. But please do not hold up the information," Belmond requested.

The woman hung up. "I will get the information for you on an informal basis. But the official transcript will have to await the doctor's written request."

Within half an hour a clerk brought the file into Mrs. Sampson's office. She examined it. She tried to conceal her reaction. But Don could read it in the way her eyes fixed suddenly on what she had read. It was a look of shock. When he held out his hand for the file, she hesitated giving it to him.

"You understand that even in the best-run mental institutions these things can happen."

Don opened the file to the first page. Near the bottom of it he read: "Patient terminated her own life on April 14. The instrument was a toothbrush handle which she had somehow honed down to a knife edge. Her body was claimed by one Max Biegenwald, listed as her uncle on admission."

His hands began to tremble. Mrs. Sampson asked, "Can I get you something, Mr. Ward?"

"No, no," he said in a hoarse whisper. "Just—just a minute or two to collect myself."

"Would you like to be alone?" she asked, about to rise.

"No, please. Just sit there. Don't move. Don't do anything."

"I'm sorry you had to get the news this way."

"Don't even be sorry," he said, "just . . . oh, God . . . Robbie. Robbie."

* * *

He was in a sweat throughout the ride back. He said nothing. Brennan said nothing. Until Don's condition made him ask, "Mr. Ward, do you want me to take you back to the office or drop you at your house?"

"The—the house," Don managed to say.

But when they were three blocks from his home, Don said, "I'll get out here!"

"It's only a few blocks. . . ."

"I'll walk the rest of the way. I need some fresh air."

"Are you sure you're all right, Mr. Ward?"

"I'm fine. I just—just need to walk a little, think a little."

"Sure. Okay." Brennan pulled the car to the curb. As Don was getting out, he asked, "Anything you want me to tell Jeannie?"

"No. I'll—I'll call her later," Don said vaguely, and started walking.

Brennan kept the car idling but did not put it into gear, waiting to see if Don could manage on his own. For he had never seen a man so shaken so suddenly. Only when Brennan was sure that Don could navigate on his own did he turn the car back toward the highway and New York City.

Don Ward did not head directly home. For some reason he felt guilty in possession of this new knowledge. He walked past large, expensive houses, past trees rendered leafless and bare by cold, wintry winds, but he was still sweating profusely. He turned up the collar of his coat to protect himself against the chill air of late afternoon.

Robbie . . . Robbie . . . Robbie, he kept thinking. Until he began thinking: *Claire . . . Claire . . . Claire. How do I tell her? No, I won't tell her. That rightly belongs to Dr. Belmond to do.* That, he realized, was cowardice. Between themselves he and Claire had always been honest, always direct. Why now seek out a paid intermediary to tell her one of the most important facts of their lives?

Once he had accepted that he was the one to tell her, he started home.

Sitting through dinner was a torment. Don tried to eat, tried to smile, tried to respond to Robbie's extravagant enthusiasms, which, under other circumstances, he would have welcomed. But it was difficult, so difficult that by the middle of the meal Claire had begun to regard him strangely, asking the first time, "Are you all right, darling?"

"Yes, fine, why?"

"Or did you have such a big lunch you can't have dinner?"

"Of course, I can have dinner." He gave a forced, if not entirely convincing, impression of a man enjoying food that no matter how hard he chewed, he did not seem able to swallow. "Maybe I did have too much lunch," he said finally. He excused himself from the table. "I've got a dozen new scripts to go over tonight. I'll be in the den."

After he left the table, Robbie asked, "What's wrong with Dad?"

"Probably overworked," Claire said. But she knew it was some event far more significant. She could hardly wait for Robbie to go up, shower, and get to bed.

The boy stopped by the den, knocked softly, "Dad?"

"Yes, son."

"Can I come in?"

"Sure. Of course," Don said, hurriedly picking up the script he should have been reading. He flipped some pages to pretend he was in the middle of it.

Robbie came into the room, went to his father, kissed him on the cheek. "Good night, Dad."

"Good night, son."

"Gee, I hope nothing I've done in the past weeks has anything to do with the way you feel now."

"Of course not." Don was too quick to assure him.

"I mean, the business you're in, you sure don't need to be worried about me, too. Well, you don't have to. I feel great. Terrific!"

"Good!" Don tried to enthuse. "Get a good night's sleep. So you'll be fresh for school in the morning. Okay?"

"Okay, Dad."

He kissed his father on the cheek once more and left.

Curious and concerned as she was, Claire made no effort to confront her husband at once. She busied herself clearing the table, stowing the dishes in the dishwasher, tidying up. She worked on the scene she was scheduled to direct the next day for the Towne Players. She did all those things waiting for the sound of Robbie's moving about upstairs to abate.

Once she was sure he was in bed, she went up to face her husband. She opened the door, catching him by surprise as he snatched a script to pretend he had been reading. She was not deceived.

"What happened? Did you have a fight with Brady? Did he fire you? Or did you quit? Either way I say good riddance. You've been there too long!" she said. "You've been too damn loyal to that network and to Brady."

"For God's sake, Claire, stop!" he said in a hoarse whisper. "It's nothing like that!"

"Then what is it? Don't you think I'm entitled to an explanation when the man I've been married to for eighteen years comes home looking the way you did, acting the way you did? If it isn't your job, is it our marriage? Some other woman? You want a divorce? For God's sake, what?" she demanded.

"Claire, just sit down," he said softly.

"But what?"

"Claire, please? Sit down?"

Silent, puzzled, frightened, she slid into the closest chair. She had never seen Don like this before.

He rose, letting the script slip haphazardly to the carpet. He started to pace, groping for the right opening words. He decided just to say it simply. As it had happened.

"Today I—I got word today. Actually I went up there."

"Word? Went up where?"

"I went up there and found out. I mean, I was up at Rockland State today. I saw her record," he managed to say.

"Record?" For a moment Claire was baffled. "Whose record? . . . Oh." She understood suddenly.

The look of fear on her face made Don think: *I shouldn't be doing this. I was wrong to come home, wrong to start to tell her. What do I do now? What do I say? Belmond would have known the right words, the reassuring way to tell her.*

"Don!" His wife was demanding an answer.

He faced her, stared down at her, realized he had no choice

now. "Robbie's mother. I saw her file. She died at Rockland State. At age twenty-three."

"How?" Claire asked.

"Suicide," he admitted softly.

"Oh, my God!" Claire said in a painful whisper. She covered her face with her hands. He lifted her, embraced her, and felt her shudder in his arms.

CHAPTER 25

They had arranged to see Dr. Belmond at an hour when they knew Robbie would be in school. They did not want him to suspect. Don had had to fabricate an excuse to be absent from a brainstorming session at the network, a meeting to explore a new tack to take on two soap operas, now that the producers had exhausted story lines of rape, incest, and adultry. Ed Brady was annoyed with Don's excuse but not angry.

They waited in Belmond's outer office, staring at each other. Don feared Claire was going to begin weeping again. Claire noted that Don's face was drained of the winter suntan he had always managed to accumulate out on the Coast by this time of year.

To Claire it felt like the time she had waited with her mother in the office of the oncologist for the results of the X rays he had taken. They had turned out to be positive, and her mother had had to undergo surgery and chemotherapy. But she had survived.

Belmond's door opened. She stood in the doorway, smiling at first. Then her smile slowly drained away. She had seen this distraught look before on the faces of patients and the relatives of patients.

"Won't you come in?"

* * *

They were seated across the desk from her. Don looked to Claire as if to say, *I must.* Then he faced Dr. Belmond.

"Yesterday I went up to Rockland State."

"Yes, I know," Belmond said.

"They showed me her record."

"And?"

"She died there. At age twenty-three. Suicide."

"I see," Belmond said softly.

Both Claire and Don strained to interpret Belmond's reaction. Was it as final and hopeless as they had anticipated? Was she writing off their son as incurable?

Belmond said only, "Well, at least it lets me make a definitive diagnosis."

"You're trying to let us down easy." Claire accused her, the voice breaking, tears rushing to her eyes.

"Not at all!" Belmond said sternly. "I needed some significant confirming facts. You've just brought them to me. I can now rule out schizophrenia. And proceed on the basis that Robbie is suffering from a bipolar affective disorder, which, believe me, is a far more encouraging condition."

"But if this kind of thing is hereditary, as you told me . . ." Claire responded, still highly emotional and weeping now.

"Claire, darling, please. . . ." Don tried to calm her.

"I don't want to be lied to," Claire said. "I don't want to be given any false assurances. . . ."

Don sat frozen by indecision. His impulse was to embrace her, comfort her. But he felt restrained by Belmond's presence, until she signaled him to action. He dropped to one knee beside his wife, embraced her, pressed her face against his shoulder, and said, "Darling, please, let's give the doctor a chance. . . . Let's hear what she has to say."

"She's already said it. This runs in families. Robbie is like his mother. . . ."

Belmond rose to her feet and said sharply, "Mrs. Ward, stop misinterpreting my words! And stop feeling sorry for yourself!"

Claire looked up at her through wet, blurred eyes. "It's only Robbie I'm thinking of. Robbie, my son!"

"If you are, you will stop crying and listen!" Belmond said sternly.

Claire glanced toward Don to invite his defense, but Don said, "She's right, Claire. Our feelings don't matter. It's what she tells us about Robbie that counts."

He used his silk pocket handkerchief to dry her eyes. When she regained control, he looked to Belmond, begging her to continue.

"Mrs. Ward, the fact that we know there is a genetic factor in conditions like alcoholism and suicide does not mean that the outcome of Robbie's case must be inevitable. Actually, in a strange way, word of her suicide is quite encouraging."

Claire looked to Don, to see if he had reacted in the same puzzled way to what she had just heard Belmond say.

"Yes, Mrs. Ward, I said 'encouraging.' With a different family history I might have had to diagnose Robbie as schizophrenic. Which would have been quite *dis*couraging. But suicide in his family history confirms for me that he is suffering from a bipolar affective disorder. In simpler terms, that means he is manic-depressive. He has mood swings between high excitement and deep depression.

"In his manic stage," Belmond continued, "he is the bright, active leader, achiever, superathlete, outstanding scholar you're so proud of. But I must also remind you, Mrs. Ward, that you've told me of some other things he does when he's in a manic stage. Dangerous things. Like crashing his father's car. Getting into knife fights in Greenwich Village. Starting a riot that ended in gunfire. All without evil intent, but still dangerous.

"Manics also tend to be extravagant. The time when he treated the whole football squad to burgers and shakes after his first victory. What did that cost? For thirty-seven husky, hungry young adolescents? Sixty dollars? Seventy?"

"His whole allowance for three months," Don admitted.

"Exactly the kind of thing I mean," Belmond pointed out. "Most things manics do are done to please and impress others. Charm them. Influence them. So people find manics not only acceptable but impressive, amusing, and delightful. Until a manic oversteps the bounds and does something dangerous to himself or others.

"Since Robbie is only in his mid-teens, his symptoms aren't as extreme as they can become in adult life. Then he may endanger his career, ruin his business, threaten the security of his wife, his family. . . ."

"But how do we restrain a boy with Robbie's enthusiasm, without killing off—" Claire broke off when that most unfortunate word intruded itself into her protest.

Belmond rephrased it for her. "How do we keep Robbie's enthusiasm within reasonable, productive bounds?"

"Exactly," Claire said.

"First, we must examine the other extreme of Robbie's condition. The depressions. He did have a serious deep depression precipitated by a great disappointment. He will have more depressions. Because he will experience more disappointments. In life that is inevitable. And those depressions can also be very dangerous."

Belmond had no need to enlarge on or explain the nature of that danger.

"Now, true, Robbie shares a genetic heritage with his natural mother. But it would be wrong to assume that both cases must end the same way. Because he has certain advantages she did not have. Robbie has a loving mother and father who are not ready to consign him to some institution when things seem to go out of control. And we have treatments now that were not available to his mother.

"While we must assume that Robbie will go through future manic stages followed by depressive stages, we will use those treatments to moderate both. Not let him get too high because extreme highs can lead to extreme lows. Not let him get too low for obvious reasons. The challenge is to avoid the worst consequences of either extreme. To keep him on track. To keep him the brilliant, sensitive, productive young man he can be."

"Can you do that?" Claire asked.

"Not I, *we.*" Belmond corrected her. "This is a joint effort. The three of us and Dr. Rissom. And, of course, Robbie. He must want to be treated. He must cooperate. Now, before I talk to him, I need assurances from the two of you."

"We'll do everything we can!" Don was quick to assure her.

"No, Mr. Ward, not yet. Think about it. Talk about it. If you wish, discuss it with Dr. Rissom. When you've done that, come back and see me. But make it soon," she cautioned.

"There's no need to talk about it," Claire said. "I can tell you now."

"Mrs. Ward, do this my way. This news is still too fresh. Right now you're impulsive. You cry too quickly. You give your promises and assurances too hastily. Think about it. Mainly let it sink in. React to it. Honestly. Then come back and tell me."

CHAPTER 26

Dinner was a tense exercise for both Claire and Don. Robbie dominated the conversation, enthusing over his progress in basketball. His play had impressed the coach, and he had been moved up to the varsity squad. Now he had determined to become the team's playmaker.

He's the old Robbie, both Claire and Don thought, reminded grimly of Belmond's warning. With Robbie's condition, getting better could actually be getting worse. His highs could be as dangerous as his lows.

They both were relieved when Robbie finally said, "I've got a paper to do for science," and went upstairs to his room.

They were silent until Don said, "I think I'll go for a drive."

Claire turned abruptly from clearing the table to stare at him. Going for a drive. Don's way of wrestling with any problem too awesome to discuss even with her.

Well, she resolved, *not this time.*

"Wait, I'll go with you."

He glanced at her, resenting her intrusion on his privacy.

"I can't stand to be alone," she said "Not at a time like this."

He appeared determined to resist, but a plate slipped from her trembling hand and shattered on the tile floor. She bent down to pick up the fragments. In her haste she cut herself on one of the shards. Her middle finger began to bleed profusely. He dropped to one knee, took her hand in his, pressed it to cut off the flow of blood. Still squeezing her bleeding finger, he brought her hand to his cheek. He was startled.

"Have your hands been this cold all evening?"

"Ever since this afternoon," she confessed.

"My fault. I never should have told you. I should have gone to see Belmond alone." Then he said, "I would have had to tell you sooner or later."

She shook her head, a warning to him to keep his voice down. He agreed in a whisper. "Of course. We can't let him know or even suspect."

He led her to the first-aid cabinet in the laundry alcove, swabbed her wound with antiseptic, wrapped it tightly in a small bandage to stanch the flow of blood.

"Let's both go. Out somewhere. Somewhere where we can talk," he said.

"What'll we tell Robbie?"

"Say anything. We're going to—to pick up some ice cream at the shopping center," he suggested.

"With two gallons in the freezer?"

"Isn't there any shopping you have to do?"

She thought for a moment. "Tonight's Thursday. They're open late at the mall," she said. "I could say I'm still looking for that dress for the affiliates meeting."

"Good idea."

Claire went to the foot of the stairs. "Robbie, darling! We're going out for a while. I want to look at some dresses at Lord and Taylor's. Something for our trip to Vegas. We'll be back soon. But don't wait up."

"Okay, Mom!" Robbie called back cheerfully and innocently.

They had been under way for only a few minutes when Claire said, "Do you realize what just happened?"

"You cut your finger," Don said, puzzled. "Does it hurt? Is it still bleeding?"

"I'm talking about what we said, what we did."

"What did we do? What did we say?

"We acted like conspirators. Criminals. We had to plot and scheme and lie just to get into our own car and take a drive. As if we were planning to commit a murder. Or rob a bank.

We whisper as if we're plotting to betray this country. We only want to discuss our son."

"We can't do it openly. Not if Robbie might overhear us," Don protested.

"Robbie?" Claire challenged him. "What about me? You weren't even going to talk to me about it. You wanted to go for a drive *alone*. Like you do when you don't want to discuss your business with me. Well, this time it is my business, too."

"I never said it wasn't," he replied impatiently.

"Then why did you want to go alone?"

"I wanted to think it through first. I didn't want to involve you until I had something intelligent to suggest," he explained.

"You didn't want to *involve* me? God, Don, who is more involved? I'm his mother! His mother!" she repeated.

"I was trying to figure it all out and come to you and say, 'Darling, I know exactly what to do and how to do it, so don't worry anymore.' "

" 'So don't worry anymore,' " she repeated, making no attempt to hide her resentment. "Good old Don Ward. The fixer. The one boy Ed Brady can rely on to fix any trouble on any network production. Well, this isn't one of your goddamn television shows! This is our son. *My* son. And he's in serious trouble. The kind of trouble you don't have any experience fixing."

Her indignation gave way to fear. She broke down and started to cry. He pulled the car over to the shoulder of the road, took her in his arms. She resisted at first, then surrendered.

"Claire, darling, please . . . crying isn't going to solve anything."

"I know, I know, I know," she repeated, but kept crying.

He held her close. Every tremor of her body felt like a blow against his chest. He sought words to comfort her. He found none. His own frustration led to anger.

"It's all the fault of that adoption agency," he exploded. "God knows we went into this with the best intentions in the world. They should have told us. It was unethical of them not to. Criminal!"

Between gasps Claire said, "They didn't know either. At the time no one knew."

"It was their *business* to know!" Don insisted. "How could they do something like this to innocent people? Let them invest so much of their lives, so much of themselves in bringing up a boy and never warn them. There must be some law. Something that makes agencies investigate more than they do!"

They both were silent for a time. Claire had stopped sobbing; her head still rested against Don's chest.

Softly, more realistically, Don admitted, "No, we shouldn't blame them. Suppose that woman, whoever she was, had been like Robbie. Bright, energetic, charming, and only later began to show symptoms. They didn't have any reason to suspect. . . ."

"Just as we didn't. Did we?" Claire said, in a way so strange that Don gently held her back from him so he could look into her eyes.

Even in the darkness he could see the guilt there.

"Claire?"

She tried to turn away. He reached out to prevent her. Again he demanded, "Claire? What is it?"

She did not respond.

"Claire!" he insisted, her guilt creating fears of his own in him.

Suddenly she broke free of his embrace. She pushed the door open and leaped from the car. She began running along the shoulder of the dark, deserted country road, the fallen branches of many winter storms cracking under her feet. He raced after her.

"Claire! Claire! Stop! You'll trip. You'll hurt yourself!"

She kept running, driven by only one thought: *I can't tell him. I can't tell anyone! I want to escape. I want—*

Before she could think the thought, her foot came down on a thick, strong branch that did not crack but rolled under the pressure, causing her to catapult forward to the frosty ground. She could feel her knee scrape the rough earth, then burn where she had injured it. The palms of her hands were bruised and gritty. She was too stunned to cry when Don lifted her.

He held her close to comfort her. "What were you running from? Me?" he asked.

"No," she answered strangely.

"Claire?"

"I was frightened. And suddenly I knew why."

"So you ran?"

"Because I now know *why* I've been frightened. Robbie's not the baby we took in. Not the boy we raised. Suddenly he's a stranger to me."

"That doesn't explain being frightened."

"Living with a stranger?" she asked, as if her question were the answer.

"Even that doesn't explain it. Claire, this is no time for holding back. If you have something to say, say it!" he insisted.

"You'll hate me," she said, struggling to break free.

"If we begin accusing each other, we'll have nothing to hold onto."

"You'll hate me," she insisted.

He seized her by the shoulders, turned her about, forced her to face the winter moon which was full and bright in the dark sky. Her look was quite different from any he had ever seen before.

"Claire, please! Tell me."

She shook her head, trying at the same time to avoid him. "You'll hate me," she kept insisting.

"Whatever it is, say it. I promise not to hate you."

She turned her head away so that moonlight outlined her delicate profile but permitted her to avoid his demanding eyes. "Robbie . . . he really *is* . . . a stranger. No part of us. Not of me. Not of you. And if he isn't, then this is not our trouble. I even wish—"

Softly Don completed the thought for her. "That we had never adopted him."

Without turning back she whispered, "You, too?"

He barely made a sound, but it was enough to admit to her that he had nurtured the same feeling.

"Was that why you wanted to be alone tonight?" she asked.

"How could I admit that to you?" he asked. "From the time we left Belmond's office I've been asking myself those questions. I sat in meetings all day and didn't hear anything. I answered questions I never heard and must have given idiotic answers. Because all through the day those thoughts kept pounding at me. After all, he's someone else's child. We took him in. Gave him the best of everything . . ."

"And is this our reward?" Claire asked.

He stared at her. How did she know?

"And when he kissed us good night before he went up to his room, I thought—"

"It's never going to be the same again," Don said.

"Exactly."

"I will call him son. He will call me Dad," Don said.

"But it will never be the same again."

"That's when I thought—"

And she joined him in saying, "I wish now we'd never adopted him at all."

When she turned to look up at him, she could see a trickle of wetness on his cold cheek.

"It's even worse," he confessed. "Promise you won't tell this to anyone—ever."

"You know I won't."

He looked away from her. What he had to say could be said only to the darkness of the night. "I even thought . . . I would rather he were dead than a walking time bomb waiting to explode. I feel so helpless. I don't know what to do. How to cope. Because you're right, Claire. I'm a fixer, oh, yes. But not of anything that really matters. When it comes to living my own life, our own lives, I'm no good at all. I want out. I want to escape. I don't know how to face it. Oh, yes, I'm sorry we ever adopted Robbie. How you must hate me now."

"Not any more than I hate myself," she said.

"Good God, what are we? Human beings? Or monsters? What kind of people have we become?"

She became conscious of the frosty night air. She shuddered. He put his arm around her and led her back to the car. She limped badly, the pain in her knee worse now. He tried to lift her in his arms, but she insisted on walking.

He started up the motor. With his hand still on the ignition key, he said, "When I think of how we've loved him, boasted about him, enjoyed him . . . and now."

"Now what?" She challenged him.

He could not answer.

"Don, we can't desert him now."

"That's the way I should feel," he confessed. "And I wish I could . . . but—"

* * *

They were back on the road and heading for home. They both had been silent, each suffering private guilts.

"If he were our own," Claire said, "and we found out yesterday that he had some terrible disease . . . cancer even, would we desert him?"

"I never said I'd desert him," Don protested. "I was only trying to tell you what's been tearing me up inside. I was testing you. Finding out was I the only one who felt this way. Testing to see how you would feel about me if you knew what I was thinking."

"And I felt the same, the same," she said.

"I never realized how little loyalty I have. Loyalty to the job? Sure! Loyalty to the network? Of course. Loyalty to Ed Brady, from whom all blessings flow? As long as he's my route to the presidency. But loyalty to my son? Now that he needs it? No, I want to cut my losses and run. I'm not much good, am I? Am I, Claire?"

She wished she could ease his torment. But all she could say was "I think we'd better go see Belmond as soon as possible."

"We'll have to tell her," he warned.

"I know," she said.

They drove the rest of the way home in silence.

They were surprised and dismayed when they drove up to the house. The light was still on in Robbie's room.

They found him in the kitchen, devouring milk and cookies. As they came in from the garage, he greeted them. "Hi. You two been out kind of late for shopping."

They both started to answer at once, overlapping.

"Your mom couldn't find the dress she wanted. . . ."

"We stopped in at the Village Lantern for some coffee," Claire said.

"I couldn't get to sleep." Robbie said, "Kept tossing and turning till I got hungry. So I came down and—"

He interrupted himself when he noticed his mother's bruised and bloody knee. He leaped up. "Gee, Mom, your leg! It's bleeding!" He came to her, put his arm around her, and led her to a chair. "Sit down. I'll take care of it."

As he went for the first-aid kit, he called back over his shoulder, "How'd that happen?"

Don and Claire glanced at each other, each demanding the other explain. Claire recovered first. "You know that entrance at the mall, the one with the revolving door. The man coming through behind me made it spin so fast that I practically got thrown out of it."

Robbie was on his knees, soaking a bandage with alcohol. "This may hurt, Mom, but it's the best way."

The sting of the alcohol was actually welcome since it put an end to the conversation. As Robbie was carefully placing a dry bandage over the raw wound, Claire looked past him and up to Don, their guilts even stronger now.

Robbie rose from beside her. He noticed the fresh Band-Aid on her finger. "Gee, Mom, you've had a rough night," he said, then added with a smile, "But don't worry, we'll pull you through. Right, Dad?"

"Right, right!" Don agreed too heartily. "You go up and get some sleep . . . son."

As Robbie started for the stairs, Don could not resist calling after him, "How come you couldn't sleep? You're usually such a sound sleeper we have to shake you to wake you."

"I don't know. Somehow tonight . . ."

"Something said at dinner, something happen?" Don asked despite Claire's furtive attempt to prevent him.

"Just couldn't sleep. But I'll make up for it." And he was on his way up the stairs.

The moment she felt they could speak in privacy Claire rebuked him. "You shouldn't have said anything."

"I was only trying to find out if somehow, without intending to, I let something slip at dinner.

"Don, we can't suspect our every word and thought."

"No?" He challenged in a hard whisper. "When he asked us why we were late, why did we both start to lie, like guilty criminals? Is it going to be like that from now on? Living a life of lies until this gets settled one way or the other?"

"What do you mean, 'one way or the other'?" she demanded.

"It's just an expression. I didn't mean anything."

"Yes, you did!" She accused him. "One way would be for

him to get better. The other would be for him to become worse . . . like that woman . . . to end the same way."

"I swear to God I didn't mean that!" Don protested, his voice rising so loud that she glared him to a muffled silence.

He took her hands, squeezing them until her wounded finger made her protest, "You're hurting me!"

He dropped her hands and embraced her.

"We can't start suspecting each other. We've got to depend on each other if we're to see this through."

Up in his room Robbie Ward was turning onto his right side, his accustomed side for sound sleep. But he seemed more alert at this late hour than he had been all evening.

What had Dad meant about something being said at dinner? Had something happened that he should have noticed? He tried to relive the dinner conversation.

How was school today? Anything interesting happen? Any tests coming up? How was basketball? Would Robbie like to go to the NFL play-off game even though the Giants were definitely out of it?

It was the usual dinner table conversation. But now that Robbie thought about it, there was a difference. Their answers were too quick. Their smiles too big. Too nervous, too. Was that what had kept him awake tonight, that sense of something different in the house that he could not understand?

Was there some trouble at the network that threatened his dad's job? Were they keeping it from him so as not to interfere with his schoolwork?

Or were they acting this way now because of all the unhappy events that had flowed from that one stupid play in which he lost the championship game? Those days when he had shut himself away from them, from school, and from the world?

He had just about got that all straightened out with Dr. Belmond. He was his old self again. Full of energy, excitement, great plans.

If everything was going along so well, why were they so concerned now?

He fell asleep puzzling over that.

CHAPTER 27

Dr. Belmond listened impassively as first Claire, then Don related in tormenting, self-conscious fragments the events of two nights ago. What they had each felt, said, the fact that they had the need to sneak out of their own house to give voice to their fears and reactions.

"Well," Belmond said, "at least you discovered that parental love is not as pure and unselfish as the fairy tales would have us believe. I have even seen natural parents confronted with a child hopelessly on drugs just give up. What they say is 'Doctor, we'll pay you anything you ask; just cure our child!' What they really mean is 'We can't cope. We want out. So you take over.'

"One thing you had better know now: Robbie's treatment will not be simple. It is not like surgery. You cannot see your son to the door of the operating room and then, as on television, hand him over to the surgeon, watch the doors swing closed, and go sit out in the corridor and wait. You will have to be part of the treatment."

"Dr. Belmond, we'll do anything you say." Claire assured her. "Only tell us what to do."

"The elements of Robbie's treatment, if he can tolerate them physically and emotionally, consist of these: First and foremost, himself. Second, the two of you. Third, myself and Dr. Rissom. Together we may be able to rescue this son of yours from a condition which is dangerous and might become fatal."

"You mean, like that woman?" Claire asked.

"You mean his *natural mother,*" Belmond corrected. "We must get used to dealing with this realistically. Using words in their proper meaning, Mrs. Ward."

Claire hesitated, then finally nodded.

"Now," Belmond continued, "first I will have Dr. Rissom do a complete physical work-up on Robbie."

"He's in excellent condition," Don protested. "He's come through a whole football season without a single serious injury. He's into basketball now and doing extremely well."

Belmond smiled for the first time. "Mr. Ward, you're not your son's doctor *or* his lawyer. Don't defend him against the treatment. What we'll be looking for is not his athletic prowess. Or even his general physical condition. But the condition of his kidneys, his thyroid, his heart, which will determine his ability to tolerate the chemicals necessary for his treatment. Some patients suffer bad side effects."

"What happens to those patients?" Don asked.

"They go untreated in the main," Belmond admitted.

"So that if Robbie is unable to tolerate—"

"Mr. Ward! I refuse to guess at the physical condition of a patient. Dr. Rissom will tell us that," Belmond declared in a way that put an end to all such discussion. "Now, then, Robbie's treatment will involve taking medication which can moderate his manic periods and thereby lessen the effect of his depressed episodes, leading to a more normal life. However, no fifteen-year-old likes to be told that he must take medication regularly, three times a day. They tend to slough it off. To see, secretly, of course, how far they can go without taking their dosage. Or how much more they can take to hurry the cure. They become daring or careless; either can be dangerous."

"But if he adheres to the regimen?" Claire asked.

"If he reacts as Dr. Rissom and I expect, he can live a very long, very successful life. But that demands strict adherence to the prescribed regimen, which both of you must help us enforce."

"We'll do everything we can," Claire promised.

"In fact," Don said, "I've been doing some heavy thinking the last two days. I'm entitled to a sabbatical, a long vacation, six months. But entitled or not, I'm going to take it. I may even quit. Take a whole year off to see my son through this."

Belmond nodded patiently throughout Don's declaration, only to ask softly, "And add to your son's guilt?"

"I want him to know how much we love him."

"No. I think you want *me* to know," Belmond countered. "Well, I would never want Robbie to feel he's responsible for your abandoning your normal ambitions. Because at the end of that particular road lies the eventual parental reproach: 'After all I sacrificed for you, is this how you repay me?' Save your sacrifices, Mr. Ward. Let's have no heroic promises. Let's go about this in an orderly, scientific manner. I'll talk to Dr. Rissom. You have Robbie at his office tomorrow after school."

The finality of her words indicated the session was over.

Don and Claire started for the door until she felt compelled to turn and plead, "Dr. Belmond, we'll do anything you ask, anything at all! Just promise me that you'll save him. Just promise—"

She broke down and started to sob. Don put his arms around her, glanced at Belmond as if to apologize, and gently led his wife out of the room.

Belmond reached for her phone, dialed. When Dr. Rissom answered, she said, "Fred? Sabrina. I just talked to the Wards. They'll have Robbie in tomorrow afternoon."

"Good," Rissom said. "I'll do a complete work-up. Cardiac. Thyroid. And renal. God, I hope he can tolerate the medication."

"I hope the *Wards* can tolerate the treatment," Belmond said thoughtfully.

Aware of a new aspect of the case she had not shared with him before, Rissom asked, "Sabrina?"

"I didn't want to add to their fears. But the psychiatric literature indicates that adoptive parents do not make the best partners in this three-way treatment."

"Oh?" Rissom replied, alert and concerned.

"Statistically we find that adopted children do not succeed as well in treatment as natural children do. We can speculate as to the reason. But that's the fact. And we both have to be aware of it."

"You mean Robbie's chances of being cured may be lessened

because of the Wards? I don't believe that." Rissom defended them. "They are two very fine, loyal parents."

"Fred, we have cases on record where, when adoptive children have gotten into serious and continued trouble, the adoptive parents have even gone to court to ask to be freed of their obligations. To *un*adopt the child, if there is such a word."

Belmond hung up the phone. Her hand rested on it; her fingers drummed on it, as she assessed this particular case realistically.

If Robbie could tolerate the treatment, *if* he adhered to all its demands faithfully, *if* the Wards could remain steadfast through all the reverses usual in such cases, then it might be possible to save this appealing, highly intelligent young man who had so much to give to society.

Robbie Ward was a case fraught with many *ifs*. Perhaps too many.

CHAPTER 28

"Why do I have to go back to Dr. Rissom again? He checked me out for steroids and drugs. I'm clean. And I feel fine!" Robbie declared, pushing back from the dinner table.

"Dr. Belmond suggested you have a more complete physical," Claire explained.

"That's another thing," Robbie said, "I'm feeling so good I don't think I need to go see Belmond anymore."

"Robbie!" Claire said in a tone she resorted to for her severest reprimands. "You have to go because we say you have to."

"I'm not crazy. Or do you and Dad think I am?" he demanded.

"Of course not!" Claire protested.

"Then why do I have to go see Belmond? Or Rissom? I've just had a physical for basketball. Rissom said I'm perfect! So I am not going to see him again!"

She heard him climb the stairs aggressively. Heard his door slam. Her first impulse was to call Belmond. She did not. She would wait until Don came home.

Routinely she cleared the table, scraped the dishes clean, stowed them in the dishwasher. Set the controls, and pushed the start button. Just as the machine began its loud washing cycle, the phone rang. It was the unlisted line which Don used mainly because she usually had the other line tied up.

"Hello, darling." She greeted him solemnly.

Reading the troubled state of her mind from the sound of her voice, he asked, "Claire, honey? What's wrong?"

"We'll discuss it when you get home."

"That's the point," Don said, "I won't be home tonight."

"You can't be leaving for the Coast. There's no plane out. Not at this hour."

"Brady's family is off on vacation to Hilton Head. So he's in town alone. He asked me to stay in and work late. Okay?"

Claire did not respond. For she had noticed a new ingenue on *The Best of Times,* the ailing series which Don had been charged with giving a shot in the arm. He had hired this very pretty actress. Blond. And talented. Very much the same as Claire had been years ago, when Don first noticed her.

What would be more natural for a man in his early forties, married to the same wife for eighteen years, than to try to recapture his youth by taking up with some young doting girl who, for professional reasons, pretended to hang on his every word and who stared at him with innocent blue eyes?

"It isn't that Hopkins girl, is it?" Claire found herself blurting out.

"That Hopkins . . ." Don was seemingly puzzled, then understood. "Hell, Claire, you don't think I'm making it with Anita Hopkins. Believe me, darling, if I were going to come on to any girl, it would definitely not be Hopkins. She's not my type."

Claire barely resisted reminding him: *She's the same type I was when you fell in love with me. And the same age, too.*

"Claire, honey, there must be something very wrong to make you accuse me of fooling around. You know better."

"We'll talk about it tomorrow when you get home."

"I want to know now," Don insisted.

"Robbie."

"Good God, what did he do this time?" Don exploded.

"I told him about going back to Rissom. He refused. He also said he doesn't want to go back to Belmond, that he feels fine."

"Damn it, he'll go! I'll make him go!" Don replied angrily. Then he calmed and said, "I'll have a nice quiet talk with him. I'll explain things. And he'll go."

"You have to get home first," she pointed out.

"Honey, please. I can't help tonight." He lowered his voice.

Claire realized Brady must be close by. "It's in these late-night one-on-one sessions that Brady lets his hair down. Talks confidentially about future plans, future promotions. Please try to understand."

"I am sick and tired of living in a family that consists of me, my husband, my son, *and* Ed Brady!"

"Darling, don't let this thing with Robbie overwhelm you. I'm telling you we'll lick it. He's going to be fine. Just promise me that you'll see it through."

"Okay, darling. I'm sorry about just now. But I needed someone, and when you said you weren't coming home . . ."

"Look, I'll tell Ed right now—"

"No, you won't." She contradicted him. "You'll do what you have to. I'll be all right. All right!" she added as firmly as she could manage.

She had never been able to sleep well alone. In their first year, whenever Don had to be out on the Coast and she was alone, she would lie awake going over her lines in preparation for her next day's taping. More than once when she showed up for the early blocking rehearsal, her director would scold her. "Claire, I'm planning on some real tight shots today. Those puffy eyes won't help." In more recent years she lay awake planning new productions for her Towne Players or listening to late-night talk shows.

This night she neither listened to her radio nor made plans for new productions. She thought only about Don, Robbie, their lives together. It was foolish and impulsive to accuse Don of having an affair.

What had led her to make such an unjustified accusation? Why, from the moment that Robbie refused to see Dr. Rissom, had she suddenly felt that her life was coming apart? Her family was coming apart?

The thought tormented her until just as she was dozing off, a single word suddenly startled her awake.

Failure.

If there was one word to which her husband was allergic, it was *failure.*

Early on Ed Brady had drummed it into him: "The moment

you get the first smell of failure, cancel the show. This industry doesn't remember a quick cancellation nearly so much as a long, drawn-out failure. Study the ratings the first two weeks, and if you smell failure, cancel!"

It was the rule Ed Brady lived by. Never mind the effort, talent, and creative potential that would be destroyed in the process. Cancel!

What did running a network have to do with her? Her feelings about Don? Or his feelings about her?

Failure.

That word persisted in her mind. Dr. Belmond had given them no guarantees. She had even warned that unless Robbie's physical checked out, treatment would not even be possible.

If Robbie did prove to be untreatable, Claire must consider what Don's response would be. Despite all his assurances, Don Ward's reaction to failure was a conditioned reflex: Cut your losses and run. Would he do that now? To his own son?

By dawn, not having slept at all, Claire Ward was forced to contemplate not only the danger to her son but the destruction of a marriage and a way of life to which she had devoted herself these last eighteen years.

She could no longer abide her empty bed. She flung back the cover and rose so suddenly that she felt a wave of dizziness overcome her.

She went down to the kitchen, put on the kettle. She was dunking the teabag in the steaming water when she heard a sound behind her. She turned swiftly, terrified. She discovered Robbie standing in the doorway. He was attired in his usual sleeping garb, his pajama bottoms. They always joked about that, she saying that someday she was going to find a store that sold only bottoms. She was tired of throwing away the tops since no charity would accept them.

"Darling, up at this hour? Don't you feel well?"

"What's happening to this family?" the boy asked simply.

"What do you mean, 'what's happening'?"

He stared at her before responding, "I heard."

"You what?"

"When the phone rang, I picked it up in the den. On that line I knew it must be Dad, and I wanted to talk to him. Instead,

I just listened," he said softly. "Mom, is that what you think? That he's off screwing some young actress? He's an old man of forty-one; what would he want with a young girl half his age?"

"You shouldn't have listened in!" Claire said. "I've told you many times it's a nasty habit."

"I didn't mean to; it just happened."

She tried to resist asking, but her curiosity overcame her. "Did you hear it . . . all?"

"Yes," Robbie admitted. "Why is it so important for me to have that physical? And why do I have to go back to Belmond? I never felt better. What's so important that you got upset and nearly cried and Dad became angry? What's happening to this family? We didn't use to be like this."

"No, no, we didn't. Get yourself some milk. Join me at the table. Maybe I can explain."

"Okay," he said.

"Robbie . . . son . . . what happened to you after that game—it's a sort of condition . . ." She groped for the word.

"A depression?" he asked, then added softly, "In the newspapers . . . when they write about someone who . . . about some kid who . . . well, you've read the papers. . . ."

"Robbie, what are you trying to say?"

"When they report on some kid who's committed suicide, they always say either that he was *in* a depression or else that nobody *suspected* he was in a depression." He reflected for a moment, then asked, "Is that what Belmond said I had?"

"Yes, Robbie," Claire admitted, trying to study his reaction without staring.

He seemed thoughtful, somewhat concerned. "So that's what it was. And those pills she gave me?"

"Antidepressants."

He took a sip of milk, and the glass was still at his lips when he managed to say, "If I tell you something, promise me you won't cry. I can't stand to see any woman cry."

"Have you seen women cry?"

"Yes," he admitted, evidently reluctant to explain.

"When? Where?"

"Oh, on TV news . . . things like that." It was an obvious evasion.

She called him to account. "Robbie?"

"Wes—Wes Parker, kid in my class. He's on the second team. But we pal around together sometimes."

"I know. He's been here. What about him?"

"One day—almost a year ago—we were out practicing passes. He's a terrific receiver. If he was taller, he'd be on the first team."

"Robbie, what about that day and women crying?"

"It got so dark Wes could hardly see the ball. So we quit. He said, 'Come on home, my mom said we're going out for pizza.' When we got near his house, his dad's car came tearing out of their driveway. Tires screeching, car leaning the way it does when someone makes a very bad fast turn. He went roaring down the street and made another sharp turn. Almost hit a car coming on his right. I could see the look on Wes's face. Suddenly he wasn't thinking about pizza anymore. He didn't know what to do. Whether to go into the house or just wait outside. So I said, 'It's getting dark. I better start home.' But he said something peculiar, 'Wait, I'll see if it's okay." I thought: *What does he mean, 'okay'?* Okay to go into his own house?"

"So I waited. He went up the driveway to look in their kitchen window. I followed him. There she was, sitting at their kitchen table. She had a cloth to her face. And she was crying. She would dip the cloth into a bowl of water. Each time she did, the water got pinker and pinker. I realized it was blood. I could see a cut on the side of her face, just under her eye. Then Wes realized I was standing alongside him, looking in. That's when he said, 'Don't ever tell anyone. Ever. Promise!' And I did.

"Then he said, 'Someday I'm going to kill him for doing things like that to her.' I felt sick to my stomach, seeing her cry like that. Why would a man do that? Why, Mom?"

"I don't know," Claire said.

Robbie hesitated before asking, "Dad . . . has he ever—"

"Of course not. Never."

"Good." Robbie seemed greatly relieved. "If he ever does . . ."

"He won't. He's not that kind of man."

"I didn't think so. But then I didn't think Wes's father was either. I wish I'd never seen it. Mostly that Wes had never seen it. But I guess he'd seen it before; else why would he say, 'I'm going to kill him for doing things like that to her' ?"

"Yes. Why else?" Claire agreed. "You said you'd tell me something if I promised not to cry. What, Robbie?"

He hesitated, then said, "I've upset your whole life. Dad's, too. Why do you two put up with me?"

"Robbie! Don't ever say anything like that!" Claire responded at once. In the same instant, she had to ask herself: *Have we done anything to make him feel this way? Does he suspect our fears and doubts?*

She reached out to embrace him.

"Never, never say anything like that again, Robbie. Never even think it!"

While she held him close, he said, "If you and Dad want me to go see Rissom, okay. I'll even go back to see Dr. Belmond."

CHAPTER 29

"Dr. Belmond, I want to know exactly what you think is wrong with me," Robbie demanded.

"What do *you* think is wrong, Robbie?" she asked.

"Hubie was right about one thing. Shrinks," Robbie said, twisting angrily in his chair. "You answer every question with a question. You're the doctor. I'm asking you. What's wrong with me? Why did you make me go through another physical? You have never seen a patient in better shape than I am!"

She noted the return of his manic tendency to describe himself in superlatives. His belligerence, too, fitted the syndrome. Primarily interested in observing, she had no intention of interrupting.

"Have you?" he demanded. When she didn't answer, he persisted. "Ever seen a patient in better shape than I am?"

He leaped up from his chair. He began to pace. His manic energy could not be contained. He began once more to handle small objects that he snatched from her desk.

"You want to know what bugs me?" he said suddenly. "There's some kind of conspiracy going on. Between you and my mother. She kept nagging me to come here. So I came. But you don't tell me anything. What's the game? What *is* going on? And why are they looking at me in such a strange way?"

Belmond's eyes suddenly fixed on him. Despite all her warnings, had the Wards begun to externalize their fears and resentments? No matter how understandable, that could be very harmful now.

"Just how *do* they look at you, Robbie?"

"You can't fool me." He accused her. "You're going to try to convince me that it's not them but me who's strange. Hubie told me no matter what you say, the shrink somehow always turns it around to blame you."

"Did I blame you, Robbie?"

"It wasn't what you said; it was the way you said it," he replied, turning away in avoidance.

She said nothing but waited. Soon he turned back to her. "Look, if I was sure I could trust you . . ."

"You can trust me, Robbie."

He hesitated. "I have to know. Are they going to hold this against me forever? Won't it ever be the same again?"

"What, Robbie?"

"They. Me. Our family. Ever since that thing happened, I feel they're looking at me in a funny way. It's like suddenly I'm made of glass. If they treat me like they did before, I'll break. You know?"

"No, I don't know, Robbie. Tell me."

"I keep asking myself: *Why are they* too *nice,* too *concerned?* Because they're scared to death? What do they think I'll do? They talk to you. What do they say? I have to know."

"How much do you want to know, Robbie?"

"Everything," he insisted, but in a whisper, betraying that he feared what she might tell him.

"Then sit down." Once he was seated, she continued: "Yes, Robbie, they are worried. Just as you'd be worried if you had a son who'd been through what you've been through these last weeks. Robbie, what your parents are concerned about is that that situation might recur."

Her words made him less antagonistic and more thoughtful as he asked, "Do *you* think it will happen again?"

"I can't promise that it won't."

"I hope not." Then he confessed, "I had some bad feelings while that was going on. Really bad."

"I know," Belmond said softly. "You feel cut off from the rest of the world. Everything becomes your enemy. Daylight.

Eating. Thinking. Parents. Friends. School. Routine. All enemies. You're so hopeless that it seems there's only one way out. Isn't that how it feels, Robbie?"

"I thought I was the only one who ever felt that way." He leaned across the desk, stared into her deep black eyes. "Dr. Belmond, tell me something. That feeling, if it does come back, what will happen to me? Because I don't know what I'll do next time."

This was one of those moments in the treatment when the patient was most open to what the doctor wished to instill. The challenge was how to tell him enough, honestly, yet not tell him those things that might do great damage to his sensitive mind. How much of the truth would serve?

"Robbie, first I promise you that if it does happen again, I will do everything I can, use everything that science has put at my disposal, to get you over it. And these days that's a great deal."

He nodded slightly, somewhat reassured.

"Of course, you have to promise me certain things, too."

"Yeah? What?"

"You will follow instructions. Follow a sensible diet. You won't overdo. You'll keep your body in control."

"My body's always in top shape," he protested. "In football season I'm on a strict diet: proteins. And, before a game, carbohydrates."

"I'm talking about a different kind of diet. Enough fluids. Enough salt. Your situation requires a delicate balance. And you must maintain it."

"I will," he promised too readily.

Mindful of all the possible consequences of the drug she was contemplating, she wondered how he would react later if the side effects altered or inhibited his way of life in a manner unpredictable now.

"You will also have to take medication regularly."

"You mean that stuff I took before?" he asked.

"No. This is different. But once you start, you must continue to take it faithfully."

"How long?" he asked.

"I don't know," she answered truthfully. Because it might

be for a year or two or possibly for most of his life. But there was no need to confront that now.

Suspiciously he asked, "Could I get hooked?"

"This is definitely not the kind of drug on which you can get hooked," she assured. *In fact,* she thought, *it's the kind of drug that unfortunately patients have a tendency to resent after a while; that constituted the main danger.*

"And if I take this stuff, then what?"

"You keep life in balance. You don't go into a severe depression like that last time."

"Those thoughts . . ." he began. "They won't come back?"

"I can't promise they'll never come back. And now you have your parents to help. You've got me. You've got Rissom. The main thing is you're not alone any longer. Always remember that. *You are not alone.*"

He nodded thoughtfully.

"I'll work out the proper dose of the medication. And I'll get in touch with your mother."

"Okay," he said.

He rose from the chair, seemed about to say something, but refrained.

"Robbie, do we have an agreement, we each do our part?"

He nodded again.

"Good!" she said.

It was four-thirty when Don Ward knew he would be very late starting home. He called.

"You and Robbie'd better have your dinner."

"Okay, dear," Claire said, as she had said so many times in the past eighteen years. "If I'm asleep, wake me."

"Sure," he said, as he had said so many times in the past eighteen years. But he never woke her when he came home that late. Guilt always prevented him.

Before she could hang up, he asked urgently, "Well?"

"Well what?" she asked, caught unaware.

Impatient because he thought that between them these days there was only one topic worthy of concern, he asked, "Robbie? Did he go to Dr. Belmond? What happened?"

"She didn't call. So he must have gone."

"Didn't he say anything? Didn't you ask?"
"I'm not supposed to ask."
"Well," Don said, disappointed, "okay. See you later."
"You always say later when you mean late."
"Claire, please . . ."
"Okay, I'm sorry, darling. See you later."

Between the press of patients whose careers demanded early-morning hours and those who could only attend after their business days were over, it was usually only after a late dinner that Dr. Belmond could retire to her den and sift through the mail she had brought home from the office.

Her phone rang. It was Dr. Rissom.

"Sabrina, I just received that copy of the Rockland State Hospital record you sent me. Pretty dismal, isn't it?"

"A very sad history," she agreed.

"They first diagnosed her as schizophrenic. Even gave her shock treatments," Rissom said. "And she was alcoholic as well. Tell me, in all honesty, so I can be guided in my future dealings with Robbie and the Wards, with a record like this, what are his chances?"

"First, you tell me, what are the results of your lab tests?"

"They're in the mail to you now. He's in excellent shape. Heart. Kidneys. Perfect. Thyroid well within the limits of normal. From the physical point of view I'm sending you a terrific youngster. Now I want *your* candid assessment. I don't want to promise the patient or his family cures that aren't possible."

"All right, Fred. Candid assessment. If he can tolerate the medication, he's got an excellent chance. *Provided* he sticks to the regimen."

"I'll do *my* best," Rissom promised.

"We can all do our best, but it's still up to him to take his medication," Belmond pointed out.

"Of course."

"There is another . . ." Belmond started to say, but stopped.

"Sabrina?" Rissom asked. "Is there something else I should know as the boy's doctor?"

Since he had put the question on such a professional basis, she felt compelled to tell him.

"Fred, what plagues me as much as anything is what's *not* in that hospital record of Emily Birch."

"What do you mean?" Rissom asked.

"We know from our studies that individuals with Emily Birch's emotional difficulties have a tendency to select sexual partners, for marriage or otherwise, who are also emotionally afflicted."

"I see," Rissom said, quite sobered by the thought. "So that the genetic effect of Robbie's natural father might make this case even more complicated and dangerous."

"If that woman followed the usual pattern, that's probably true, Fred."

"Sabrina, when I sent him to you, I never promised it would prove an easy case. I know only one thing: This is a boy worth saving. He's got so much going for him. So much to give—" Rissom interrupted himself. "Sabrina, stop me. Because I'm beginning to sound like a patient now. I'm demanding promises and reassurance. I know you'll do your best."

She was reading a newly published psychiatric paper on emotional disorders in juvenile delinquents when her phone rang. Instinctively she looked at the desk clock. Past eleven. Surely no patient would call this late just to postpone tomorrow's hour. She lifted the phone. As soon as she recognized the voice, she put aside the paper. It was Robbie's voice, sounding furtive, secretive.

"Dr. Belmond?" he asked in a hushed voice.

"Yes, Robbie?"

"One thing I forgot to ask you today."

She smiled. Every patient always thought of the important question to ask right after he left her office.

"Yes, Robbie, what is it?"

His voice dropped even lower as he asked, "There's no chance—I mean, you aren't thinking of having me locked up, are you?"

She felt a chill come over her. "Of course not. What makes you ask such a question? Anything anyone said? Anything?" For her greatest fear now was that by accident or otherwise, Robbie had come by the knowledge of his mother's history.

"I was just thinking, that's all."

"Robbie, where are you now?"

"Home."

"Where at home?"

"I'm in my father's den. On his office phone. And I had to know. Before I could go to sleep."

"I give you my word, Robbie, no one has ever said anything about putting you in an institution. No one!" she repeated firmly.

"Okay," he said, sounding greatly relieved. "Sorry I bothered you, Doctor."

"One thing I always want you to remember, Robbie. Whenever you have any question, especially a question like that, call me! No matter what time of day or night, call me! Understand?"

"Yes, ma'am, I understand."

"Now get some sleep, Robbie."

"Yes, ma'am," he said.

Just before she could hang up, she heard a sound that forced her to ask, "Robbie?" She could hear him breathing, but he did not respond at once. "Robbie—" She coaxed him.

"If I did call you . . . if I did talk . . . they wouldn't know about it, would they?" he asked in a small, plaintive voice.

"No, they wouldn't."

"Okay then. Because times I have some pretty bad thoughts. And if they knew, they might not want me anymore," he whispered.

"Never think that, Robbie. They love you. They want you. Always. But we'll still keep our secrets. Don't worry."

"Yes, ma'am," he said.

She hung up more concerned than she had been.

CHAPTER 30

"Dr. Rissom's medical findings indicate that Robbie should be able to tolerate the drug. However, I must warn you, Mrs. Ward, that we can never be sure until we administer it," Dr. Belmond said.

"What happens if Robbie takes it and can't tolerate it? Is that dangerous?"

"We'll stop it before it gets to the dangerous stage. But to make sure of that, he'll have to be monitored regularly. In the beginning three times a week."

"That often?" Claire asked, reflecting her doubts about Robbie's acceptance of such close and frequent surveillance.

"His blood levels will have to be checked to prevent a dangerous buildup. We will have to monitor his salt intake. In this case, since salt helps the excretory process, the more the better. He must never become dehydrated. So his fluid intake has to be monitored, too. His kidney reaction tested. His thyroid. Once he levels off, testing can be less frequent, maybe only twice a month. I will also have to observe him for side effects. And so will you."

"Side effects?" Claire was startled by the first mention of that possibility.

"You must watch him for signs of fatigue, muscular weakness, nausea, vomiting, slurring of speech. Possibly even a slight tremor of the hands. If you detect any of those, you're to let me know at once."

Claire nodded, even more tense now.

"Of course, we must be observant without being obvious, Mrs. Ward."

"He won't like being regimented. Not Robbie."

"Does he practice football regularly in season?" Belmond asked. "Or basketball now?"

"Yes. But that's different," Claire said.

"You mean, he will accept regimentation if he thinks it's worth it. We've got to convince him that it is."

"The drug?" Claire asked.

"Lithium carbonate. By maintaining a proper balance of it in his blood, we can level out his highs and thus his lows. Should his depression recur and become severe, we can add the antidepressant as well. But he must adhere to his regimen religiously to avoid any dangerous consequences. Take exactly what is prescribed. Appear regularly for his tests."

"Do you want me to explain it to him, or will you?" Claire asked.

"Since we should get Robbie started at once, I'll explain it to him. Then, when he discusses it with you, you can reinforce me."

The session at an end, Claire started to rise but sat down again. "I hope I can do it," she confessed. "At the outset I thought: I'm an actress. A damn good actress. I can see this through. Smile when I have to. Be encouraging when I have to. Stern when I have to. But somehow I find I can't."

She fell silent for a moment, before adding, "I'm asking for encouragement, something to hold on to. I want to be hopeful about my son. But I want the truth, too."

Belmond nodded, then smiled sympathetically.

"Why is it that patients think psychiatrists are solitary people without spouses or children? Problem children. I'm a mother, too, Mrs. Ward. I've had my share. You're wondering about your adopted son. Well, what would you say if your natural son turned on you and accused you: 'I must be adopted. You'd never treat me this way if I really were your son!' That's what I used to hear from time to time when I disciplined my son.

So don't let the idea of adoption get you down. In fact, from one point of view, his birth mother's case history can be of some comfort."

"That sounds impossible," Claire protested.

"No. Experience indicates that patients with a family history of manic depression respond better to lithium carbonate. So let's get started. I want to see Robbie on Monday!"

Staring down at the little white pill in the palm of his hand, Robbie asked, "Is this it?"

"Yes, Robbie, that's it," Belmond said. "Lithium carbonate."

"Something new?"

"If something two thousand years old can be new, yes," Belmond said, smiling. His glance of puzzlement invited more. "Almost two thousand years ago ancient Greek and Roman physicians used to prescribe mineral waters to cure people who were depressed. One of them, a physician named Soranus, wrote it up in his notes. Then, recently, modern scientists have discovered that those same curative mineral waters are rich in lithium carbonate.

"So, as I said, it is new and old," Belmond continued. "Even today, in Europe and places here in America, people go to spas to drink mineral waters which contain lithium."

Robbie turned the pill over and over in his hand, saying, "Looks sort of like the salt tablets we sometimes get during a tough game on a hot day."

"It's not very much different from ordinary salt. But different enough," Belmond said. "I'm going to start you on three of those a day. In ten days I will increase the dose. Until we achieve the proper lithium level in your blood."

"And I have to go to Dr. Rissom to be checked out three times a week?" he asked grudgingly.

"Only at the beginning."

"It'll cut into my basketball practice."

She wrote out the prescription. "Have this filled right away, Robbie. And start taking them today. Three times a day. Best to do it at mealtimes because those usually occur at the same hours every day and are spaced enough apart."

* * *

It was almost past midnight when Don Ward's red Mercedes pulled into the garage. Claire heard him. Came down to greet him. His first question was: "How did it go, Robbie and Belmond?"

"From what he said, fine," she was relieved to report. "I had the prescription filled, and he's already taken two pills, this afternoon and at dinner."

"Good!" Don said.

"Can I get you anything? A sandwich? A drink?" Claire asked. "How did it go today?"

"Last night's special did well in the overnights," Don said, loosening his tie and unbuttoning his collar. "So we can relax for twenty-four hours. Brady's trying to make a deal with the same producer for a series of three more specials for next season." Then he seemed to remember and said, "Yeah, a sandwich, something bland."

"Stomach acting up again?"

"If it isn't the ratings, it's Robbie. And if it isn't Robbie, it's the ratings," he said wearily. "But driving home, I got an idea. A way to get him to keep taking his pills religiously. And it won't make a bad sixteenth birthday present either."

"Oh? What?" Claire asked, at the butcher-block counter top, cutting his cheese sandwich into two triangles. "Milk?"

"Yeah," Don said, slipping his jacket over the back of the dinette chair. "I'll have a talk with him tomorrow. I've got an idea he'll like. Like a lot."

Robbie was just finishing his cereal when Don came down.

"Hi, son, good morning!" Don sang out.

"Hi, Dad."

Don came around the table to lean down and kiss Robbie on the cheek.

"Man, have I got news for you," Don said.

"Yeah? What."

"Saturday morning. Say, you don't have a game this Saturday, do you?"

"No. Why?"

"Boat show!" Don announced, beaming.

"Boat show?"

"The Coliseum. In New York. Saturday's the boat show. And we are going down there and look over the new line of sailboats. Including the new Hobie Cats."

"We've already got a cat."

"You call a fourteen-footer a cat? A real cat?" Don scoffed, smiling.

"Dad . . . you mean . . . that one I found in the catalog? The sixteen-footer?" Robbie asked, eyes beaming in anticipation.

"Sixteen." Don agreed, then added temptingly, "Or maybe even eighteen."

"An eighteen-foot catamaran! Awesome!"

"After all, you've got a big birthday coming. A guy doesn't get to be sixteen years old more than once in his life," Don said.

"An eighteen-foot cat. Wow!"

"Well, next Saturday morning."

"Unless you get called out to the Coast," Robbie said, unable to give way to total, unreserved optimism when his father's time and availability were concerned.

"Not this time, laddie, I promise you. Saturday morning. The boat show. And if that thing looks like I expect, we'll buy."

"Aw, great, Dad, great!"

He leaped up and embraced his father. While they held each other, Don said, "There's only one thing, Robbie."

The boy looked up at his father, sensing he had let his enthusiasm run away with him.

"You get that cat, provided you take your pills exactly the way Dr. Belmond said. The right number at the right time every day. Deal?"

"Sure! Deal!"

Robbie held out his hand to shake with his father. Don glanced across Robbie at Claire, his confident eyes relaying the message *I knew that would do it.*

If one were to judge by the number, variety, and size of the seagoing craft on display, the high, wide expanse of the New York Coliseum on Columbus Circle in midtown Manhattan could have been one vast indoor marina.

With some disdain Don and Robbie ignored the powerboats,

despite the busty bikini-clad models who smiled continuously while reclining in languid poses on the decks of costly yachts. They tried to give the impression that any man who bought one of those large, expensive pleasure craft would automatically ensure himself of such sexy company.

Instead, Robbie seized Don's hand and dragged him toward the display of double-hulled Hobie Cats. The center of the Hobie exhibit was an eighteen-foot catamaran, in full sail, poised on only one of its blue plastic pontoons, the other suspended high in midair as if executing that daring sailing maneuver called flying a hull.

Robbie and Don circled the craft, admiring its graceful design. It was far more boat than the fourteen-footer on which Don had taught Robbie the art of sailing.

This boat, largest in the Hobie line, would prove a real challenge. But Don felt that if it were a little beyond Robbie's abilities as a sailor now, he would be able to master it by end of summer.

Besides, if it would induce Robbie to continue his lithium faithfully, then the mere thought of owning such a boat, no matter the expense, was worth it.

"Well, Robbie, what do you say?"

"She's a beauty, Dad."

"Think we should pick out the color of the sail?" Don asked.

"You mean we're going to order it now?"

"Sure. By the time it's ready for delivery, it'll be March. Maybe even April. Let's get hold of that salesman."

Robbie pored over the various samples of colorful sails. There was the Silver Streak, all marine blue. The Carumba, two shades of blue stripes alternating with several shades of red and one band of purple.

Robbie selected the one called Cat Fever. Blue, red, orange, and yellow stripes. He liked the name.

CHAPTER 31

In the weeks following the commencement of Robbie's treatment he appeared to respond well. At the outset he resisted being monitored three times a week to ensure the proper lithium level in his blood. So he considered it a marked advance when Belmond informed him that from now on he would only have to appear at Dr. Rissom's once every two weeks.

In the Ward household time and Robbie's recovery had its beneficial effects as well. Whenever Don was out on the Coast and made his nightly call, his first question was no longer "How is *he?*" With the accent on the pronoun.

Conversation between Don and Claire was back to normal. About the club and would they go to the next holiday dance. About the new Mercedes, hers, which always seemed to need tuning up. About her mother. About the house and some repair that was necessary. About whatever network problem Don was troubleshooting this trip. About how Claire's rehearsals were going. About the next network affiliate meeting. Then, somewhere along the conversation: "And how's Robbie doing?"

He was no longer the twenty-four-hour concern which had shadowed even their sleeping hours. Claire's periodic visits to Dr. Belmond were no longer traumatic experiences that she feared. Belmond's reports on Robbie's progress matched Claire's own observations. Robbie's problem seemed to be solved or at least under control.

They could put their minds to considering colleges, about which Robbie would soon have to make some decisions. This coming term he would have to take his preliminary SATs. On the basis of his results, which they now had every reason to expect would be excellent, Robbie would have his pick of colleges.

Their often-discussed and long-cherished ambitions for their only son were falling into place again, as if the dangerous episodes of recent months had never occurred.

Dr. Belmond, however, continued to view the situation with caution and professional reserve. During her two years of residency at a large state hospital, later at a small private clinic, and in her own present practice, she had become accustomed to the progress and the remissions of patients with similar conditions. Always the patients trod a fine line. Under control they were usually bright, sometimes excessively bright, productive, happy people. Out of control they were either morbidly depressed or wildly elated and ofttimes dangerous.

She saw no purpose in alarming Claire Ward, so she did not dwell on the negative posibilities. But both she and Rissom maintained a cool and careful watch over their young patient's progress.

As long as he took his lithium pills, appeared regularly at Rissom's office for his blood checks, and kept his hours with her, Belmond felt she had the situation under control. But to assume that a teenager would continue to follow such a routine without occasional lapses was unrealistic.

Robbie took his accustomed seat across from her. He looked clean, if not neat, freshly showered after basketball practice, his dark hair glistening. His face was ruddy and unmarked, except for a slight red bruise high on his right cheek where he had been elbowed during a scrimmage under the basket to retrieve a rebound.

Belmond looked beyond his handsome face to focus on his eyes, blue, alert, far more tranquil than she had seen them in those early days.

"Dr. Rissom tells me your latest lab reports are excellent. Your lithium level is perfectly stabilized. And all your other signs are good. Now, tell me, how do you feel?"

"Okay, I guess," he said, smiling.

"Any problems."

"Not that I know of."

"Schoolwork?"

"Well, that's getting tougher," he admitted. "I find I have to study more. But I find I like it."

"And other things? Athletics? Social things?"

"You mean Susan?" he asked self-consciously.

"Yes, Susan."

"We're going to go to this concert. Catastrophe. That's a new hard-rock group. I got one of their albums. They're playing at the civic center down in White Plains. So we're planning to go. But this time no riot," he said, smiling sheepishly.

Belmond nodded, wondering about the fascination of present-day adolescents with savage, deafening music and the eccentric practitioners of that incomprehensible art.

"How is your relationship with Susan otherwise?" Belmond asked.

She noticed that Robbie seemed suddenly uncomfortable at being seated. He was poised to rise and move about as had been his habit. But the only action he took was to pick up a little toy which a patient had brought Belmond after a trip to Fort Ticonderoga. It was a miniature of one of the cannons used at that fort during the Revolutionary War. Small enough to heft in the hand, it was one of Robbie's favorite objects to play with during moments of stress in treatment.

"I think . . . I think she's . . . she's more . . . more . . I don't know."

"More adventurous?" Belmond suggested. When he did not respond, she asked, "More willing to make out?"

He did not answer; his eyes did that for him.

"And you're not," she concluded.

"I—I'm afraid to. . . ."

"Of what?"

"The balance you keep worrying about, maybe it would be upset if I did," he said. "I wouldn't want that to happen again."

"It won't upset your lithium balance. But as for making out, you have to decide when you're ready. Girls develop faster than boys at this age. They prefer older young men. And young men your age feel more at ease with girls just a bit younger."

"I sometimes wonder . . ." But he shook his head, abandoning the subject.

"Wonder what, Robbie?"

"The woman," he finally said, "that woman who gave birth to me . . . and the man . . . I often wonder what they were like. And did they fall in love? Or was it just making out in the back of some car? Or in somebody else's home, while she was baby-sitting? Like Elise Wiswell. She had to leave school. Was that how I came to be? From something like that?" he asked. "I'd like to know sometimes."

In similar situations Belmond often advised adopted patients to make such a search and to settle their troubled minds on their origins. But knowing so well the file of "Birch, Emily" and its final entry, she decided not to.

"Someday," he began, but ended it, limiting himself to that. "Someday . . ."

"And how is basketball coming along?" Belmond asked, to direct his mind into other channels.

"Pretty good. We won all our warm-up games. And we're down to fourteen guys now. One more cut, and that'll be the squad that goes into the prep league tournament," Robbie said. "League rules say only ten men to a tournament squad."

"Remember what I told you, Robbie," Belmond cautioned. "All that running, all that physical stress produces lots of sweat. Without being aware of it, you may dehydrate yourself. So keep drinking water."

"Oh, I make sure of that. First signs of thirst I always down two or three cups of water."

"You can become dehydrated long before you feel thirsty. So whenever you get a time-out, drink at least one cup of water. Between halves drink as many as you feel comfortable with. Okay?"

He nodded.

"Now, your pills? Three a day? With your meals?"

"Yes, ma'am."

"Good!" She encouraged him. "How are things at home?"

"Back to normal."

"What does that mean?"

He smiled. "Dad gets called out to the Coast. Mom hates the idea. So she keeps busy with her Towne Players, with her charity drives. But she keeps *looking* at me."

"Looking at you?"

"Yeah. Like she's expecting to see some miracle. She's always asking did I take my pill at lunchtime. Breakfast and dinner she can see that I do. But lunchtime I'm on my own. So she keeps looking at me. Like when I'm having dinner, every once in a while I look up and she's staring at me. Am I supposed to *look* any different because of those pills?"

"Of course not," Belmond said, smiling. "But you can't blame your mother for being interested in the way you look, the way you eat, the way you sound, what you say. With mothers, that's only natural."

"Especially after I scared the hell out of her, out of both of them. Right?"

"I wouldn't put it that way, Robbie."

"But I'm over that now. I'm all right!" he declared proudly. Then asked, more modestly: "I *am* all right, aren't I?"

"You're doing very well, Robbie, I'm proud of you."

Robbie's recovery had had substantial effects on the private lives of his mother and father as well.

During the time of his crisis lovemaking between Claire and Don had been infrequent, hurried, tense. Almost (Claire resisted the word but could find no other), almost mechanical. Not truly an act of love but an act of duty, a way of securing a release from tension for him, a less than satisfying emotional exercise for her.

Their talk afterward was inevitably about Robbie, about what she had come to call in her mind the Problem. It reminded her too much of the fretful time when she had been trying to conceive and their love was arranged and managed by gynecologists and other specialists. After that she and Don had never recaptured the lusty, uninhibited abandonment of the sex of their early marriage. Later Don's advancement at the network had begun demanding more and more of his time, energy and concentration. When she began to resent that he used to promise "We'll get away to one of the islands. We'll just lie on the beach all day and make love all night. We'll go someplace where they won't be able to reach me. It'll be just you and me, like it used to be, in the old days."

They had managed to get away. A few times to the islands. Once even to Gstaad for skiing. For the first two nights it had been everything she had dreamed it would be. But on the third night, when they were in bed, aroused to a degree of passion they had not experienced in some time, the phone rang.

"To hell with it!" Don whispered into her ear. But the phone had continued to ring insistently until she could feel his hardness subside. Once that had happened, he rolled over onto his side, saying, "Sorry, darling . . ." He picked up the phone. It was an overseas call. From New York. Sorry for the intrusion, the hotel clerk apologized, but New York insisted. Ten o'clock at night Gstaad time was only three in the afternoon New York time.

From Don's clipped, eager responses she knew it was Ed Brady calling.

"Yes. Sure. Of course. First thing in the morning. Great! A coup! A real coup! Of course, first thing in the morning. Right! Right!"

Until Claire had said to herself: *If he says "yes" or "right" one more time, naked as I am, I am going out into that corridor and scream!*

But at the same time she had felt her own passionate desire ebbing away. When Don hung up and turned back to her in an attempt to resume making love, neither he nor she was any longer in the mood. She eased to her own side of the bed, the cool side. He turned on his back, stared up at the ceiling, and said, "Sorry. But it was important. The network just closed a deal for the rights to the Winter Olympics. Brady wants me to inspect the site, let him know what I think will be required in crews, cameras, teams of announcers and commentators. The works."

When she did not respond, he said, "This could be my first big break, darling. Maybe I could get to produce the entire Olympics. That would be a terrific credit." He knew she was hurt and feeling abandoned, so he said once more, "I'm sorry. I couldn't ignore a call from the office. Especially Brady."

Later they had made another attempt to have sex. But it was mechanical, routine, dry, loveless. She was not fulfilled, only relieved to turn on her side and fall asleep. Which she had done, but not without some tears.

But these nights, released from the constant concern and fear about Robbie and what he might do, their intimate relationship had become warmer, more relaxed. Sex had become more frequent, less planned, more impulsive, far more enjoyable.

Though she and Don had never discussed it, she was sure they shared that same overwhelming feeling of relief that people experience after narrowly avoiding a fatal accident. They look back at the moment of the near disaster and resolve to make the most of their new chance at life.

Some nights she lay awake after Don had fallen asleep from sexual exhaustion, and she thought: *Now that Robbie's well again, all our fears and worries were worth it. Now that he's well again, it's even given our marriage new life.*

CHAPTER 32

It was almost three o'clock. Robbie's last class was Spanish. He had been called on only to be caught thinking about basketball instead of the proper declension of a verb. It took him a moment to recover and provide the right answer. But his teacher, Mrs. Carnahan, shook her head. "It's not like you, Robbie. Not at all like you."

Every teacher who had a chance to examine Robbie's scholastic record or see his unusual IQ score always expected brilliance from him. Whenever he faltered for lack of preparation or, as now, because his mind had wandered from Spanish to the more important subject of basketball, the teacher always expressed disappointment.

At last the three o'clock bell sounded. He bounded out of class, met Susan under the hall clock only long enough to confirm their date for Saturday night, and raced down the corridor to the exit closest to the gym.

He changed into his basketball shorts, sweat shirt, socks, and sneakers, drank two cups of water, then charged out onto the court, where Mr. McNaughton was surrounded by his eager candidates for those final ten places on the tournament squad. Robbie was the last of the fourteen to make it to the circle.

"Okay, men," McNaughton said, "next week we start league play-offs. When every game counts. And this year we want to go all the way to finals. Like our football team did. Right, Robbie?"

"Right!" Robbie called back obediently, though he hated to be reminded of that disastrous game.

"So we'll divide into two squads. Five regulars, two subs on each side. We'll play regulation quarters. At the end of the first quarter the two subs go in and two others come out. We rotate until every man has played at least two full quarters. We do that for our two games this week. By Friday I'll have picked my ten men. Okay?"

There were okays all around from the fourteen finalists, McNaughton selected his two squads, dividing them evenly for height, weight, speed, accuracy in shooting, and aggressiveness. He picked Robbie to be on the Skin team, meaning the team that played without shirts. The Shirts would wear old Canaan jerseys that were now used only for practice.

Before McNaughton sent them out onto the floor, he took Robbie aside. "Robbie, I'm looking for the same thing you gave the football team: leadership. You're not as tall as Converse. Or as muscular as Linburn. So let them do the heavy work under the basket, fighting for position, getting the rebounds. But once we get that ball, I want you to direct the move down the court and set up the play. I want you to be my playmaker."

"Yes, sir, Mr. McNaughton."

"Use your quickness, your peripheral vision, your instincts. We need all that."

Robbie nodded, eager to get out on the floor, where the others were warming up with shots that looped through the baskets or else spun around and fell out. Balls came at the baskets in such profusion that at times two balls perfectly aimed collided in midair and fell off to the sides.

McNaughton blew the whistle that hung from his neck by a rawhide leather thong. He called his two teams to attention and ordered them to take up starting positions. Converse came to the center circle for the Skins; Clinton jumped for the Shirts.

McNaughton looked around, made sure all ten men were where they should be, threw the ball up, blowing his whistle at the same time. The game was on. Clinton got the tap, batted it off to his forward, and the Shirts started down the floor. Robbie stayed with his man, almost intercepted the pass to him, but in so doing lunged out of position. The man faked a dribble toward the basket but instead straightened up and shot over Robbie's outstretched arms and scored.

The Skins took the ball out. Converse and Linburn raced downcourt to give them height and weight advantage under the basket, while Evenger, a blond-haired senior, about Robbie's size and weight, threw the ball in to him. Robbie started to dribble downcourt. Evenger preceded him, moving to the corner of the court. Robbie looked to his four teammates. They were well positioned. Except for Evenger. With his free hand Robbie signaled him closer. But it was a diversion. For Robbie arced the ball to Converse over the head of Clinton, who was guarding him. Robbie placed the ball high enough so that Converse only had to leap for it and stuff it into the basket. The play had worked perfectly.

McNaughton noted that with quiet satisfaction. In addition to his excellent physical responses, Robbie Ward had a keen sense for court tactics. With a playmaker like Robbie and two tall, strong boys like Converse and Linburn, McNaughton had visions of making it to the championship round of the prep school league. Possibly even going on to the all-state finals.

Tough play continued through the quarter. At the end the score was Shirts 10, Skins 14. McNaughton blew his whistle, called two men from each team off the court, and sent in the subs. But he did not substitute either man for Robbie. He wanted to see how long Robbie could function as playmaker without letting down or having his judgment impaired by fatigue.

Caught up in the excitement of competing, encouraged by the manner in which his teammates had reacted to his playmaking, Robbie was eager to start the second quarter. The others might be wet and panting. Though he was equally perspired, Robbie was anxious to keep going. He did not want to upset his rhythm or the rhythm of his teammates. They were hot. He wanted to stay hot. The thought vaguely crossed his mind; *Get some water.* But he banished that by thinking: *I'll drink twice as much at half time. I don't want to risk a cramp now. Not when McNaughton seems impressed. Well, if he's impressed now, wait till this next quarter.* Robbie felt all the intensity and excitement he used to feel when he quarterbacked the football team until, of course, that one fatal play.

Of the two substitutes McNaughton put into the game for the Shirts, Scott Andrews was detailed to guard Robbie. A digger, a ferret, small but agile and quick, Scott harried Robbie from the instant the ball was passed in to him. While Robbie dribbled upcourt, surveying the position of his teammates, until the instant he passed the ball, Scott clung to Robbie like a second skin. Twice Scott managed to get the tips of his fingers on the ball as Robbie passed it, causing it to be deflected. Once it went out of bounds. The second time it was picked off by a Shirts guard, who went down the court to score.

No matter how intently Robbie tried to shake him or take him out, Scott hung close. Robbie resolved to pick up the pace, outhustle him, but he felt tired, slow. Late into the second quarter, attempting to get off a quick, hard pass before Scott could get set, Robbie lost control. The ball went wildly out of bounds.

Without a word being said, Robbie had the sudden and disturbing feeling of replaying that fatal football pass which resulted in the loss of the championship game. He felt his teammates staring at him, as if they, too, remembered.

McNaughton blew his whistle, calling, "Time!" Robbie and his teammates came to the side of the court. Some knelt on the floor, leaving circles of sweat where their knees touched it. Others gathered around the water bucket to drink quick swallows of water.

Robbie simply dropped to the bench, wondering: *That last bad pass, was it intentional or did I just lose control?* He stared down at his hands, as if they were at fault. He tried to relive the play. He had wanted to get the pass off to Converse, who was just to the side of the basket. It was a perfectly sound play. It was just that the ball slipped out of his hands. That had never happened before. Why this time?

When he went out on the floor again, he would try that same pass from that same place on the court and see what happened.

"Okay, men," McNaughton said, "let's go. Second half!"

As Robbie rose to race out onto the floor, the coach said, "Robbie, let Eddie Richter take over this quarter."

"Why?" Robbie demanded.

"You've been going at top speed for a full half," the coach said. "This is only practice. Ease off, man. Rest awhile."

Robbie sank back down onto the bench. Through the second half he watched as Eddie Richter ran the Skins. Eddie might be a step faster right now, being fresh, but he was not as good as Robbie knew himself to be. Yet that pass that eluded him still clung to him like a nettle. From time to time he stared down at his hands. Something had gone wrong. Something unusual, something highly unusual for him.

He sat through the entire second half. Once excused, he went into the shower. After he had dressed, instead of going out to the lot to where his bicycle was parked, he went down the cinderblock corridor to where the light emanating from McNaughton's office indicated the coach was still there.

He was making his notes on the practice session, checking each candidate's performance based on today's play. When he noticed Robbie in the doorway, he looked up, smiled.

"Yeah, Robbie?"

"I wanted to explain . . ." Robbie began.

"Explain?" McNaughton was puzzled. "Explain what?"

"That pass."

"Which pass?"

"The one that got away."

"What about it?"

Suddenly faced with the opportunity to explain, Robbie found himself at a loss for words.

"Well, what happened . . . I mean, it was not like in that football game. I wasn't trying for a spectacular play. I was just trying to pass it high and hard to Converse. It would have been a hanger for him. But somehow, somehow it got away."

"Of course, it got away," McNaughton said. "You'd been playing at top speed for almost a full half. Your hands were sweaty. You had too much momentum going. I'm surprised it happened only once. Forget it."

"Yeah, but you took me out right after that."

"You were in that phase of a player's game when his intensity gets beyond him. He starts to make mistakes. Son, if we were in the finals of the NCAA and my playmaker reached that point, I'd take him out even if he were an all-American. Every human body has its limits. Part of a coach's job is to know when that happens. So don't worry about it."

McNaughton turned his clipboard around but kept his large, powerful hand over it. "If you promise not to tell anyone, I'll let you see."

"Promise."

"My top candidates for those ten places."

McNaughton removed his hand. Robbie read the top ten names. His was third on the list.

"After Friday's game, unless something startling happens, this list is it, Robbie."

It was dark by the time Robbie made the last turn into his own block. The garage door was open. Mom's new Mercedes was parked. She was home. He leaned his bike against the garage wall and went in. She was on the phone again.

And, he noticed, she did not retreat into her secretive voice when he appeared. He had become very sensitive to that during the time of his recent troubles. She was, in fact, talking in more than her normal voice as he heard her say, "If she thinks that role is too small for her, she doesn't have to take it! I've been on shows with stars who had smaller parts. Besides, if you want my honest opinion, it's too fat a part for her."

Robbie stood in the doorway, smiling. "Attaboy, Mom! Give 'em hell!"

She waved him off, half amused, half annoyed. She put her hand over the mouthpiece to say, "Sally Binns. She's complained to everyone in the cast about her part."

"You could also say *she's* too fat," Robbie volunteered.

"Shhh!" his mother said, but she nodded in agreement.

He went up to his room, automatically flipped on his stereo, dropped his books onto his desk, fell onto the bed, exhausted. He lay there, hands behind his head, listening to the music, his whole body resonating to the rhythmic, monotonous beat which held him in its grip. Gradually the music became only a distant throbbing. His mind focused more and more on that one bad play of the afternoon.

He tried to relive it and realized that his difficulty had actually begun as soon as Scott Andrews was substituted into the game.

For some reason, for the first time in any athletic competition, Scott was faster than he. Was it due to the fact that during those dark days (which he was now able to refer to as his depression) he had allowed his body to deteriorate? He had read an article on fitness in a sports magazine that said that, after only three days of a layoff, muscles begin to lose their tone. He had laid off for more than three days, more even than three weeks. Perhaps to make up for that he needed not to bike to school but to run. Running there and back would add up to almost seven miles a day. A week or more of that and he'd be back to top form. He would start tomorrow.

When he mentioned it to his mother at dinner, she encouraged him. To her it was a sign of ever-further improvement. He was once again the Robbie who was looking for excellence, for ways to extend himself. Running might have a tonic effect on him.

The next morning, when she packed his lunch, as she had become accustomed to doing for some weeks now, she wrapped a white lithium pill in a small piece of clear plastic. Carefully she placed it in with his sandwich, fruit, and a thermos of hot soup.

"Don't forget . . ." she started to say.

Robbie anticipated her. "I know, I know, take my pill!" He laughed.

"Robbie, this is not funny."

"I was only thinking, right now half the girls in our class are hearing the same thing from their mothers: 'Don't forget to take your pill.' "

Claire's impulse was to ask, "Susan? Is she on the pill? Is anything going on between you two?"

But she refrained. Somehow, if it were, she would rather not know about it. She kissed her son and sent him off to school.

Because he was burdened by his books and his lunch box, running was a nuisance. But that only added to the challenge. By the end of the third mile he could feel that he was breathing harder than he expected. And sweating more. He was sure now that his original suspicion had been correct. Those dark days had robbed him. Well, by the end of this week he would overcome that. By Friday's game he would be ready. Anyone who wanted his place on the squad would have to fight him for it. That thought carried him through the last half mile easily, almost effortlessly.

But the game that afternoon was less satisfying than the day before. McNaughton took him out in the middle of the second quarter.

"What's the matter, kid?"

Robbie just shook his head. His legs felt tired. His arms did not respond as he wanted. He blamed it on his long run that morning. Conditioning would take time. More time than he had expected. He wanted to explain to McNaughton, but that would sound like a lame excuse. He would see this through by himself. He was determined to be ready for Friday.

On his run home the thought first came to him. He would have to consult that sheet of instructions Dr. Belmond had given him. Something on there kept nagging at him, like a bit of thread on a frayed shirt cuff, large enough to see but too small to grasp. The longer his run, the more it tormented him. He must consult that sheet the moment he reached the house.

The garage door was locked. Mom was not home yet. He went around to the back of the house and let himself in, careful to turn off the alarm system. In their affluent neighborhood every home had an alarm system. He dropped his empty lunch box in the kitchen, went straight up to his room, and dug out of his top desk drawer the *"Patient's Guide for Lithium,"* which Belmond had given him on the day he took the very first of his three daily pills.

He raced impatiently past what he considered the routine instructions and warnings: "Never take more than the prescribed amount. . . . Never double up on pills if you have forgotten to take one. . . . Do not restrict the amount of table salt you use."

Finally he found it: "Read the following symptoms very carefully. If you feel any of them beginning, tell your doctor at once. If you cannot reach your doctor, then do not take any more medication. The symptoms should disappear within a few hours."

There followed a list of three different sets of symptoms: "Mild, Moderate, Severe." Under "Mild" there were only two: "Nausea" and "Shaking of the hands." Under "Moderate" there were many, including "Difficulty walking, talking; Excessive thirst; Weakness;

Muscle twitching; Drowsiness; Silliness (lightheadedness)."

His eyes fixed on the symptoms "Weakness" and "Drowsiness." Perhaps they were the cause of his less than effective play this afternoon. They might even cost him his place on the final squad if he allowed them to continue. Especially during the game on Friday, on the basis of which McNaughton's final cut would be made.

Robbie held out his hands, studied them to see if they shook. They were perfectly firm and strong. No, not so strong, he felt. He flexed them. Opened them. Flexed them again, stared at them. He opened them once more. They were big enough to control a basketball. Why today had that ball eluded him not only once but three times in the course of the game? Why had it got away when he tried to pass to Converse, high, hard passes over the heads of the defenders? Now that he thought of it, during the last few practices Scott Andrews, a kid who was never as fast as he, had clung to him like a second skin. Why? There could be only one reason. Those damned lithium pills had slowed him up. Didn't it say very clearly on this instruction sheet that difficulty walking was a possible side effect? If walking might be difficult, then surely running must be.

He had always had confidence in the ability of his body to respond to anything he demanded of it. It was swift, strong, able to recuperate from the sudden jolts and shocks of football, a far more bruising game than basketball. Why was it now failing him at the crucial moments in these practice games? If it happened now, what would happen during a tournament game, when the competition would be much tougher?

He determined there was only one thing to do before Friday's crucial game: skip his pills. But Mom watched him like a hawk. Every meal at home, breakfast and dinner, she was there, insisting, "Robbie, darling, take your pill. Robbie, don't forget your pill. Robbie, your pill. Pill, pill, pill." Until he could anticipate her words simply by the look in her eyes.

His damn pills had become more important than anything else in her life. Even the times they ate out, just before they left the house, she was always sure to ask, "Robbie, do you have your pill with you?" The one time he forgot, she produced a pill from her purse. To her his life depended on those damn pills.

He had begun to question if they were necessary at all. He felt fine. He had not experienced another episode of that dread depression. So what did that prove? That the pills were responsible? Not if you figured it out. After all, except for that one time, he had never had a depression before. And without any pills. So how could anybody be sure that the pills were responsible for his recovery?

When he thought about it, the pills could be affecting him in another way, too. And not for the better. Only last Saturday night at the arcade, when he and Susan were hacking around with the group, she made a remark. It didn't trouble him at the time, but it did now.

"What is it, Robbie? What's come over you? You're not the same anymore."

Those were her words. They were the same words he had been using about himself. When he was out on the court, when he was running, handling the ball, passing, a skill at which he had always excelled. *It was not the same anymore.*

Not the same anymore. The only thing that had changed were those pills. They were to blame. Had to be. They had not only slowed him down but made him dull and uninteresting to Susie. They were changing him into something he wasn't. And, more important, didn't want to be.

There was only one way to find out. He would only pretend to take his pill when his mom was looking. Or if she were not looking and asked, he would say he had just taken one. Then he would flush it down the toilet. The one in his lunch box would be easy to dispose of. The others would take a little skill at deception.

But between now and Friday he would take no pills. And on Friday he would play the game of his life. He had determined that when it occurred to him there was always that damned visit to Rissom's office every first and third Monday of the month.

So what? That was Monday. Friday was the important day. He could make up for the pills he'd skipped by doubling up on Saturday and Sunday. It might even improve things between him and Susie if they had their regular Saturday night date. And this time maybe they would go all the way.

In his more serious solitary moments he asked himself with

the urge so hot and strong *why* hadn't he? Sometimes, in some unexplained way, he suspected it had to do with being adopted. Why? Adopted kids have the same feelings all other kids have. From the way the guys talked, he knew that. Susie was much the more adventurous of the two of them. She had a way of wriggling into positions that presented her young breasts to him. She always seemed disappointed when he was the one who broke off physical intimacy.

That, too, had grown more obvious ever since the damn pills. He decided he would not double up on the pills until after Saturday night. If he skipped three days' worth and tripled up on Sunday, he should be ready for his blood test on Monday afternoon. Especially if he doubled up on Monday morning as well, even though Belmond's printed instructions stated clearly, "Do not take any pills the morning of your blood test."

CHAPTER 33

Robbie woke on Friday morning with a tingling sense of great anticipation. His first moments he lay in bed with an uneasy awareness that he had intended to do something on waking. Then he remembered. Just before falling off to sleep he had determined that first thing in the morning he would consciously determine the way he felt, to discover if skipping his pills had really had any effect on him. He lay still, breathing deeply, assessing the feelings in his arms and legs. He felt stronger. More his old self again.

He leaped out of bed, confident that today he was going to be fine, great, better than great. If nothing else, skipping those pills had restored his confidence. Tomorrow night with Susie he would go all the way. . . .

He was in the shower, soaping and washing himself, when he was afflicted by a thought that troubled him, pursued him, at the oddest times: *Whoever they are, those birth parents of mine, if they hadn't gone all the way, I wouldn't be here with the problem I have.*

He was toweling himself when he thought: *One day I'll find that woman and ask her how it happened and what he was like. What did he look like? What kind of guy was he? Was he good at sports? Were they in love? Or was it just a one-time thing? Was he a chance happening? Were they so hot for each other that they didn't give a damn, so I was conceived and born?* And she had better have all the answers and be willing to tell him!

But beneath his anger and his resentment against his unknown natural mother and father was the feeling that what inhibited him with Susan was guilt. That he might be fathering and inflicting on some other child all the uncertainties and problems of being unwanted by one woman and adopted by another.

Breakfast went by in the usual way. His father drank his orange juice but skipped his coffee because there would be a coffee meeting at the office. Mom was making phone calls to all the members of her cast to alert them to when their scenes would be rehearsed. So when she turned from the phone to remind, "Robbie, your pill!" he could say, "Already took it," and she did not question him.

She gave him last-minute instructions. "If I'm late from rehearsal, there's some fruit in the fridge. And also some of yesterday's beef if you want a sandwich. But try not to eat too much. Dad's taking us to a new Italian restaurant in Stamford. Everyone says it's terrific."

"Dad?" Robbie asked skeptically.

"If he doesn't get home, the two of us'll go," she promised.

She packed his sandwich, an apple, a fruit tart, and, of course, his pill, wrapped in plastic. To quiet her suspicions and give protective color to his deception, he said, "Mom, from now on can't you use waxed paper instead of plastic? Plastic's too tough to take apart. It clings so."

"You sound like a television commercial," she said, laughing. "Okay. From now on, waxed paper."

She kissed him to send him on his way, completely secure in the knowledge that her son was dutifully following Dr. Belmond's orders. She watched from the front window as he cycled down the circular drive, turned, and was on his way to school.

Since his recovery she was free to go about her life again without those poisonous thoughts which had been her constant torment in the weeks gone by: *What is Robbie doing up there alone? What is he thinking? Or worse, planning? What will I discover if I dare open his closet door?*

Dr. Rissom assured her that Robbie's blood tests checked out extremely well, his lithium component at exactly the proper level. He and Belmond had even discussed the likelihood that after a year, two at the most, if progress continued, Robbie might get along without any pills at all. Both doctors were extremely satisfied and optimistic.

Then all of Don's and her plans could proceed as they had always anticipated.

Robbie, with his excellent record, would be off to a good school, the best, possibly even Harvard. She and Don would spend more time together. She could go out to the Coast with him. Instead of watching him go off alone on those sudden but frequent trips, only to have him fly home overnight on the red-eye so as not to waste another whole day traveling. He would always get home about quarter to seven in the morning, try not to disturb her when he got out of his smoke-infested clothes and into the shower. But always she woke. Aware, even in her sleep, of his presence. She would slip out of bed, call a welcome to him over the shower, and hurry down to make him a good hot breakfast. However sophisticated and unlike her mother she was, Claire still believed in the sanctity and life-sustaining qualities of a good hot breakfast.

Once Robbie was off to college and she was free to travel with Don, there would be no need for those exhausting overnight flights home. They would spend more time out there. She would luxuriate in a bungalow at the Beverly Hills Hotel, have breakfast in bed, spend her daytime hours at the pool, and her evenings dining at Chasen's, Laserre, Ma Maison, and other restaurants which had sprung up since the years when she used to go out there on a rare picture assignment. Perhaps—she allowed herself to daydream—she might even secure a good character role in a film now and then. Mature women had come into vogue ever since Shirley MacLaine won her Oscar for *Terms of Endearment.* Studios were now looking for properties for mature women.

Yes, since Robbie had responded so well to the lithium, Claire was a woman full of plans and ideas, not dreads and fears. Her life had taken on a whole new, bright outlook. When she recalled how she felt that first time she had gone to see Dr. Belmond and now how well things had worked out, she could honestly say she was a new woman.

Perhaps, she thought, all people needed such a crisis in their lives to appreciate the good times, the safe, relaxed, comfortable, normal times.

Through classes all day Robbie paid only scant and absolutely minimal attention. Barely enough to be able to respond to the questions his teachers asked. He did not volunteer at all, unusual for him. He was satisfied to coast through the day, his mind on only one thing: that final practice session.

Robbie stripped and slipped into his basketball uniform. Today no shirt again. McNaughton had designated him playmaker for the Skins, and he knew that his performance would determine whether he would make the tournament squad.

He felt confident. As in the old days, Robbie was *up.* Alert! Raring to go. He would show McNaughton; he would show them all. He stared hastily into the mirror inside his locker door to assure himself that he looked his old self again. Today not always one step too slow. But himself. Quick. Agile. He would handle that ball as it had never been handled before by anyone! His old elation was running again, and he gloried in it.

He was first out on the floor. McNaughton noticed. Smiled. He, too, seemed to recognize the old Robbie Ward. His teammates came onto the floor excited, tense. Aware of what hung in the balance. McNaughton selected the teams. Robbie was teamed up with Converse and Linburn again. That was significant since everyone knew that Converse and Linburn were sure to make the final squad.

The four nonstarters sat on the bench, awaiting their turn to demonstrate their abilities. But the ten men out on the floor were prime candidates. All Robbie had to do now was prove himself. With a confidence he had not felt in weeks, he trotted out onto the floor. He shook hands with his teammates. Converse slapped him on the back. "Go, Robbie, go!"

He felt a sense of elation when McNaughton came onto the floor, whistle in mouth, ball in hand, and brought Converse and Felter, the Shirts' center, together for the tip-off. Robbie was ready. His hands felt strong and secure. He knew there would be no mistakes today. No carelessly thrown balls. He was ready.

The tip-off went to the Skins. Clinton received it, passed it back to Robbie. He started down the floor, dribbling slowly, giving his team a chance to set up for the play. Converse to the basket, Linburn to the perimeter of the foul circle, from which point he was deadly with his hook shot. Clinton and Pauley were acting as safety valves in the event Robbie had to pass off. He moved the ball slowly. Passed off to Clinton, who dribbled, tried to work his way in, could not force an open lane, passed back to Robbie, who suddenly whipped the ball high toward the basket, so that Converse, leaping in precise timing, had only to intercept the ball and drop it into the basket.

The ball went over to the Shirts. Robbie started downcourt to his defensive position. He caught a quick glimpse of McNaughton's face. The coach seemed delighted with the way Robbie had engineered the play. Robbie felt the confidence he used to feel quarterbacking the football team.

He had control. *Without those damn pills he would always have control.*

Practice continued. It was tough, sweaty, strongly contested physically. The teams working against each other with all the ferocity of traditional opponents. Robbie felt bruised and aching by the time the first half was over. But his Skins were ahead by 24 to 19. When he left the floor, replaced by Scott Andrews, he was confident that he had staked out for himself the position of playmaker for the first team. McNaughton greeted him with a slap on the back and a cheery "That's more like it, Robbie. You're really yourself today."

He sat on the bench, his sweat shirt thrown loosely over his bare shoulders. He felt the sweat run down his chest in rivulets. He was still breathing hard but eager to go back in if McNaughton called on him.

The rest of the practice session, which included the four alternates, was tough, hard-fought basketball played by ten young men each of whom was determined to make the squad, all the while knowing that four of them would not succeed.

By the end of the second half, under Scott Andrews's playmaking, the Skins had fallen behind. They lost 42 to 39. Scott Andrews was no longer a threat to Robbie.

That fact was established when McNaughton assembled his sweaty squad in the locker room and read off the names of the ten anointed. Converse and Linburn, of course. The third name he announced was Robbie Ward.

He took his shower, enjoying the hot water that beat down on him, dispelling all feeling of fatigue as well as the aches and pains in his arms and legs. But the dominant feelings—confidence, pride, and triumph—were worth it. In the next weeks of the tournament he would play such sensational basketball that they would forget about his one blunder, that bad forward pass.

To accomplish that, he had to devise for himself a regimen that would protect him from the side effects of those damn little white pills, while at the same time so controlling his blood level that no one, not even Dr. Rissom, would suspect.

Susan was waiting for him in the parking lot. Tall, slender, flaxen-haired, she reminded many people of Claire Ward. People who saw the three of them together always assumed that not Robbie but Susan was Claire's child. People who knew them always thought: *That girl's the nearest thing to his mother he's ever going to find.* She lacked Claire's good triangular facial structure, but she could never be called less than very pretty. Today she was dressed in a pleated plaid skirt and a pink cotton sweater, which accented her look of freshness and youth.

"Well, Robbie?"

"Made it," he said, smiling. "Hands down."

"Terrific!" She kissed him. He drew her close and inhaled. She always smelled good. Her skin was always cool and smooth, not like some girls on whom you could count each oily pore.

"We'll celebrate. Tomorrow night," he said, "the Parrot Cage," naming the rock disco where all the gang went on Saturday nights.

"Tomorrow night?" She apologized. "You didn't ask me, so I made a date with Swede."

Though he was disappointed, he said, "Then next Saturday night."

"Terrific!" she said. "I'll ask my dad to drive us over."

"Okay," he said.

She turned to go find her bike, but he reached out and caught her hand and pulled her back.

"Still love me?" he asked.

"Uh-huh," she said in a breathy whisper. "Much as ever. More."

"Maybe next Saturday night we'll—" he started to say but broke off.

"Saturday night we'll what?" she asked provocatively.

They both knew what he meant. He was now ready to go all the way. She was not one of the sluts. But there was no doubt, based on what had happened between them, on what little had been said, that she was ready, and he was not. She had even told him that her mother had given her instructions in how to take care of herself in the event it did happen. That was as good as receiving permission.

He watched her get on her bike, wheel about, wave enticingly, and roll out of the parking lot. He climbed onto his own bike, determined not to disappoint her. Next Saturday night, he decided, would be the night.

He arrived home. Lily had been there, had done her usual efficient cleaning, and was gone. Good! He would be alone in the house. He needed access to those pills, which his mother guarded so zealously. They were in the same cabinet where she kept her vitamin pills and the stress pills she had had Dr. Rissom prescribe for his dad, which his dad never took.

His own pills, his lithium salts, were one among many little plastic bottles that lined the shelf. He popped the cap, poured a dozen into his hand, and stopped. He suddenly realized that he had gone about his plan in the wrong way. Those pills he had furtively flushed down the toilet, he needed them now. Those pills he had discarded with his sandwich wrapper, the ones his mother always tucked into his lunch box so neatly in waxed paper, he needed those now. Else, if he were to double up tomorrow and Sunday, his mother would surely notice that the pills were being rapidly and strangely depleted. She would become suspicious. She would question him.

If it did become an issue, he would have to brazen it out. But from now on, whenever he skipped his regular dosage, he would accumulate the pills, take them all at double-up time, and no one would ever suspect.

He must start now to make up, trusting that by Monday he would have restored the lithium level in his blood to the required concentration.

As he swallowed two pills, he heard Mom's Mercedes pull into the garage. He had to take an extra slug of water, for the pills stuck in his throat. He was unable to answer when his mother called from the garage, "Robbie, you home?"

A moment to force the pills down, and he called back, "Yeah, Mom."

"How did you make out?" she asked as she came through the door, loaded down with two heavy brown bags from the supermarket.

"I made it," he said, lifting the bags out of her arms.

"Good." She kissed him as a reward. "I knew you would. Though I could tell you were worried. You thought your pills would interfere, but they didn't, did they?"

"No," he said, turning away to set down the bags. "They didn't."

He had never mastered the ability to deceive her while looking into her eyes. If she had not been so relieved that he had made the squad, she might have been more discerning and noticed his evasion. But she had been greatly concerned that a failure might trigger a new episode. Belmond had warned that in Robbie's kind of case disappointments could precipitate new depressions.

CHAPTER 34

Robbie biked straight from practice to Dr. Rissom's office for his blood test. After his early visits, which used to occur three times a week, Claire had given up driving him, a sign of her increasing confidence.

Both Belmond and Rissom agreed. "If we want Robbie to act maturely, we must treat him as a mature individual."

He was particularly tense on this day, reluctant, almost unwilling, to surrender his arm to Rissom's attractive young nurse so she could take a blood sample.

"A little tense today, aren't we?" she remarked.

"Exhausted," Robbie said. "We had a tough practice session. That won't affect my blood level, will it?" he asked, preparing his excuse if the results did not measure up to Belmond's expectations.

"I don't think so," the young woman said. "You've done well so far. We'll wait for the lab report."

All the way home he was troubled by her observation. Did he appear tense because he was covering up his deception? Or was his tension due to staggering his lithium in violation of his prescribed routine? He would have to wait out the results.

Dr. Fred Rissom leaned forward in his chair, studying the lab report which his nurse had placed on his desk. He said a soft "Damn," then turned and lifted his phone. "Get me Dr. Belmond!"

He waited impatiently until he heard her voice. "Sabrina? I am sitting here looking at Robbie Ward's lab report. Something is wrong. After weeks of a good steady lithium level suddenly it shoots up. Have you changed his dose without telling me?"

"Of course not, Fred."

"Something's wrong," he repeated with great concern. "Terribly wrong. I just hope it hasn't reached a dangerous stage."

"He's due here tomorrow afternoon. Get that report over to me. I'll find out what's wrong!" she said determinedly.

Robbie sat across from her. She appeared the same as always. Neat, pleasant, her gray-streaked black hair framing her strongly featured face, she listened with a benign attitude, nodding from time to time as Robbie reported on the events of the past week.

". . . so I was even more determined I was going to make that final squad. Anybody get in my way I was going around him or through him with that ball. Twice I dribbled behind my back and drew fouls. Made 'em both. Once, when Scott had position, I faked him out and dribbled right by him. That time I didn't even pass off but went in for the lay-up myself. I was hot. Real hot!"

Belmond smiled, nodded, pretending to enjoy his exultation. "It felt like the old days. Right, Robbie?"

"Yeah! Yeah, like the old days." He agreed.

Whereupon Belmond's smile slowly dissolved into a grave look of concern. "It *was* like the old days, wasn't it?" When he did not reply at once, she insisted, "Robbie?"

He started to turn away, as he would have with his mother.

"Robbie?" Belmond waited until he turned to face her once more. "Want to tell me about it?" She allowed him time to respond. When he did not, she drew a sheet from a leather folio on her desk. He knew at once what it was. He had seen it from this same angle before. The lab report.

"Dr. Rissom was very disturbed by these results. So am I."

He felt sweat begin to ooze from his forehead. His chest, which earlier in the day had run hot with the sweat of physical exertion, now felt cold and damp.

"I had to do it," he blurted out, "else I never would have made the squad. Never."

"What did you do, Robbie? Skip your dose?"

He nodded.

"When? For how long?"

He told her. She could conclude the rest. "And then you doubled up over the weekend?"

He nodded once more.

"Didn't Dr. Rissom explain to you? Isn't it clear in my printed instructions? If you skip a dose, *never, never* double up."

He turned away.

"Robbie, this medication can be your greatest friend or your worst enemy. Don't abuse it. It can have far worse side effects than any you might have experienced thus far. You could go into seizures, like epileptic fits. It might even be fatal. *Yes, fatal.* Do you understand?"

"Yes, yes," he said softly.

"Now, what made you do it?"

He explained his fear of not making the squad. Of Scott Andrews beating him out. He blamed the pills for slowing him down. For robbing him of that extra step he had always had on Scott. So for the tryouts he had decided to avoid them.

"And it worked," he insisted, "it worked!"

Belmond shook her head and said very firmly, "No, Robbie, it didn't work."

He interrupted. "But it says right on your instruction sheet there can be side effects—weakness, muscle twitching, difficulty walking, even."

"Not on the mild dose you're taking." Belmond corrected him. "The effect was all in your mind. You blame the pills for everything you did wrong. You didn't take into account your nervousness at not making the cut. Your overeagerness. The possibility that this boy Scott might have been playing over his head on one particular day. It could have been a dozen other things. But your mind fixed on only one thing. The pills. So when you cut them out, you thought: *Now, now I can be my old self again.* And just feeling that way gave you extra energy, that one step you felt you were missing. Renewed confidence, not avoiding the pills, is what did it. Do you understand?"

Robbie nodded.

"If you go on believing that you can improve your athletic ability by manipulating your pill taking, you will be tempted to do it again. Before some special game. Or if you feel that the coach is losing confidence in you. Or if you have a bad game or two. Everyone who plays any sport regularly has a bad day every so often. Even Doctor J will come down the court, do one of his fancy midair maneuvers, evade all the defenders, and then fail on the dunk."

Robbie's eyes reflected his surprise at Belmond's knowledge of the game and its heroes. She smiled. "I have a son just a little older than you. He plays basketball, too. He's on the squad at Princeton."

"He is?" Robbie was impressed to learn that.

"When he's home and not studying or listening to rock, he's watching the NBA," she said. "Nowadays he has discovered classical music. So he listens to rock less and watches basketball less. Which is a great relief. But he still can't resist the play-offs."

Her confession seemed to restore the closeness and mutuality that had existed between them before Robbie's deception.

"You mean that those pills won't affect my play at all? Ever?"

"I mean, Robbie, that neither Dr. Rissom nor I can answer that question if the words *at all* and *ever* are in it. We can't give you any blanket promise. But even if it means you have to taper off on competitive sports for the benefit of your future life, it is worth it. You are a bright young man, yes, brilliant. Don't endanger that for the sake of shooting a ball into a basket. There is more to life. Think of it that way. And promise me you will not do this ever again. It can be dangerous."

He nodded. It was as good as his promise.

"Now, if there's nothing else . . ." Belmond said. It was her usual way of either ending a session or else evoking from him those last-minute questions that he might have been reluctant to raise before.

"Well, I . . ." He was tempted to ask her about the effect of the pills on his sexual urges.

"Robbie? Anything?"

"No." He decided not to ask finally.

He had heard other guys talk, the ones who had been to shrinks. They said once you opened the subject of sex with them, it almost always led to talk about being gay and the like. Since he had vague fears that his shyness with Susan might be related to that, he refrained from mentioning it to anyone. It made him only more determined that Saturday night would be the night on which he would prove to himself and to her and anyone else who wondered about it that he was not gay.

He left Belmond's office with two resolves: He would not tamper with his pill routine again, and Saturday night would be the night.

CHAPTER 35

Saturday night. For Robbie and Susan an evening of vigorous dancing, joking, little hints, and squeezes. They were finally at the top of what all the guys called Makeout Hill in Wally Converse's car. Robbie and Susan in the back seat. Wally and Aimee Foster in the front. Wally was Robbie's teammate on the squad and the only one old enough to drive legally.

At first, mingled with rock music on the radio, there was the usual nervous joking among the four of them. But then, except for sighs and whispers, a sultry quiet settled over the car. Between Robbie and Susan there were kisses, reachings, touching, increasing hot desire, body straining against body. He was aware of and familiar with every curve and outline of her body. Finally his own body was straining almost to the point of bursting. With her moist mouth open to him and with her body beneath him positioned, as he knew it had to be, he was ready for the moment he had been desiring yet avoiding all these long weeks. He knew one thing about himself now: He wanted her. In that moment he wanted her more than he had ever wanted anything in his entire life.

She was helping him with his zipper when suddenly there was a blare of sirens. The whole hill came ablaze with harsh, glaring searchlights. Angry voices on bullhorns issued orders. The headlights of all the other cars lit up as if on command. Makeout Hill seemed to be under siege.

Robbie felt his burning desire slowly shrink into guilty flaccidness. Susan wriggled free from underneath him to straighten her dress and attempt to pull it down to some presentable length. A man preceded by the strong beam of a powerful flashlight was poking into the car, examining each face. Susan tried to hide. Robbie blinked at the strong light, which assaulted him suddenly after the total darkness.

As his eyes adjusted to the harsh light, Robbie was able to distinguish the uniform of a police officer.

"We didn't do anything," Robbie protested at once.

"That's okay, kid. We're not after anyone up here. We got an alert that there was some nut on the loose. Rapist. Armed. So the word is get off the hill. Find some other place to have your fun."

The light went out. They were in the dark again. Whatever had been their hot, feverish desires moments earlier had been totally dissipated. Fear of a rapist, an armed rapist, had replaced all other thoughts in their young minds.

"Maybe he's the same one who killed that computer operator they found just off the parkway last week," Susan said, whispering fearfully.

"Yeah, maybe," Aimee said. "I want to go home."

"Home. Yeah." Susan agreed.

Wally dropped them in front of Susan's house. There were lights on in the upstairs bedroom, which meant her folks were still awake. Her parents' rule, strictly enforced, was that her door was always to be open when she was not alone in her room. And the living room was far too open and vulnerable, being in full view from the stairs. There was no safe, secret place in this house for Robbie and Susan tonight.

He kissed her at the door, his hardness pressed against her. But she said a soft but forbidding "Uh-uh. Not here. Not tonight."

"That was scary up there. All those lights and sirens. And that thing about a rapist."

"Yeah." Susan agreed.

But their talk was merely evasive. So he said, "Sorry."

" 'S all right," she said, but they both knew it wasn't.

"If that damned cop hadn't shown up . . ."

"I know," she said, then added, "Except if you'd been faster . . ."

"Gee, how fast was I supposed to be? You never said—never said you were ready."

"The man is supposed to know those things. He shouldn't have to be told. That's what it says—"

"Says where?"

"In all the books," she replied impatiently, betraying her disappointment.

"Not in the sex ed book we got from school, nothing in there about a man supposed to guess when a girl is ready."

"Other books," she said angrily. "Gee, Robbie, what's wrong with you lately? You're not the same anymore."

"What do you mean, I'm not the same?" he demanded. "It never happened before, and it never happened tonight, so what's not the same?"

"Before you were . . . more exciting, different. You used to do crazy things, exciting things. Now you're like—like dullsville. Like tonight. I can tell you now, I was ready a long time before you were. You just didn't . . . I don't know, Robbie. I think maybe we just ought to be friends. . . ."

There was no more devastating end to a youthful romance than that. "Let's just be friends" meant that any sexual relationship, actual or in contemplation, was over. That even friendship was most unlikely.

"Yeah," Robbie said, hurt as well as angry. "Let's do that. Friends!"

He turned away, started down the walk and went the rest of the way home, kicking at the ground, cursing to himself, blaming those damn pills for having slowed him down sexually, too, so that whatever secret signal she was supposed to have given him, he had missed it.

No matter what Belmond or Rissom said, those damned pills were taking over his whole life. They had almost cost him his place on the team. They had cost him Susan. How much more would they deprive him of? He could be facing years of being hobbled by the effects of those pills. He would be like Benjy Moss, that kid in sixth grade, who had diabetes and had to have special food and was always being watched so carefully by his teachers because at any moment he could have some kind of spell or something. Once he did have one, right in class. They had to feed him orange juice in a hurry before he came around.

Am I going to be like that for the rest of my life? Robbie pondered. *No, not me,* he decided angrily. *Not me!*

Following a call from Dr. Belmond, Claire was more alert and exacting about Robbie's pills. She insisted on seeing him take his morning pill at the breakfast table. At dinner, even when they ate out, she made sure that Robbie took his evening pill in her presence. The only one left to chance was his midday dose. He was able to skip those without being detected. Whenever Claire questioned him, he was quick to answer, "Of course I took it. You didn't find it in my lunch box, did you?"

She had worked out her own method for keeping a balance in his young body between water intake and salt. She simply added more salt to every recipe. If it was not recommended for adults like Don and her, she had decided that by comparison, the harm to them was less than it would be to Robbie if his salt or fluid dropped below the level essential to accommodate his lithium.

She continued to supervise his pill taking so vigilantly that he rebuked her for being a combination of the KGB and the CIA. Ofttimes he accused her of watching him when she was busily occupied with other things.

Though she disliked the strain it put on their relationship, she accepted that the responsibility devolved on her and her alone. For Don was now clearly established as Ed Brady's successor as president of the network. The one remaining step in the corporate shuffle was a shake-up in the top executive echelon of the parent company so that Brady would move up to being chief executive officer. Once that had happened, Don Ward would succeed to the job for which he had sacrificed so much of his life and their lives.

In recent months all his time was spent with Brady, virtually day and night. Brady wanted him to learn every facet of the job of president. That was not a charitable act on Brady's part. For when he moved up, the earnings of the network, twenty-two to twenty-four percent of the profit of the entire entertainment complex, would be crucial in measuring his success as president of the parent company.

Don was now away more often and for longer stretches. He was included in all executive meetings of the parent company. At Brady's side virtually every moment, he handed him reports, figures, ratings, competitive studies of all three networks, planned programs and series, pilots in work, pilot scripts assigned, their progress, casting plans, stars signed for specials, movies of the week now shooting, those in postproduction, commitments to stars, commitments from stars. Whatever Brady referred to in the course of any meeting, Don was by his side, slipping him a folder, a file, a list, a fact sheet.

The Ward home had become, for all practical purposes, a single-parent household. Don was so deeply involved that when he called, as he still did every afternoon at five, whether in New York or on the Coast, Claire told him little, in order to say nothing that would cause him any worry. She never did tell him of Robbie's deviation from his pill routine. It was over now. There was nothing Don could have done except reprimand Robbie, and she had already done that.

She decided to handle all problems by herself so as not to distract or disturb Don in these, the most crucial weeks of his career. Once he was ensconced as president, things would be different. He would be master of his own time.

It had taken relentless bird-dogging by Don's secretary, Jeannie, who hounded the dealer, the distributor, and the main plant out in California to make sure that the new eighteen-foot Hobie Cat was delivered in time for Robbie Ward's sixteenth birthday.

In mid-March the boat, in knocked-down condition, with its multistriped Cat Fever sail, was delivered to the Soundside Marina on the Connecticut shore of Long Island Sound.

The week before Robbie's birthday Don arranged for the two of them to go out and supervise the assembly and the launching of the craft. But the night before, Don had to fly out to Denver, where the affiliate channel was rumored to be considering switching to one of the other networks. That would have been a disastrous, possibly even fatal, blow to Brady's ambitions. So Don was forced to call the marina, order it to assemble the boat, and put it into the water to await Robbie's birthday, when he and his son would come up for the christening and for Robbie's first lesson in handling so large a craft.

Claire had made all the plans. Her two men would go up to the marina. Robbie would have his first sail in his new boat. When they returned, her mother would join them for cocktails and then dinner at La Crémaillère in Banksville, where she had arranged with the maître d' for a birthday cake. Robbie's favorite, a rich chocolate mousse cake. And as a surprise she had invited Susan and her mother and father. After the difficulties of the past few months Claire was determined that her son's sixteenth birthday would encompass all the favorite things and people in his life.

From brief snatches of Robbie's end of telephone conversations she was vaguely aware of some strain in the relationship between Robbie and Susan. But she was confident such a night of celebration would patch things up.

The afternoon of Robbie's birthday. He waited anxiously for his father to return from New York. Just after the appointed time of three o'clock there was the sound of a car pulling up in the garage. Robbie leaped to the door, calling, "Dad?" Claire turned to the door expectantly, too.

It was only the delivery man from Au Maison, a small, expensive bakeshop in town that specialized in fancy hors d'oeuvres for at-home entertaining. He brought two cartons full of their finest. Once Claire had paid him and he was gone, Robbie seemed even more depressed than before.

"He said this time he'd positively be here. He promised."

"Robbie, I'm sure your father must have a good reason for being late." Claire tried to console him.

"That's the best thing about my dad. He always has a good reason for being late. Or not showing up at all."

"It's the nature of his business. Especially these days. You know what's going on at the network. The executive changes."

"Why the hell doesn't he go into some other business? One that makes more sense!"

"Now, Robbie," Claire began sternly, "you know that without your father's job—"

Robbie picked up the familiar refrain. "I know. We wouldn't have a private school, two Mercedes, charge accounts at all the expensive restaurants. He's great with everything except keeping promises!"

Frustrated at being forced to contain her own anger with Don, she was doubly harsh with her son.

"He promised you a new eighteen-foot cat if you followed Dr. Belmond's orders. And he got it for you. They don't give those away, you know. They cost money. Lots of money!"

"So what?" Robbie challenged. "What good is a big, expensive eighteen-foot cat if it just sits there in the water? It takes two to sail it. And today's the day he was going to start teaching me. So where is he?"

"There's still enough daylight left," Claire pointed out. "He'll be here. Don't worry."

"Sure," Robbie said in a desultory manner that rejected his mother's assurances.

Almost half an hour had elapsed. Claire had tried to occupy herself by arranging the hors d'oeuvres on flat bakers' tins and placed them in the oven ready to warm up in time for cocktails. Robbie sat staring grimly at the clock on the dinette wall.

Finally he exploded, "I told you he's not going to be here!"

"He will," Claire insisted.

"It'll be like last weekend when he had to fly out to Denver!" Then he confessed softly, "I—I biked down to the marina last Sunday."

"All that way?" Claire asked. "It's almost twenty miles each way."

"Twenty-four and a half," Robbie admitted. "I wanted to see my boat finally. She's a beauty. And what a sail! You could pick that sail out anywhere on the Sound. I was itching to take her out. But Mr. Hazlitt, he's the owner of the marina, he said it needed more weight to right her if she went over. And also I needed more experience. So I just sat there, polishing her pontoons with my sweater. But I thought surely today—"

The phone interrupted.

"That's Dad!" Claire anticipated. "Tell him I'll drive you to the marina. It'll save time if he meets us up there."

"Hello!" Robbie answered enthusiastically. "Dad? Yeah. Oh,

oh, I see." His voice sagged suddenly. "Sure, sure, I understand. Yes, Dad. Next week. Yeah. Right, next week the weather'll probably be warmer. Yeah, I know. Sure, Dad, sure."

He hung up the phone. If he were nine, he would be crying. As it was, she saw his blue eyes film over.

"He can't make it?" Claire asked.

Robbie shook his head; talking was too difficult.

"What happened?"

"Something about a sudden meeting with Brady. About some figures for the parent company. What difference does it make? He's not coming."

"Robbie, I could drive you to the marina. You could see your cat. Maybe talk to Mr. Hazlitt. Get some advance pointers on how to sail her. How about that?"

"I didn't want that boat to talk about. I wanted her to sail," he said. Then, disappointment turning to anger, he said, "Look! Do me a big favor? Cancel the cocktails. Cancel the dinner! Cancel everything! Including my adoption!"

He burst out of the room. He climbed the stairs in a fury. She heard his door slam. In a moment she heard his door open once more. She heard him shout, "Happy birthday, Robbie Ward! Happy birthday!"

His door slammed shut again. Soon she heard him playing one of his rock tapes so loudly and aggressively that the house shook.

CHAPTER 36

It was Friday afternoon. Another league tournament game. Canaan had already won its first three. This fourth one was against Hillside, the same team that had beaten them for the football championship because of Robbie's ill-fated forward pass. The same end who had intercepted that pass was a guard on the Hillside team. So Robbie was more eager to win this game than any other.

To insure that he would be in peak form, he had begun to skip his midday pills on Monday. Today he even tried to palm his breakfast pill, but Claire detected that and made him take it with his orange juice. Out of sheer perversity he pretended to choke on it.

She added an extra caution when she wrapped his midday pill and placed it in with his lunch. She handed him the box, kissed him, and said, "Come straight home after the game." He nodded and left.

She watched from the front window as he went tearing down the driveway on his bike. She thought: *Two years from now he'll be doing that in a sports car. Before we know it, he'll be off to college.*

He was impatient to get through the schoolday. Every class was a bore, even science and math, which he really liked. But not today. He was determined to show Hillside and everyone.

He was first into the locker room, first into his basketball jersey and shorts, pulling up his long wool socks with the crimson and gold stripes, double-knotting the laces of his basketball shoes so they could not come loose to trip him. He raced out onto the floor, grabbed a ball from the team manager, began to dribble up and downcourt, at first slowly, then with increasing pace and changing direction, finally dribbling behind his back. He had adopted a complete routine which he executed religiously before every game. Once he had warmed up, he went to the side of the basket to practice his one-handed jump shot, though scoring was not considered his forte. He was the brains, the playmaker, the steady hand with the ball, while the others did the scoring. "Good hands," Coach McNaughton always said, "Robbie Ward sure has good hands."

From the first jump-off it was obvious it would be a tough game this afternoon. Hillside Academy had a physically big team. What they lacked in finesse and speed, they more than made up for in height and weight. They were tough under the baskets, coming off with more than their share of rebounds. With fewer opportunities the Canaan players had to make good on a higher percentage of their shots. Robbie had to be more cautious in the way he handled the ball. He had to guard against any of those larger men taking the ball away from him on the dribble. He had to be more precise and careful when he passed off to Converse or Linburn. A number of times he chose to pass to his guards because Linburn and Converse were so effectively covered by even taller Hillside men.

In an effort to slow Robbie down and throw him off stride, the Hillside guard subjected him to constant physical harassment until he was forced to signal McNaughton that he needed to be substituted for, so he could recover. McNaughton sent in Scott. But on the second play Scott, under pressure, threw the ball away. Hillside took over and scored, putting them in the lead. McNaughton sent Robbie back in, even before he had caught his breath or been able to down some badly needed water.

He played out the half and was relieved that they came off the court only one point behind. The second half would be even tougher since Hillside's superior size and weight were beginning to wear down Robbie and his teammates.

In the locker room McNaughton outlined on the blackboard

three additional formations they had not used against Hillside, two offensive plays and one new pressing defense.

"Let's put our speed against them," he said, "harry them, make them cough up the ball. Converse, Linburn, you two stay out from under the basket to draw their big men out and cut down their rebounding. Robbie, that puts more pressure on you and the two guards to do the rebounding. But it's the only way we can counter their size and weight advantage."

Intent on studying the new formations, Robbie paid no attention to the team manager, who kept urging cups of water on the sweaty, dehydrated players.

Robbie was eager to get out on the floor for the second half. But McNaughton stopped him, wiped his sweaty face with a fresh towel. "You okay, Robbie?"

"Never better."

"Good. Because this game is in your hands."

"Don't worry, Mr. McNaughton, I owe those bastards one," Robbie said. He trotted out on the floor to take one of the balls and start shooting one-handed jumps from the side.

The warm-up over, the game resumed. Converse was able to tap the ball on the jump-off. Robbie took over, resumed control of the game, started dribbling down the floor. With the two big Hillside men kept outside, Robbie passed off to one of his guards, then started in, took a return pass, and was under the basket in position to shoot. He made the shot, regaining the lead by one point. The coach's new tactic succeeded. If it increased the burden on the smaller men, it put even greater pressure on Hillside. The main thing, it worked.

Canaan succeeded in getting a greater share of rebounds, which meant more plays for Robbie to set in motion and direct. He began to feel the elation he used to love in the old days on the football field. The sense of being in command. Directing the others, giving signals with his left hand while dribbling with his right. Setting up his men, Converse and Linburn, faking to go in but then pulling up short to keep the big Hillside men out. Thus letting Robbie or one of the guards slip into scoring position.

By the end of the third quarter they had stretched their lead to six points. Hillside, feeling the pressure, was beginning to foul, a sign of their frustration with the new Canaan attack. Robbie enjoyed going to the foul line, where he was considered deadly, his one-handed shot a weapon of almost unerring accuracy.

He had scored three times from the foul line and was lining up for his fourth try. They had stretched their lead to eight points. The Hillside coach had put in a new man to guard Robbie, his original opponent being in foul trouble.

Robbie toed the foul line, bounced the ball six times, a ritual he had adopted, believing that any less than six did not relax him sufficiently, and any more than six overtaxed his concentration. On the sixth bounce he suddenly felt his hand go out of control. Rather than try the shot, he stepped back from the line, gripped the ball as hard as he could with both hands, seeking to steady them. The harder he pressed, the more weakness he sensed. Determined, he went back to the line and started to bounce the ball once more. One, two, three, four, five, six. Instead of shooting, he backed off again. McNaughton came up off the bench to stand even with the foul line.

Robbie started bouncing the ball once more, in rhythm, one, two, three, four, five, six. This time, because he was aware of McNaughton and his teammates staring at him, he let the ball fly, despite the unsteadiness in his right hand. The ball not only failed to touch the hoop, it never reached the backboard; instead, it sailed into the row of seats behind the basket.

Robbie stared down at his hands, clenched them, pressed them against his sweaty thighs in an effort to steady them. Hillside took the ball, passed in, worked it in close, and one of the big men scored easily. The ball went over to Canaan. It was passed into Robbie, a routine pass with no interference from the opposition. Robbie started to dribble toward center court. But after he had taken only three steps, the ball eluded his hand, skittering off to his right and out of court. A totally unforced turnover.

He felt both his hands start to tremble. The long muscles in his forearms began to twitch. He clenched his fists to conceal his difficulty. But McNaughton knew Robbie too well not to recognize these were bizarre reactions. He slapped Scott on the back, sending him out onto the floor to replace Robbie.

Robbie looked to the bench. He shook his head, refusing to come off. McNaughton gestured firmly, ordering him to the sidelines. Robbie continued to resist. McNaughton called a timeout. Though all his teammates came to the bench, Robbie refused.

McNaughton went out onto the floor.

"Robbie, come on! You need a rest! You're exhausted!" Still, he refused to move. "You've already cost us an unnecessary time-out. You don't want to cost us a technical foul as well. Do you? Now come on!" McNaughton insisted.

"I can't," Robbie said.

"What do you mean, you can't?" McNaughton asked, greatly concerned.

"If I come off now, I won't ever come back," Robbie replied, unaware of what he was saying.

McNaughton placed his hands on Robbie's sweaty shoulders, stared into his eyes. "Robbie, what is it?"

"What is what?" Robbie demanded impatiently, as if not he but McNaughton were talking strangely. Then a wave of nausea swept over him. He brought his hand to his mouth to prevent it, but it was too late. The bitter, smelly green mess was pouring from his mouth, overflowing his hand, dripping down the front of his damp jersey.

He shrugged off McNaughton's hand, raced toward the dressing room, noticing as he passed the grandstand that Susan was there, watching, a witness to his disgrace.

Once inside the dressing room he regurgitated so violently he felt that his stomach would be ripped out of him. When the siege was over, he sank to the floor and lay there, exhausted, in a cold sweat and covered with his own foul mess. He heard the door open. Instead of looking to see who it was, he curled into a tight ball, attempting to shield himself from view. He heard footsteps approach him. He heard McNaughton speak to him, softly and with great concern. "Robbie, what is it? Are you sick? Are you in pain? What happened?"

"The game . . . you better go," Robbie protested.

"Forget the game," McNaughton said, "I want to know what's wrong. What did you eat?"

"Nothing!" Robbie exploded. "Just leave me alone!"

"I can't leave you alone. Get up; take a shower; get into your clothes. We're going to see your doctor. Robbie! Robbie, get up!"

"It's nothing," Robbie protested. "I know what it is, and it's nothing."

"I want to hear that from your doctor," McNaughton insisted. "Robbie!"

The stricken boy refused to move. The coach reached out, gripped his arms, and lifted him up. He saw the boy's tears and sympathized. In the most vulnerable time in a young person's life, those teen years, when nothing that happened was ever of minor importance, Robbie Ward had been disgraced and embarrassed before the opposition, before his teammates, before the entire student body.

However emotionally traumatic that might be, to McNaughton the more serious concern was the state of his health. If Robbie had not been a leader and a control player since his sophomore year, McNaughton might have attributed this unfortunate episode to nerves. But not this boy. Not Robbie Ward. He was too mature, mature beyond his sixteen years. He had always been too steady, too in control for nerves alone to cause this. It must have a different and more deep-seated basis.

"Robbie, the doctor who signed your athletic eligibility form, wasn't that Rissom?" McNaughton asked. "Robbie?" When the boy refused to answer, the coach said, "I'm going to take you to a doctor, Robbie. It would be better if he were your own."

"Yeah, Rissom." Robbie finally confirmed it.

Robbie submitted himself to Rissom's general examination. As Rissom took Robbie's pulse, blood pressure, listened to his heartbeat, peered into his eyes, he made little concerned sounds that hinted at discoveries he did not reveal either to Robbie or to McNaughton.

Meantime, he commented, almost to himself, "Threw up, did you?" He did not wait for an answer but rechecked Robbie's pulse, listened again to his heart. Then he took his blood pressure again.

Another taciturn "Uh-huh," and Rissom asked, "Robbie, are you taking any of those gimmick medications young athletes think are going to make them into supermen?"

"No, sir."

"Then it can only be one thing," Rissom concluded. "Robbie, have you been taking your lithium regularly?"

"Uh . . . more or less," Robbie said.

"Robbie, you know damn well that 'more or less' is not regularly. In fact, more or less is downright dangerous. I've told you that. Dr. Belmond's told you that. What have you been doing lately?" Rissom asked, his sharp eyes peering from behind his glasses to demand a specific answer.

Robbie had no alternative but to confess to Rissom how he had juggled his dosage to conform to the demands of his basketball schedule.

"Figures," Rissom said gravely. "Irregular heartbeat. Tremors of the hands. Likelihood of thyroid abnormality. Robbie, never fool around with any medication. Especially that one. Too little one time, too much another. The idea that if some medicine is good, more is better has killed more patients than even the negligence of doctors. I'll talk to your mother."

"Please don't!" Robbie begged.

"Got to, Robbie. For your own sake. But I'll tell you what I'm going to tell her. What I think happened is this: You've got your system so hyped up from taking too little sometimes and too much others that it's out of whack. And today, during the game, when Coach tells me you played a tough first half and didn't drink anything, you got dehydrated besides. Nothing'll bring on the side effects of lithium faster than dehydration. It hit your stomach, and you threw up. Nothing serious, *if* you don't continue to abuse your lithium. I do have to tell her that, Robbie."

Rissom looked at the tense sixteen-year-old who stared up at him from the white metal stool. He could read the boy's inner torment from the look in his eyes.

"But telling her isn't going to solve your problem, is it?" Rissom asked. "You threw up like a sick little kid. So you feel you've disgraced yourself in front of the whole school. And maybe there was a girl or two out there, a girl you've been trying to impress. So now you feel your whole life is over. Well, it isn't, Robbie. We've all done worse. And lived to tell of it. My advice is: Go home; confide in your mom what you've been doing. And never do it again. And I think you'll outlive this and a hell of a lot more."

"But it was awful." Robbie tried to explain. "All that stuff gushing out and I couldn't stop it—it just—"

"Robbie, believe me, more people in that crowd felt sorry for you than looked down on you. I'll bet most of them felt, *Tough break; with Robbie Ward out of the game there goes our chance to win.* Right, Coach?"

"Right!" McNaughton agreed.

"You're the only one who felt it was a cause for shame. Now, let me take a blood sample and send it out to the lab for a rush reading. Find out what's really going on inside you. Then I'll call your mom."

McNaughton drove Robbie home. When Claire saw him get out of the coach's car, her instant reaction was to look for bandages, a cast. When she saw neither, she was even more alarmed. Breaks, fractures, bad muscle tears were not uncommon or necessarily dangerous injuries for young athletes. But unseen troubles immediately registered as more life-threatening. Especially since the afternoon three years ago, when a youngster at Canaan Prep had keeled over during early football practice and died of an undetected heart condition. She flung open the door, raced down the circular driveway, calling, "Robbie! Robbie! What happened?"

"Nothing, Mom. Nothing."

She ignored his disclaimer. "Mr. McNaughton, what happened?"

"He's okay now. He'll tell you. So will Dr. Rissom."

"You had to take him to the doctor?" Claire asked, even more alarmed.

"Just to check him out. He's all right now."

"All right *now?*" Claire responded. "What about before? Why did you have to take him to see Rissom?"

"Mom, please, don't make a scene," Robbie begged, with the usual oversensitivity of teenagers.

"You had to go to the doctor. The coach had to drive you home. And you're asking me not to make a scene? Well, I damn well will make a scene until someone explains what this is all about!"

"Mrs. Ward," McNaughton interceded, "do as Robbie says. No scene. Give him a chance to tell you. Then call Dr. Rissom. Meantime, your son is not in any danger, believe me."

Impatiently at first, Claire listened as Robbie explained his unfortunate experience on the court. Then she embraced him.

"You must have been terribly embarrassed, darling. Well, don't worry about it. Your real friends will understand. Those who won't are not worth having as friends."

It was small consolation for a highly sensitive young man of sixteen. Abruptly Robbie withdrew from her embrace. There was such an air of decision about the manner in which he did it that Claire asked, "Robbie?"

"I am never going to take those pills again," he said in a low, firm voice that bespoke irreversible determination.

"We'd better talk to Dr. Rissom and Belmond about that."

"I'm not talking to anyone about it. I've made up my mind!"

"Robbie!"

"I'm not. No one can make me!" he insisted.

He barged out of the room. Despite the thick, luxurious carpeting, she heard his heavy aggressive steps mount the stairs. She heard his door slam shut. She hesitated for only an instant, reached for the phone, touched the numbers she had come to know quite well in recent months. She was rewarded only with a recorded announcement that Dr. Belmond was engaged at the moment and would call when she was free.

Claire waited impatiently, debating whether to go up to his room and try to convince him to reverse his decision. But experience had taught her that so soon after such a strong declaration as he had made, it was useless. Tomorrow perhaps or several days from now, she might revive the discussion with some hope of convincing him.

She called Dr. Rissom. He told her of his findings, his warning to Robbie.

"Doctor, he says he won't ever take his medication again."

"Frankly, Claire, between taking it the way he's been doing and not taking it at all, I don't know which is worse." Then he added, "He's got to take it! Belmond, you, Don, I, we've got to work on him. He's too great a young man for us to let slip into his extreme moods again. It could be dangerous, Claire, very dangerous. Especially after such an embarrassing disappointment as he suffered today."

CHAPTER 37

Claire had deliberately refrained from making other calls to keep the line open for Dr. Belmond. But the doctor failed to call. Claire had to fight her compulsion to phone Don. She stifled the impulse by reminding herself that he was due to call any moment now. It was just past five. Meaning just past two o'clock Coast time, when he usually returned from one of his business lunches in order to call home at five New York time. People who worked with Don, even Ed Brady, knew that and made allowances for it. Screenings of new pilots were never scheduled until two-fifteen, after Don Ward had made his faithful call home.

She resolved to wait until five-thirty. Seven minutes before five-thirty she could no longer restrain herself. She dialed the network offices in Hollywood. Don was not there and had left no message. She dialed the Beverly Hills Hotel. She asked for Mr. Ward, Don Ward.

"I'm sorry," the operator announced in her professional lilt, "but Mr. Ward is no longer registered here."

"What do you mean, he's no longer registered?" Claire demanded. "I happen to know he's there. And it's important I talk to him."

"I'm sorry, madam, but our records show that he checked out this morning."

"He couldn't have checked out this morning," Claire insisted.

"He is due to stay there until Friday evening!"

"I'll connect you with the front desk. That's the best I can do," the operator announced in a cool, detached manner.

"Front desk. May I help you?" the voice of a young, eager male clerk responded.

"Ward. Don Ward?" Claire said.

"Yes, madam. What about Mr. Ward?"

"Your operator tells me that he checked out. There must be some mistake."

"No mistake, madam. I was at the desk early this morning when he checked out."

"Is he on his way back to New York?" Claire asked.

"No, madam. Mr. Ward has moved to the Bel-Air for the rest of the week," the clerk informed her. Then, as if to cast some doubt on Don's motives, he added, "At least that's what he said."

"I see," Claire replied, the last remark creating strong suspicions about Don's strange conduct. Why would Don have moved suddenly from the Beverly Hills to the Bel-Air? And not told her? Only one reason. Privacy. The Beverly Hills, with its crowded pool area, hectic Polo Lounge, busy front entrance, was no place for secrecy. Everyone in the business knew what everyone else was doing and with whom. But the Bel-Air, secluded, and with its spread-out private rooms and bungalows, was the place where a man seeking to have a discreet affair could shack up and run little risk of being detected.

She spun the rotary phone index Don kept alongside each phone in the house. In his methodical but impatient way Don never liked to be frustrated when he was searching for some actor, actress, producer, director, or agent. He had all the numbers of all of them, even those of little importance. He also had the phone number of every hotel in or around Los Angeles, Palm Springs, and Las Vegas, where anyone in show business might be found. Don Ward was like Ed Brady in one respect. When he decided to do something, he was impatient, active, finger-snapping, hair-triggered, impatient.

Claire found the number. She dialed. The Bel-Air switchboard answered. "Mr. Ward? Mr. Don Ward of New York? Just a moment, madam."

Claire heard the ring. It seemed to keep ringing for an eternity.

Finally there was an answer. It was Don. He practically snarled his "Hello!"

Why not, she thought, I caught him in the act, really in the act.

"Remember me?" Claire demanded, her voice steely with hurt.

"Claire? Honey? What's wrong?"

"Maybe *you* can tell *me,*" she responded angrily.

"What are you talking about—" He paused. Then, as if he had just looked at his watch, he said, "God, I'm sorry. But we got so wrapped up in the scene that I forgot to call. I'm terribly sorry. . . ."

"You got so wrapped up in the scene, did you? I'm here in Connecticut with all kinds of trouble and you're hiding out in the Bel-Air, working on the 'scene.' What's she like, Don, that 'scene' of yours?"

"Claire! Claire, get hold of yourself! What's happened to you? What do you mean, 'all kinds of trouble'?"

Finally, in a disconnected way, she was able to articulate her problem with Robbie, about his threat to refuse any more pills. She also confessed her suspicions about Don.

"Listen," he said to mollify her, "I'm putting someone on the phone who'll explain."

"Mrs. Ward? Claire? I'm Abner Crystal. Maybe you've seen my credit on some comedy shows. *Suddenly It's Love* or *Family Affair?* or *What Did We Do Wrong?*"

Claire was not only familiar with Crystal's name, she asked, "Didn't you and your wife have dinner here at the house about four years ago?"

"Right!" Crystal said. "Didn't think you'd remember. Well, I'm in a jam, Mrs. Ward. The new series I'm developing for the network did not work out. Ed Brady blew his top. He not only canceled my deal but wants to make a big stink about it in the industry. Well, I can't stand that, Mrs. Ward, not at this time in my life. Because I may not get many more chances. Maybe not *any* more chances. You see, I'm . . . the doctors say I'm terminal. I am a man of forty-three and terminal, and Brady wants me to be funny, inventive, and fresh. I have a wife and two kids. The only thing I can leave them is a percentage in this new series I'm developing, which, if it works, could see them through school and college and maybe a little more. But my name has to be on that pilot script as 'developed by.' That's the key to my future percentage.

"So I confided in Don. And Don said, 'We'll hide out in the Bel-Air, where we can work in secrecy. We'll lick this story and make this the best damn pilot this business has seen in years.'

"And you know something, Mrs. Ward, he's done it. If he weren't such a three-piece-suit type, he'd be one of the best comedy writers in this business. Another day of polishing, and we'll have it. My name'll be on it. But it's his ideas. His ideas . . ."

She heard a gasp, then heard Crystal say, "Excuse me, please, Mrs. Ward."

In a moment Don came back on the line. "It wasn't necessary for Ab to tell you all that. And if the subject should ever come up, you don't know anything about it. Understand?"

"Yes, yes, of course. I'm sorry for what I said, and even more for what I thought."

"Now, about Robbie, don't worry, honey. I'll be home no later than Sunday morning, and I'll take care of everything."

"All right, darling, I'll wait. And I want to say—"

He interrupted. "You don't have to say it. I know how it must have sounded to hear that I moved to the Bel-Air. Now don't worry. Sunday!"

"Okay, darling. Sunday. I'm sure nothing much can happen in just a few days."

"I said, don't worry about it." Don comforted her.

She lowered her voice, fearing to be overheard. "Darling, about Ab, is that true? Terminal? At forty-three?"

Pretending to answer a quite different question, so Ab wouldn't suspect, Don replied, "Yes, yes, I paid that bill."

"Two kids?" she asked.

"And that one, too," Don answered.

"Oh, God," Claire whispered as she hung up.

"Come on, Ab, back to work," Don said. "The final scene, and we've got it."

"Right," Crystal said, "the final scene."

"Meantime, I'll get a secretary over here so she can start typing a next to final draft," Don said.

"Next to final?" Ab protested.

"Use your head, Ab. We can't say this is the final final. The network is going to want some input. Don't they always?" Don said, smiling.

"Man, now you're talking like a real writer," Ab said. "Okay, the next to final."

CHAPTER 38

It was just past midnight when the emergency typist pulled the last page out of the typewriter. She had typed steadily for nine and a half hours, handing over, page by page, the script of the half hour show so that Don and Ab could go over each page, make corrections, change lines, insert added laughs, added bits of comic business, hand them back to her so she could retype them. There had been four complaints from the occupants of the next suite about the late-night noise of the incessant typewriter. Despite that, Don and Ab worked continuously. Before Don would release the typist, they had her wait another two hours so they could go over the next to final draft. Once satisfied, Don dug into his pocket, pulled out his money clip, and peeled off fifty dollars.

"This is for you personally. Tell your typing service to send its regular bill to the network, my attention."

"Thanks, Mr. Ward. And good luck. It reads very funny to me," the typist said.

She was gone. They were alone, the two of them, Don Ward and Abner Crystal. Wearing forty-eight-hour growths of beard, they looked as if they'd been on a two-day binge. Ab sank down on the bed nearest the window, glanced out at the blue glow shining up through the water of the lighted Bel-Air swimming pool. Before the inevitable postpartum writers' depression could set in, Don said, "Let's go out to the bar and get a drink. Maybe two drinks. Three."

"Like this?" Ab asked, referring to the way they looked.

"Right. Shave. Shower. Then the bar," Don agreed. "You first."

While Ab shaved and showered, Don reread the script. It was good. It was fresh. It was funny. He could already cast it with two stars and two featured name players. It would work. Brady would like it. Love it.

While Don shaved and showered, Ab reread the script. He picked up two lines of dialogue he thought could be improved by being shortened. In comedy lines even syllables make a difference. When Don came out, slapping aftershave onto his handsome face, Ab said, "Don, there are two lines—"

"I know, I know," Don said. "I deliberately want them left that way. That'll give Brady his chance to show what a genius he is. He'll spot those two lines. You'll change them. And everybody'll be happy. Now for the bar."

Ab Crystal smiled and said, a bit apologetically, "Don, would you mind if we didn't go to the bar?"

"No. Why?"

"It's the strangest thing, but lately I get this tremendous yen for the foods I used to eat as a kid. Lox and bagels. Scrambled eggs and onions. What we used to call *heimisheh* food back in New York. I feel like that now."

"Nate and Al's?" Don suggested.

"Right," Ab agreed.

"You got it, kid!" Don said, starting for the door.

"Don, before we leave this room, I want to say something."

"Christ, after forty-eight hours aren't you all talked out?" Don joked.

"No, Don, this is serious. There're not many guys in this business would have done what you did."

"Ab, unless this is the setup to a very funny joke, forget it."

"I can't forget it. I'll remember this for the rest of my life. . . ." Then he smiled strangely. "Boy, that *is* a joke. Isn't it? Not a very good one, but a joke."

"Come on, Ab, let's go. Nate and Al's isn't open all night, you know."

* * *

They were driving toward Beverly Hills along Sunset and had stopped for a red light when Don said, "I know what it's like, what you do for your kids. I've got a boy, too. You do things for them you'd never do for yourself. Maybe that's why I did it, Ab."

They had had all the nostalgic food that Ab Crystal's ailing stomach could take. Then they went to the Polo Lounge at the Beverly Hills. Except for a young television star, whose eyes were glazed from either drink or cocaine and who was being hustled by a high-class call girl, the place was empty. The two bartenders were slowly polishing already polished glasses just waiting to close for the night when Don and Ab walked in. The young star stared at Don, finally recognized him, and waved.

Don waved back, smiling at him, then fixed his stare on the girl who was with him. She seemed to take the hint. She grabbed her purse and said, "Sorry, honey, got to go to the ladies' room."

As she passed them, Ab whispered to Don, "Boy, that's a euphemism if I ever heard one. Talk about funny."

"Come on, Ab, let's have one drink and get this young idiot out of here."

Together he and Ab took that young star home and put him to bed to sleep off whatever it was that had numbed his addled brain. They hoped he would recover to resume shooting on his series tomorrow. But Don had his doubts.

Don drove Ab to his home on Coldwater Canyon. The lights were still on. Ab's wife was up, waiting. When they pulled into the driveway, she came rushing out to greet them. She kissed Ab, clung to him, asking, "Are you all right, darling?"

"I'm fine, fine. Never been better," he said. "Well, not lately, that is." He tried to laugh. "You know Don Ward?"

"Of course. Hi, Don, come in? Coffee? Some breakfast?"

"We've already had breakfast. What we need, both of us, is some sleep. Take care of him," Don said softly.

"I will," she promised, tears filling up her eyes.

As Don turned back to his car, Ab suddenly said, "Don, wait!"

Don turned back to him. Ab put his arms around him, kissed him on the cheek, and said, "Thanks. Thanks for everything. And I mean everything."

Don watched as Ab's wife shepherded him into the lovely New England-type cottage that years of comedy writing had earned for Ab Crystal's family. If the work Ab and he had done during the last two and a half days were as good as Don believed, this house would shelter Ab's family long after the unfortunate writer was gone.

Dawn was breaking in the east by the time Don's rented red Continental rolled into the quiet, unattended parking area of the Bel-Air Hotel.

Don doubted that he could catch up on the sleep he had missed during the last two days. He was bad enough sleeping in daylight back East. Out here with the three-hour time difference the chances were even worse. But he decided not to take a sleeping pill in case Brady called. He would depend on sheer exhaustion to act as a soporific.

He was crossing the small, deserted, newly decorated lobby of the Bel-Air when the night clerk intercepted him.

"Mr. Ward?"

"Yes," Don said, turning to the desk.

"Two messages. Both insisting they're emergencies." The clerk handed him two slips. To one of them there were stapled two follow-up messages. He looked at that one first. It was from Claire: "*Call the first moment you can.*" The other message was from Ed Brady: "*Just arrived at Bev Hills. Call! At any hour!*" The operator had appended her own note: "*Sounds very angry.*"

Don reached his room, slumped down on the bed. Five in the morning California time, eight o'clock New York time. He would call Claire first. She might be awake, especially if she'd had a night of big problems. Why else would she have called and left such a message? It had to be Robbie. Undoubtedly still refusing to take his medication.

He dialed. Before the first ring was completed, Claire answered.

"Yes?" she asked, breathless. "Don, is that you?" She had not completed that last word when she began to cry.

"Claire, Claire! What is it? Answer me! Claire!"

He heard a man respond. He recognized Dr. Rissom. He was afraid to ask his next question.

"Doctor, Robbie—he didn't . . . I mean . . . he hasn't done anything foolish, has he?"

"We don't know, Don. He's missing."

"Gone? Ran away?" Don asked, sounding almost relieved, because of what he had feared.

"Don, get back home. The fastest way you can."

"Let me talk to my wife." He heard her crying on the line. "Claire, honey, just control yourself. I'll get back as soon as I can. On the first plane out of here. The nine o'clock. I'll be at Kennedy by five this evening. Just—just hold on; just don't go to pieces." He was rewarded only with more tears.

Rissom took over again. "Don, I'll stay with her until you get here. But hurry!"

"Of course, of course," he said softly, feeling a cold sweat begin to form over his entire body.

He sat there on the side of the bed, feeling helpless. It would be a long, tormenting four hours before flight time. There was nothing he could do till then. But first, call the airline. Make sure to get a seat on the first nonstop plane out at nine o'clock. He dialed the airline. It rang interminably before anyone answered. Then a recorded announcement told him, "All our reservation personnel are busy right now. But you will be attended to by the first free representative." He held on for an eternity that lasted almost five minutes.

"Yes, may I help you?" a cheerful female voice said.

"I have to get on the nine o'clock to New York. First class."

"Just a moment," the voice said. In barely longer than a moment she was back. "I'm sorry, sir, our computer shows we're full in first class."

"Then what about coach?"

"Just a moment, sir." She was back quickly. "Sorry, sir, coach is full, too. After all, it's the weekend. Seems like everyone in Los Angeles likes to be back home in New York on the weekend."

"Look, young lady! I have to be on that flight this morning at nine! Now, I'm with the Intercontinental Television Network, and I know you've always got one or two seats in first class set aside for emergencies. I want one of them!"

The young woman sounded flustered and apologetic. "I'm sorry, sir, but my computer shows we're full up."

"Let me talk to your supervisor!" Don demanded.

"Sir, it is now only twenty-one minutes after five o'clock in the morning. There is no supervisor on duty at this hour!" She was beginning to sound sharp and testy herself.

He slammed down the phone. He tried the other two airlines that flew nonstop LA to NY. But with the same frustrating results.

To the last one he shouted, "Damn it, there's got to be one airline with at least one empty seat to New York!"

There was a hushed, timid, almost frightened voice at the other end saying, "Gee, I'm awfully sorry, sir . . ." when he hung up.

In a few minutes, more calmly, accepting the realities of his situation, he called back each airline and had himself wait-listed for the nine o'clock LAX to JFK.

His hand was still on the phone as he frantically contemplated his next move. The phone rang. His first surge of hope was that one of the airlines was calling back to say it had bumped someone to make room for him. He answered eagerly.

Instead of the airlines, it was the familiar, impatient deep-chested, barrely voice he knew only too well.

"Don? Where the hell have you been? Don't you return phone calls anymore? What's going on? What the hell are you doing holed up in the Bel-Air? Screwing around? When I need you!"

It was a typical greeting from Ed Brady. He always asked four or five questions before you could answer one. He always tried to make you feel guilty because you had not anticipated all his unreasonable demands.

"I've been here, and I've been working," Don said, his own patience on a very short fuse.

"Maybe," Brady said to impress on Don that he was extremely skeptical of that explanation. "It doesn't matter. The real problem is this, Don. There is going to be an emergency board meeting of the brass at the parent company here on Monday morning. I don't have to tell you what that means. Now you and I have to spend the whole weekend going over every program we have in development for the next eighteen months. Everything! I have to have at my fingertips, every story line, every star, every director. Plus the demographics that justify why we picked the properties and stars we have.

"Because I've been tipped off that this is the crucial meeting.

If we score on Monday, I move up to become operating head of the conglomerate and you take over as president of the network. Do I have to say any more?"

He expected Don's immediate and enthusiastic response. When it was not quick in coming, Brady asked, "What's the matter, Don, did you drop the phone? Didn't you hear me? This is it! D-day! Don? For Christ's sake, at least breathe, so I'll know you're there!"

There was still no response from Don Ward. Now Brady's voice took on a different tone, less accusatory, less bullying, far more concerned. "Look, Don, if just the thought of that meeting scares you, what are you going to be like when you really have to face all those directors on Monday?"

"Ed . . . I am not going to be there on Monday," Don Ward said in a flat, even voice.

"What the hell do you mean, you're not going to be there on Monday?" Brady was shouting. "Listen. Get the hell over here to the Beverly Hills. I want to talk to you. Breakfast. Nine o'clock!"

"Nine o'clock, by whatever means it takes, I am going to be on a plane to New York."

"*You* are crazy!" Brady was bellowing. "Now get over here!" Brady paused, awaiting surrender to his command. Furious at Don's silent refusal, he said, "Don, did you hear me? It's either get over here or you are fired. Clear?"

"Did you say fired?" Don asked, without raising his voice.

"I damn well said fired!"

"You mean that I am no longer Ed Brady's man for all emergencies? I am no longer required to jump at Ed Brady's every command? I am free of this crazy industry in which nothing ever gets settled or done? Where the demands never stop? The pressure never lets up? Where the most important thing in the world is to hold the hand or kiss the behind of some overpaid, overdrugged star to make sure that the series continues? Or that we don't go too far over the budget? You mean you are going to deprive me of the joys of all that?" Don Ward asked. "Mr. Brady, how can you do that? And how could I possibly live without all that stomach-turning, nerve-shattering happiness? Really, Mr. Brady, you go too far. Too far."

"Don, I don't know what's come over you since I saw you

on Wednesday, but I honestly think you've flipped out. Hey, you're not on coke, are you?"

"No, Mr. Brady, I am not on coke."

"Stop calling me Mr. Brady. It sounds—sounds like you're off your rocker. Now get hold of yourself. Get on down here. Breakfast in the Polo Lounge at nine."

"Mr. Brady, I've already told you. At nine o'clock I will be on my way to New York."

"Will you stop saying that!" Brady shouted.

"And will you stop shouting?" Don Ward responded. "Because it won't change anything. I am going back to New York. My wife needs me. My son needs me."

"Don, use your head. Not many men your age get a chance like this. President of a network at forty-one. Don't blow it!"

"Sorry, Mr. Brady, but I have just spent two days with a man who taught me a great deal about life and living. I'm lucky! I don't have the same problem he does. But I can at least be as devoted a father and husband as he is. I am going back to New York."

"Don, listen to me . . ." Brady struggled to keep him on the line.

"I've already listened to you. Now you can take your whole network and shove it! I am through!"

"Don, Don, wait—"

"Look, Mr. Brady, as my one last official duty for this network I will give you an important piece of advice. Get hold of a writer named Abner Crystal—"

"I know Ab," Brady said. "I just fired him off his last assignment."

"Well, he's got a new series concept and a pilot script. Get hold of that script. Before any other network does. It's worth its weight in gold. Whatever deal he wants, give it to him. I promise you won't be sorry."

"Okay, okay, Abner Crystal. Now about you—" Brady persisted.

"Mr. Brady, please, don't embarrass yourself. The answer is no. And I can tell you now that for the first time in eighteen years I feel free. *free!* Now all I have to do is get a seat on the nine o'clock."

He hung up before Brady had a chance to fire another salvo of either threats or promises. He sat holding the phone. That seat on the nine o'clock. He had already listed himself as a standby with all three airlines. He would go to the airport and wait. But what if nothing opened up? Then what?

There had to be a way. There had to be. He could call his contacts at the network's largest sponsors, companies that had their own jets. But it would take a sheer stroke of luck to find one with a jet headed LA to NY that also had an empty seat. He tried. Luck was not running with him today. Even if he could still prevail on the manager of transportation at the network for a favor to which he was no longer entitled, that woman did not reach her office until nine-thirty.

He called all three airlines again. Again he was informed that his only chance was to appear at the terminal before takeoff on the chance there would be a no-show. There usually was, each service agent informed him. But to Don Ward "usually" was small consolation. And the next flights out would not arrive in New York until late at night.

There was one more hope. A long shot, but at least a hope, before he was forced to take his chances at the airport. It was now twenty-four minutes to six Pacific coast time. That would make it twenty-four minutes to seven Rocky Mountain time. There was a chance, an outside chance, that Danny Caputo having finished his second show for the night, the one that ended at 4:00 A.M., he would be in the casino playing blackjack, his favorite aftershow relaxation.

Don found the number of the hotel in the thick address book that traveled with him everywhere, like the black box that accompanied presidents of the United States in the event of a nuclear emergency. Don riffled through the pages under the Gs. General Electric, General Mills, General Motors, each with a half dozen executive names and numbers, then on to what seemed an endless number of hotels, resorts, entertainers, actors, directors, with names beginning with *G.* Finally he found it. The Gold Coast, Las Vegas. He dialed the number.

"Danny Caputo, please!"

"I'm sorry, Mr. Caputo is not taking any calls."

"Look, lady, I know him. I know where he is now. He's in

the casino playing blackjack. Get him. This is urgent. Just tell him Don Ward of Intercontinental Network is calling and it's an emergency."

While he held on, Don assessed if it was politic in dealing with this highly emotional singer to start off by reminding him of what Don had done for Caputo's son when the kid was just coming off a drug habit that had almost killed him. Don had got the boy a job with the network, in production. The kid had done well. He was working there now and advancing on the basis of his merit. Or would Caputo dislike being reminded that he was beholden to anyone? He was a strange man, unpredictable in his reactions. But a man with heart, whose charities were numerous and, in the main, anonymous.

It was barely minutes, but seemed hours, before Don heard the singer's familiar voice on the line.

"Kid, that you?" Caputo was asking. "What kind of trouble are you in?"

"Danny, it's my son—"

"Oh, God!" Caputo said. "All right, lay it on me. Booze? Drugs?"

"He's missing . . . and he's sick . . . he needs to be found."

Caputo interrupted. "Just tell me where he disappeared. I got friends in police departments everywhere."

"You don't understand. I have to get back to New York, and I can't get on a plane."

"Where are you now?"

"The Bel-Air."

Caputo took a moment to figure the logistics. "Look, I can have my jet in LA in fifty minutes after they gas up here. You be at the private landing area at LA International in an hour and a half. They'll be waiting."

"Thanks, Danny, I can't tell you what this means," Don began to say.

Caputo interrupted. "*You* are going to tell *me* what it means. I have a son, too. Remember? Be there! By the way, do you have transportation to the airport?"

"I've got a car."

"I can tell by your voice you're in no condition to drive," Caputo insisted. "I'll call my limousine service. There'll be a car at the door before you're packed. And good luck. If you need any more help, I got connections, kid. Everywhere. Remember that!"

"Thanks, Danny, and if I can ever return the favor—"

"Kid, every day my son gets up and goes to work you are returning the favor. Get going!"

The longest four hours and sixteen minutes Don Ward ever spent, he spent within the confines of the luxuriously appointed cabin aboard Danny Caputo's private jet. Tired as he was, he was unable to fall asleep. He finally gave up and took, instead, to drinking coffee to stay awake.

When the plane landed at Kennedy, there was a limousine already waiting to speed him to his home in Connecticut. Danny Caputo was an extremely thoughtful, concerned man.

CHAPTER 39

His first sight of Claire shook him almost as much as the shattering news she had phoned to tell him. She looked suddenly older. Her face, normally beautiful in the way that beautiful women grow more so as they mature, was now drawn, the skin stretched tight. Her eyes were red from weeping. Her honey hair was straggly and ill arranged. He took her in his arms and said very softly, "Don't worry, darling. I'm here. And I'll handle it. I won't let anything happen to our son. Just don't worry."

He had to steel himself from trembling because he was so affected by what Robbie's disappearance had done to his wife.

But looking beyond his wife's tormented face, he was staring at two doctors, Rissom and Belmond, who by their demanding eyes were telling him that they had to speak to him alone.

"Isn't there anything you can give . . ." he started to ask Rissom.

Rissom anticipated his question. "I tried. She won't take anything."

Don led Claire up to their bedroom, made her lie down, drew the shades to shut out the remaining daylight. He sat alongside her, holding her hand. Tenderly he closed her eyelids, hoping she would drift off. Eventually the tense muscles in her face relaxed; her breathing became more regular and shallow. His presence seemed to have afforded her some comfort.

One time she whispered, "We can't let him . . . we can't let him go," when she meant "die."

"We won't, Claire. I promise you, we won't," Don said, summoning all his conviction since for hours now he had been haunted by that moment when he had first seen the final entry in the record of Robbie's natural mother at Rockland State Hospital.

Soon Claire's grip on his hand eased. He knew she was asleep.

He went down at once to confront both doctors.

"Mr. Ward, we have to be prepared for all developments," Dr. Belmond began. "That's why we both are relieved that you're here. Your wife would not be able to bear this by herself."

"What developments?" Don asked.

"Don," Rissom intervened, "We're far more disturbed by Robbie's absence than we allowed Claire to suspect. You see, when Robbie disappeared, he took his lithium pills with him."

"It shows that he knows what he needs. I think it's a good sign," Don said.

Rissom shook his head gravely. "Don, what made Robbie rebel was his embarrassment before a crowd at a basketball game. He blamed the lithium for that. Now, if he were rebelling against the lithium, why would he take it with him when he disappeared?"

Don looked to Dr. Belmond for some explanation of his son's conduct.

"Mr. Ward, lithium, taken in overdose, can be fatal."

"And he knows that," Rissom said. "Dr. Belmond and I both have warned him. Now do you see what we're so worried about? And why we have to find him before he does anything—anything dangerous."

Don did not respond but sank slowly into the nearest chair. He cradled his clasped hands between his thighs. He stared at familiar objects in this very familiar room and saw none of them. He was mute for several very long minutes. When he spoke, it was with the voice of a man who felt called upon to launch into some action, the nature of which he had not the vaguest notion.

"We have to do something. We have to organize a search. Notify the police. Make announcements on the radio. On TV. I've got connections. I'm well known in the industry. I can get the word around. I'll call Danny Caputo. The police owe him favors. He's done lots of benefits for them. . . ."

He was doing the only thing he had learned to do in the past eighteen years. He was being the assertive executive. Instead of retreating in the face of a problem, he was taking action. "Always take action" had been Ed Brady's motto. Never appear to be defeated or discouraged; always be upbeat and aggressive in the face of any problem. That's what had made Don so terrific as Ed Brady's problem solver.

"Look," he tried to persuade Rissom and Belmond, "don't worry about a thing. I'll call Security at the network. I'll call . . ." His voice slowly trailed off. He looked up at Rissom, who stood over him.

"I—I quit. This morning. At five twenty-four, Pacific coast time. Don Ward, executive vice-president, successor to Ed Brady, president of the network, told him to take it and shove it. So there is no network. No Security." He repeated the words—"No security"—for the words had more than one meaning now. "It'll be in the trades Monday, *Hollywood Reporter, Daily Variety.* Maybe it'll even make the front page of *Weekly Variety.*"

He tore at his collar to free his constricted neck. The button burst loose, but he seemed able to breathe again.

"What do we do about your son?" Belmond said. "Your wife was afraid of the effect the publicity might have on your career."

"To hell with publicity. We notify the police. Right now!" Don said. He crossed the room in quick steps, grabbed, the phone, and punched in 911. When he got a response, he said, "I want to report that my son is missing. He is Robert Ward. Sixteen . . ." He followed with a description. Dark-haired, blue-eyed. Five feet eight. One hundred thirty-nine pounds.

"Last seen?" Don was repeating the question, to which he had no answer. He looked to Rissom.

"Thursday. After he came home from the Canaan school gymnasium. He disappeared during the night."

Don repeated the information to the policewoman, who was taking it down.

"We'll send out an all points." The woman tried to reassure him.

"Do whatever you can," Don insisted. "Please!"

When he put down the phone, his hands were trembling.

* * *

Because it made him feel less guilty than merely waiting for the police to do their work, Don got into his red Mercedes sports car and began to tour the neighborhood. He slowly covered the route Robbie usually took between home and Canaan Prep.

He followed the same route home, the same streets, searching for some signs, but found nothing. There was a patrol car in the driveway when Don returned. He entered the house to find two officers questioning Claire. She was giving them what little information she could. Where Robbie might have gone, in whom he might have confided. Robbie's favorite hangouts.

One officer kept making notes, nodding little signs of assent. But his attitude was far from optimistic. When Don appeared, the officer turned to him, asking the same questions again. Why, in Don's opinion, had the boy disappeared? Had he been acting strangely? Had he said anything out of the ordinary that might be a hint of his intentions, his goal, his reason? Don could tell him even less than Claire.

Finally the officer said, "We'll turn this over to Missing Persons. But frankly it's not very much to go on, Mr. Ward. However, I've seen cases start with less and work out very well."

The looks on the faces of both officers, which were directed at Don, clearly indicated that this last was said to calm a distraught mother rather than to offer much hope to a distraught father.

Don asked himself: *Why does everyone assume that a man can bear these troubles more bravely than a woman? Are fathers supposed to love less, worry less? Or be stronger despite their worries? If anything happens to that boy, I know whose fault it is. I know better than anyone. All those times when I had to be away, when I disappointed him, when any other father would have been there and I wasn't. I used to console myself: He's a terrific kid; he can cope, even without me. Look how well he's doing. But all the while something was missing. Me. And now, when he needs me more than he ever did, there's nothing I can do. Nothing.*

But what good would it do to tell that to two strangers, policemen on a routine call about a missing young boy?

The officers were gone. In Don's absence Belmond had left a note for him: "*Call me at once if anything develops. Anything at all.*"

Before Rissom left, he pressed a small white envelope into

Don's hand. "Try to get her to take one of these. And keep me posted. If there's anything I can do . . . anything. After all, I've known that boy since he was eleven days old."

Left alone, Don thought: *Why is it that everything everyone says to console us sounds so final? He's out there. He must be. And he's alive! He is alive!"*

In the solitary silence of his dark living room Don Ward began to weep.

By sheer habit and the need to be occupied Claire went through the ritual of preparing dinner for them. They ended up not eating any. But sat in the dark breakfast room having coffee. Even in the darkness he could see the glazed look on Claire's thin face.

"I searched the neighborhood," Don said suddenly to explain and excuse his present helpless inertia.

"Good," she said, equally detached and helpless.

They were silent. The phone rang. They both lurched toward it. Don seized it first.

"Yes?" he demanded anxiously.

Dr. Belmond's voice replied, "Any word yet? Anything?"

"No."

"Let me know. I'll be home all evening. Call at any time. Anytime at all."

"Yes, yes, of course. Thank you," Don said and hung up. "Belmond," he explained to Claire.

For some reason the name made her begin crying. He went to her side, knelt beside her, took her in his arms. "Angel . . . sweetheart . . . now of all times we've got to hold on. Robbie will need us. We've got to . . ." and he left it unsaid, because he no longer knew what they had to do, or were capable of doing. "I'll go down to the police station. Maybe I can help."

He was in the foyer, putting on his coat, when he heard her call. "Don, no! Please, don't leave me now!"

He went back to her.

"Hold me," she pleaded.

He lifted her to her feet, embraced her, held her tightly, and could feel the difference in her since four days ago, when he had embraced her and kissed her good-bye. He held her even closer.

"My fault," she said. "This is all my fault."

"It wasn't anything you said or did. It was what happened. You had nothing to do with it." He tried to console her.

"Tell me, honestly, would you have been for adopting if I hadn't been so insistent? Did you really want a child? A son? Did you?"

He held her off from him to look down into her tormented face, visible even in the dark. "You know we both wanted him. Both of us!"

"I always felt that *I* wanted him. You only went along. If I hadn't been so insistent . . . if I—"

"Claire! Stop it! Stop blaming yourself! We both wanted him. It's not your fault. In fact, if it's anybody's fault . . ." He paused, then admitted softly, "On the way back I had four hours to think. Four long hours. And I figured it out. Not your fault. Mine. Did I push him too far? Did I show so much pride in him that without knowing it I put pressure on him? I have this need to brag about him at the office, to the other fathers, to Ed Brady. Was I using him in some way?

"Or did we pin all our hopes on him? Since we couldn't have a child of our own, did we say: 'We'll take this child in and he is going to justify us and our lives'? Did we use him for our satisfaction? I asked myself all those questions," he confessed.

To assuage his torment, she said, "I've done my share of thinking, too. Maybe we shouldn't have told him he was adopted. Maybe there's such a thing as being too honest. Maybe we were putting too much of a burden on him. Maybe . . ." Her maybes trailed off into unspoken fears and doubts.

"Why *did* he take those pills with him?" Don asked suddenly, his mind operating in that disconnected way in which minds tend to in moments of crisis. Too late he realized that he was revealing Rissom's fear, Belmond's fear, expressed to him but kept secret from Claire.

"What do you mean, '*why?*' Her eyes searched his in the darkness.

"Just a crazy thought." He tried to evade her.

"What crazy thought?" she insisted.

"It's nothing, nothing at all, just—just curiosity, idle curiosity," he said, seeking to close off that avenue of macabre speculation.

"Where my son is concerned, there is no such thing as idle curiosity!" she asserted. He could feel her thin body grow tense against him. "I want to know what you mean!"

"I didn't mean anything."

"You're afraid to say it, aren't you? I can think it, you can think it, Rissom and Belmond can think it, but no one is allowed to say it. Well, I'll say it for you. Those pills, the first time Belmond ever mentioned them to me she said the danger with giving them to a teenager with depression was that an overdose could be fatal. Good God, what do you think I've been worrying about these last fifteen hours?" she demanded, beginning to weep again.

"Claire, darling, this is no time to go to pieces. No matter what we fear, we've got to hold on. Hold on. Hold on," he kept repeating aimlessly.

"Yes, hold on," she said, "hold on." Then she added, "To each other. Don, have you thought what it would be like if there were no Robbie anymore . . . no—"

"I never thought of that," he lied. Because he was lying, he repeated, "Never!" But he clung to her more tightly than ever.

CHAPTER 40

Dr. Sabrina Belmond stopped by her office before going home. As soon as she had found out about Robbie Ward's disappearance, she had canceled all her patients for the day. She owed them the responsibility of picking up their telephone messages in the event any of them was experiencing an emergency.

The messages were all routine. Requesting a change of hour. Or informing her that they could not keep their appointments. But one message, left by a woman whose voice betrayed unusual tension, requested that Belmond call her as soon as possible, at home. The woman's name was Betancourt. Since Belmond had no patient by that name, the message was unduly disturbing. Possibly it was a new patient, a referral, suffering a critical anxiety attack. The call demanded an immediate reply. As she reached for her phone, Belmond repeated the name Betancourt . . . Betancourt. It seemed familiar after all. She riffled through the files in her drawer, pulled out the one marked "*Ward, Robert*." She looked through it. She found it. *Betancourt.* The woman at the adoption agency, who had been involved in the legal action to release the name of Robbie's natural mother.

Belmond dialed the number swiftly.

"Mrs. Betancourt? Dr. Belmond."

"Thank God you called!" the tense woman said

"Is this to do with Robbie Ward?'

"He called me. At about noon. Demanding answers to questions, lots of questions," Mrs. Betancourt said.

"Was he very verbal, loud, pointed in his language?" Belmond asked.

"How did you know?"

"As nearly as you can remember, what did he say?"

"He wanted to know his natural mother's identity."

"Did he say why?" Belmond asked.

"He said something about doing some research at the library, research in psychiatry."

Belmond asked sharply, "Did he say *what* he was researching, and *why?*"

"He said something about manic-depressive disorders being inherited. He wanted to find out," Mrs. Betancourt said.

"What did you tell him?"

"I had no chance to tell him anything. He spoke so rapidly he was unstoppable. He would ask a question, never wait for an answer, and go right on to another question. He kept insisting that I knew but wouldn't tell him. That the whole world was in a conspiracy to keep him from finding out."

"Now think carefully, Mrs. Betancourt, did he say anything at all that indicated what he would do if he found out?"

"No. He only said, 'If you don't tell me, you'll be sorry.' "

"Was he threatening you?"

"I don't think so," the woman replied.

"Did it sound as if he might be threatening himself?" Belmond asked.

"Yes," Mrs. Betancourt admitted.

"Did he give any indication, direct or indirect, of where he was, what he might do, where he might go?"

"None."

"I trust you didn't mention Rockland State Hospital," Belmond said.

"I didn't. *He* did."

Stunned, Dr. Belmond asked, "Did he say how he knew about that?"

"He had been searching through some papers in his father's desk in the den."

"I see," Belmond said, in a soft, breathless whisper. "Thank you for calling, thank you very much."

She dialed Rockland State at once. Yes, there had been a call from an agitated young man, asking for information about a patient named Emily Birch. But the operator had avoided his demand by saying that all such requests had to be in writing. When the young man added vulgarities to his insistent demand, the operator had hung up.

Belmond called Dr. Rissom. She briefed him on the distressing information she had just acquired.

"He told me once," she said, "that he liked to go to the library and look things up. Naturally. He's a bright, highly intelligent young man. I've had such patients do that before. They have an intolerable curiosity about their condition. And the treatment. Either they don't trust the doctor, or else they want to become equals in the treatment."

"Yes," Rissom agreed, and added sadly, "But they don't often make the same unfortunate discovery that Robbie made: that he was born with the genetic elements of his condition."

"That could have had the same effect on him as a diagnosis of cancer," Belmond said. "A patient with an active mind, a bright mind, tormented by the knowledge that there was something within himself that could eventually destroy him."

"That poor boy's like a walking time bomb," Rissom said. "And no one knows when he might go off."

"He's in a highly manic state," Belmond pointed out. "That should prevent him from taking any intentionally suicidal action."

"And if he does something foolhardy in his manic state," Rissom asked, "how much safer is he? We've got to find that boy!"

When Rissom and Belmond arrived at the Wards' home, they found them with a Detective Francisco Melendez who had been assigned to the case. He was a short man, with a sallow complexion and a drooping black mustache. He had eyes that darted from one object in the room to another, as if each were a potential suspect. Nevertheless, he listened intently to Belmond's recounting of her latest distressing discovery.

"You mean," Claire asked, "that Robbie knows about his natural mother? And what happened to her?"

"I'm afraid that's true, Mrs. Ward," Belmond said.

"He's probably imagining all sorts of dire things about himself," Don realized.

"Most likely," Belmond said.

"Poor Robbie. Poor Robbie . . ." Claire kept repeating. "If only he knew how we feel about him—"

"Look," Melendez interrupted, "I am very sorry about your son and his condition. But my job here is not to treat him; it's to find him. Now, unless one of you doctors can tell me how I do that, I would appreciate it if you let me do my job!"

"We'll do anything we can to help," Rissom offered.

"Good! I want to know if there is any person, a close friend, a teacher, someone in whom this boy would confide things he does not tell anyone else." He turned to Belmond. "During his sessions has he ever mentioned anyone?"

"There is one person on whose reaction he seemed most dependent. A girl named Susan."

"Susan Spencer," Don said.

"They'd been going together almost exclusively. Until recently. When she broke it off. He took that very badly," Belmond said.

Melendez tugged at his untidy mustache. "This girl, where does she live."

"Meadow Lark. Not far from here. I could show you," Don volunteered.

"I think we might just run over there," Melendez said. "Just the three of us," he emphasized.

Mr. and Mrs. Neil Spencer stood on each side of their daughter, Susan, who sat stiffly straight-backed in a wing chair in the corner of the large early American living room. Claire and Don sat on the couch facing her. Melendez stood to one side to avoid any appearance of confrontation.

Most witnesses were so tense and frightened to be involved in a police interrogation that they became defensive and withheld rather than revealed vital information. So the short, swarthy detective addressed her as gently as he would his own teenage daughter.

"Now, Susan, first thing I want you to know, whatever you tell me not only is confidential but will not get you or Robbie into trouble. In fact, we want to find him *before* he gets into trouble. So whatever you can tell me, it might help. Okay?"

Her pretty face grim, her brown eyes guardedly seeking reassurance, first from her father, then from her mother, Susan Spencer said, "Yes, sir, I understand." But she was very tense nevertheless.

"When was the last time you saw Robbie?" Melendez asked.

Before answering, she looked to her father for permission.

As tall as Don Ward, and the same age, but overweight, Spencer seemed ten years older. He stepped between his daughter and Detective Melendez. "Maybe I'd better answer that."

"I'd rather she was the one who told me," the detective insisted.

"And I would rather *I* told you," Spencer replied.

Claire rose from the couch to protest. "Mr. Spencer, my son's life is involved. I insist your daughter answer the man's question!"

Don rose to embrace Claire, who was trembling now. "Easy, darling." He glared across her at Spencer. "Do this the way Detective Melendez wants! There's such a thing as impeding justice, you know!"

It was an empty threat, sheer bluff, but Spencer eased back, giving Melendez direct access to his daughter.

"Robbie was here yesterday . . . last night. . . ."

"Last night?" Melendez asked. "And? What did he want? What did he say?"

Spencer intruded once more. "He wanted her to go out with him. But, frankly, on the basis of his condition, I refused. He was like a—like a . . . if you want my candid opinion of your son, Mrs. Ward, I think he was high on drugs!"

Susan defied her father enough to say, "Daddy, Robbie's never used drugs. Never!"

"Well, he looked damn high to me!" Spencer said. "Doesn't matter, I wouldn't permit any daughter of mine to go out with him. Don't know what the hell's come over that boy. A few months ago he was as nice and well behaved a kid as you'd want to know. But lately . . ." Spencer shook his head grimly, his flabby jowls emphasizing his dismay.

Melendez nodded thoughtfully, turned to Susan. "So then what happened? Your father said no, you couldn't go. What did Robbie say?"

"He said . . ." the girl hesitated before revealing it. "He said, he said it would be like old times . . . better than old times . . . he said he was himself again. . . ."

"What did he mean, 'old times'?" Melendez asked.

"Till that time when he got sick he used to be so exciting. He had ideas going all the time, you know. I mean you never knew what he was going to come up with next. It's what made him so much fun. But after that last football game he's never been the same."

Claire broke from Don's embrace to move to Susan's side.

"Susie, last night, when Robbie said that, did he *seem* like the old times? Was he as excited and full of ideas? It's important, dear, tell me."

Unaware of the gravity of her answer but fearing she might be imparting a secret, Susan nodded.

"Did he say anything that could give us a clue to where he might go, what he might do?" Melendez asked.

"No," Susan said quickly.

Too quickly, Melendez perceived. "Did he ask you to go anywhere with him?"

"No."

"A disco? A roadside rock joint? Did he mention any special place? Any place from the 'old times'?"

"No."

"Then what was he going to do that was like the old times?" Melendez asked.

"I don't know," Susan said. "Just that he sounded excited, like he used to."

Her father intervened. "Look, she's told you all she knows. I think you've imposed on us long enough."

"Yeah," Melendez said. He gestured to the Wards that it was futile to continue this interrogation. "Well, thanks," he said to the Spencers. "Thanks a lot. You've been a help. A big help."

As they stepped out of the Spencers' door, Melendez said softly, "You want to know what's going on in there now? That fat son of a bitch is accusing his daughter of making it with your son. He was afraid she might say something that would reflect on her reputation. He's the kind of father who insists *he's* the only one who has the right to do that. No help, no help at all."

As they approached his car, in what seemed an afterthought, Melendez said, "I better talk to those doctors."

* * *

"Look, Doctor," Melendez was saying, "don't give me his whole case history. I probably couldn't understand it anyway. Just tell me if Robbie said to his girl friend 'It's going to be like old times' . . . whatever the hell *old times* can be to someone who's only just become sixteen . . . what would he mean?"

"To Robbie *old times* would mean that he is experiencing his old manic high. That he is apt to do something wild, impossible, most likely dangerous. Something that would show the world that he is the Robbie Ward he was when he was a football hero at school," Belmond said.

"Then what we are looking for is a kid who might do something dangerous. Possibly steal a car? Drive like a maniac?"

"He did that once before. But it was my car," Don said.

"Since both your cars are here, we have to consider maybe he would steal some stranger's car. Which would be very unfortunate," Melendez said. "Strangers, and especially insurance companies, are not very understanding about things like that."

"He's never exhibited such tendencies before, even in his manic state," Belmond said, "but he's never been this manic before. So anything is possible. The best thing is to find him as soon as possible, so we can get him regulated on his lithium."

"The best thing . . ." Melendez repeated sadly. "Lady, in my business the best thing rarely happens." He turned to Don and Claire. "Okay now, Mr. Ward, Mrs. Ward, *think!* What kind of thing would Robbie do when he was in that state of mind? Something daring. Something from the past. Something that he has done before and might want to repeat to show off."

"Well . . ." Don began, but looked to Claire to receive permission.

Melendez interrupted angrily. "Mr. Ward, this is no time for holding back! I don't want to contend with looks and gestures and permission. Whatever you were going to say, say it!"

"There was the time," Don Ward began, "when we had to go take him off the Windsor Street bridge."

"The bridge over the railroad tracks?" Melendez tried to identify it.

"Yes," Don said. "On a dare he was walking the narrow rail of the bridge. There's barely enough room to put one foot in front of the other. We got a call from the mother of one of his friends. We went there, and I haa to take him down before he could fall."

"Yeah," Melendez said grimly. "Last few years two kids have fallen to the tracks trying that stunt. One of them didn't live. The other became a paraplegic. So you think he might—"

Belmond intervened. "Mr. Melendez, on the possibility that Robbie would not revert to anything he might have deemed daring at thirteen, we've got to look for some more immediate challenge."

Rissom agreed. "I've known that boy all his life. Just tell him something is impossible today, and he'll find a way to do it tomorrow. Or try to."

The phone rang. Melendez turned abruptly to answer.

"Melendez! . . . Yeah, Bill. Stolen car? . . . Yeah. And? . . . Trooper made the identification on the Merritt. Gave chase. Going over a hundred miles an hour? Didn't want to endanger other vehicles, so he lost him. . . Of course. Any description? . . . I see. Yeah. Got it. If there's any follow-up, let me know."

He hung up, turned to face them. He directed his words to Belmond. "So he's never exhibited such tendencies before? The trooper says all he could tell under nighttime conditions, the driver was a young man about sixteen, seventeen, dark-haired."

"Robbie!" Claire exclaimed.

"Could be," Melendez said. "Could very well be. Trooper said once he turned off the Merritt, he headed east. In the direction of Westport. Any reason that boy would want to go to Westport? Did he have a friend there? Another girl friend, maybe?"

Don shook his head, puzzled. But Claire said softly to herself, " 'I didn't want that boat to talk about. I wanted her to sail.' "

"Mrs. Ward, what did you just say?" Melendez asked.

"It's what Robbie said. The day my husband promised to teach him to sail his new cat and then couldn't make it."

Belmond joined in. "He mentioned that to me, too."

Don said, "Of course. Westport. The marina."

"Do you think he could be there, trying to sail that boat? Now? In the middle of the night?" Melendez asked.

Belmond answered, "In his condition he might well try anything!"

And Rissom nodded sadly.

Don turned to Melendez. "You'd better come with me!"

"Wait," Claire protested. "I'm going, too."

"Claire, please . . ."

"Mrs. Ward, your husband's right," Melendez said.

"He's my son and I have a right to be there. If he's in trouble, I have a right to know it. If they find him, I have a right—" She stopped. "I didn't mean to say *if* they find him. They've *got* to find him!"

Because Melendez had had previous tragic experiences with such cases, he urged, "Mrs. Ward, take my advice—"

"I am going!"

She said it with such finality that Melendez glanced at Don. They both knew it was the simplest, albeit possibly the cruelest, thing to permit her to come, considering what they might discover.

CHAPTER 41

Soundside Marina was closed and deserted. It appeared ominous in the grim, cloud-shrouded dawn. The water, black and angry, beat against the pilings, a film of old oil forming rainbows on its surface. The wind swept across Long Island Sound. Heavy with moisture, it felt like light rain on Claire Ward's face as she stood on the dock, staring out at the dark sky. Beside her, her husband, Don, felt her shudder. He put his arm around her. Her kind of cold could not be warded off by a comforting arm or the tweed coat wrapped around her. It was fear. If her son, Robbie, was out there, he was lost. Not only hidden by the dark night but swallowed up by the angry waters.

Detective Melendez stood alongside them, speaking into his walkie-talkie from time to time.

"Where the hell is that police boat?" Melendez demanded. "You said it was on the way half an hour ago!"

There was some cross talk back which neither Don nor Claire Ward could make out. But it obviously infuriated Melendez, who replied, "Look! You know what exposure can do in this kind of weather. And we don't know how long the kid's been out there!"

More cross talk.

"What do you mean, we don't even know if he's out there?" Melendez replied angrily. "We found the stolen car here. His father has a boat at this marina. That boat is gone. Two plus two equals four! He is out there somewhere."

It seemed that hours had gone by. It was less than thirty minutes. Through the mist of early morning appeared the silhouette of a vessel, which played a powerful searchlight across the darkness in their direction. A voice came over the water by bullhorn. "Detective Melendez?"

Melendez shouted back to acknowledge.

"Any instructions? Any direction?"

"Just sweep the area. It's a Hobie cat. Eighteen-foot." Melendez turned to Don Ward. "What color was the sail?"

"Mainly blue with red, orange, and yellow stripes."

Melendez relayed the information and asked, "Anything said about a copter?"

"Not till this mist lifts," the bullhorn responded.

"Okay. Get going!"

Claire could make out the shadowy form of the police boat as it turned to head out into the Sound. Its searchlight probing ahead of it, as if cutting a path, it started away from them, the throb of its powerful engines growing faint as it disappeared into the mist once more.

A police car pulled up behind them. One of the officers emerged, carrying a paper bag with containers of hot coffee. He passed one to Claire, one to Don, but used the third one to lure Melendez away from the Wards. Once at a confidential distance, the officer spoke. "We got another report. That kid is really on a tear."

"You mean he's not out there?" Melendez asked.

"I mean he damn well may be out there. But before that, even before the stolen car thing, he may have been spotted walking the Windsor Street bridge railing."

"How do you know?

"Duane was thumbing through the nine-elevens to make up the daily report. Earlier last night there was a call from someone who lives on Windsor. A kid about sixteen was spotted walking the rail. The caller said he stood there, balancing himself, while two trains went by underneath."

"No jumper," Melendez concluded.

"Evidently just wanted to see if he could balance himself against the rush of the wind as the trains went by. When our checkup got there, the kid was gone. We think it was the Ward boy."

"Could be." Melendez agreed. "Could be."

He did not attempt to drink his coffee but tossed the container in the direction of the dark water. He seemed even more harried than before. He turned his walkie-talkie on again. "Melendez. Spot anything?"

"Not a thing."

"Nothing at all?"

"Nothing."

"Well, keep at it," Melendez said, because he could think of nothing else to say that would not admit the feeling of defeat that was beginning to grip his stomach. His wife always said, "Frank does his best detecting with his stomach. What he feels there generally turns out to be his best hunch."

Now he was wishing it were not so.

Dawn was beginning to break far to the east over the Sound. The mist, giving way slowly to daybreak, was whirled about by the fresh, moist ocean breeze that came with the light. Melendez had confined Claire to the shelter of a squad car. He hoped she would doze off. She did not. As much as possible he avoided any conversation with Don, not wishing to reveal his own hopeless estimate of Robbie's chances.

He had learned from experience that to lie to people in the Wards' situation led only to eventual disillusionment with the police and loss of confidence in the system. Whereas time, and some gentle half-truths, could lead the family to arrive at their own unhappy conclusion. Then they felt that the police had at least been truthful with them.

The weather, the early spring, the reckless attitude of the boy, the sheer size of the boat he was grappling with, the rough water, the number of hours he might have been out there—all militated against a hopeful outcome.

Melendez felt he must start getting the Wards ready for such a resolution in this unfortunate case. He was no novice at this kind of thing. He knew, and he suspected Don Ward knew, that if the cat heeled over, no 139-pound kid could generate enough leverage to right it. On his own, in water of such low temperature, prolonged exposure would be fatal.

"Mrs. Ward, you better stay in the car. If there's anything, I'll let you know right away," Melendez said.

He gestured Don to follow him to dockside. They both peered out over the water. Neither expected they would discover anything but the heaving black water and occasional ripples of white foam. But they stared nevertheless.

Melendez felt it was time now. "Mr. Ward, you good with those cats?"

"Pretty good."

"And the boy?"

"Good as a boy that light can be. But an eighteen-footer is a handful for two adults. Let alone one boy."

"Yeah." Melendez agreed. "I got a brother owns a small supermarket on Third Avenue down in New York, you know?"

"Yeah?" Don replied, puzzled by the apparent lack of connection.

"Financial-wise he does very well. Better than me, I can tell you. Now he has got such a cat. Not eighteen feet. Only sixteen. So he kept nagging me, 'Frank, come out on my boat, you'll love it. I'll teach you how to sail; it's the greatest way in the world to relax.' So I went out with him. Twice. Once would have been enough. I mean, you're out there with no protection against the elements. Either you get a terrible sunburn or else you come back wet through, cold and miserable. And that's in the summer yet."

"Yeah, in the summer." Don agreed, to pretend he was interested in the detective's seemingly pointless recitation.

"Then it gets caught in a sudden wind, over we go, into the water. That sail, which should be standing up proud, is lying flat in the water, and I am floating around, taking a swim I never wanted. My brother is laughing at my discomfort and saying, 'Half the fun is in going over.' I think, *Who the hell needs that kind of fun?*

"So then we have a job to right that big sucker. We both climb out on that pontoon, grab ahold of that rope . . . what do they call it?"

"The righting line," Don said, beginning to grow impatient.

"Yeah. The righting line. We grab hold of that, plant our

feet against the pontoon, and lean as far back as we can. Gradually that big, heavy son of a bitch begins to come up out of the water. In a while that sail is up there, big and colorful. We are sailing again, but we are wet clear through. And he claims that's fun."

"Under the right conditions it is."

"Yeah. So I'll tell you what I'm thinking," Melendez said, getting to the point. "There am I, one hundred sixty-eight. And my brother, Domingo, one hundred eighty-two. And we can only get that sixteen-foot sucker out of the water with a lot of effort. Now a big one, like eighteen feet, must take at least as much weight to get it up, no?"

"Yes. They recommend more than two hundred twenty pounds."

"See what I mean? Suppose that boat out there is over and your kid, what is he, a hundred forty? What is he going to do if that thing went over, which in this kind of wind is a possibility. Maybe even a probability. Or worse, suppose that thing pitchpoled on him?"

With that word Melendez inadvertently betrayed that he knew a good deal more about sailing a cat than he had admitted. Only a man experienced with such boats would know that particular term. It meant that under certain conditions, in the hands of a less than expert boatman or one who might not keep his weight properly placed, the leading edges of the two pontoons might dig into the water. Whereupon the forward momentum of the craft would lift the rear of the pontoons, thus sending the craft somersaulting end over end and causing it to land sail down, pontoons up. The pilot, wherever an accidental fate deposited him, could be unconscious from a blow against the side of one of the pontoons.

Don turned to confront Melendez. The detective pretended to be staring out across the dark waters. But he was aware of Don's questioning stare.

"What I mean is, I don't know your wife, but she's a mother. So she is bound to get very hysterical if things don't go according to plan."

"Which they are not doing, am I right?"

"Mr. Ward, would you rather I lie to you? Or tell you the truth?"

"The truth," Don insisted.

"The truth you can see for yourself," Melendez said, pointing out in the direction of the dark waters from which the mist had now lifted. "They will sweep the whole area. What they'll find . . . who knows? I'll keep checking with them. They'll keep telling me the same thing. We already got the Coast Guard working on it. But even if they find him, I can't guarantee, well, uh . . ."

"You can't guarantee he'll be alive." Don said it for him.

"I think that is a fair statement, Mr. Ward. I tell you this, so you can prepare your wife in whatever way you know. Because I am not good with hysterical women," Melendez said. "Not even my own wife."

They heard a car pull up behind them and stop abruptly. They both turned, saw a man getting out. Don recognized him.

"Dr. Rissom?" he called.

Rissom approached him. "I couldn't stand just waiting. I had to be here. Anything?"

"Not yet," Don said, unwilling to accept Melendez's fatalistic assessment.

"And Claire?" Rissom asked.

"Barely holding on."

"I thought so," Rissom said, reaching into his pocket for a small white envelope. "Try to get her to take this sedative."

Don went back to the car. Claire sat still and stiff, staring.

"Take this, darling," Don said softly.

"It's a sedative, isn't it?" she demanded belligerently.

"Dr. Rissom brought it for you."

"My son is out there. And no matter what they find, I don't want to be asleep when it happens. If there is joy, I want to feel it. If there is pain, I want to know it. Else I am not truly a mother, and never was. Never was."

She began to weep.

He edged in beside her, embraced her, and spoke softly into her ear. "Claire, darling, listen to me. You may not have given birth to him, but you gave him all the love, care, and attention that any child could have. You gave him more of that than most mothers. Because my damned job took me away from him so much."

He stared out at the mist, at the dark waters of the Sound

as he said, "In a way, if anything happens to him now, it's only right that it's because of something that I bought him. It points the finger to where the blame really belongs. Me! So don't go accusing yourself. And don't punish yourself now by refusing this pill. Take it!"

He brought the pill to her lips. She turned her head away, protesting, "I want to know the truth the moment they know it."

He knew it would be futile to persist. He left her, sitting there, staring.

The three men—Don Ward, Dr. Rissom, Detective Melendez—heard the sound before they saw it. The sound of copter blades whipping the air above them. Soon they could see it descend toward them across the water, out of the mist, a ghostly presence. Its searchlight seemed to seek them out. It hovered over them, then touched down, its blades continuing to rotate.

Melendez exchanged some words with the police pilot. As he was about to slam the hatch shut and lift off again, Don called out, "Wait!"

"Yeah?" the pilot asked, expecting some additional information to aid him in the search.

"I'm going with you!" Don said.

"Hey, now wait a minute, mister . . ." The pilot started to argue.

"He's my son. And I am going to search for him!" Don insisted.

"It's against regulations to board a private citizen," the pilot shouted back.

Melendez interceded. "Christ, Joe, give him a break. Bend the rules a little. After all, it's his kid."

The pilot hesitated, looked to his copilot, who finally nodded. The pilot waved Don aboard.

Calling to Rissom, "Take care of Claire," Don climbed into the copter, slipped into the seat behind the pilot. The hatch closed, the pilot lifted the craft off the pier, and the copter disappeared into the mist.

Rissom watched until it was gone; then he turned to Melendez, his eyes inviting a report. But the detective said only, "You better take care of that lady."

CHAPTER 42

Don Ward sat with his face pressed against the cold plastic bubble of the copter, staring down at the choppy waters of Long Island Sound. He saw nothing but the waves in the dark waters which gave rise to little bursts of white foam when one broke.

Ahead, he could see the wake left by a stubby tug that was urging a heavy barge toward the open waters of the ocean. But he could see no sign of any small craft, no multistriped sail, no blue pontoons, no yellow life jacket, the kind Robbie would have worn or should have worn.

On the other side of the bubble the copilot kept his own vigil, straining to see, in an effort that both he and his pilot were coming to accept as futile. They transmitted their unhappy opinions by glances, by shrugs, by sympathetic looks in Don's direction, which he was too intent to notice.

Finally the pilot delivered a firm, regretful shake of his head to his copilot, pointed at his gas gauge, and said, "Mr. Ward, sorry, but we've got to turn back."

"You can't turn back! Robbie's out there somewhere. We know that!" Don protested.

"Mr. Ward, see that needle on the gas gauge. What's it read?" the pilot asked.

"You've got almost half a tank," Don said.

"Just over a quarter," the pilot corrected. "Rule is, when you get below half, if not engaged in actual rescue activity, head back and fill 'er up. We've been below half for some time now. Sorry," he said, at the same time banking the craft to make a graceful turn back toward land.

"You can't do this! Not to Robbie! We can't desert him now!" Don said, seizing the pilot by the jacket.

"Mr. Ward! If you endanger the safe operation of this craft, we will have to use force on you!" the pilot warned. "Now I know how you feel. I'm a father myself. But there come times we have to accept reality. There are two craft out searching for your son now. If he's out there, if he's still . . ."

"Still alive?" Don asked.

"Mr. Ward, all I know, we have to turn back," the pilot said, completing his turn and heading for base.

Below, Don could see the wake of the police boat heading out. Through filmed-over eyes he could see the strobe lights of four commercial aircraft circling to await permission to land at Kennedy Airport. The red-eyes. Overnight flights from Los Angeles to New York. Planes he had flown many many times, never imagining that one day he would see them from this perspective and for this solemn reason.

All those times, all those years, when, tired as he had been, he looked forward to coming home to Claire, to Robbie. To having breakfast with his son. Hugging him. Kissing him. Tousling his silky black hair. Just calling him son was a great satisfaction.

And now . . .

What would he say to Claire? How would she face it? Thank God Rissom was with her. He leaned his head against the plastic bubble and started to weep.

The pilot looked to his companion. Both shook their heads in sympathy. Suddenly the pilot sat upright, alert. He had been hearing the usual cross talk. But now a fresh voice cut in on the police band, announcing, "Emergency! This is American Flight Ten. I spot a strange configuration in the waters of the Sound. Just off the Connecticut shore. In the general area of Bridgeport Harbor."

The copilot pressed his own phones close as the airline pilot continued. "Looks like a capsized sailing craft. Can't make out any signs of life."

The voice gave an estimated compass reading. When he began to repeat the information, the copilot slipped off his headset and leaned over to hold one of the phones against Don Ward's ear.

". . . just off the Connecticut shore in the general area of Bridgeport Harbor. Looks like a capsized sailing craft. Can't make out any signs . . . sorry, just got landing instructions." The airliner cut out.

The pilot banked the copter, heading east and slightly north toward the indicated area. When his copilot tapped the gas gauge, the pilot said, "Both boats must have picked up the message. They'll be there in case we have to ditch."

The copter whipped its way through the dawn across the dark waters of the Sound. To the left Don could see the outlines of the Connecticut shore, a vague, ghostly presence. To the right the bare outlines of fog-shrouded Long Island. Above them several commercial planes hovered in wide circles, waiting the word to land, their strobe lights blinking in the mist.

Ahead, Don could see only dark, choppy water, white foam, where the waves broke. The pilot kept his eyes on his instruments, especially his gas gauge, on which the needle now flickered between one-quarter and empty.

Suddenly the copilot pointed to their right. The pilot leaned forward. Alerted by their movements, Don jumped from his side of the copter to peer out the right side. The copilot indicated his sighting. Don stared, kept staring to make sure. He saw it. There was no doubt. The multistriped object flat on the black water, with striations of blue, red, orange, and yellow. Bright, festive, colorful as that sail might have looked on a sunny day on the Sound, those colors and contrasts served a far more vital purpose now.

Don tugged at the pilot, who nodded and nosed the craft down in the direction of the sail. When they hovered over it, Don could make out the uppermost blue pontoon. Hunched over it was a motionless figure, attired in a yellow life jacket. Trailing alongside, like a lazy, useless watersnake, was the righting line. Evidently Robbie had desperately tried to right the craft but had failed.

The copter wheeled closer at a lower altitude. Don pressed more urgently against the plastic bubble. He could make out the dark hair, the youthful face, a lifeless gray.

Both pilots looked at each other. The copilot shook his head hopelessly. The pilot gave a gesture which said, *Report it.* The copilot picked up his microphone.

Two craft were streaking across the rough waters of the Sound. Both the police patrol boat and the coast guard cutter had picked up the same message from the airliner. They had started at top speed in the general direction indicated. When they came in sight of the hovering copter, they were both tuned in to the message.

"Police Copter Three to all craft. Sighted foundering cat. One occupant." Then added: "No apparent signs of life."

Since the copter copilot could see the long white wakes of both rescue craft, no further message was necessary.

At the time the two rescue vessels were closing in on the overturned cat, Detective Melendez was standing on the edge of the dock at the marina with his walkie-talkie up against his right ear. Alongside him Dr. Fred Rissom was straining to hear anything that came over the detective's radio. To make sure that he did not, Melendez pressed the instrument tighter to his ear.

All he would report was "They sighted him."

"And?" Rissom asked anxiously.

"They're moving in now to pick him up."

"And then what?"

"Best thing would be for the copter to fly him to shore. To City Hospital. That's where they take most immersion cases."

It was an evasion but, Melendez thought, one crisis at a time.

"I'd better go tell Claire," Rissom said, turning away. But Melendez caught him by the arm.

"Maybe you'd better not. The last part of the message was 'no apparent signs of life.' "

Both men stared at each other. Rissom finally spoke.

"We'd better start for City Hospital."

The Coast Guard vessel was first to come alongside the capsized cat. A coast guardsman in a black rubber wet suit dropped overboard, swam the short distance to the cat. With one arm around the pontoon, his free hand reached out. He turned the face.

From the low height of the hovering copter Don Ward could make out the face of his son. Eyes closed, cheeks hollow, he appeared as lifeless close up as he had from a distance. Don saw the diver signal for a line. It came flying through the air, landing just feet from him. He reached out, lashed it around the body several times. With the help of the men on the vessel he began to nudge the body toward it.

In the copter pilot and copilot exchanged glances, expressing by means of looks what they would have said if Don were not aboard.

He saw them lift the body on deck, saw the captain kneel beside it, cover it with a warm blanket, all except the face. He saw the captain feel for Robbie's pulse and evidently find none, for he slapped Robbie across the face briskly, hoping to stimulate some reaction. There was none. He stared at Robbie's gray, youthful face, then said something to his radioman. The message came up to the copter: "Take him away."

The copter dipped low over the patrol boat. The copilot lowered a basket stretcher. When it touched the deck, the captain and his first mate lifted the body into it, making sure to keep the blanket tightly wrapped around it. Don could read the captain's lips: "Such a young kid. Too bad."

The stretcher was reeled up into the copter. Don helped the copilot receive it and set it down. He dropped beside it, pressed his face against Robbie's. It was cold, icy cold. He reached under the blanket for his son's hand. It seemed to resist him, as if refusing to be held; it was so stiff and frigid.

He pressed it against his own warm face because he could think of nothing else to do. All the while he kept thinking: *What will I tell Claire? What will I tell her?*

The pilot had alerted the emergency room at City Hospital. When they landed at the copter pad on Twenty-third Street and the East River, an ambulance was waiting. The resident who was riding the wagon took one look, stared across Robbie's body at the copter pilot to say, "You should have delivered this down the street to the medical examiner."

"Shut up, you idiot! This is the boy's father!" the pilot reprimanded.

"Oh. Sorry," the young resident said.

He proceeded to take Robbie's vital signs. Shook his head, indicated to his driver to lift the stretcher to the ambulance. He turned to Don.

"You'd better come along with us."

CHAPTER 43

In Emergency at City Hospital Dr. Alton Singer came rushing into the room to be met by the resident's gloomy shake of the head.

"Sorry we bothered you, Dr. Singer."

"Half my life consists of being bothered," Singer said, a gruff man, short, stocky, and resigned to the biological fact that after middle age a man will put on weight. It allowed him to indulge his appetite without any qualms of conscience.

"Okay. What do we have here?"

"Immersion hypothermia," the resident informed. "Estimate he might have been in the water as long as five hours."

"Five hours?" Singer demanded, outraged. "Didn't anybody look for him? Wasn't he listed as missing? Stand back!"

The resident moved aside. Singer found himself confronted by another man, not in hospital greens or whites.

"Who the hell are you?" Singer demanded.

"I'm the boy's father," Don Ward said.

"Oh. Sorry. Stand back, please," Singer asked, gently removing Robbie's hand from Don's grasp. "In fact, it might be better if you waited outside."

Don nodded stiffly, took one more look at his pale, motionless son, and slipped out of the room.

Singer took charge of Robbie Ward's case.

"Thermometer!" he ordered, holding out his hand.

"I already took it. Mouth and rectal. I get no reading," the resident said. "And no vital signs."

"Then why the hell don't you have a thermopile in here?" Singer asked. "What did they teach you in medical school about immersion cases? If the rectal temp doesn't register, just throw the body away?" He turned to call his young colleague. "Young man, and anybody else who happens to be listening"—it brought several young doctors running into the room from the corridor—"when dealing with immersion cases, do not be fooled by the usual indicia. Vital signs. Temperature. And the rest.

"Now come in close. You are looking at a victim of immersion who, I would judge from his physical development, is between seventeen and eighteen. He presents no detectible vital signs. He has no temp that the usual thermometer will pick up. That means he is at least below ninety-five degrees Fahrenheit. But below ninety-five is not necessarily the end of the world. So what do we do? We find what his actual temperature really is. Assuming, of course, that he has any temperature at all."

He turned to one young woman resident, obviously of East Indian extraction, petite, black-haired, dark-skinned. "You!" Singer commanded. "Examine this patient!"

She pushed back the blanket, to test Robbie Ward for pulse, and could find none. She tried to raise his arm, but it was stiff and unyielding. She tried to raise his head; his neck was rigid. She turned back to Singer.

"We are much too late. Rigor mortis has already set in," she announced.

At that moment the door to the ER opened. Without turning to look, Singer made an angry gesture to accompany his command. "Bring that damned machine over here!"

Instead of the thermopile he had ordered, he was greeted by a loud, tearful outcry.

"Robbie!"

Thrusting aside Dr. Rissom's hand, breaking free of her husband, Claire Ward rushed past Dr. Singer to reach the examining table. She lifted Robbie into her arms and held him closely as if her body heat could revive him. "Robbie, Robbie, my baby," she kept crooning to him. "Robbie, Robbie." She was beyond tears.

Singer glared at Don and Rissom. "Get this woman out of here! Out!"

It took considerable force for Don and Rissom to pry Claire away from her son. Rissom gestured Don to keep her outside the room, but he himself remained.

"And who are you?" Singer demanded.

"I'm Fred Rissom, the boy's doctor."

"Oh," Singer said, "then, by all means, stay." But by his attitude he indicated to Rissom that his patient's chances were very slim.

They brought in the thermopile, a small instrument consisting of dissimilar metal plates connected together, which would, under the influence of even a slight degree of warmth, produce an electric current that would register low body temperature, if indeed any existed.

Singer brusquely motioned the residents to gather around while he inserted the lubricated sensor into Robbie Ward's rectum. He turned on the apparatus and stared very hard at the readout. His eyes invited Rissom to look. Neither detected any discernible indication. Finally it began to flicker, then to register, mounting slowly until it recorded a temperature of sixty, then sixty-five, then seventy-five degrees, settling finally at seventy-eight. Singer glanced at Rissom with his first sense of hope.

"Well, distinguished colleagues, we do not have a case of rigor mortis here after all, do we?"

He glared at the young East Indian resident, bringing a blush to her dusky cheeks.

"That being the case, first we must assure that an airway is established and maintained. Which we do with this tracheostomy tube and respirator."

Once he had affixed the tube in Robbie's throat and set the respirator going, he turned to the more basic problem.

"Now, one of the first things to remember about immersion hypothermia is that the body is divided into two zones. The core, or inner zone, where all the vital organs are centered. And the outer zone, the part consisting of the skin and fat layers. Now, the only time it is of benefit to be fat, healthwise, is in such cases. Where fat can be a protection. If I should ever suffer from hypothermia, you would have no trouble. But unfortunately this patient is not fat. Still, we do what we can."

Despite Singer's sarcastic manner of presentation, Rissom was well aware that the man was greatly concerned, though not very hopeful about any treatment. Singer's look to Rissom was an apology, as if to say, *If I can't do much for your patient, at least it will serve to teach these young physicians.*

"Normally one would resort to immediate use of a warm bath. A nice, safe, orthodox procedure. Except for one little thing. It could prove fatal.

"Yes, fatal," Singer emphasized. "Why? Because this patient has a temperature of less than eighty degrees. His pupils are miotic. He presents no discernible heartbeat. I won't even bother to take his blood pressure. And if we took an electrocardiogram, the results would be very discouraging. So that if we did prescribe a warm-water tub, what would result?" Singer waited only briefly for a response before inviting him. "Dr. Rissom?"

"A marked difference in response between the inner core and the outer, with consequent rewarming shock," Rissom explained.

"Exactly," Singer said. "Immersion in cold water tends to constrict the blood vessels. A warm-water bath would, of course, dilate them. However, the outer blood vessels would dilate first, drawing away the blood from the inner core, where the vital organs of the body are contained. So the blood would be drawn away from where we need it most, in the vital organs, to where we need it least, the outer core of skin and fat.

"Therefore, to avoid rewarming shock, we must warm this patient from the *inside.* Otherwise his core temperature will not reach a desirable level. And that would mean that his myocardium, his heart muscle, would not be sufficiently restored to respond to antiarhythmic procedures. Which, I suspect, we may need in this case."

Singer turned from the table to instruct the charge nurse, "Mrs. Linkroum, call upstairs and tell them that we are going to do a peritoneal dialysis at once. I want everything ready."

As Singer and Rissom came out of the ER, followed by a retinue of residents, they were confronted by Claire Ward, who broke from her husband's embrace to seize Singer by the lapels of his white lab coat.

"Doctor, please, my son's life depends on you. Do something!"

Singer had been confronted too many times by such pathetic

pleas. He had run out of answers, especially in cases where the prognosis was so grim. He looked to Rissom to intercede.

"Claire, your son is in very capable hands. Let the man do his work. He knows what he's doing."

"Robbie, is he—"

"No, Claire, he is not dead. And in a case like this 'not dead' is a lot more than we expected," Rissom said.

Singer took Claire's hand. "We will need time. Hours. But we will be working, and watching, and maybe even praying a little. As soon as we know anything, you will know it."

Singer turned to Don Ward. "Take care of your wife, my friend. We will take care of your son."

As Singer and Rissom strode down the hall followed by his staff, Singer said softly to Rissom, "Damn it, for all we know, when she held him close to her warm body, she may have been giving him the only treatment that could help."

Don tried to restrain Claire in his tight embrace, but she broke free to follow Rissom, Singer, his staff, and the rolling stretcher bearing her son.

Claire Ward peered through the small square glass insert in the door of the operating room to watch what she could of the dialysis procedure. But Rissom, Singer, and his staff surrounded Robbie, obscuring him from her view.

All she could see, from moment to moment, was the gray face of her young son. She kept thinking: *Sixteen years can't end this way, not this way, dear God.* But his motionless hand, protruding from the blanket that hid most of his young body, warned her otherwise.

She was conscious now of someone close beside her. She turned, expecting to face Don. It was Dr. Belmond.

"I came as soon as Fred called," Belmond explained. "What did they say?"

"A chance," Claire said. "Not a good chance, but at least a chance."

She turned back to peering through the glass.

Inside the small OR Dr. Singer was gruffly charging one of his residents, "Keep check on his electrolyte balance and the level of his body fluids, else this whole procedure may be a waste of time."

He turned to the head OR nurse. "Trocar!"

She handed Singer a sterile blunt stainless steel needle. Palpating the right side of Robbie's rigid belly, Singer chose a place which would insure that the trocar did not puncture his liver or any other vital organ. He pushed the blunt end of the needle against Robbie's skin, pierced it, pressed it into the boy's peritoneal cavity. He could feel the gut give way, as it should. He demanded a second trocar and inserted it in the same manner on the left side of Robbie's body.

"Catheter!" Singer ordered.

The nurse handed him the thin colorless plastic tube, which he carefully inserted into the first trocar. He snapped his fingers. The nurse read his instruction, attached the catheter to the steel container of dialysis fluid, and released the clamp. The warming fluid started to flow into Robbie's peritoneal cavity. In moments it began to spurt out of the second trocar, thus setting up a constant flow of the warming medium through the core of Robbie's body.

As Singer supervised the procedure, he instructed, "While we do this to avoid rewarming shock, it does not always work. In a case this far gone, nothing may work."

He continued the process, more containers of warm fluid, more glances at the thermopile readout. He began to detect a slight rise, which he discounted as merely reflecting the warm fluid itself.

He did another test of Robbie's vital signs. He paused and retested them. His look to Rissom indicated: *At last a response, slight, but some response.* His staff, alert to every one of Singer's reactions, since he was not always verbal about his deductions, began to take heart. They looked from one to the other, giving eye signals that acknowledged the first hopeful development in the case.

Their reaction was noticeable even to Claire and Don as they stared through the glass insert. She turned to look up at Don, who nodded, not daring to say a word for fear his optimism might anger fate and jeopardize his son's life. Standing behind them, Belmond peered through the glass between their heads.

She whispered, "He's on to something."

"Yes, please, God," Claire said. Then realized that in these past hours she had had closer contact with God than at any time in her life. A strong guilt accompanied that, and silent vows of more faithful observance in the future.

Inside the OR Singer was now attempting to flex Robbie's arms, then his legs, one at a time, slowly, with steady pressure. Arms and legs, on the basis of whose rigidity the resident had made a diagnosis of rigor mortis, began to give. Singer invited Rissom to try. He was able to move them more freely. On Robbie's youthful face, gray gave way to paleness, paleness eventually yielded to the more natural-looking skin for a sixteen-year-old.

Singer ordered them to discontinue the respirator. He observed Robbie's naked chest as it rose and fell without assist. Breathing was shallow; intake and exhalation were both brief but at least perceptible. He looked to Rissom for his approval. Securing it, Singer ordered the tracheostomy tube in Robbie's throat disconnected from the respirator but kept in place in the event the boy suffered a sudden relapse. For the time being, Robbie Ward seemed able to breathe on his own.

"Keep him warm. Continue with the dialysis for another half hour. Then move him to a bed in a private room," Singer ordered.

One of the male residents said, "If I may say so, Doctor, this was a very informative lesson. I would have given him up for dead."

"You may say whatever you like, young man," Singer replied still gravely concerned.

"He's going to make it," the young man insisted.

"Oh, he's going to make it all right," Singer agreed, "but I would like to talk to him half an hour after he regains consciousness."

"What do you mean?"

Singer and Rissom exchanged impatient glances, but neither answered.

Once outside, they were confronted by Claire and Don Ward.

"He's going to be all right," Claire insisted. "I saw the way you both moved his arms and legs. Then he moved them by himself, didn't he?"

"Yes, yes, he did," Singer quietly agreed, always self-conscious in the presence of the unjustified optimism of relatives of a patient.

"Then he's going to be fine, fine!" Claire enthused with great relief.

"Yes, he could be," Singer said, refusing to make any outright commitment. He broke free and started down the corridor.

Having noticed Singer's reticence, Don glanced at Rissom and detected an equally concerned look in his eyes. Leaving Claire in the care of Rissom and Belmond, Don started quickly after Singer. He caught up with him.

"Doctor?" was all that Don said.

The short, portly man stared up into Don's face. "Mr. Ward, don't embarrass me with thanks or congratulations. What I did any competent doctor could have done. But what we have really accomplished we won't know until your son is conscious and able to speak."

"What do you mean?" Don asked.

"Hypoxemia, Mr. Ward, hypoxemia," Singer said. "We may have done your son no big favor by pulling him through."

"Brain damage?" Don asked. Singer nodded grimly. "I know what you mean. We did a show on the network about that once."

"Well, if this happens to your son, it won't be over at the end of an hour. It won't even be over after a few episodes, like in a miniseries or a soap opera. You and your wife will have to plan the rest of your lives around it. Who'll take care of him? Now! And after you're both gone! Will there be someone? Will there be money enough? You'll worry about that till the day you die!"

In the face of such an unexpected onslaught Don Ward drew back, paled, and felt himself trembling.

"I'm sorry, Mr. Ward," Singer said. "But when I see life threatened in this way, when I see what could be a bright young man possibly turned into a vegetable, I hate everybody. Myself. Medicine. And the foolish human race that does more damage to itself than nature or any enemy. Some days I hate to practice medicine."

He started down the hall, took only a few steps, turned to call back. "I'll look in in a while. We should have a pretty good idea by then."

Don watched as the short, stocky figure receded down the corridor, his white lab coat flapping loosely and his shoulders hunched. He was indeed a tired man, a discouraged man.

CHAPTER 44

In the room assigned to him, in the neatly made hospital bed, patient Robbie Ward was breathing easily. Not deeply but not nearly so shallowly as only a few hours earlier. His mother and father stood at the foot of the bed, observing as Dr. Rissom administered basic neurological tests to him. Dr. Belmond's eyes were fixed as she studied every one of Robbie's reactions.

Rissom held Robbie's right eye open, then his left. He directed his pocket flashlight at them, passed it from side to side. The boy's pupils reacted, responsive to the light. When Rissom pricked his legs with a surgical needle, Robbie withdrew them. Rissom took the boy's pulse, which was now strong enough to be palpable to his touch.

Rissom glanced at Dr. Belmond. "No heart arhythmia."

"So far, so good," Belmond said.

Her words were a great relief to Claire. But not to Don, whom Dr. Singer had warned about the worst of possible consequences.

"He should be coming out of it soon," Rissom said to Belmond. "We'd better wait."

In less than an hour Robbie's eyes flickered open for the briefest instant, then closed. Rissom gestured Claire to speak to her son.

"Robbie . . . Robbie . . . can you hear me?" Claire entreated. "This is Mother, Robbie. Mom. Can you hear me?"

The boy opened his eyes, kept them open for a moment, then

as if disbelieving, closed them. He seemed motionless until he spoke, very faintly and haltingly. "Mom? That you? Really you?"

"Yes, darling," Claire said.

Rissom urged her to keep talking.

"We're here. Me. Dad. Dr. Rissom. Dr. Belmond. And you're okay now. They found you before it was too late. They brought you here to the hospital. You're doing fine, just fine."

"I am?"

"Of course, darling." She leaned forward to kiss him on his warm cheek. She took his hand, pressed it to her face.

He opened his eyes once more, this time to look at Don, then at Dr. Belmond.

"Sorry," he said. "Very sorry. I don't know why people bother. Not worth it."

"Don't say that!" both Claire and Don protested at the same time.

"Let him say it," Belmond said, smiling. "Right now let him say anything he wants."

In response to her rebuke Don asked, "You mean there's no brain damage?"

"Not if he can talk as coherently as this," Belmond said.

"Brain damage?" Claire asked, aware for the first time of the jeopardy that had hung over her son. She embraced him fiercely.

Dr. Belmond said, "There is nothing more I can do here now. But I want to see Robbie the day he is discharged. We are going to get him back on track with his medication. And make sure he sticks with it."

As Belmond reached the door, it opened before she could touch it. Singer was in the doorway, his white coat flecked with spots of dried blood and brown stains from medications he had had to use during his usually hectic morning in Emergency.

"Well?" he asked.

"Responses normal. And he talks very coherently," Rissom said.

"Now that's what I call a recovery," the little man said, beaming. He approached the bed, stared into Robbie's face. Took his pulse. Then clapped him gently on the side of the face. "How old are you, son? Seventeen? Eighteen?"

"Sixteen," Robbie said.

"Some body for a sixteen-year-old," Singer said. "My own son is nineteen and not nearly so developed. But then he listens to records all day and all night. Lying down yet. If they could teach medicine through records and cassettes, he could become the world's greatest doctor. Otherwise God knows. So what'll happen? He'll become some kind of computer genius and make millions. A hell of a lot more than his old man, I can tell you."

Singer had carried it all off as a joke. But his feeling of enormous relief was quite apparent to the professional eyes of Rissom and Belmond. Evidently the boy had been on Singer's mind constantly through the whole busy morning in Emergency.

Once Singer had gone, Belmond said, "I will expect you in my office, Robbie, the day you come home."

"I'll be there," Robbie promised.

"Well," Rissom said, "no more need for doctors around here. And there must be lots of children with croup up in New Canaan. I'd better be going, too."

He started for the door, which Belmond held open for him. Then he stopped, turned, and looked at Robbie.

"Son, whatever else this whole mad business means to you, remember one thing. You've got two of the finest parents in this world. To me, your parents, like all other loyal parents who've seen young people through so many troubles lately, are the unsung heroes of our time. After two generations in which parents have been taking the blame for almost everything, it's time we started to appreciate them."

The Ward family was alone for the first time since Robbie's disappearance. Claire and Don stood at the foot of Robbie's bed, staring down at him, beaming. Out of Robbie's view Don took Claire's hand, and for once in many, many hours it was neither cold nor trembling.

"I want to say . . ." Robbie began.

But his mother interrupted. "You don't have to say anything, darling. Just lie there. With your eyes open. And look at us."

Don added, "Of course, you can smile a lot if you feel like it. But don't strain yourself to talk."

"But I want to talk," Robbie insisted.

"Okay," Claire said. "If you want to."

"When it got bad—I mean real bad— You see, Dad, till I got out quite a ways, I didn't really know how much difference there was between a fourteen-footer and an eighteen-footer. I had her in control pretty good. Till she caught a sudden wind from behind. The boom started to oscillate. Then suddenly she jibbed. Came clear across from port to starboard. So fast it knocked me out of the boat. Clear out.

"But I remembered what you taught me when we first worked with the fourteen-footer. 'Son, no matter what, stay with your boat. Hang on to your cat. She can't sink, but you can.' So I fought my way back to the boat and hung on. When it got tougher, I lashed myself to one of the pontoons.

"I looked up. All I could see was mist and darkness. I heard planes overhead but knew they couldn't see me. I was alone, real alone in this whole world. That's when I knew I didn't want to die. Only it was too late.

"Because by that time I knew I wasn't going to make it. So I thought: *Before I die, I would like to go back and thank them for everything they did for me. They didn't owe me anything. I was nothing to them.* Like we used to hear in Sunday school . . . 'I was a stranger and you took me in.' But I guess I didn't do my part. I tried. Honest, Mom, Dad, I tried. But that thing, that big, overwhelming feeling, kept running away with me. Until Dr. Belmond.

"But I began to miss that feeling, that excitement. So I skipped taking my pills. Till the old feeling came back. That's how I felt the last few days.

"I wanted to come back to explain it to you. But then I knew I never could. So I thought: *They're terrific people, my mom and dad. Even if I don't get a chance to tell them, they'll know, they'll understand.* I hope you do."

Claire moved to his side, knelt beside the bed, and put her arm around him. "Robbie, after the first day that we saw you, you were never a stranger. You were ours. And we were yours. So never, never think of yourself as a stranger or of us taking you in. We're a family. Always were, always will be."

"And we'll have more time now to be a family," Don said. "I've quit the network, son. Told Brady off. And I'm free. We'll have plenty of time to learn how to sail that cat. And do a lot of other things."

"Terrific, Dad," Robbie said, then asked, "But what about—"

"A job? Money?" Don asked. "Don't worry. Your dad's no dummy. But this time he'll do it his way, not their way."

The boy nodded, smiling.

"Of course, you've got to do your part. Dr. Belmond. Dr. Rissom. Your lithium. On schedule and in the right doses. And instead of that old feeling, new feelings. Good ones. Constructive ones. Okay, son?"

"Okay, Dad."

Four days later, after Dr. Singer had checked him out for the final time, Don and Claire Ward took their son back home to Connecticut.

The phone was ringing when they rolled into the garage. Don's first, and conditioned, impulse was to turn off the motor and rush for the phone in the kitchen. But Claire reminded, "You don't have to, darling. Not anymore."

The three of them laughed. The phone had stopped ringing by the time they reached the door.

Once inside, Claire said, "Robbie, while I'm preparing lunch, get on the phone and arrange your appointment with Dr. Belmond."

"Okay, Mom."

But as he reached for the kitchen phone, it rang again. He answered.

A frosty female voice asked impatiently, "Is this the Ward residence finally?"

"Yes," Robbie said.

"Donald Ward, please! Mr. Brady calling."

"Dad, for you," Robbie called out toward the den.

"Yeah? Who?"

"Guess!" Robbie said, laughing.

"No! He wouldn't."

"He is!"

"Well, let him wait. I'll take this in the den."

Don Ward settled down in his leather club chair, swung his feet up onto the ottoman, before deigning to pick up the phone. "Yes, Mr. Brady?" Don said as Robbie came into the doorway.

Even that far from the phone Robbie could hear Brady shout,

"What the hell is this Mr. Brady stuff? I thought we were friends, Don. Friends!"

"Okay, sorry. Ed. How's that?"

"Better. Much better. Now, tell me, how's your son?"

"He's back home, looking and feeling terrific." Don glanced at Robbie and smiled. The boy smiled back and made an okay sign, his three fingers straight up, his thumb and forefinger forming a circle.

"Good! Glad to hear it. Give him my best."

"Oh, sure," Don said.

"Now that you're past that crisis, I've got some really important stuff to discuss with you."

"We just discussed the important stuff, Ed," Don said. "My son is okay. And he's home. That's important. Anything else doesn't matter now."

Brady reverted to his old agitated, autocratic, unreasonable bellow again. "Well, we can at least discuss it! Can't we?"

"Sure, let's discuss it, whatever it is."

"Okay," Brady said. "Now, when you told me about Ab Crystal's new series . . ."

"Did you read the script?"

"Terrific! Fresh! Funny! Different!" Brady said. "So we made the deal."

"Good!" Don said, thinking: *That provides for Fanny and Ab's two kids.*

"There's only one hitch," Brady said.

Oh-oh, Don thought, *is this greedy bastard trying to cut in on Ab's percentage of the show?* "What hitch, Ed?"

"Ab tells me he didn't write this by himself. He says you spent three days and nights with him."

"I gave him a suggestion or two. So what?" Don said evasively. He motioned to Robbie, who came into the room, sank down onto the ottoman, as he used to when he was a small boy and Don would tousle his hair while talking business on the phone. Don reached out to Robbie's head again.

It felt good to Robbie to have his dad's hand running easily and lovingly through his hair, as in the old days. Meantime, Robbie could hear Brady's voice changing from his usual rasping, belligerent tone to one more placating and coaxing.

"Don, don't play the shy boy with me. When a writer with Ab Crystal's credits says you did more than help with an idea or two, I have to believe him. So I'll tell you what I told Ab. The deal is firm. A pilot and the first eight scripts, with an interest in the series for him, if you work with him."

"Ed, I live in the East. From now on, I work in the East. I'm a family man. I can't be flying out to the Coast for every story conference."

"We figured that. So I went you one better. We decided, Ab and I, that we shoot the series in New York. For some reason that he wouldn't tell me, Ab says he'd like to move back to New York for the next six months."

Don nodded, stopped tousling Robbie's hair in a way that forced the boy to look up at him questioningly. But Don signaled that he would tell him later.

"Ed, if that's the deal and we can settle on the money, then okay."

"Great! Listen, Don, tomorrow let's meet at 'Twenty-one' and finalize things. Okay?"

"Ed, I am spending tomorrow with my son, who is just home from the hospital and feeling great. I want to share that feeling with him. So no 'Twenty-one.' Anything you want to finalize can be done over the phone."

Don Ward hung up.

"Dad?" Robbie asked.

"You mean, about New York and Abner Crystal? Remember about four years ago Mom and I had a couple up here for dinner. Abner and Fanny Crystal. He was a very funny man. Remember?"

"Oh, sure, the man who wrote the *No Time for Fathers* show."

"That's the guy," Don said. "Well, his kids are going to lose their father in about six months. So he wants to spend his last months with them here in the East, where he was born and grew up. He wants his kids to discover his roots and theirs."

Don reached out to embrace his son and hold him. Robbie clung to his father.

At that moment Claire came to the door to announce lunch. One look, and she decided lunch could wait.